Survive
for
Now

BOB HOWARD

DEDICATION

For Dawn who works endless hours to market my books with the determination only a spouse can show, Julie who challenges me to write in a way a father cannot ignore, and Drew who motivates me with a son's pride in the accomplishments of his parents.

CONTENTS

	Acknowledgments	i
1	Safe Haven	1
2	Revelations	26
3	Jetties	39
4	Escape from Conway	61
5	Outside Contacts	103
6	The Mission	135
7	Jean	159
8	Guntersville	177
9	Friends and Enemies	204
10	Green Cavern	212
11	Dark Passages	234
12	Hope	250
13	SOS	263

ACKNOWLEDGMENTS

Writing is work that can be fun, frustrating, and satisfying. At the end of the day I have found that I throw very little away because it is a creation only a writer can understand. The decisions are usually final because I know why I made them.

There is still room for discussion and technical advice, and for that I want to thank some collaborators who reached out and offered their advice.

Jay High, Chief of Police in Jamestown, South Carolina offered me insights about weapons and tactical details, but most importantly he offered point of view. My discussions with him helped me to develop the action. We didn't agree about everything, but our exchanges were an outlet for me to visualize what I wanted to write. He has also given me direction I will use in the future.

Samantha Case helped me to remember that sometimes writing the way I talk isn't always a good idea. As an editor she spotted colloquial expressions that I sometimes wondered if readers would even understand. Editing is tedious work, and I hope she is willing to edit for me as this series continues.

Jeff Roberts, Fire Marshal, gave me technical advice about the day to day life of a firefighter. I took some liberties with his information because this is a work of fiction. Nonetheless, I was able to see life in a fire station through his eyes.

My deepest appreciation goes out to my collaborators and to the many readers who contacted me with comments and ideas. Even those critical of my work played a part in the development of this second book.

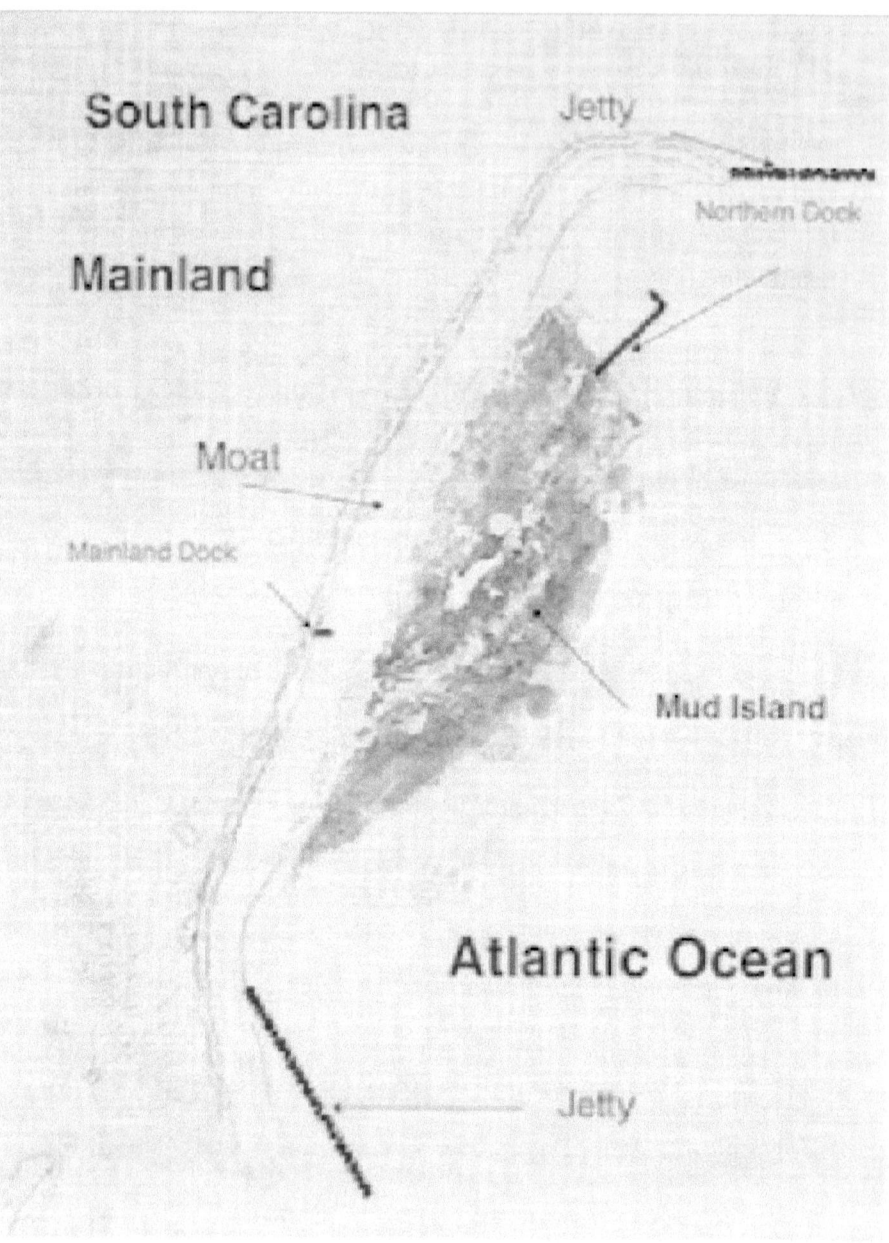

South Carolina

Jetty

Northern Dock

Mainland

Moat

Mainland Dock

Mud Island

Atlantic Ocean

Jetty

1 SAFE HAVEN

When I pulled open the big vault door to the Mud Island shelter, both the father and daughter stared with stunned expressions and wide eyes. No one had been there to see my face when I had opened the door the very first time I had been to Mud Island, but I probably had the same expression.

I took a moment to myself and went back in time to the day when I had first brought Jean, Kathy, and the Chief to the shelter. We had met offshore, me in my Boston Whaler and the three of them in a raft that seemed much smaller than it was because of the Chief. He was a mountain of a man with the personality of a faithful Irish Setter, and we had all taken an instant liking to each other.

Pulling open the shelter door for them had been a great moment for me. Seeing the looks on their faces was rewarding. I guess it was like the first time a kid gets to see Disney World, and just like Disney World, the surprises inside the shelter of Mud Island just keep on coming. The entrance is impressive, and the decontamination area gives the feeling of security and safety, but it doesn't give a clue as to what lays in store beyond that.

Tom and Molly followed us inside the shelter, but they seemed to huddle closer to each other as if they weren't sure of what was happening. Tom was tall and kind of rugged looking, but there was something about him that also said he was not the outdoors type. He was athletic, but not due to hardship. It looked like he had been in some kind of training program. Despite the hardships of the previous months of surviving from day to day, he was fairly well groomed. He had managed to shave at some point in the last day, probably after finding the houseboat.

Tom also looked like he had either scavenged clean clothes for them or was in the habit of finding ways to wash their clothes. The backpacks they had with them were not overstuffed with supplies, so my guess was they were trading old clothes for new whenever possible. He was wearing jeans, work boots, a sweatshirt, and a good winter coat.

I also figured that Tom's height and rugged appearance would have been almost imposing if not for a recent weight loss. He wasn't as big as Chief Barnes who sometimes made me feel like I was in the room with a smiling Grizzly bear, but of the three men inside the shelter, I was definitely the smallest. It made me think all the way back to high school when we would pick football teams in Physical Education class. If I wasn't picked last, it was always close to it.

I noticed I wasn't the only one who was appraising the newcomers. Kathy, our blond and beautiful Charleston City Police Officer, seemed to be a bit taken with Tom. Kathy had been a rookie cop when the dead began trying to bite the living, but her poise and confident personality had made her into a hero when she took singlehanded control of the chaos at the Charleston cruise ship terminal. She'd saved the lives of thousands of people by organizing the defensive stance at the terminal long enough for them to board the cruise ship, Atlantic Spirit, and pull away from the port.

Now Kathy looked self-conscious about having her hair pulled back in a ponytail, dressed in coveralls, and not wearing makeup. It looked like she was trying to discreetly pull the rubber band out of the ponytail without Tom noticing.

The fourth member of our family, Jean, was fixated on the little girl. She was studying the child with an adoring look that was lighting up her face like a Christmas tree. Jean was what I would call naturally cute. Maybe she was seeing a connection between the way she probably looked as a child and Molly's appearance.

Unlike Kathy, who was tall and athletic, Jean could only reach five feet if she stretched a bit. Even though her dark hair was cut short, it matched the color of Molly's shoulder length curls so well they could be sisters. I was head over heels in love with Jean almost from the first moment we had met, and the joy on her face as she studied Molly made me love her even more.

Tom asked, "You people all live in here?"

He looked around at the sparse surroundings of the entry room and into the adjoining area we called the decontamination room.

The Chief gave a deep chuckle and said, "Not in here, Tom. You'll see where in a few minutes."

I sealed the big outside door into place and gestured for our new guests to go ahead of us into the next room. They moved hesitantly through the door and Tom studied the room that looked more like a locker room than anything you could live in.

Uncle Titus, my sometimes crazy survivalist benefactor who had left me this shelter in his will, probably expected this outer room to be needed for decontamination after a nuclear war rather than a zombie apocalypse. That's why there were showers for washing off after going outside, and special suits with breathing apparatus and radiation monitors attached to them. He also probably considered the possibility of a biological war, but I seriously doubted he gave much thought to zombies.

"We'll be going through this room into the main part of the shelter," said Kathy, "but first we have some unpleasant business to take care of."

"Unpleasant business?" asked Tom. "What kind of unpleasant business?"

He had one hand loosely hanging near the back of Molly's head, and he gently drew her closer to his left leg.

She sensed his tension and looked up at him with a slightly frightened expression.

Jean reacted immediately and went down onto one knee in front of her to make eye contact.

"Don't be afraid, Sweetie. There's nothing here that can hurt you," said Jean.

Kathy had succeeded in getting the rubber band out of her ponytail, so her long blonde hair had fallen free. The effect on Tom Bergman was obvious because the thought of unpleasant business suddenly didn't seem to be making him quite as tense.

The Chief had been quiet other than his brief response to Tom a minute earlier, and I could tell he was thinking ahead to the same question we had to broach when he, Kathy, and Jean had first floated into the vicinity of my boat while I had been out doing some target practice.

I had a boat, a shelter, and plenty of guns, but I didn't know how to shoot, so I had to take the boat far enough from shore to get some target practice where I wouldn't be heard by the infected dead that were wandering around in the dense coastal trees.

After a bit of practice with the guns, I found myself facing a raft carrying two attractive women and a mountain of a man who was wearing some kind of uniform. As a matter of fact, so were the women, but the blond was dressed as a cop, and the cute pixie with the dark hair was dressed as a nurse in hospital scrubs.

We had faced the same unpleasant business at that chance meeting as we were facing now, but with a child and a protective father in the room, it wasn't going to be quite as funny as it had turned out to be on that day.

I had asked if any of them had been bitten, and Jean had immediately begun pulling off her clothes to show she was okay. She was completely natural about it, probably because she was a nurse, but I had felt like some kind of pervert. I had stopped her from stripping, which had made me look good in their eyes, but it was still a dumb move in more ways than one. Cute or not, the world had changed, and you couldn't just take someone's word that they hadn't been bitten.

This time there wouldn't be any joking about it, and we had to be careful. If Molly had been bitten, Tom was going to protect her. If Tom had been bitten, we were going to be faced with making a very unpleasant decision to go along with the unpleasant business. None of us had thought it through before rushing out to the houseboat and bringing Tom and Molly inside, but if he was hiding a bite from an infected dead, he would become dangerous to us all. The only alternative would be ugly.

Kathy made firm eye contact with Tom and asked, "Were you or Molly bitten by any of those infected dead out there?"

Tom understood immediately why we were all watching for his reaction, but that may only have been because he knew the consequences of the wrong answer. He looked from Kathy to the Chief, then toward me and Jean. Out of reflex he pulled his daughter behind him.

It was the reflexive move that made me realize what he possibly did for a living before the infection had spread like wildfire around the world. Combined with his athletic build, his fast but smooth reflexes made him appear ready to move in any direction in a split second.

I remembered an interview I had heard on TV when Chipper Jones had retired from baseball, and the reporter asked Derek Jeter to describe Chipper Jones.

Jeter had said, "Chipper Jones 'looks' like a baseball player."

When Jeter said Jones looked like a baseball player, I thought to myself, "Jones and Jeter both 'look' like baseball players."

It couldn't hurt to relieve the tension in the room, so I asked, "Tom, were you a pro baseball player before all this craziness started?"

I saw Jean glance my way with a look of appreciation, and when the Chief and Kathy realized I had easily defused Tom, they gave me the same look. Tom seemed to be looking inward at a distant memory for just a moment, and his shoulders dropped as the tension let go.

"Yes, I was, Ed. How did you know?"

"Just a guess," I answered, "but I've always been a real fan of the game. Were you with the Minor League team in Myrtle Beach?"

Tom looked like he was going to answer, but he stopped and faced Kathy instead.

"How are we going to do this?" he asked.

Tom had reasoned that we were going to have to get by this part of surviving every time we met someone new and opened our doors to them, and the only thing to do was get it over with. We would be vulnerable, and it had to be dealt with.

"To tell you the truth, Tom, we didn't give it a lot of thought before we came outside and got you. We had to stop you from eating the seafood because it may be contaminated," said Kathy.

"Contaminated? Contaminated by what?" he asked, looking from one of us to the other.

Jean said, "Let's be mindful of the little ears in the room. We can explain that to you at a better time, Tom."

Everyone looked at Molly at the same time which made her hide behind her dad's leg. I think the tension had gotten bad enough to make everyone, even her father, forget that we had to remember that some rules still applied in this screwed up world, and one of those rules was to watch your mouth when children were around.

"So," said the Chief, "we have to be sure no one is a danger to the others if we are going to bring you in, and we've had some unfortunate experiences with parents protecting their children. How do you want us to do this, Tom?"

Maybe it was asking Tom Bergman how he wanted to deal with the unpleasant business that made the difference to him and everyone else. Telling him or his daughter to strip wasn't half as funny as it had been when it was contemplated between me and the trio in the raft.

Tom said, "I still have my dignity, and I'm still modest enough after everything that's happened to be embarrassed about how this has to be, so I'm not too happy about anybody having to inspect my body."

"I'm a nurse," said Jean, "and I've inspected Ed's body plenty of times."

That did the trick. If anyone had been chewing gum, they would have choked on it. Molly didn't know why all the big people started laughing, but she joined in anyway.

"Thanks, Jean, but you're still far too cute for me to be comfortable with that," he said. "Besides, if I have a bite, you're all going to want the upper hand, so it has to be him." He gestured at the Chief who couldn't have looked more uncomfortable if he had tried,

The Chief still managed to say, "What, you don't think I'm cute?" He feigned a hurt look and shifted from one foot to the other.

This time the laughing was real instead of just being a release of tension, and it was agreed that the ladies would take Molly inside to the master bath where she would get the first hot bubble bath she would have in months. They could use the opportunity to check her for bite marks without her even being aware of what they were doing. It was a relief to see Tom found it immediately agreeable because it probably meant she had not been bitten, or he would have been trying to hide the bite from us.

Tom pulled Molly out from behind him and handed her over to Kathy and Jean. They each took one of her hands and led her toward the circular hatch that led to the main shelter. Tom watched with wide eyes as they went through the hatch that entered the main part of the shelter and didn't look at me or the Chief until it had closed behind them. Molly looked back and forth between the two women as they walked away, obviously feeling some comfort in the familiar contact with two mother-figures.

When they were gone, he looked at us and asked, "How big is this place?"

"We'll give you a complete tour after we finish your bubble bath," said the Chief.

None of us laughed at first because the Chief always had a way of delivering a line with such a straight face.

The thought of us giving Tom a bubble bath was just a little disturbing, but I had to add, "No matter how hard he tries, don't let him kiss you, Tom. I've had to keep an eye on him since the first day he got here."

We all broke down laughing again. Tension would wind you up like a spring, and there was nothing like laughing to unwind it.

The Chief and I talked privately for a moment and agreed that Tom would feel more comfortable if we let him use the shower in the decontamination room to get himself clean. There wasn't anything we could do about modesty, but we could help with dignity. Tom was used to having teammates around when he showered, so we would try to keep it natural.

While Tom showered, we unsuccessfully tried to do a discreet survey of his body for bite marks. The Chief and I were like a couple of uncomfortable idiots and we were happy when Tom started talking about what he and Molly had been through.

Even though we had been back outside of the shelter, risking our lives and ignoring the good advice of the man who had built the whole thing, I asked Tom what it had been like for them when the world ended.

When Molly and her father, Tom Bergman, had discovered our houseboat parked along our secluded dock, they thought they had reached heaven on Earth. They had been surviving from day to day by staying on the move for a long time. There were some places that were just naturally safer than others, and when they had to move on, they always looked for the ones that had a laundry list of qualities.

Tom explained to us that he never accepted that any place they ever found could be permanent, even when they had found a well-stocked place a couple of months ago. He said the houseboat was the first place they stayed that he gave more consideration to as a permanent place where they could live, but even it had its drawbacks.

For a place to be completely safe, their shelter had to protect them from three things. It had to keep the infected dead from getting in, it had to keep the uninfected living from taking what little they had, and it had to withstand the unpredictability of Mother Nature. Tom said when he saw the houseboat, it had only one out of the three things, but that was better than anything they had found so far.

He said they were in Myrtle Beach when the reports started telling people to stay home, but Tom knew a hotel room on the fourteenth floor wasn't what anyone in their right mind would call home. He did a quick inventory of the little refrigerator in their room and saw they would last three days at most.

There was a snack machine in the hallway, but there was already a line of people pumping it full of dollar bills and coins as if the thing was stocked with seven course meals. Tom saw that it would be empty long before he got to the front of the line.

A quick check of the floor above and the floor below produced the same results, and two floors below theirs the machine was facing certain death as a bag of chips got hung up. A big guy had it leaning over at a forty-five degree angle and was letting it fall back onto all four legs with a crash. Each time the stubborn bag of chips stayed where it was, but eventually the glass didn't. When it shattered, people risked their lives by sticking their arms through broken glass. It was Black Friday at a vending machine.

Tom finished showering and toweled off. He was waiting for one of us to say what to do next, but we weren't exactly survivalists who had the sense to think the simple things through, so we were just sort of stuck where we were.

He said, "I would ask if you guys were satisfied, but I've already seen what your sense of humor can do with a question with a double meaning, so I'll just stick with the obvious and say thanks for the shower, and maybe I could get dressed."

The Chief and I could be so juvenile sometimes, but we gratefully said together, "Don't mention it."

......

I spun the locking mechanism on the circular hatch and led the way through, followed by Tom and then the Chief. Tom had that look of awe on his face again. As we passed through the living room his mouth was hanging open at the sight of the modern comforts and the technology.

"I imagine we looked the same way you do right know when Ed brought us through that hatch the first time," said the Chief.

Tom looked like he was going to say something, but he closed his mouth and just kept soaking it all in. He was a patient man, and there would be plenty of time for questions.

By the time we gave Tom a clean bill of health and were ready to bring him into the main part of the shelter, Kathy and Jean had Molly sitting at the kitchen table eating a plate of spaghetti and drinking chocolate milk. For a nine-year-old she was doing a pretty good job of not wearing too much spaghetti sauce, but she had a respectable milk mustache. Kathy gave us a discreet thumbs-up and a wink to indicate they had found no bite marks on Molly.

We had given Tom a set of the Navy coveralls we had become accustomed to wearing, and he was overcome with joy to see his daughter shoving in hot food with her feet swinging under her chair. It was the same thing we had seen her doing through the houseboat camera.

Tom risked spaghetti sauce and chocolate on his clean clothes and gave her a big hug. He noticed that she smelled like bubble gum shampoo, and her clothes were brand new. She had on a pair of blue jeans and a tee shirt. The jeans fit well, but the tee shirt was an oversized deep blue shirt that said Go Navy on the front. Seeing his daughter look like a clean and normal child again was almost more than he could stand.

Kathy said, "Have a seat, Tom. Your daughter told us spaghetti and chocolate milk were your favorite."

"She's right," he said, but Kathy saw the slight wrinkle around his eyes at the thought of washing down spaghetti with chocolate milk.

Kathy handed him a bottle of cold beer. "We need to ration the chocolate milk, so this will have to do."

I don't know if it was the reprieve from the chocolate milk or the surprise of the cold beer that lit up Tom's expression, but he twisted off the cap and took a long swallow. He sat down next to his daughter, and I could see something in his expression as he looked at her that said he would sleep better tonight than he had in a long time.

We all took a seat and dished out the spaghetti. I think all of us were dying to hear about what Tom had seen. I was sure he would be surprised when we would get around to telling our stories and that we had left the safety of the shelter, not once but twice.

Tom described those first hectic days as if he was recalling the one nightmare that you remember better than others because you've dreamt it over and over again.

He had been playing baseball for the Triple-A club in Myrtle Beach and had a good enough season to hope for a shot at the big leagues next year. That was one dream he wouldn't get to live in real life.

When the season ended, his wife had sent their daughter from Guntersville, Alabama to spend the winter with him. He explained to us that his wife didn't want to be a baseball widow, so she had divorced him. He had hoped it would make a difference to her if he made it to the big leagues, but he's hadn't gotten there fast enough for a second chance with her.

"Were you able to contact her when everything started to happen?" Jean asked.

"We were able to talk for about five minutes before the line went dead, and I never got an answer after that. She said it was all happening there just like it was here on the coast. Guntersville only has about eight thousand people living there......or had, but she said it was really bad."

Tom stopped talking and ate a bit of his food. Hunger was making him eat, but it was clear that he would have just drank beer if it was up to him. Molly was shoveling in her second helping of spaghetti, and that's what held him together.

"She said she and some neighbors were going to try to make it to Huntsville because it was a big city, and they have the Marshall Space Flight Center there. She said there were rumors that the Army at Redstone Arsenal and NASA had things under control. It's only about forty miles, so we figure she had a good chance of making it," he said.

I traded looks with Kathy, the Chief, and Jean. There would be time to tell him our side of the story, and there was no reason to bring him down. We all gave silent agreement to let him have at least one evening of peace.

Tom reached up and brushed a lock of his sandy brown hair off his forehead. In a different light we could see that his rugged appearance was really his athletic demeanor. I could tell Kathy found him attractive, and Jean probably did too, but I was getting to see another side of Jean that I hadn't known was there. Up until this night I had always considered her to be just a fun loving free spirit, but now I was getting to see a maternal instinct that could only come out when a child was around. I might not have known about that side of her for a long time if Molly had not appeared in the houseboat.

The Chief scooped a second helping of spaghetti onto his own plate and added some to Tom's without asking if he wanted more. The Chief was giving Tom a good reason to stay at the table to answer more questions.

Tom took the hint and told us about those first days of the outbreak and what it was like in the hotel where he had been staying. He said there were people who were literally assaulting the hotel management over things like no room service and no clean towels.

"There were people who just weren't getting the big picture," he said.

Kathy and the Chief looked across the table at each other and looked like they might spit out their food because of some shared secret.

"What's so funny?" I asked.

Kathy said, "When we escaped from Charleston on the Atlantic Spirit, we had people on board like that. One guy said it was the worst cruise he had ever been on."

We all laughed at the absurdity of the man thinking they were on a cruise just because they were on a cruise ship. The same applied to the hotel.

"There's one big difference between the cruise ship and the hotel," said Tom. "Were they trying to charge the passengers to be on the cruise ship?"

We were all stunned by the question, but I had to ask anyway. "Are you going to tell us the hotel was still trying to collect money while the infected dead were attacking anything that moved and was still alive?"

"They told me I couldn't leave without paying my bill, and my car was in their garage. Then they tried to book someone else into my room who could pay with cash. They also increased the cost of the room to about nine hundred dollars a night."

"What did you do?" asked Jean.

"Well, I don't think we would have stayed even if the rooms were free. I didn't like knowing there were hundreds of people in the hotel who were going to be hungry and angry. If they were willing to loot a snack machine, they would be even more desperate in a few days. To make matters worse, there were about twenty hotels all packed into a few blocks. That's a lot of people without supplies in a very small area. As a matter of fact, that's probably more people than there are living in Guntersville."

Around another mouthful of food, Tom explained that they had gone to a suburban area to get away from the congested tourist district. What they found there wasn't much better. People with enough cash and vehicles that could carry supplies had stripped the stores bare already. Whole neighborhoods looked like they were getting ready for a hurricane. Windows had plywood nailed over them, and it seemed like everyone had a gun.

Tom never thought he would do anything illegal, but it wasn't long before he had stolen a car and they had begun leap-frogging from one place to the next. He said the gated communities seemed safe at first, but if you could prove you lived there, they would let you in even if you had an obvious bite mark.

Once again my companions and I shared a look of remembrance. The same thing had happened on Kiawah Island south of Charleston. The armed security guards who were paid to protect the lives of the people who lived there felt like they were rescuing their residents, but eventually the attacks began inside their protective boundaries, and the guards found themselves fighting for their own lives.

"We found pockets of people who were kind enough to take us in, but if you hung around too long, you got to see it happen every time. There was just no way to be prepared for the sheer numbers of those things. They would either overrun your defenses, or someone would get bitten and not tell anyone."

Tom paused for a moment and looked over at Molly. She was contentedly downing her chocolate milk as her father was reliving what it was like to keep her alive. I tried to imagine what it must have been like to be so worried for such a long time about someone else. Children would be so helpless to defend themselves. I wondered when Tom had been able to sleep the last time.

"What made you head south when you left Myrtle Beach?" asked the Chief. "We've been trying to figure out if there's a pattern to their movements."

Tom said, "We didn't choose south originally. I couldn't think of where else we should go, so we headed west. I don't know if I thought we could make it all the way to Guntersville, but that was the direction toward home, so that's the way we went. We only made it to Conway, though. It seemed like everyone was trying to go straight west, and the infection was moving faster than the people."

"I think," Tom continued, "it was like pouring water into a funnel. Thousands of people were trying to squeeze out of Myrtle Beach using one main road, and Conway was like a big dam. People just kept pushing from behind, and what we didn't know was that the infection was also in front of us. There were people trying to escape toward Myrtle Beach, and we were colliding with them as the infection spread outward. To tell you the truth, I don't think it would have been any different no matter which way we went."

"If you were heading west through Conway, how did you wind up directly south of Myrtle Beach?" asked Jean.

Tom answered, "Well, I guess I would have to call it dumb luck. We were stuck on Highway 501 with a few thousand other people as the sun was going down. Everything had come to a complete stop just as it was getting dark, and headlights were coming on. The police were trying to keep everyone moving west without getting all jammed up, and one of them recognized me. A Conway police officer who said he went to all of the games when he wasn't on duty recognized me and asked for my autograph."

"I was the same way," said Kathy. "When I would do traffic duty over by the minor league ballpark in Charleston, I'd watch for the players to leave, and I'd get their autographs. You never knew when one would be famous."

Tom laughed, "How many asked for your phone number when they gave you an autograph?"

Kathy blushed, which we weren't used to seeing. She knew she was pretty, but she wasn't one of those attractive women who had to hear it all the time. If anything, she was a bit self-conscious about her looks.

"There were a few times," she said.

He flashed her a smile before he went on, and I could tell she liked it. She returned the smile but then looked down at her plate.

"The officer saw Molly in the car with me and asked if she was my daughter. When I said she was, he told me to make the next left turn and pull over to the side of the road. He didn't say why he wanted me to get out of traffic, but he had this really serious look on his face. I could tell he was worried, so I did what he told me to do."

"What did he want you to do?" I asked.

Tom told us that the officer had come up alongside him in a police cruiser and motioned for him to follow his car. Not knowing what else he should do, he followed the officer as he sped down a dirt road that sloped toward the Waccamaw River.

We were very familiar with the Waccamaw River but further south than Conway. If things had gone as we expected, the bridge over the Waccamaw River where it passed through Georgetown, South Carolina was in the water rather than above it. The mudflats around that bridge were probably packed full of infected dead.

Tom continued without noticing that each of us had retreated into private memories of our attempt to rejoin civilization by flying down to the Naval Weapons Station in Goose Creek. On our way back from there, we had to leave the plane parked at a dock a few miles south of Georgetown because a bullet had clipped a hose in the engine compartment.

The police car Tom was following braked to a hard stop at the bottom of a boat ramp, something else we were familiar with because we had two boats and a seaplane. That wasn't something everybody could say these days. It also seemed like everywhere we went, we wound up at a dock or a boat landing.

Tom said he expected to see boat owners at the bottom of the ramp, but all of the boats were either military or manned by the police, and there were a lot of them. There was also some serious firepower mounted on the bows of the military boats. The officer he had followed from the crowded highway came over to his window in a rush and told him they had to hurry. He told Tom to leave their luggage in the car.

They had listened to the officer because they didn't know what else to do, but also because of his sense of urgency. When they got out of the car, Tom saw that the officer kept glancing upward. He followed the officer's eyes and saw that they had a good view of the bridge over the Waccamaw River.

What he saw made him feel a chill. The bridge was bathed in the bright lights on poles, but there were also hundreds of cars sitting still with their headlights on. Shadows were rushing in and out between the cars, and everything was moving. People seemed to be attacking each other, and the attacks were coming from the other side of the river moving rapidly toward the spot where Tom had pulled out of traffic only a few moments ago. He took Molly's hand and started to follow the officer to the boats. Like everyone else, he kept glancing up toward the chaos that was moving like a wave from car to car.

As the wave of infected dead moved along the stopped cars, people would try to get out and run, but there were so many infected already mixed in with the living that it was too late to escape. The mob of attacking infected dead and the helpless victims appeared to be moving in a swirling motion, and eventually people began to jump from the bridge. Many of them fell with their attackers still hanging on by their teeth.

The police officers and soldiers in the boats couldn't do anything to help. Part of the bridge was still over solid land, and it was more merciful than landing in the water because the fall would either kill the people trying to escape, or it would at least knock them unconscious. As much as the police and soldiers wanted to help, they knew that to do so would place everyone in their boats at risk. No one falling was likely to be unbitten, and even if they weren't, there was no way to sort them from the infected who fell with them, at least not until they hit the ground. The infected would be the first to rise from the ground, and if the shocked people on the boat landing waited long enough, they would see the victims begin to push themselves into a standing position, too.

Tom scooped Molly into his arms and ran with the police officer to the last of the boats that were casting off from the ramp. It looked to him to be about ten or twelve boats, and each was carrying six or seven heavily armed men and women in uniform. There were no other civilians who had made it to the boats, and Tom felt guilty, but he had to keep his daughter safe. He would deal with the guilt later if he had to deal with it at all.

He handed Molly up to another officer in the boat and then climbed aboard himself. Tom said he was amazed by how calm Molly was. With the exception of her pink sweatshirt, she seemed almost to be a smaller mirror image of the people around her. They were all grim faced, knowing that they could have tried to help the people up on the bridge, but they also knew it was a lost cause. It was worse than a lost cause. It was certain death.

One of the officers raised both hands in the air and waved them across each other. One by one he got the attention of someone in each boat. They, in turn, got the attention of their companions. When everyone was looking in his direction, he spoke just loud enough for them all to hear.

Tom said that he told everyone to stay as quiet as possible. No one was to shoot their weapon unless it was absolutely necessary. He said they were going to go downriver to the South and try to join up with other military and police units that were trying to fortify positions and make a stand against the infected.

His last instructions made Tom realize just how lucky he had been to have the police officer recognize him. He said the man in charge told the others there would be people on the riverbanks wanting to be rescued, and there was no way to know who had been bitten. He told them to keep their boats in the center of the river and to keep plenty of distance between themselves and private docks. There were to be no rescues, and he made sure someone on each boat answered that they understood.

One of the soldiers called out in a low voice and asked what they should do if they encountered other boats with people who were escaping. It was a logical question because there were hundreds of boat owners in the area. Some of them had escaped by water, and many could be seen on the river already.

The man in charge answered that private boats were to be told to let them pass and then to follow. When they were far enough downriver away from the populated part of town, they could try to set up a screening process. Anyone who was not bitten could remain with the group. Any boat that was even carrying a bitten passenger would stay behind or be sunk.

The officers in charge on each boat then tuned their radios to the same channels and did sound checks. They were given call signs by the officer in charge and one by one they idled their engines a little higher and steered toward the center of the river.

They kept their speed low at first, and all of the boats were dark with the exception of one red running light on the bow. The river was eighty to one hundred yards wide and was fairly deep even along the banks. If they stayed in the center, they should be able to see trouble before trouble saw them. That was when bullets started flying over the boats. Tom said he didn't know where they were coming from until two of their boats began returning fire.

The crew told Tom that the boats were armed with the Ma deuce, or M2 .50 caliber machine guns. They and the M134 mini guns were spitting out four thousand rounds a minute and quickly silenced whoever was shooting at them. They were also using tracers, so he could see the eerie glow of every fifth bullet as they streaked toward the boat landing.

Tom said that he and Molly were just trying not to be in the way, and there were no words to describe the gratitude he felt to the men and women who had snatched them from the jaws of death. He told us he remembered having that thought, and the phrase seemed so appropriate to describe the hideous creatures that were shambling toward families on the bridge. The screams had blended into one high pitched sound that didn't begin to die down until they were out of sight from the bridge.

Tom looked like he had reached his limit for one night, and all of us could see it. The man looked completely exhausted. I had a feeling that one more beer would put him under the table.

"Tom," said Jean, "you and Molly both need sleep. Finish your food while we get a room ready for you." She mussed up Molly's hair as she left the table, and Molly gave her a little giggle.

......

Once we had our new friends settled in for the night, the four of us returned to the living room. We had gotten into the habit of spending time talking over the daily events. It was usually just a social gathering because there hadn't been anything significant happening for a while, but we also used the time to talk about strategies and the future.

We had a roof over our heads, weapons, clean clothes, and food, but we always remembered what Uncle Titus had told me about thinking like a survivor. We had to continually remember that it could all be taken from us if mistakes were made. We also had to remember that our supplies, while plentiful, were not infinite.

Taking in a child and her father was not going to impact our supplies to a great extent, but we had been toying with the idea that we could hide our heads in the sand and ignore what was happening in the real world, or we could be proactive and prepare for the time when we would be forced out of Mud Island. As I had said to my friends before, it's like shucking an oyster. You have to pry at them to get them open, but sooner or later the oyster gets opened and gets eaten. That was one reason why we had also started monitoring the shortwave broadcasts continually.

Tonight's social gathering was like putting closure on the idea that we could just sit tight and wait until this all blew over, but we needed to know more from Tom about what was happening on the mainland. He wasn't in any shape to go on, though, and we were all left with the same question. How bad was it if a dozen boats carrying well-armed men and women didn't make it through safely with Tom and Molly?

The Chief broke the silence as we settled in on the couch and a couple of recliners. When you considered what was happening in the rest of the world, we certainly couldn't complain. We didn't have the opportunity to give Tom a complete tour before showing him to his room, but there was no doubt he would be amazed when we showed him the rest of the place.

"So," said the Chief, "anyone want to take a guess about what happened? How did they wind up here?"

"I don't follow you," said Kathy. "I'm sure Tom will have a lot more to tell us when he wakes up. Something must have gone terribly wrong for over seventy police officers and soldiers to not make it out, but one man and his child did."

"That's not what I'm getting at, Kathy. How did they get here, not how did they survive?"

Now it was my turn to be confused, and Jean didn't look like she was doing much better. She had deep frown lines on her forehead and was eyeing the Chief like he was an alien.

I said, "Chief, you're getting all of us worried. Are you having a stroke or something? You sound like you're saying the same thing twice. How did they get here, and how did they get here?"

"Oh, now I see why everyone's looking at me like that," he answered. "I'm asking, how did they get from the Waccamaw River, which is to the west of Highway 17, over to the east of Highway 17? The last time we saw Highway 17 it was the Infected Dead Memorial Highway."

All of us were intimately familiar with the coastal rivers and the main highway that ran parallel to the Waccamaw River. The four of us had made two insane trips by plane and boat away from the safety of Mud Island. We made it out and back by a combination of crazy luck and teamwork.

The Chief continued, "The Waccamaw River is about one hundred and twenty miles long. One hundred of it is in South Carolina, and it goes past us right through Georgetown. So, Tom and Molly either got off the boat before Simmonsville or after Georgetown, but there's no way they could have gotten off in between and then made it across Highway 17."

"I can't imagine how they could have gotten past Simmonsville on land," I said. "The accident that blocked Highway 17 had those infected dead backed up through Simmonsville. That's one town that had a population increase after the infection started to spread."

"And," Jean added, "if they went as far as Georgetown, how did they get turned around and come all the way back up to Mud Island? As a matter of fact, I can't wait to hear how they got across the moat to the dock."

"I imagine the most interesting part of Tom's escape with Molly is yet to be told," said the Chief. "Breakfast should be interesting."

The Chief got up and walked over to a corner of the room where he had been keeping rolled up maps and navigational charts. He searched through the collection until he found the right one and took it to the dining room.

He didn't say anything, so the rest of us followed out of curiosity. He moved a few things off the table and spread out the map. Kathy sat heavy bowls on two of the corners and passed a matched set to me to do the same on the other end.

The map was longer than the table, but the Chief had everything he needed to see in the middle. He sat a salt shaker on one spot and said, "This is Simmonsville."

I put the pepper shaker on the map and said, "Here's Georgetown."

The Chief reached over and moved it from the city to the bridge over the Waccamaw River. He said, "I think whatever happened, it had to be somewhere between these two places. Here's the Waccamaw River running parallel to Highway 17." He ran his finger along the river starting at Simmonsville and ending at Georgetown.

I looked at the land between the river and the highway, and I could see there was no possible way that anyone could have survived trying to walk from the Waccamaw River to Highway 17. There were only three roads going from Highway 17 toward the river, and they didn't go all the way to the water. The closest of the three was the dirt road that I had traveled to reach Mud Island. It went in the other direction too, but just like on my side of Highway 17, it was a dead end.

The problem was that even if they could have made it from the river to Highway 17, they couldn't have crossed that highway. It was just too crowded with the infected. As for the woods, they were worse between the highway and the river than they were on our side of the highway. The woods were so dense on that side that a person could be lost in there for days without food and water, and they wouldn't be able to go more than two feet before they were tangled in the brush. It was that bad even without the infected trying to get through there themselves. It really was no wonder that the infected stayed on the main roads. They were following the path of least resistance.

"That's only about a ten mile stretch of road," said the Chief, "but any open ground gets you spotted by the infected dead, and trying to go through the trees would be impossible."

"So, that leaves going around, either above Simmonsville or below Georgetown," said Kathy.

Jean added, "And Simmonsville is the capital city of the infected dead, so it had to be Georgetown."

I was listening to them, but I was really stuck on the question of crossing the moat more than I was on how they got to our side of the highway. Regardless of which way they had come, they had managed to breach our best security barrier.

"Guys," I interrupted, "we have a problem. I know Tom just got to sleep, but we need to find out how they got across the moat. If they could do it, then somebody or something else could do it, too."

"When was the last time any of us went out to the end of the dock?" asked the Chief.

We all looked at each other as if we needed confirmation, but we all knew there was a blind spot on the other side of the houseboat, and the last time any of us had gone that far down the dock was a long time ago.

One of our trips away from Mud Island was to bring back the plane, and we had also wanted to bring back a boat trailer so we could tow the Boston Whaler out of the water and hide it. In the process we had gotten lucky and brought back another boat. It was parked in line with the seaplane across from the houseboat.

When we parked the boat and the seaplane, we had passed behind the houseboat, and as far as I knew, none of us had been near the end of the dock since. We didn't even go that far out on the dock when we brought Tom and Molly inside.

Kathy said, "I think we can wait until morning to find out, Ed, but you're right. We have a blind spot behind the houseboat, and we took it for granted because the current was too strong through the entrance of the moat."

The Chief went back to his stash of charts again and started rummaging through them. He came back with one and rolled it out on top of the first map.

"That's a navigational chart of Mud Island," said Jean, "but there's something different about it. Is there something missing?"

"You're right, Jean. This chart was made before the jetties were built."

The Chief put one finger on the map and showed where the jetty would be built across from the northern tip of Mud Island. Where the land ended on the other side of the moat, there were markings and depths that showed there had been a large sandbar pointing straight at the island.

"I'm almost afraid to say it," said the Chief, "but I think Uncle Titus had all of this dredged when he built the jetties. The moat probably didn't even have water in it at low tide."

The moat was what we had unofficially named the body of water that separated the island from the mainland. Most of the small islands along the coast have tidal pools or marsh between them and the mainland, but we had something that looked more like a river. The only way to cross it was by boat, and we had seen countless infected dead disappear under the surface when they tried to cross it.

Jean looked at me and asked, "Did your Uncle have any pictures of the island before the work was done?"

"Not that I know of," I said. "If he did, they weren't on the island."

"Chief, are you saying you think they walked across on a sandbar?" asked Kathy.

"If they did, it means the jetty didn't keep the sand from getting deposited across the mouth of the moat, and if that's true there will come a time when the moat won't be as effective keeping us safe," said the Chief.

Jean may not have been the technical genius that the Chief was, and she tended to be quiet when we started brainstorming, but she didn't get through nursing school by being dumb.

She said, "We need to move the houseboat so we can see that blind spot, and I think we might need to move the plane and the boat to the southern tip of the island so they won't be landlocked at low tide."

She didn't notice that we were all looking at her until several moments of silence passed.

She finally looked up and said, "What? Isn't it obvious to everyone?"

Kathy said, "I don't think we need to wake Tom up. We know what we're going to find out there, and it's just a good thing that we found out before it became too shallow to move the houseboat."

"That bigger boat we brought back last time out should be able to tow the houseboat, right Chief?" she asked.

"Yeah, but that oyster Ed's always talking about is one step closer to being pried open and eaten."

2 REVELATIONS

Tom probably would have slept longer, but the smell of fresh coffee, bacon, and eggs was more than he could stand. He appeared at the entrance to the dining room looking like he wasn't sure where he was. Before he came out of his room we had all agreed that we would give him a chance to enjoy his meal before we assaulted him with our questions about how he got here. Instead, it was more important for him to know how we got here.

Once he was situated at the table with his first steaming cup of coffee in his hands, we began by telling him about how Mud Island came to be. Molly was still asleep, so it was a good opportunity to tell him about the bad things we had seen, too.

Mud Island was literally carved out of an uninhabitable stretch of beach on the coast of South Carolina. My Uncle Titus was a survivalist with money, and the rest of the relatives didn't even know he had money. That's likely to be why he had so much. Anyway, he was a survivalist with money, and he used it to prepare for every type disaster he could think of.

Tom asked, "Did he plan for a zombie apocalypse?"

"I doubt it," I said, "but this shelter and all its trimmings would have been as close as anyone could have gotten to being prepared for zombies. I think he would have done more if he hadn't died. There were some plans in his safe that showed he was looking at the idea of putting more protection in the woods on the other side of the moat. The plans had a note in the margin that said a wall was pending approval of the government after an environmental impact study."

"I guess it worked out in my favor that he didn't finish that part," said Tom.

"We've talked about that, Tom," said the Chief, "but we'll get to that after you're more awake and you've had a chance to enjoy your meal."

Jean and Kathy finished sitting plates down in front of everyone and joined us at the table.

"Wow," said Tom, "I never thought I would sit down at a table and have another meal without being worried that something was going to come up from behind me and rip into the back of my neck."

"You and Molly are safe here," said Jean. "Enjoy your breakfast while we bring you up to speed about what we know. Afterwards, you can do the same for us, but for now we want you to make yourself at home."

I went on telling Tom about Uncle Titus and the will. The rest of the relatives didn't even find out about the shelter, the houseboat, the seaplane, or the Boston Whaler which we had safely hidden in a section of the woods near the southern tip of the island.

"When I found the houseboat, I saw the plane and a boat parked across from it," said Tom. "Do you know what my biggest fear was?"

"That's an easy question," said Kathy. "You were afraid of the owners coming home and finding you living in their home. We've thought it all out, Tom. We think Uncle Titus left Ed the shelter to live in, and the nice stuff outside was all a distraction. No one would even bother to check the rest of the island if they thought everything was right at the dock."

"So," I went on, "I inherited all of this from my Uncle, and when I came down to look it over, the world went to hell. I drove up to Surfside to get some essentials."

"Some what?" three people asked at the same time.

Tom looked at the Chief, Kathy, and Jean and saw their accusing grins. Each had stopped eating and were looking at me.

"Okay, let me explain something," I said. "When I got here, there was no apocalypse in progress. Nothing was on the news about dead people attacking live people and biting them. I was thinking of this place as some sort of beach house without windows, and I was planning on living here. My uncle left me a wall safe full of money, and I figured I would quit my job and just hang out here until I decided what else to do."

Tom asked, "Doesn't that sound a bit unlikely? A shelter conveniently falls into your lap, and we have a zombie apocalypse?"

"Some people would say that," I said, "but when you think about it, people win lotteries, too. Also, there's a more realistic answer. All over the world there are survivalists who have built places like this. I doubt anyone knows how many there are, but before the zombie apocalypse, a lot of survivalists grew old and died. I don't doubt for one minute that there's another Ed Jackson out there somewhere who's holed up in a shelter because a survivalist relative left him a rabbit hole."

"That's the first time I've heard you say that," said Jean, "and it was well put. You were just the luckiest lottery winner because you got your shelter right before the apocalypse. Someone had to be last, right? Imagine how many rabbit holes might be uninhabited."

"Now get back to that part about going into town for essentials," said the Chief. "What was it that your uncle forgot to stock? Was it food, water, weapons, or ammunition?"

"It was video games," I said. "My uncle put TV's in every room with a great video library, but he knew I was into video games and didn't think to leave me an X-Box, a Playstation, or a Nintendo."

My friends were all grinning around their forks as they continued to eat, and I could tell they were just yanking my chain. Tom was clearly enjoying the way we all got along with each other, because he was grinning as he ate, too.

"Anyway," I said, "there wasn't anything happening yet, and I had rented a Jeep to make the drive down to Mud Island. When I found all the money Uncle Titus left me, I decided to return the Jeep and get some videos games at the same time. That's when it all began."

"I made it back to the shelter and closed myself in. I just holed up and watched the world go to hell and back in a handcart until the rest of this group showed up."

"So, the rest of you weren't friends of Ed's before the apocalypse? He didn't invite you guys down for a visit, and you got lucky, too?"

"Oh, we got lucky all right, but that came later," said Kathy. "Did you get to see any of the early news reports on TV about what was happening in other cities?"

Tom thought back and realized how little he had thought about what was happening elsewhere. He had been so concerned about keeping Molly safe that he had changed the channels looking for FEMA and South Carolina Emergency Management broadcasts. When he passed by the local channels, he wouldn't pay as much attention to the broadcasts as he did the red and white ticker running across the bottom of the screen.

Sometimes there were FEMA messages, but mostly he felt like the stations were just going for better ratings by being the first to report who had just gotten their throats ripped out. He remembered thinking there was probably at least one idiot reporter who had tried to get an interview with a zombie.

Tom's cynical attitude was really not his normal character. He was just frustrated and scared for his little girl, and all he wanted to know was how to keep her safe.

He said, "It all happened so fast. I turned on the TV, and I caught bits and pieces of what was happening, but I missed a lot of the real stories. At first FEMA said to go to shelters, hospitals, and schools. Then they said to stay where we were. I started to pack, then I started to unpack. Sometimes I turned off the TV when I got mad enough at it, but then I would turn it back on thinking I might miss something important."

"Did you catch any bits and pieces about a cruise ship named the Atlantic Spirit trying to get out of Charleston harbor?" asked Kathy.

Tom thought for minute and remembered seeing something about the cruise ship. There was something about the people barricading themselves into the terminal long enough to get everyone on the ship. He also remembered thinking he wished he was escaping with Molly on the big ship. There would be food, shelter, water, and people wouldn't be tipping over the vending machines.

"Yes, I saw something about that," he said. "Why?"

"Because that's where we come in," said Kathy. "We were on that cruise ship. Jean and the Chief were members of the crew. I was a Charleston City Police Officer. Jean was a Registered Nurse on the medical crew, and the Chief was in charge of ship operations. As I understand it, that means the Chief was the senior non-commissioned officer on the crew, and he was responsible for just about everything that happened on the ship."

Tom said, "So you three met each other on the ship before you met Ed. I didn't see everything that was reported about the ship, but I knew it was a safe place to be. I mean, you guys are living proof of that. You wouldn't be here right now if not for the cruise ship."

Tom looked from one face to the other and couldn't understand why he wasn't seeing something that confirmed his feelings about wishing he had been able to get Molly onto a cruise ship. All he was seeing was long faces.

The Chief said in a sober voice, "There were about five thousand souls on that ship, and you're looking at the only survivors. Jean almost didn't make it when we were trying to deal with the infected passengers who had boarded."

"Others may have made it to rafts, but we didn't see them," Jean added.

Tom's expression said he understood something better than he had before.

"That's why we had the business about inspecting us for bites when we came in last night," he said.

"People on your ship did the same thing I've seen since this all started. Families protecting bitten loved ones until it's too late. Then they turn on each other until they wind up killing other people along with their whole family."

"Exactly," said Jean. "One of them almost got me when we were trying to move his body to a better place after he died from the infection."

She didn't think she needed to tell him that they were trying to toss his body overboard. "We were trying to identify bitten people when the whole thing fell apart, and the ship was overrun by the infected. I think we were close to getting it under control at the start, but now I wonder if it's even possible. People just aren't willing to admit when they've been bitten."

"What happened to the ship?" asked Tom.

The Chief said, "As far as we know, the Navy sank it after it became a floating cemetery. We made it to a raft, and the only movement we could see was infected dead wandering around looking for more victims."

"The Navy? We still have a Navy? I got firsthand experience with what was left of our Army, but I didn't think about the Navy," said Tom.

"They're having their own problems," said the Chief. "On our first trip away from Mud Island, their base at the Naval Weapons Station in Goose Creek was getting overrun. They told us by radio it was the same at other bases up and down the coast. There were some Navy ships still doing rescue operations out of that base, but only Navy personnel and their families. The infection had gotten behind their lines because of civilians looking for help."

"And some were infected," added Tom.

I said, "On our second trip out, we encountered a Navy warship that looked dead in the water, but it looked like a Navy SEAL team was trying to board it. Our guess is that it was overrun, and the Navy was taking it back. As long as they're busy saving themselves, we can't expect them to do much for us."

Jean brought the story back around to their escape and said, "We found our hero when our raft got close enough to shore, and Eddy was out in the Boston Whaler getting in some target practice. If you think we were rough on you last night, you should have seen how bad he was. He ordered us to strip right there on the spot."

The Chief saw that I was about to object to what Jean was saying, so he came to my defense, or at least that was what I had thought he was going to do.

"Now, you know that's not true," he said. "He ordered the women to get into his boat and strip, and he told me to start paddling."

I turned beet red, but I knew better than to try to defend myself. The Chief was a straight-faced comedian when he wanted to be, so people who didn't really know him could never be sure when he was kidding.

Instead of denying what he told Tom, I said, "That's close but not exactly true. He got naked as soon as I asked how I could be sure none of them had been bitten. It was not the high point of my day."

After sharing a good laugh with us, Tom said, "I could tell from the moment I met your group that you guys are very close. You're lucky to have each other."

We acknowledged his sentiments all around the table, but my eyes lingered on Jean's, and hers did the same. It was Jean who had started whipping off her clothes as soon as I had asked them how I could be sure none of them had been bitten. I had stopped her before she had gone too far, and that moment of trust had allowed her to immediately see me for the kind of guy I am......an idiot with the chance to see two good looking women get naked, but a gentleman who would rather believe a stranger.

It was sort of sad that we reached a point where I couldn't be that trusting again. Back then it was just me, but now I would be placing others at risk by being so trusting.

Kathy said, "Tom, we trusted a couple of people on our first trip out of here. It was a married couple. They had a chance to join our group and come back with us, but the first chance they got they tried to take what we had and leave us stranded. We need to know that you're not like that."

"Did the other people have a nine year old daughter with them?" asked Tom. "It's not hard for me to tell that we're safer with you than without you, and if something happens to me, I don't think you guys would turn your back on Molly."

Jean said, "I think you hit the nail on the head, Tom. So now that you know how we ended up here, the boys can give you a tour of the rest of the shelter while we get Molly up and make her some breakfast. We still have a lot we want to know, but you need to see the rest of what we have here."

We all agreed it was time to give Tom a tour. The Chief led the way while Kathy and Jean went to get Molly. Tom was all smiles as he watched them go down the hall that led to the individual rooms.

The Chief couldn't wait to show Tom the armory, and he was like a proud father himself as he showed off the wide variety of hand guns and rifles. Tom wasn't a stranger to weapons, first because he had grown up around them, but second because he had spent time in the company of heavily armed soldiers and police. Even though he was a civilian, they had appropriately armed him as if he was one of them, and there had been no shortage of target practice.

Tom didn't have the same interest in the power plant as he did the armory, but he was definitely impressed. He listened as we explained the details to him, understanding that this was a tour, but it was also instruction that could save their lives.

We showed him the expansive storage areas and how well stocked they were. It was hard to put ourselves in his shoes since none of us were parents, but he said more than once how grateful he was that we had brought them in.

Tom said, "You mentioned something last night about the fish being contaminated. What was that all about?"

I asked him if he had seen many of the infected dead that had been in the water or out in the surf, and he said that he hadn't, but that he had seen plenty of them stuck in the mud along the Waccamaw River.

"Have you eaten any of the blue crabs or fish that you caught?" I asked.

"I didn't get a chance to before you showed up," he answered. "I was looking forward to frying the fish when you stopped me."

"How about before we came along?" asked the Chief.

"No," he said, "I found the fishing gear in the houseboat. The first thing I thought of was fresh fish. You guys left a few cans of food in the houseboat, but the thought of cooked seafood was making my mouth water."

"It won't anymore," I said. "When you see one of those infected dead standing on the beach with six or eight blue crabs hanging from it, you'll lose your taste for seafood."

"I don't think I need to see that to lose my taste for it, Ed. Just hearing you describe it is enough for me," he answered. "You think the fish are contaminated too?"

The Chief winced a bit and said, "It's the food chain, Tom. The crabs, the fish, the infected dead, and even living people are all in the food chain. I don't know if it's safe or not, but I don't want to find out."

"Come on, Tom," said the Chief. "Ed and I are going to show you something that will help take your mind off of the seafood for now. We're just glad you didn't eat any of it. We don't really know if it's bad for you, but we don't want to find out the hard way."

We took him to the workout room, and the Chief was right again. Being a professional athlete, Tom had a real appreciation for the variety of equipment.

"There's no excuse for not staying in shape with this stuff in here, and look at all the entertainment equipment to give you something to watch while you do the really boring stuff," he said.

I told him that Jean had gotten me to spend a little more time in the gym and a little less time on the video games. I had managed to gain a few pounds in the right places while losing a few around the waistline. I wasn't quite buff yet, but I liked the way I looked and felt.

We eventually made our way back to the dining room where Molly was digging into a stack of pancakes soaked in maple syrup. She couldn't have looked like she was enjoying herself more.

"Hi Daddy," she said with a big smile.

Tom circled the table and gave her a big hug, but on the way by he gave Kathy and Jean an appreciative look. The way to Tom's heart was definitely through that child.

After Tom was done talking with Molly for a few minutes, he came with us to the living area so we could talk about the question that was burning a hole through our brains. How did they get here? Not just their escape from Conway, but literally how did they get to Mud Island? Molly would be content with her food for a bit, and we could get some information.

The ladies followed us to the living room, and we all got comfortable with fresh cups of coffee. Tom looked around the room and realized he was still the center of attention, but he couldn't know that it was more than just his journey we needed to know about. It was our long term safety.

Since Molly was eating at the dining room table, the Chief just handed a sketch pad to Tom and said, "Take a look at this, Tom. This is Mud Island." He pointed at the northern tip and said, "Here's where the dock would be, and the houseboat would be right about here." He drew a rectangle next to a straight line.

"This is the moat, and this would be the mainland. Did you cross from the mainland to Mud Island from somewhere around this area?" asked the Chief.

Tom studied the rough drawing for a moment to get his bearings and said, "Yes, this spot right here wasn't more than knee deep at low tide. When I saw the houseboat the tide was going out, but the water was too deep for us to cross, and the current was so strong we couldn't make it two feet without it starting to pull me along with it. Molly and I sat on the rocks and watched the tide go out, and gradually the bottom appeared all the way across. I carried her over and I lifted her onto the deck of the houseboat, then I climbed up after her."

Tom saw our concerned looks and easily guessed what the problem was.

"There was a man-made jetty extending outward from the mainland. The rocks we were sitting on were part of the jetty. There was a big gap in the jetty about twenty yards out, and a sandbar was forming from the gap all the way to your island."

The Chief said, "The good news is that the infected aren't problem solvers. They aren't going to wait for low tide. The bad news is that some will stumble out of the woods at low tide. Jean was right when she said we need to move the houseboat so our camera will have a clear view to the other side of the moat where the jetty begins. That won't be so hard to do."

"What about the seaplane and the boat?" I asked. "Are we in danger of the southern exit of the moat being closed, too?"

The Chief drew the southern tip of Mud Island and showed them how the sand would be deposited over a long period of time. "As long as the sand keeps building up in this area," he shaded in the drawing with his pencil at the place where the southern jetty touched the beach, "Mud Island will just grow a larger beach. Eventually, the sand will start going around the tip of the jetty, and a sandbar will form."

"How long will that take?" asked Kathy.

"Maybe years," said the Chief, "but we should start a regular program of monitoring the depth of the water. Years may seem like a long time, but since we're likely to be here for years, we need to be thinking about what we're going to do then."

"When do we move the houseboat?" I asked.

The Chief switched on the TV screen and brought up the camera view of the dock. It was a clear day, but we could tell it was windy. That might mean there was a storm offshore.

"I don't see any reason to wait," said the Chief. "The tide is coming in, and the wind is from the East. That should help us move the houseboat once it clears the end of the dock. Let's park it facing to sea in the channel right along the L shaped part of the dock. We won't have protection for the plane and the boat during bad weather, but they should be okay. We'll also have a new blind spot, but the water is deep at the end of the dock. Nothing can cross there."

Kathy looked around and said, "Looks like a nice day for some fresh air. Anyone care to join me for a stroll?"

Jean said, "Count me in. I could use some fresh air, and I think it will do the baby some good, too."

One thing I had learned about our group that was really fun was that each of us was capable of saying totally absurd things while keeping a straight face. Then we would all exchange looks with each other like we were in a movie and looking right at the camera.

This was one of those times, but instead of the usual fits of laughing that would follow whatever absurd comment had been made, this moment went on for a few more heartbeats. I don't know if we were waiting for a punchline or what, but Kathy was the first one to make everyone snap out of suspended animation.

"Oh, my God, Jean," she said as she wrapped her arms around Jean and pulled her into a really sweet hug. "You aren't, I mean really?"

Jean hugged her back and said, "Yes, really."

I was still standing there looking like I didn't have a clue about how to react. I looked at the Chief and Tom, who were both looking at me, waiting for me to do something. The Chief had his tongue in his cheek, probably to keep from swallowing it, and Tom had a neutral expression. Since Jean had just said what she had so naturally, Tom wasn't really picking up on the fact that this was news to me.

If I had been a cartoon character, a lightbulb would have appeared over my head. I looked at Jean, first at her face and then lower. I didn't know you could be paralyzed by hearing such things, but apparently you can.

Kathy let go of Jean and turned to me next. When she put her arms around me, I was still looking at Jean. She had a big smile on her face, and then I finally understood that glow I had been seeing every time she looked at Molly. She really had been seeing what a little Jean would look like.

My paralysis ended just as Kathy finished hugging me, and I managed to get my arms around Jean next. I couldn't think of what to say, or I wasn't capable of speaking. I wasn't sure which one it was.

I finally managed to croak past a big lump in my throat, "I love you, Jean"

The Chief, always looking for the right time when I would provide him with comedy material he could use, said, "I told you he can talk. You just have to wait for it, and by the way, what happened to Uncle Titus' private stock of optimism?" That's what Jean had called the big supply of condoms she had found in the infirmary supplies.

Jean answered before I could, "You know how it is, Chief. Sometimes enthusiasm is stronger than optimism."

I was glad she answered so I wouldn't have to take all of the blame for that enthusiasm.

3 JETTIES

It was somewhere near the end of the first week in January, and it was anything but a nice day for a stroll, but the fresh air was a welcome change. We were bundled up and armed. Tom was going with us, and it felt good to have a fifth person in the group. It felt safer.

I expected Molly to get upset when Tom told her she would be staying inside, but her separation anxiety didn't show. Tom told us he had tried his best to help her understand what had happened to the world. At her age she was just past the stage where she had to look under the bed at night before she could go to sleep, and she was still young enough to have an irrational fear of losing her father. Of course these were unusual times, and if I didn't have Jean in my bedroom with me at night, I would probably look under the bed for monsters. Molly also had every right to be worried about losing her father.

I looked around to see what Molly was doing as we were getting ready to go outside, and I saw both Jean and Kathy huddled around her over at the shortwave radio. They were showing her how to press the microphone key and rotate the dial until the digital numbers changed. Jean helped Molly to get the headphones over her ears without catching her hair, and then they adjusted the volume to where she said it wasn't too loud.

I heard Kathy ask her, "Molly, what's rule number one?"

Molly answered, "Do not tell anyone where we are."

"That's very good, Molly, now what's rule number two?"

She answered, "Don't tell anyone how many people are here with me."

"You're a very fast learner, Molly. Can you tell me what rule number three is?"

Molly looked like she was thinking it over for a moment, but then she said, "If anyone talks to me, ask them where they are and how many people live with them."

I had to laugh at that, and Jean looked like she was barely keeping it in herself. She leaned over to be closer to Molly and said, "Do you remember rule four?"

Molly gave her head a nod first and then said, "Every time I talk, press this button. When I'm done talking say over and let go of the button."

We all applauded Molly for answering correctly and watched as she situated herself in front of the dial. She turned it a little, listened, and then turned it a little more. Jean had told her she may hear nothing but noise, but we needed her to try.

The Chief and Tom were waiting for us in the decontamination room. I was surprised to see that the Chief was wearing a wetsuit and had a complete set of SCUBA diving gear at his feet.

When he saw my expression, he said, "It's about time we find out how deep the moat is and what's at the bottom."

"I hate to ask, Chief, but do you expect to find something at the bottom?" I wasn't particularly fond of deep water, which meant anything that was deeper than my own height, and I didn't want to think about why the Chief expected something to be at the bottom, but I couldn't stop myself from asking.

The Chief said, "I've noticed when the infected go into the water, they just disappear, so we know it's deep and there's a swift current. Hopefully, the dead have just been carried right out through the southern exit to the moat, but if they are getting stuck on the bottom by the oyster beds, I want to see what kind of condition they're in."

The Chief was a big man, but the wetsuit made him look bigger for some reason. I had never asked him how tall he was or how much he weighed. It just didn't seem like the polite thing to do for some reason. My guess was that he was an even six and a half feet tall, but I couldn't guess the weight. He was mostly muscles and his workouts with the weights were impressive.

We all gathered at the door after checking the cameras one more time to be sure the area outside was clear. We stepped through the big vault door into a brisk wind and took a defensive stance in case there was something outside we hadn't seen. I closed the heavy door behind us and gave the combination lock a spin.

Other than the quick trip outside to bring in Tom and Molly, we hadn't been finding reasons to put ourselves in danger by opening that door. Uncle Titus had left messages for me, and the number one rule he had given more than once was not to leave the shelter. If he only knew how many times I had broken that rule.

The brush and trees of Mud Island had been turned brown by the cold wind blowing in off of the ocean. The leaves were thinner on the trees, and we could see further than usual, so there was less chance that any infected dead that had strayed onto the island could get near us before we saw them. It was a good thing we could see further, because the wind would cover the sounds they make as they shambled around in search of a victim to bite.

We moved in single file, and we moved fast. It was cold, and we wanted to get the job done as quickly as we could. Planning the move of the houseboat was easy. We would hook the bigger of our two boats to the stern and give it a tug. While one person handled the boat that was earning its keep as a tugboat, the rest of us would handle steering lines and just let the current carry the houseboat into position. The Chief would wait to dive into the moat until after we were done.

When we got to the dock, the Chief jumped into the big boat and got it started. We were all happy to hear it start up so easily since it hadn't gotten much use. As most boaters know, the best way to treat an outboard engine was to flush it with fresh water. That was a luxury we hadn't been able to afford, and we hoped we could one day make a trip along the coast and find a dock with a fresh water supply where we could get it done.

While the Chief assumed his position, I went to the far end of the dock to get a look at the other side of the moat. I wasn't happy with what I saw. There was a group of about a dozen infected dead just standing at the spot where the breach in the jetty had let the sand pour through. They were doing what the infected tend to do when there were no victims to pursue, just hanging around.

I yelled in their direction, and they immediately became agitated. Kathy, Jean, and Tom came over to where I was when I yelled, and we watched together as the infected tried to come to us.

"Why'd you yell at them, Ed?" asked Kathy. "They weren't going to be a problem."

I had to raise my voice a bit over the sound of the wind and the outboard engines as the Chief revved up the boat. "I wanted them gone when the Chief goes into the water, Kathy. By the time he goes in, they should be washing out to sea on the other end of the island."

Once our visitors were all swimming, or rather sinking, we took our positions at the lines, and the Chief brought the boat around to the stern of the houseboat. We hooked him up, and he took up the slack on the lines. There was nothing at first, but with a slight jolt the houseboat began to slide along the dock. We played out the longest lines at the stern and kept the lines at the bow short. At the same time, the Chief started to turn inward toward the moat. The houseboat pivoted nicely at the end of the dock and neatly slipped into its new position. It was now behind the plane, but we would have an unobstructed view of the hole in the jetty with our camera, and it had been as easy as we had hoped it would be.

"Okay, kids," said the Chief. "Let's find out what's on the bottom of the moat."

"Remind again me why we need to do this," I said.

The Chief pointed at the spot where the sandbar was forming at the breach in the jetty. "If that grows enough to fill in the end of the moat, we could see a time when the moat is empty at low tide. At the very least, it could be shallow. One thing we need to find out is whether or not your uncle buried the power, water, and fuel lines, or if he figured the moat was deep enough. If they get exposed at low tide, they're vulnerable......and so are we."

Jean leaned over and looked into the water. "Are you going to be able to see down there, Chief?"

"I have some underwater lights, but I won't be able to see too far in front of me, Jean. That's why I need you guys to keep tension on the lines I'm hooking to my weight belt."

"How will we know if you need to come up in a hurry, Chief?" she asked.

He lifted a very light but tough cord and said, "This is my emergency tether. If I give a hard tug on this, everybody get me to the surface as fast as you can."

Every time I had ever seen someone SCUBA dive on TV or in a movie, they would either step off the edge of something and disappear feet first, or they would sit on the rail of a boat and just fall over backwards. The Chief laid down on the end of the dock near the stern of the houseboat with his upper body extended out over the water. He put his mask over his face and lowered himself until his head was in the water. We watched and waited as his head swiveled to the left and right.

When the Chief lifted his head, he sat with his legs crossed and took off the mask.

"Ed, did your uncle say anything about staying out of the water?"

I thought for a moment, but I couldn't remember him mentioning it.

"No, Chief, he said not to leave the shelter. That was the only rule. Why? Is there something down there?"

"Seeing is believing, folks. When I go in, whatever you do, don't let the lines play out too fast," said the Chief.

Kathy said, "Chief, I brought my cell phone with me. Think we could put it inside a sandwich bag or something? You could get a few pictures or some video."

"Good idea, Kathy. There's a box of Zip-Lock bags in the houseboat," I said.

Kathy went into the houseboat and rummaged around through the kitchen cabinets. As a bonus she found a roll of clear tape they could use to get a good seal on the sandwich bag. She dropped the cell phone inside and sealed it shut. Then she rolled the zipper end of the bag a couple of times and taped it shut.

As soon as she handed it to the Chief, he leaned back over into the water and aimed it at something. A few seconds later he sat back up on the dock and looked at the video. He handed it over to Kathy, and she watched for a moment. She looked like she went pale.

Jean, Tom, and I took our turn, and it was easy to see why the Chief was concerned about going in the water. There was an infected dead stuck under the houseboat.

We couldn't tell why it was stuck. It probably had some piece of clothing or body part caught on a nail. Whatever was holding it in place, it was the fact that it was still moving and still reaching for the Chief that made us nervous. They don't drown. We had suspected as much because of the people we had met on the Stono River when we went to get the seaplane, but we hadn't seen it for ourselves.

"How long do you figure it's been there?" asked Tom.

Kathy said, "Judging by the skin that's hanging off of its face, I think maybe it's been there a long time. Something has been eating him."

In the video it just looked like loose flesh on the side of its head at first, but as it moved a bit, we could see that it was a small crab. Tom turned away from the group and retched.

Jean knew the feeling since she had done the same thing once before, and she rubbed his back to help him get over it.

"Now I understand why you said not to eat the seafood," said Tom. "I don't think I'll ever look at seafood the same way again."

Kathy said, "Brace yourself, Tom. We came across an entire floating community that was using the infected as crab bait. We had to leave our plane behind on our first trip away from the shelter. When we went back for it, we had to go by boat, and the mouth to the Charleston harbor was a death trap. Armed survivors in Fort Sumter shoot anyone who tries to go in that way. So, we had to use the Stono River to get in. The people at the Stono Marina had managed to separate themselves from the infected, but five hundred people got hungry and started to eat the seafood."

"They were using the infected as bait?" asked Tom. "How did they catch the infected?"

"There was no shortage of infected in the water," said Kathy. "As a matter of fact, they were still falling into the river from a bridge by the marina. The people were hooking the infected and just lowering them back into the river. An hour or so later they would pull them back up to harvest the blue crabs hanging on for their own meal."

"I've been thinking about that a lot," I said. "The people at the marina had to cook the crabs in something, right?"

"People usually boil blue crabs, Ed. Why do you ask?" said Kathy.

"Well," I said, "they didn't have a fresh water supply. That means they were boiling river water. I imagine you would have to boil it a long time before it was safe to drink, so they were really poisoning themselves."

Jean had been listening to us talk about the marina. Even though she was a nurse and had seen her fair share of trauma, the thought of eating the infected crabs had hit her particularly hard. Jean walked over to the end of the dock where the Chief was waiting for Kathy to bring him the cell phone.

"Do we really have to do this, Chief? I don't think I could take it if something happened to you."

The Chief looked up at Jean and said, "I'll be okay down there as long as I know I have you guys up here worrying about me. Let's do this, Kathy."

Kathy brought him the sandwich bag with the cell phone in it, and he started the video recording.

"I don't want to be fiddling with this when I should be looking at what's in front of me," he said. He flashed that big smile of his, and turned back toward the water.

I tied the main lines we would use to retrieve him to his weight belt, and Kathy tied the lighter line around his right wrist. She said, "If you give any sudden jerks on this line, be ready to get yanked out of there even if it's a false alarm."

"I'm counting on that," he said. "I would rather get yanked out on a false alarm than to have you guys up here debating about whether or not it was a signal for help."

Jean looked sick as the Chief eased himself head first into the deep water at the side of the dock that pointed inland. This time he didn't stop with just his head submerged.

Jean looked at me, and I could see tears in her eyes. I hadn't really been worried about the Chief until I saw that look on Jean's face.

I started concentrating on what was happening to the ropes that were attached to the Chief. I had one of the main rescue lines, and Tom had the other. Kathy had the signal line and was already focusing closely on the tension of the line. She had to play the line out carefully so it would be just tight enough for her to tell his normal movements from a signal that he was in trouble.

The bubbles from the Chief's SCUBA gear were moving further from us toward the center of the waterway that we called the moat. It completely surrounded the island that hid the shelter inside it, and it had proven to be a good defense again the infected. We had seen plenty of the infected walk into the moat and just disappear under water. The beach on the mainland side didn't slope into the water. It just dropped straight down like a ledge. On the island side, there were massive beds of oysters that would shred the flesh of anyone who tried to cross through them, infected or alive.

There was an added bonus of sharks swimming in the moat when the weather was warmer. Thankfully, there wouldn't be any sharks in this area in January. If the sand managed to come through the hole in the jetty enough to block off the northern entry to the moat, there wouldn't be sharks in the moat on a regular basis for a long time.

The Chief was making good progress and had gone so far that he was likely to be able to see the widest part of the moat between the island and the mainland. The cold water was a bit more clear than usual, so visibility might be better where it was deeper.

The main line I was holding was a bit slack, so I pulled it in a bit. I saw that Tom was doing the same with his line. Kathy's brow was furrowed as she focused all of her attention on the signal line.

Jean was alternating between the bubbles and looking at the lines. Her head was going back and forth between them.

"Something's wrong," she said. The urgency in her voice made all three of us look at her. The rescue lines weren't moving much, and the signal line wasn't pulling hard enough for Kathy to get concerned.

"What makes you think he's in trouble, Jean?" I asked. My voice was probably an octave higher than I would have liked, because it made me sound a little panicked.

"The bubbles have moved all the way over there," she said. She pointed in the general direction of the bubbles which were at least ten yards farther away from us.

"I've been watching your lines. Kathy has been playing out signal line, but you guys haven't been playing out rescue lines." Jean's voice made mine sound calm.

Tom and I looked at each other and at the coils of rope by our feet. She was right. Kathy had played out much more line than we had. I tested my line and felt movement on the other end, so I knew I was still hooked to the Chief's weight belt. Tom tested his and shrugged his shoulders.

"Feels the same to me," said Tom. "See what happens if you retrieve him a bit."

I pulled on my line and felt it go tight. It felt like when you go fishing and a turtle grabs your bait. The line gets tight, and then you feel like you're dragging something, but you gradually get the turtle out of the water. Tom's line wasn't getting slack as my line was being pulled in. We exchanged looks again, but this time we both saw the same urgency Jean had shown.

"Kathy," I yelled. "Anything happening over there? We're pulling him in."

"Hurry, Ed. Please hurry." Jean sounded like she was choking on tears.

Kathy's signal line continued to gradually go out and to the right where the bubbles were coming to the surface.

She yelled, "Should I try to pull him in with the signal line, Ed?"

I didn't have all the answers. As a matter of fact, I didn't have any of the answers. The only one of us who knew what was going on down there was the Chief, and this wasn't part of the plan.

"Wait, Kathy," screamed Jean, and she began frantically pointing toward the bubbles. "They're moving faster. I think he's going for the opposite shore. Let the line play out."

The air bubbles were definitely moving away faster than before, and the rescue lines were tight but still in front of the dock, not more than ten yards away. Tom started to pull his line harder and was being met with strong resistance.

I said, "Wait a second, Tom."

He stopped pulling for a moment as I looped my line around a piling on the dock. Then I helped him start to pull in his line.

We had our fears about what would be on the other end of the line when it came to the surface, but we knew it wasn't going to be the Chief unless something had stolen his breathing gear.

"Kathy, keep to the right," I said. "Jean, you stay behind us. Whatever it is on the end of this rope, Tom and I are going to tow it to the left and tie it off right behind the plane. Then we'll get the other line."

When the water soaked head of an infected dead broke the surface of the moat, it wasn't really a surprise anymore. I was relieved because it wasn't hanging onto the Chief, and only he could know how he traded places with this thing. As a matter of fact, there was still one line left to pull in, and the odds were in favor of the Chief having traded places with two of them.

We moved to our left along the dock until we got to the plane. The infected dead was like an anchor because he was so bloated with water, but the line was securely pulling him along.

"Guys," Jean said. Look at the second line."

We tied off the line and went back to Jean. The second line had pulled tight in the direction we had dragged the other one.

"It's following the splashing noise of the first one," she said.

"Let's not stop it," I said. "That first one was heavy, so if this one wants to do some of the work, let him."

Tom untied the line, and we just followed as it pulled itself along the bottom to where we had tied off the other one. Once we had it tied off, we ran back to where Kathy was handling the signal line.

"The air bubbles have almost reached the other shore," said Kathy. "What's he doing?"

The Chief broke the surface just short of the opposite side of the moat not too far from the place where the jetty started. He pulled himself out of the water and sat down in the sand. When he pulled off his mask, he was too far away for us to be sure, but it looked like he was smiling again. He held up his right arm and then gave a tug on the signal line. I couldn't wait to find out what had happened down there, but the first thing we had to do was get the Chief back on our side of the moat.

Tom cupped his hands around his mouth and shouted, "Can you swim back to us?"

The Chief emphatically moved his head from side to side. He pointed toward the jetty, and it was my guess that he planned to walk back across at low tide. In the meantime, he would need to have us covering him. We hadn't forgotten that those woods were sometimes crowded with the infected. That was why he had shaken his head from side to side rather than to yell back at us. I was glad we thinned them down by twelve before we moved the houseboat.

"Kathy, you qualified as a sharpshooter, didn't you?" I asked.

"Sure did, Ed." She grabbed one of our scoped rifles and ran over to the houseboat. She disappeared through the door and then reappeared as she reached the roof. She didn't waste time looking for the perfect position and started scanning the tree line behind the Chief.

Chief Joshua Barnes had spent almost his entire life on one type of ship or another, so he trusted the water. He particularly trusted the open sea, and he didn't trust the woods. You just couldn't see far enough, but there wasn't anything wrong with his hearing.

I joined Kathy just in time to see the Chief carrying his gear along the beach, and he was in a big hurry. He had left the signal line behind.

I scanned with my scope where he had been sitting just as the first of the infected came out of the trees. It was stumbling as it tried to get free of the trees and then stepping into the soft sand. It fell down once but went from a crawl to a standing position with determination. I couldn't hear it from so far away, but I had been close enough to them to know it was undoubtedly making plenty of noise. That would draw more of them in the same direction.

Kathy had also seen it come out of the trees and was sighting in on it. Her first shot dropped it just as the tree line became a target rich environment.

Jean appeared on my left, and Tom was to my right on the other side of Kathy. The four of us started shooting as fast as we could acquire a new target, and the Chief was strapping his tanks back on even as he ran.

I hoped he wasn't going to try to walk on the jetty because the rocks were far too slippery. The infected couldn't follow him onto the rocks, but living people were likely to break a leg or worse by trying to walk on them. The Chief had worn diving shoes inside his flippers, but they wouldn't be much help.

Some of the infected were attracted to the noise of our guns and began turning in our direction. After a few steps, they were falling into the water and sinking out of sight. That thinned the horde down faster, and we were able to focus on the infected that were still following the Chief.

By the time he was faced with a decision on where to go, the last of the infected had either been shot or had walked into the water. Through my scope I could see the Chief's chest was heaving. He was a big, strong guy, but he had just crossed the moat against the current and then jogged down a sandy beach with SCUBA diving gear on his back. Even he would be tired. As I watched, he sat down heavily on the big rock where the jetty began.

Tom was probably the only one of us he could hear over the wind, so he cupped his hands around his mouth again and yelled, "Are you okay?"

The Chief gave us a thumbs up and went back to watching the tree line for more company. Jean wrapped her arms around me and I felt a faint sob as she let go of her pent up fears.

We kept watch over the Chief for the next three hours when we saw the tide was going back out. Before long it had become low enough for him to walk across. It was still hip deep, and the current would have been too much for the average person, but the Chief pushed against it. He kept looking down into the water, keeping his eyes on the bottom. It wasn't likely that any of the infected would come back out through this end of the moat, but he didn't want any surprises.

......

There are a lot of words you could look up in the dictionary that mean good things, and you would find a picture of Chief Joshua Barnes next to each of them. As big as a bear, but he had a kind heart and a gentle way about him that made everyone feel like they were protected when he was nearby. Seeing him stranded on the other side of the moat made us feel separated from the safety we were used to feeling. He was under the protection of our rifles, but having his solid personality over there instead of over here with us made us feel like we were the ones who were stranded. Even Tom seemed unnerved by having to wait for the tide to go out.

As we watched the Chief carefully crossing on the sandbar bridge that was forming across the northern entrance of the moat, I thought about what it was like when we first met, what we had been through together, and what it had been like living with him in the shelter.

When the raft that carried the Chief, Jean, and Kathy had appeared out of nowhere, one of my first thoughts was how impossible it looked to see a man that big in a raft. His full, reddish beard made him look a bit like a Viking in a tiny ship. When he smiled that first time, I felt like a friend was smiling at me. Of course he had a way of joking with me that always seemed to catch me off guard. It was just his way of enjoying life, not at my expense, but along with me. We may be facing the end of society as we knew it, but he was going to enjoy the company of his friends. Of that I was sure.

In the raft he was still wearing a white uniform from the cruise ship, Atlantic Spirit. His expression sitting in the raft with a long paddle across his lap was a look of amusement, and as much as I tried to find something else that was amusing, I was pretty sure he was amused by the sight of me standing at the stern of my Boston Whaler with a weapon in my hands.

What I learned later was that he wasn't the kind of person who was amused at someone else's expense. It was just his way of letting everyone know it was always safe to find enjoyment in the moment, and as amazing as it seemed, he was smiling as he crossed the dangerous gap between the mainland and the dock.

It wasn't as if the Chief was our leader. It was more like we worked together in everything we did. We had made two trips away from the shelter, and we had been a team each time. If we tried to make the Chief our leader, he probably would have deferred to Kathy, and even though she was an assertive, trained Charleston City Police Officer, she would have deferred to him, not because he was a big man, but because she trusted him.

As the Chief came the last few yards, he pulled his air tanks from his back and easily lifted them up onto the dock. He barely had a chance to stand up straight after pulling himself up onto the dock before both Jean and Kathy had their arms around him. Of course, he looked amused about their concern. He gave them both big hugs, reassured them, and then started to guide them toward me.

"Ed, we need to get back inside and talk about what happened down there."

Tom came over and joined us. He no doubt felt like an outsider at times, but only because he could see how close we were. When we had the time to tell him about our past adventures, he would really begin to understand just how close people could be.

"Where's the cellphone, Chief?" I asked.

He handed it over, and I put it in a safe place so nothing could happen to it before we got back inside. The tide was going out, but a strong wind was kicking up, and along with it the rain. Wind and rain could hide the sounds made by the infected, so we gathered up our weapons and other gear and headed back for the shelter.

"Hey, Chief," I said. "Care to give me a clue about what you saw?"

The Chief laughed as he started for the end of the dock, but this time he didn't look amused.

"You guys pulled in two lines with two of the infected hooked onto them instead of me. What do you think was down there?"

That wasn't the answer I wanted to hear.

With the sun more to the West, the ocean side of Mud Island was all shadows and cold breezes. We were in a hurry to get back because we wanted to see what was on the video, and we also didn't feel safe. The outside seemed more sinister than I could remember from the past. We made good time, and I dialed in the combination of the door quickly.

Molly was where we had left her, intently listening to the noise in her headphones as she slowly turned the dial. She looked up and gave us a little wave before going back to her work.

I crossed to the sofa and brought up the camera view of the dock to see if we had accomplished what we had set out to do. The screen came to life. Where the houseboat had been there was now a clear view across to the tip of the mainland. There was a horde of infected crowding around the area where the Chief had been sitting, literally too many to count.

Tom let out an exclamation of surprise. "That's right where Molly and I crossed the water and where you crossed today, Chief. I never realized there were so many of those things out there."

We all gathered around the TV screen and watched, for the moment forgetting about the video and what the Chief had seen below. One by one the infected dead broke away from the horde and tried to cross the water, but they apparently had no depth perception because they couldn't tell deep water from shallow water. Some went straight into the deep water and sank below the surface, and some stumbled into the shallow water above the sandbar.

The end result was the same because they didn't tend to walk in a straight line, drawn only in the direction of the last noise they heard. Sooner or later they would lose their forward motion to the current and stray off of the sandbar into deeper water.

Some fell down, got back up, and started walking back in the same direction from which they had come. They would shamble into the other infected dead walking behind them, and the collision would cause two or more to fall into deeper water.

We were fascinated by their inability to reason out that they could cross safely if they stayed on the sandbar, but our fascination was also sheer horror at the number of infected that came out of the trees as the ones in front continued to get washed away.

"What do we do if any of them make it across?" asked Tom.

"The same thing we've always done," said Kathy. "Nothing. They can't get in here. If nothing else, they are a deterrent to the wrong kind of people trying to get to the dock."

Jean said, "Eddy, where's the cell phone? I want to see what the Chief saw."

I dug it out of a zipped pocket on the inside of my coat. No water had gotten into the sandwich bag, so it should be okay. I switched the TV to receive the image from the phone and turned on the video playback mode.

The first minute or so was the blurred image of the infected dead that was stuck under the houseboat. It was reaching with one hand in the direction of the Chief. The Chief explained that he wanted to be sure that one couldn't reach him before he went deeper.

The cell phone rotated back to the left, and the view became murky. There wasn't much light to begin with, but the depth of the water made everything look black up ahead. The Chief gave a little kick to go deeper and kept the camera aimed down at about a forty-five degree angle. He turned on a flashlight and aimed it in the same direction.

"This is about when we were playing out your lines slowly," I said. "We weren't too worried about what was happening at this point because your bubbles were coming up not far from the lines."

Everyone moved in closer to get a better look except the Chief. He knew what was down there, and he knew what was about to happen next. If we hadn't been packed together so tightly in front of the TV, maybe all of us wouldn't have screamed when a face appeared right in front of the camera.

The Chief had shown the presence of mind to keep the camera aimed at the infected for a moment longer before he tucked it into his weight belt. We all looked at him for an explanation because the view was pitch black.

He said, "The infected was bloated from being in the water a long time, and body gases were probably making it start to float to the surface. It tried to grab me as it floated by. I was just lucky that it didn't start floating to the surface directly below me. It managed to get a grip on one of the rescue lines, so I unclipped it from my weight belt and managed to loop it around the infected. No sooner had I finished with that one when a second one drifted up from below. I decided it was time to get out of there. I looped my second line around that one and started swimming against the current toward the other side."

"Why didn't you just come back to the surface, Chief?" asked Jean. "You had us scared to death."

He reached over and put his arm around Jean's shoulders and pulled her close as he said, "I only wanted to go down there once, Jean, so I needed a picture of what I saw."

"I don't need a picture that bad," she answered. "A description will do just fine." She sounded angrier than she was, but she went ahead and punched the Chief in the chest. I'm not sure he noticed.

Right on time the camera view got lighter as the Chief had pulled the cell phone out of his weight belt. The view went all over the place but finally settled on something big in the distance. The Chief was swimming almost parallel to something, but he was getting a bit closer at the same time.

It was a horrifying sight straight out of a nightmare description of the gates of Hell. There was a net stretched across the moat from the island all the way to the other side. It didn't go all the way to the surface, and its purpose could not have been guessed without a clue from Uncle Titus, but right now it was a body catcher. Sharks had room to go over the net, and when I had gone through the area in the Boston Whaler, I probably had passed over it with at least ten feet of clearance. The infected hadn't been as lucky.

The Chief must have stopped moving forward because the camera panned back and forth to take in as much of the scene as possible. There were hundreds of the infected tangled in the net. Most of them were moving, and blue crabs roamed freely over them.

A large portion of the captured infected dead were bloated from their extended stay in the water, and we watched in sick fascination as a body came loose from the net and started drifting toward the surface. When it reached the top of the net, the current caught it and carried over the net and into the darkness beyond.

"You can't see it," said the Chief, "but it looked like there was a second net about twenty to forty yards past the first one."

"What will this mean to us?" I asked. "As long as we stay out of the water we should be okay, right?"

"For now it's not a problem," said the Chief, "but if the sandbar gets big enough to stop the flow of water through the moat, it will eventually all collapse to the bottom. How many tons of wet bodies do you figure those nets are holding?" he asked the group.

Kathy was the first to understand why that mattered. "Chief, were you able to see the conduits that run from Mud Island to the mainland?" she asked.

The Chief ran the video of the nets backward and then froze the picture. He said, "Look closely right across the middle of the net." He put his finger up to the TV screen at the area he wanted us to look at. There appeared to be a straight line under all of the bodies.

"Is that what I think it is?" I asked.

He answered, "If you think that might be a big pipe that crosses the moat, then it's what you think it is. I think your uncle may have put up the nets to protect the pipes, but he couldn't have guessed the nets would become dangerous if they got too heavy."

"Let me see if I understand you, Chief," said Tom. "If the nets hadn't been there, and the sandbar completely stopped the flow of water, the pipes would probably have become buried in mud over time. That would have been a good thing."

Kathy picked up the thought from there, "But the nets have been catching hundreds of the infected for months. If the water goes down too fast, the weight of all those bodies could crush the pipes that carry power to the island. We would have to start tapping our fuel reserves."

"How long can we live off of those fuel reserves, Chief?" asked Jean.

The Chief had lived and worked on ships for a long time, and he was used to calculating fuel needs without a calculator. One hand went to his beard. That was his body language that meant he was thinking something through. It only took a couple of minutes before he answered.

"If we begin a power consumption plan as soon as the landline fails, we could probably stretch it out for a couple of years. Hot meals could be decreased to one per day, and leftovers could be eaten cold. Hot showers can be on a schedule rather than every night the way we do it now."

I said, "We always knew that the power might fail just because of reactors going off line and hydroelectric plants needing repairs. It was just a matter of time."

"Any chance we can prolong the inevitable?" asked Kathy.

"What have you got in mind?" asked the Chief. "I don't think we can get a dredge and bring it here if that's what you're thinking. Dredges are usually not able to move under their own power. They get pushed and pulled into place by a tugboat. Besides, we can't patch that hole in the jetty. Those rocks are too heavy."

"I wonder how the hole got there in the first place," I said.

"Something must have rammed it," said the Chief. "Whatever it was, after it hit the jetty and knocked some rocks out of place, it must've gotten free and went back to open water around the jetty. It may have even sunk in deeper water. Those rocks would punch a pretty big hole in most ships. The point is that we have a hole in the jetty, and we can't do anything about it no matter how it got there. Any other ideas?"

We all looked at each other helplessly, but no one had anything to contribute. The Chief said, "At the present rate of sand build up, we could begin to see a drop in the water level within a month. After that it will move faster because less water will come back into the moat. In a week or so after that, we'll see the top of the net and the first of the bodies."

I was picturing the net above the water line, and I could see it pulling at its moorings. That's when an idea hit me.

"Chief, how are the nets anchored to the mainland and to Mud Island?" I asked.

"I already thought about that, Eddie. They already support a lot of weight, so they must have concrete moorings on both sides."

Kathy, the architect of the plan that saved thousands of people at the Charleston cruise terminal felt like she had the answer.

"Why not cut the net loose?" she asked. "We could wait for the top cable to be exposed when the water level drops, and just cut it."

The Chief didn't get excited the way the rest of us did, so it must be more bad news. "Here's the catch," he said. "For the nets to collapse the power conduits, the weight has to fall all at once. For that to happen, it will take the weight of the fully loaded nets to be completely above water. I don't doubt that their full weight could pull the moorings out in a few days, and the whole thing will come crashing down. If we were able to cut each mooring cable as they become exposed, the weight would gradually settle over the power conduits and actually protect them from damage. The problem is that the cables look like they are the same cables used on suspension bridges. They're probably woven steel, and I would guess about four inches in diameter."

It didn't take a rocket scientist for all of us to understand that there was no way to cut through those cables, and there must be a lot of infected dead in them if they were heavy enough to pull the moorings out.

4 ESCAPE FROM CONWAY

The mood in the shelter was not the best, to say the least. We all felt like we were one step closer to being the oyster that got eaten, and it was Tom who brought things back into perspective. He looked at each of us one at a time. I could almost feel his gaze.

"Guys, did someone tell you there was no Santa Claus? Did someone tell you there would be no Trick-or-Treat this year?" he asked. "I made an error once that cost us the ball game. I'm glad I didn't have your attitudes or I would have quit then."

I think he did a good job of putting us in our place, and we couldn't help but grin. He took Kathy by the hand and said, "Everybody in the dining room."

We all followed behind Tom and Kathy. Jean nudged me and hooked a thumb in Kathy's direction. She was blushing beet red. We all knew she was attracted to Tom, but it had been a long time since a man had taken her by the hand.

When we were all seated around the dining room table, Tom passed out beers and sat down next to Kathy. He said, "It's time for me to tell you how Molly and I got here. Maybe after hearing our story you will know just how lucky you have been, and you won't cry because someone licked all the red off of your candy."

"I know where the red went," said Jean. She looked at Kathy and smiled, and Kathy turned beet red again.

"See, there it is."

Kathy gave Jean a mock scowl, and Jean mimicked it. The Chief started doing a full body laugh, and the mood got better. When it started to die down, and everyone was wiping tears from their eyes, Tom caught his breath and started to tell them about that first night.

"Do you four remember where you were when you found out about the infected?" he asked. He knew the answers, so he didn't wait for us to speak.

He went on, "From the moment it started until the night that we escaped from Conway with over forty armed saviors, I had one clear thought, and that was we were going to die. I knew I would do anything to keep Molly alive, but I also knew it was only a matter of time. That's what hopelessness is, folks, and I would have been right if not for a baseball fan."

He took a long swallow of his beer and got a distant look. We could tell he was going back to that night and picturing their escape. A dozen boats running in single file with one red light on the bow. Well-armed, well trained men and women who gave him and his daughter a chance to live.

"I can only think of our trip down the Waccamaw River in something like fragments, or number of miles," he said. "The first fragment was only four miles long, and we had nothing to fear from the west bank except people who had dropped anchor along the dense forest that ran along the river. The east bank was lined with about three dozen large houses and private docks. If we were going to run into shooters, it was likely to be from that side."

Tom took another long swallow from his beer before going on. Before he started, he put his head down and was staring at the table. I figured eye contact wouldn't be easy.

He continued, "I learned from one of the soldiers that the man in charge was a National Guard Captain with a good reputation named Anthony Marchant. The soldier told me Captain Marchant was from the area, and he had a good idea of what to do to survive. He said we were lucky."

Tom was quiet for a moment, and Kathy told him to take his time. Details were important no matter how small or trivial they might be. Tom said he was okay, and that he could go on.

"When we formed up in single file and started down the river, Molly and I were in the fourth boat. There were quick introductions all around, but something kept me from hearing names. I think it was all too unreal to be exchanging pleasantries as we were watching people die."

Tom told us that getting clear of the boat landing wasn't a problem because civilian craft had given the armed boats a wide berth. Many of them were content to just stay out in the middle of the river to wait for something to happen. After all, they had nowhere to go.

When the military and police boats began to idle into formation, civilians who had dropped anchor began pulling them in so they could follow the firepower. I think that's what all of us would have done if we had been there in our boats.

"As we pulled away from the boat landing, we got a better view of what was happening up on the bridge. The screaming, the running, the cries for help that were being ignored......there was nothing anyone could do," he said.

"We could see from the center of the river that cars were pulling out of traffic onto the shoulder of the road, trying to make it to the same turn where the police officer had told us to go. A steady stream of cars were making it to the turn and trying to reach us before we pulled away from the boat landing. None of them would make it to us in time."

"The lead cars started honking their horns to get our attention, hoping we would wait for them. I could see the infected starting to make the same turn down the road toward the boat landing. The honking horns attracted more infected dead and weren't helping the people who were trying to escape. It wouldn't be long before those people were trapped where they were."

Jean said, "It's not your fault, Tom. If the Captain had told the boats to pick up more people, the boats would have been overwhelmed."

"I know," he said, "but how many times have you asked yourself why you were one of the chosen? One of the people who got to live?"

Kathy said, "There isn't a day that goes by that we each don't think the same thing, Tom. I can't count the number of times we've been spared by luck or by the courage of someone in our group."

Tom went on, "One of the first cars to the boat landing was carrying weapons, and they began firing at us when we didn't stop for them. Everyone kept their heads down, and our convoy increased speed to get out of range. Two of the boats received the order to lay down cover fire, so they began shooting over heads or at the ground in front of the desperate people who were shooting at us. I don't think we lost anyone, but I'll never know for sure."

"When I looked over the railing on the boat the next time, we were away from the boat landing. It was getting darker as we moved away from the boat landing and the bridge. All I could hear as the shooting stopped was the sounds of powerful boat engines and occasional radio chatter. There was something being said about covering the first four miles faster than we normally would, and about the road traffic on the east bank of the river."

Tom said, "The boat landing filled up too fast with drivers who thought it was an escape route, and when the shooting started those people who couldn't make a right turn to the boat landing just kept going straight. That put them parallel with us and moving faster on the straight road. I didn't know the area, but the Conway Police Officers did, and they said the road was appropriately named Waccamaw Road. It ended at the river about four miles downstream."

"It was obvious to all of us," he said, "that a large number of cars would get there ahead of us. There wasn't a boat landing at the end of the road, but there were a couple of private docks. If those drivers had guns, they would be as close as anyone would get to the military convoy."

Tom said, "To make matters worse, the private docks faced the river just before a bend. We would be swinging outward to the right to avoid the docks, but then we would have to start making a sharp left across the river back to the eastern bank because there was a boat landing on the western side as we came out of the first turn."

"If you can picture it," he said, "We didn't know what we were going to find when we came out of the turn, but radio chatter said the boat on point could see plenty of light coming from that general area. That meant boats would be in the water or just leaving the landing. If we ran into traffic blocking the river, there would be a mess. And as if it couldn't be worse, there was about a one hundred yard stretch of river that narrowed to about forty yards wide."

"I heard a radio order come from Captain Marchant that told the first three boats to go through fast as we made the first turn while the rest should cut their speed in half immediately after they were past the private docks," he said. "I heard the order to have weapons hot."

"I could feel our boat start to lean toward the right, so I knew we were coming to the end of Waccamaw Road. I took a risk and pulled myself up where I could see over the railing, and I could see the two private docks. Both were loaded with people waving their arms at us. They had nowhere to go but back the way they had come, but by now it was a four mile long solid line of cars all the way back to Highway 501. The infected dead were probably working their way down that row of parked cars."

Tom finished his beer and got another for each of us. He said, "I'm going to need a few beers if I have to relive the experience."

We could tell he was trying to lighten the mood a bit, but it fell on deaf ears. We all knew what it was like to see people who weren't going to make it out alive, and the scene on those docks must have been heartbreaking. They wanted to help, but it was a lost cause.

"I could see parents holding up their children," said Tom. "They wanted us to at least take them. I don't think anyone could have survivor's guilt worse than mine because they helped us but not those people. If our crew had cut the engines to take them on board, I would have been right there helping them."

"And you would probably be dead by now," said the Chief. "What were the odds that everyone on those docks was bite free?"

"I don't know anymore, Chief. I know to be careful now because the infected outnumber living people, but I can't help thinking about those children. They were probably dead within minutes after we passed them," he answered.

Jean said, "I can tell you this much, Tom. The outbreak was on both sides of the river. You probably had as many people behind you in traffic who were already bitten as you had in front of you. When Kathy took over on the Atlantic Spirit and started a screening process to see if any of the passengers had been bitten, it was surprising how many people we had let board the ship who had been bitten, and we had a screening process out on the dock. You guys would have brought someone on board from those docks who had been sentenced to death already, and they would have taken you with them."

"You're probably right," said Tom, "but I guess you know it doesn't make me feel better. It does help to know that Molly is alive for now."

"She's alive because you didn't stop to help," I said.

Tom nodded his agreement, but it would take a lot of time and a lot more beer for him to really start to accept it.

He said, "We were leaning to the right at high speed, and then we started to level off and go to half speed. That caused a big cheer from the people on the docks. As they saw our bows settle lower in the water, they thought we were stopping for them. When we didn't stop, the cheers turned into screams."

Tom told us that he suddenly realized there was more light ahead. As they came out of the turn and started to lean over to the left, his view was temporarily blocked because they were on the port side of the boat. He took a chance and stood up to his full height so he could see.

"One of the police officers told me that was the Sidewheeler Road boat landing on the western side of the river. I could see a large parking area that was packed full of cars with boats on trailers. So far, there wasn't any chaos because access to the area was so limited, which meant there wouldn't be any infected dead yet. People were just waiting for their turn to put their boats in the water, but for every person with a boat there were ten who were trying to buy a ride. I don't doubt that some were able to escape for a price, but there weren't enough boats."

"As we came out of the turn and started back toward the left bank of the river, I could see the first three boats up ahead. They were still moving fast and pulling away, but the main thing was that their path was clear of boat traffic. The radio order came through to increase speed after clearing the area across from the boat landing," said Tom.

"The people at the boat landing had the same reaction as the people on the private docks. At first there were cheers. Then there were screams, some of them angry because twelve military and police boats can throw up one hell of a wake. Our wake hit the people who were on the water but not under power, causing some of the occupants to be tossed overboard. Others who were trying to release their boats from the trailers got knocked down. All in all, we weren't too popular," Tom said.

"We expected the shooting to start sooner," he said, "but maybe it didn't because people thought we were there to help. When it started, we didn't really know who was doing the shooting, nor did we know if we were the targets. From what I could see, it was probably someone trying to take a boat rather than to buy a ride. It didn't matter because bullets eventually started tossing up the water around our boats."

"Did you return fire?" asked the Chief.

"Not immediately," answered Tom. "Since we were boat number four, we were almost past the boat landing before the people on the landing caught on that we weren't going to stop. Most of the shots missed because we were already putting distance between us and them. I saw someone on boat five fall over into the boat, and that was when the Captain gave the order to return fire and to target shooters if possible."

"After only a few seconds it became easier to identify shooters because the unarmed people were all hitting the ground or diving for cover. The really smart ones were the people who jumped into the river. We knew they couldn't be shooting at us. The gunners from eight boats opened up on the boat landing, and the shooting from there was quickly stopped."

"Once we were clear of that landing, I saw that the boats on point were slowing down and waiting for us. I didn't know it yet, but there was a large, natural cove up ahead that went in behind a big island. Someone in the boat with the Captain told him it would be a good place to set up a floating triage center. Boats could enter on one side of the island then exit the other side after everyone was checked."

Jean said in a low voice, "Nothing can go wrong here."

"We didn't know," said Tom. "We just didn't know how far people would go to protect their families by hiding the bites. We weren't likely to be beaten in an armed attack, but we were as susceptible as anyone to an inside attack."

Jean said, "I promised a long time ago that I would jump overboard with the infected if one of them bit me, and that promise still stands. As bad as it may sound Tom, we have to look out for our group. If you want Molly to survive, you have to make that promise, too."

She was looking him straight in the eyes, and he could see how serious she was. He said, "If I get bitten, I won't hide it from you. I would only want you to protect Molly after I'm gone."

"You have our word," said Jean. "Now, what about Molly? What if she gets bitten? Will you hide it from us?"

Tom looked like he was thinking it over for a minute, but then he said, "I don't know, Jean. I honestly don't know."

Kathy said, "If you had answered without a doubt that you were sure you would tell us, Tom, I don't think any of us would have believed you, and that would have damaged our trust in you. Take some time to think about it, and after you've reached a conclusion you can let us know. If you still aren't sure, then we will give you some supplies and a ride up or down the coast, whichever you prefer."

"You've got to be sure," said the Chief. "There's no in between."

The conversation had taken a really dark turn because Tom was honest and admitted that he didn't know if he would tell us if Molly was bitten. I decided to get us back onto the topic of Tom's escape until he had a chance to think it over.

"Tom, what happened when you pulled into the cove?" I asked.

"It looked perfect, even at night," he said. "We had two boats take up position at the mouth of the cove, and the rest of us moved into the center of a lake that was about two hundred yards square. Down river we could see the next boat landing on the west bank, and it looked crowded."

"The Captain gave the order to have two other boats go around the island to the only other entrance to the lake. He told them to keep the back door closed to traffic. If anyone tried to enter from that direction, they were to be told to come up to the entrance we used, and that they would be protected. The red running lights on our bows were perfect for showing people where they had to go."

"The next thing he did was to have the eight remaining boats form two straight lines in pairs," he continued. "There was a gap between the lines of the four pairs they could use for inspection of civilian boats, and they could inspect four at a time. The idea was to have four boats enter the gap between the two lines of military and police boats and come to a stop. The crew of one boat would stand guard while the crew of the opposite boat would inspect the passengers for bites. We were in the first of the boats that was guarding people."

"The first four boats entered between us, and the Captain used a loudspeaker to explain to the people on the boats what was happening. The first four civilian boats were inspected without a hitch, and they were told they could either exit and wait on the river, or they could drop anchor behind us on the lake," he explained.

"Four more boats entered for inspection, and after a few hours there was a huge floating colony of about a hundred boats filling the lake. We had to start sending everyone else out the exit to wait on the river."

"I'm not exactly sure who began shooting, but it came from somewhere in the middle of the civilian boats. They were all anchored close together, and there were screams first. From what I could hear, there was an infected man trying to bite someone on a boat that had tied up alongside his boat."

Tom reached over and picked up a pad of paper and a pencil from a shelf across from the dining room table. He drew a big rectangle with two openings at both ends but on the same side of the rectangle. He made eight dash marks the length of the rectangle. They looked like the lane markers on a three lane highway. Then he filled in the entire area of what looked like the third lane with dashes. "This is what it looked like," he said, "and one whole row of our boats had their backs to the civilian boats. When the screaming started, and someone began shooting, people started trying to get out. Some made it because they were waiting near the entrance and exit, but it was chaos in the middle."

"What about your boats?" asked Kathy.

"We were surrounded, and to make matters worse we had a row of civilian boats between ours. The passengers on those boats started trying to climb over into our boats."

Tom told us that he could see boats trying to force their way out of the cove, but there were too many trying at once. More shooting started, and the inevitable happened when a bullet hit a fuel tank. The explosion destroyed every boat close to it, but the fireball shot out in all directions and hit the four military and police boats that had their port sides facing the civilians. The crew on Tom's boat went into action quickly because they knew their boat was close enough to the exit to break away from the inspection line and head for freedom.

Tom said he saw one man trying to pull a woman out of the water into his boat. He almost had her over railing when she turned her head and bit him on the cheek. He let go, and she fell back into the water, tearing half of his face off as she fell. The man disappeared into the boat, but there was no doubt about his fate.

There was another boat that was starting to sink because it had been rammed by a larger boat. The passengers were all gathered on the bow trying to jump onto the deck of a third boat. What they didn't see was that the passengers of that boat had already died from the infection and were waiting with open jaws as the people jumped to the deck of their boat.

He said the worst thing he saw was a mother handing her child to a man on another boat because her boat was sinking. She didn't see that the stranger was an infected dead, and Tom didn't need to give us the details of what followed. The mother realized her mistake too late and tried to pull the screaming child back, and in the process she fell into the water. He lost sight of her, and he couldn't watch what was happening on the boat. The child had stopped screaming.

The water in between the boats was a sea of bobbing heads. The infected that fell in just sank out of sight because they didn't have the sense to shut their mouths, but many of them fell on top of people who were not infected. Before they sank, they managed to catch hold of flesh with their teeth. Many more people would die from the infection as they reached for the safety of boats and were pulled aboard by friends, relatives, and strangers.

The fire continued to spread, and there were more explosions. Tom said he had a fleeting thought that it would be a blessing to blow up rather than to be bitten. He saw the fireball take out the four boats from their convoy, and Captain Marchant was on the lead boat. Most of the crews jumped into the water, but the fireball started to light off their munitions. As cases of ammunition began to explode, bullets were flying everywhere. The four civilian boats that were in between the two rows of military boats acted as a buffer and protected the remaining four military boats.

Tom looked behind them to see if they were being followed by the three boats that had been lined up behind his. They were there and moving forward, but he watched with a sinking feeling as a boat crossed the path of the military boat that was closest to their stern. All three of the military and police boats crashed into each other as they hit the civilian who had cut them off.

On the far end of the cove where boats were entering for inspection, the two military boats broke free and started downriver at high speed. They passed by the exit just as Tom's boat and the two boats at the exit entered the Waccamaw River. They lost all seven boats that had been in line doing inspections with Tom's crew. Almost fifty of their companions were dead, including their commanding officer. In a matter of minutes they had gone from being a formidable power of twelve boats on the river down to five. They had lost over half of their boats and people because they were trying to help survivors.

As they sped away and passed the crowded boat landing on their right, they saw their mistake. The infection had already reached this far even though the landing was in a remote area. People who were escaping in boats had seen the row of armed military and police boats turn into the cove, and they naturally expected that rescue had arrived. Unfortunately, plenty of those boats were carrying bite victims. It was only a matter of time before there would be a repeat of what had happened at the bridge.

When they started down the river in a row of five boats, they were at their maximum speeds, and they quickly overcame the civilian boats. Each of their boats were equipped with twin outboard engines while the civilians typically had one. The result was that they passed them and the last of the private homes on the west bank of the river.

Tom said, "Our lead boat was being driven by a crew that was from the Conway area, and they knew that we weren't far from a major section of the river that had no boat landings or roads for a very long stretch. Once we reached the turn we would be able to reduce our speed to save fuel. In only a few minutes we made that turn. Five minutes later, the radio call came through to cut speed."

"We stayed at low speed for about two miles where we came to a campground that had no access by road. There were a few boats already anchored near the bank, but not too many. If there were no bite victims among the boaters, it would be a good place to spend the night. I know we were a welcome sight to the campers when they saw the Army and Conway Police emblems on our boats."

"Our five remaining boats pulled up to the bank and tied mooring lines to trees. There wasn't a dock or any facilities. It was just a place where people had stopped to camp so many times that it had become a place to escape from civilization."

"It felt good to have my feet on firm ground again and for the first time since Highway 501 I got to meet face to face with the officer who took a leap of faith and let us come along with them. His name was Ron Barrett, and he looked like he was from New York. You know, jet black hair and a bit of an accent. I found him and shook his hand, thanking him over and over again."

Tom told us that Officer Barrett looked at him at first as if he had no idea who he was. It never occurred to him that the officer was looking around at the survivors and seeing not just who was still there, but who wasn't. So many of his friends were gone.

When Officer Barrett snapped out of whatever dark place he had gone, he remembered helping Tom and Molly escape from the death trap on Highway 501. He smiled at Tom and started looking around for Molly. When he saw her clinging to my knee, he pulled her to him and gave her a big hug. His friends had died, but he had saved a little girl and her father. It was at least a small consolation.

"I know how I felt about my teammates in baseball," said Tom. "You would get close to someone, and one day they would be gone. Sometimes it was good news because they got called up to the big leagues, and sometimes they got traded. That was okay because at least they were still in the game. What hurt was when you found out someone was cut. It was like getting fired from a job when you don't have any other skills."

Tom lowered his eyes to the table and said, "I'm not saying getting cut from baseball is as bad as dying, but I knew how Officer Barrett felt. His friends were gone in the blink of an eye, and he hadn't been given the time to process it. When he let go of Molly, I gave him a hug, too."

"We spent the night at the boat landing. It didn't take long for us to check out the campers who had arrived there before us. They were as anxious as we were to be sure no one was in our group who had been bitten. There were five civilian boats with families on each of them, so there were men, women, and children. I felt like the odd man out being the only civilian with the soldiers and the police, but they didn't act like I wasn't supposed to be there. We had already shared an experience that created a bond."

"Tom," said Kathy, "are you okay with going on?"

"Yeah," he said. "I'm okay. It's just that I didn't even know most of their names before they died, and as you can guess by us showing up on your doorstep, things didn't get much better. At least for a few hours that night Molly got to be a kid again. The campground was so remote that it was safe to let her play with the other children. I thought they were playing tag or something, but it turned out to be a variation. The child who was trying to catch the other children was pretending to be an infected dead."

Tom said the new man in charge was Sergeant Gathers. He wasn't an officer, but he had combat experience in the Middle East. He was an African American who was much like the Chief. Deadly serious about his job, but able to find a bright side to almost any situation. He considered this campsite to be the bright spot in our day.

Even though we posted watches, the area wasn't accessible by land, so we didn't have to worry about those dead things stumbling into our camp at night. If a boat approached, we would all hear it coming long before it got there. Sergeant Gathers figured we would have a chance to catch our breath and to make some plans.

Some reasonable sized tents were set up, and people pitched in to help get a meal cooked for the survivors. Sergeant Gathers had the senior people from each boat around a folding table, and they had maps spread across its surface. I could hear him talking about their possible escape routes, and he was making it clear to everyone that it was an escape from behind enemy lines.

The Sergeant told them there were three sets of combatants in the area. There were the infected that were not capable of reason, there were the armed forces and police, and then there were the civilians who were capable of digging in for the long haul. At this point, he considered them to be just as dangerous as the infected.

The group discussed the options we had, and it seemed clear to everyone that we should work our way to the coast. Sergeant Gathers said he thought their best bet would be to try to make contact with a Navy ship that could extract them. He traced his finger down the Waccamaw River which meandered through largely unpopulated areas until it reached a stretch just before Georgetown. There was a muddy looking island in the river that looked like it had a small marina behind it where they could leave the boats. It was about forty miles downriver, and it had a road that would lead directly to the coast. Tom heard the Sergeant say it was Butler Island and Rice Bluff Road.

The Chief looked over at me and said, "Does that sound familiar to you, Ed?"

"Sure does, Chief," I answered. "That's the extension of the road from Mud Island back to Highway 17 just below Simmonsville. There's no way they could have known what a hotbed that place had become, but if they got there before it became really bad, they could have made it across through there."

"Well, as it turned out, there was no way we were going to get there before it became bad," said Tom. "What should have been a few hours turned into weeks. We were fairly safe from the infected unless we got out of the boats, but the river became a good place to get shot. People set traps at the narrow spots, and they guarded fuel stations at marinas. We had to fight every inch of the way."

When they left the camping area the next morning, the civilian boats left with them. They alternated the five civilian boats with the five military and police boats, and even though they were still a well-armed force, they were easy targets for survivalists who had dug in along the river.

"We spent a lot of time camping along the river, and we even became more and more like the survivalists, fighting for fresh water, food, and fuel. We lost people and boats and made very slow progress getting down the river."

Tom went on, "One of the worst days was when we reached a place called the Bucksport Marina. We were down to five boats again, partially due to a fuel shortage, but also due to damage taken during attacks. It was a great place for a trap, and we lost three more boats. One of them was carrying Sergeant Gathers."

The boats had just come out of a large bend in the river when they were faced with a big island right in the center. They passed to the left of the island and didn't even see the civilian boats that came out from behind the island into their wakes. The boats closed in and started firing small arms at them, but they were having to drive straight at the Bucksport Marina, which was apparently the base of operations for the river pirates.

"Someone at the marina had an RPG, a rocket propelled grenade, and they opened up on us. Since our boats were full of ammo, the RPGs were effective, and no one survived on the boats that were hit. My boat and one other outran the attackers, but we were down to twelve people on two boats. I was grateful to see my friend Officer Barrett was still with me and Molly."

"We limped into the small marina behind Butler Island several weeks after leaving Conway. From what we could tell, we were less than five miles from the ocean, and we felt like we could cover that distance on foot in three hours if we didn't run into any trouble. We didn't know that those five miles were so populated by the infected dead."

"We considered going through Georgetown out into the ocean, but decided we had lost too many people on a desolate stretch of river. If we met any serious resistance we wouldn't be able to defend ourselves, and a more populated city like Georgetown was likely to have more people with weapons."

"All of us thought the area we were in was unpopulated enough for an easy hike to the shore, and the military had portable radios called MBTRS. They had good range, and they said we could reach the naval ships for extraction."

"You were in the worst place you could be," I said. "You were just west of Simmonsville. An accident on Highway 17 caused a big log jam in Simmonsville."

The Chief leaned toward Tom and said, "Try to picture this, Tom. The infected dead were attacking the living, and there were so many people in the area that there wasn't any place for them to go. The living tried to retreat from the log jam by going back the way they had come, and that caused even more dead to be in that area. It was like a wave washing up onto a beach and then going back in the opposite direction. It just kept doing that until the town of Simmonsville was a mass of infected dead."

Tom said, "That would explain the welcoming party. They were spread out, but there were plenty of them. We tied our boats up as far out on the marina dock as we could, and we were unloading our gear to get ready for the hike to the coast when they started coming out of the trees. Fortunately for us, most of them tried to walk across the mud to get to us. Some stayed on the dock, and we didn't waste bullets on them. We just pushed them off the dock into the mud."

"We've seen that behavior, too," said Kathy. "But we just shot the legs out from under the ones in front. The dead behind them weren't coordinated enough to step over them, and the dead that went down flailed around, causing more of them to fall off of the dock."

"We were a long way out on the dock," said Tom, "so the infected had a long walk without good balance. One of the guys spotted a rack that was holding long boat oars, and they were perfect for silently sending the infected over the edge. While the rest of us stowed our gear in backpacks, a couple of the guys used the boat oars to clear the docks. We were glad we didn't shoot them, because they just kept coming and coming. If we had fired shots, we probably would have had more of them arriving at one time than we could handle."

"When we were ready," said Tom, "we started for Rice Bluff Road at a trot. The temperature had dropped and it looked like it was going to rain, so we wanted to cover the five miles and get it over with. Things didn't go too well, though. Less than a half mile from the start of Rice Bluff Road, we started to make the turn that would take us toward the coast, and it was wall to wall infected dead. As far as we could see, the entire road was packed. We didn't have any choice but to keep going straight into a suburban neighborhood on the edge of Simmonsville."

Tom said the infected were just standing around in a big crowd, not really showing interest in anything until his group showed up at the end of the road. They didn't need an invitation as they all began to follow the first living things they had seen in weeks.

Simmonsville was so overrun by the infected that they had wiped out the population in a few days. People who had been told to stay at home by the FEMA broadcasts in the first few days lost all hope of escape as more and more people died. The only chance any of them would have had to survive would have been a fortified place with a large amount of supplies.

Tom said, "At the end of the paved road we followed a dirt path that led to the back of the first cul-de-sac. The good news was there was still power, so we knew we could at least find a warm place to sleep. Some of the homes still had their HVAC units humming outside, undoubtedly because someone had left the thermostats set too high or too low.

Whichever it was, the infected were drawn to the sounds of the running units, and they were less likely to hear us."

"I guess the bad news was that our group was a mixed bag of survivors, but not necessarily skilled people," he said. "There were a few who wouldn't listen to anyone. They did their own thing like it was a game. To them, the first house was fine, so a bunch of them broke away from the main group and just rushed into the first house. Five people ran in despite the warnings from me and Officer Barrett. They didn't work together like a team clearing the house. They split up and rushed from room to room looking for the infected, but instead of finding and eliminating them, it was the other way around. They ran straight into waiting arms and teeth."

"Ron and I hung back at first, but then we went to the door of the house and saw that the five had run into trouble. I had Molly staying back with a woman in the front yard because the shooting and screaming from inside was so bad. The rest of us knew that even if we took this house, it was going to be surrounded in minutes because of the noise. We needed to either take the house fast or keep moving."

Tom ran his hands through his hair. He looked like he was reliving a nightmare. "I think there were at least two infected for every living person in the house," he said. "And each of the living people had already been bitten. As they had split from each other and gone to separate rooms, they had all apparently retreated to a large living area, each with the infected in tow. There were more infected than normal, so the house must have been a last refuge for a bunch of neighbors when it had all begun. All Ron and I could do was pull the door shut and get our remaining group moving again."

As soon as Tom and Ron had gathered up the last of their people, they saw there was no safe place inside the neighborhood. Even if they got lucky and found a house that had no infected inside, which wasn't likely, they would be surrounded in minutes, and there would be no escaping.

They passed the homes one at a time looking for a gap that was free of the infected. There were infected everywhere they turned, and it seemed that they were trapped. Tom said they were tired, hungry, winded from running, and losing all hope when Officer Barrett said he had an idea.

He pulled Tom close to his face and said, "You have to get your little girl and the others to safety. We're going into the next house and clearing it. Then I'm going out the back door to take care of distracting these things. I have an idea that should keep them busy long enough for you guys to get out of the area. If it works, I'll catch up with you."

Tom didn't want to see his friend do anything crazy and said, "No, you're not going to be able to do anything by yourself. We need to stay together."

Before Tom could stop Officer Barrett, he ran up the steps onto the front porch of a modern home and went through the front door. Tom and the rest of their group had no choice but to follow. Molly, two men, and two women followed Tom and Ron into the house. Ron had already killed two of the infected before Tom came inside, and there weren't any others in the main part of the house. Ron told them to all wait in the kitchen at the back of the house while he distracted the ones outside away from the house. He said that he wanted Tom to take the rest of the group out the front door and run like hell when the time was right.

Tom asked him when they would know that it was safe to go, and Ron just smiled and said he would know when it was time. They could already hear the groaning from the front of the house as more and more of the infected had gathered at the front door trying to get in.

Officer Barrett took a quick look out the kitchen window. He gave Tom and Molly each a quick hug and then disappeared out the back door. Tom went to the window to see where Ron was going and caught on to what he was doing.

The house Officer Barrett had chosen was facing inward toward a suburban street, but the back was facing one of those necessary evils of suburban living. The kitchen window faced an electric power relay station with a chain-link fence surrounding it. Tom realized that he had been able to hear the incessant hum coming from the station and had blocked it out. Officer Barrett was running straight for the only gate in the chain-link fence.

One of the other men left in their group asked what was going on. Tom had never asked his name. He had already gotten in the habit of not getting to know people because so few were surviving. As he watched out the window, he realized he was watching the last person from the convoy of boats that had left Conway with him, and Tom didn't believe he would be seeing his friend catch up with them later.

Officer Ron Barrett ran the fifty or sixty yards to the power relay station with everything he had. When he got to the gate, it only took one shot to blast the lock apart that kept people safe from dying inside. He fired two more shots at approaching infected, but his goal was to draw attention to himself. Three shots was all it took. Every infected he could see turned in his direction at the sound of the first shot, and he was sure that every infected he couldn't see did the same thing.

The gate was only a bit larger than the average door, and Ron Barrett didn't plan to lock it behind him. He closed it and dropped the U shaped latch into place, but the sheer numbers of the infected dead bumping into it were more than likely going to cause it to eventually open. He looked around at the chain-link fence and saw that the warning signs on the fence about keeping out were probably not necessary because the concertina wire was going to keep anyone from climbing in or out. He began circling the high voltage equipment, staying as close to the fence as possible without getting close enough to be grabbed by the reaching hands that were extended through the fence.

The number of infected dead grew and grew until Tom couldn't see inside the enclosed area, but he could see when the gate was finally pushed open. There was a logjam at the opening as too many of the infected tried to go through at once. Those in front were pushed to the ground, and the ones right behind them were landing on top of them.

Tom watched in horrid fascination wondering if the infected weren't doing a better job of blocking the entrance than the gate had, but eventually some of them managed to tumble over the tangle of bodies and roll into the enclosure.

One by one the infected fell into the open area between the gate and the high voltage equipment that hummed its warning. Tom could guess that Officer Barrett had circled the danger zone to get to the back corner judging by the large number of infected dead that had gone around to the back side of the fence. Tom also guessed that the total number of the infected had grown to three hundred. It was time to move to the front of the house, but before they left, Tom had to see what Ron was doing.

Tom told the others to wait in the kitchen while he checked to see if their way was clear out front. He circled back through the living room and ran up the stairs to the second floor. He made sure a bedroom on the front of the house was clear before crossing to the window. From there he saw that there were a few stragglers still making their way through the gaps between the houses over to the power relay station, but it was definitely better than it had been. Ron's plan was working.

Tom crossed the hallway and checked a bedroom on the back of the house. His luck was holding up, because the room was also empty. He went to that window and looked out at the rear view behind the house. The Infected crowd had swollen in size, and the fenced area around the power relay station appeared to be smaller and insignificant in their midst.

Inside the enclosure, he could see Officer Ron Barrett sitting on the ground at a spot directly across from the gate. The entire size of the station appeared to be about two hundred feet on each side with a safe zone around its inside perimeter, and as Tom watched the first of the infected had gotten their feet under them and started for Ron. True to form, they were going to take a direct path to him, and as they stepped from the safe zone of the perimeter into the proximity of the high voltage equipment, it was obvious what was about to happen.

Their ungraceful, shambling way of walking caused them to go as much left and right as it did forward, and one by one they made contact with the wrong things. Blue electric arcs of lightning began shooting through the bodies of the infected. They erupted into flame as their tattered clothing caught fire and spread. Those nearest to them didn't even need to be electrocuted because their clothing caught fire so easily. Hair and skin were ablaze, and smoke was billowing above the entire scene. Tom knew the sacrifice his friend had made for him and Molly one more time, but he thought to himself that it must smell like hell down there.

Those infected that had spread out to the left and right to go around the melee in the middle were not spared by the fire or electricity. The crowd of groaning, snapping dead were packing into the area so tightly that the electric charge crossed through them and reached the surrounding fence.

Tom was mesmerized by the sight of hundreds of infected dead being electrocuted all around the outside of the enclosure. They were falling and colliding with the dead behind them, and they were also catching fire. There was a large buffer zone around the outside of the fence, and the infected filled that zone. The smoke, fire, and bolts of electricity were amazing, and in the middle of it all sat Officer Barrett. He had stood up and turned in a circle to watch as he personally brought about the end for an untold number of infected dead.

Tom had to tear himself away, but just as he started to leave the window, he saw Officer Barrett look in his direction. He doubted that Ron could really see him through all of the smoke, but Tom could see him clearly waving his arm in a motion that said it was time for Tom to get the others to safety. He gave a silent wave to the brave man who had been responsible for giving him and Molly a chance to live once again.

He crossed the hall again and looked out the window. The streets were so clear that all of the infected must have been drawn to the bonfire and chaos at the power relay station. Tom quickly ran down the stairs to the kitchen where he found all four adults crowded around the little kitchen window.

One of them turned and asked him if he had seen what was happening, and despite the fact that he had been watching from a better vantage point, he had to take one more look. He was surprised to see that the infected so completely filled the area that they were almost to the back of the house where they were hiding. He knew it wouldn't be long before the fire traveled across the infected and found a new source of fuel as the homes caught on fire. Ron was going to thin the population of Simmonsville by at least a thousand. Homes that held infected dead inside were going to join the fun.

Tom told the others the way was clear out front and it was time to go. They didn't hesitate, but each one gave an unseen wave in the direction of Officer Ron Barrett. They quickly ran out the front door and ran in the general direction of the coast, but they had a long way to go.

They stayed close to the houses and made their way to the front of the neighborhood, looking back from time to time at the massive fire and plume of smoke. The noise was incredible, and the infected from miles around were probably moving toward them. They needed to keep moving as long as there was a gap between them.

At first it was better to be in front of the homes running parallel to the street, but they gradually started seeing more and more of the infected that had come a long way, drawn like moths to the huge fire. Behind the homes was an access road that ran directly to the power relay station, and it had become the most popular route for the infected to use. Whether they were streaming out of the neighborhood or the forests to the South, they were converging on the access road and were packed together so tightly that the entire parade was being pushed forward from behind.

Tom said the last block of houses had trees behind them that gave them some cover, and the street in front of the homes was beginning to be too populated, so they crept low to the ground between the buildings until they were in the trees behind them. Even if the infected saw them, the push from behind would carry the infected forward toward the fire. If they were spotted by any infected, they weren't aware of it.

They kept creeping along until Tom was surprised that he could see an intersection sign that said they had reached Highway 17 in record time. The dirt road that had become Infected Dead Turnpike was the crossroad with Highway 17, and it was named Overland Drive. From what he could see, it was crowded with the infected that were being drawn across from the other side of Highway 17.

Tom gathered the four adults in close with him. Molly was squeezed in the middle of them. He told them that the bad news was that they had to cross Highway 17. That meant they would be in the open crossing four lanes of road, and the median and shoulders had no cover. The good news was that there was a fire station across the road, and better yet, one of the fire trucks was outside.

He explained to them that getting across the road was not impossible if they kept moving. Stopping for any reason was as good as a death sentence. Tom told them to just run for the truck and climb it. If he could get it started, he would drive it out onto Highway 17 using the northbound lane to go south. He told them that the map showed a road less than two miles away that would lead directly to the coast. We didn't want to interrupt him to tell him he was talking about our road, but we were all wondering if he was going to say anything about the big accident that had blocked people from leaving Simmonsville.

"Tom," I said, "did you see anything that looked like a big wreck on Highway 17 near where you were?"

"As a matter of fact, I did," said Tom. "That's what changed everything. I thought we were going to be home free once we made it to the truck, but I was wrong."

"What happened?" asked Kathy.

Tom told us that he knew they were in trouble as soon as they left the cover of the trees. The plume of smoke was still rising, and the noise from that direction was drawing the infected straight toward them in a steady stream. The wood line on the other side of Highway 17 was a mass of movement as the infected stumbled out of the dense brush onto the open shoulder, and the entire highway was a swarm of dead. They were spread out, but it was going to be a gauntlet for them to run in order to reach the fire engine.

Tom said he scooped Molly up and started to run, and the others automatically followed. They made it across the grassy shoulder onto the pavement before they got a good look down Highway 17. They were on a slight rise in the road so they could see the massive wreck that made the road look like an auto salvage yard. From shoulder to shoulder there were cars and trucks turned in every possible direction. Some were destroyed beyond recognition while others had probably come to a stop soon enough to join the others, but the drivers and passengers had been caught up in the wave of infected that were going from vehicle to vehicle in search of living flesh to bite.

There wasn't time to stop and take it all in, but Tom did have time to realize that cars were against the trees on the far side of the road, all lanes and the median were blocked, and large numbers of cars had tried to go around the wreckage by crossing a small open field on the right. Once cars and trucks began getting stuck in the soft soil of that field, it had filled with people trying to drive through the gaps between them. In some places there were cars on top of cars, and many trucks had rolled over smaller vehicles. In the moments when the chain reaction began, it must have been total mayhem just avoiding running over people who were fleeing for their lives. The infected didn't have to search for people to bite. They only had to stand still and wait for the unsuspecting living to run directly into their arms.

Tom didn't know how long this many infected had been wandering around near this impossible barrier, but many of them had been doing what they tended to do when there was nothing drawing their attention. They had been just standing around and staring at each other. Sometimes a breeze would blow and move a tree, and they would all look that way. Sometimes it was nothing more than moving grass that drew their attention, but given nothing new for a really long period of time, they often did nothing more than stare at their own feet.

This crowd of infected was on stimulus overload. After countless weeks of nothing new to attack, there was a roaring pillar of fire and smoke, and a handful of living people running through their midst. The horde was growing by the second as the highway filled with more and more of the infected, and they were coming from all directions.

Just when it seemed to Tom that they had made a terrible mistake to think they could run through so many of the infected, something exploded near the power relay station. The sound momentarily blocked out the chorus of groaning that had also increased to a deafening roar, but as the explosion rolled across the trees, the houses, and the infected, the groaning changed to a fevered pitch. Tom said it sounded like desire, and the thought made him shudder. He said he heard them groan plenty of times, but he said the explosion seemed to awaken in them a more desperate sound.

Tom looked around himself and saw that he was completely surrounded, but he kept moving from side to side and mostly forward. He didn't have time to look back to see if the last survivors in his group were still with him, but he was sure he heard a scream rise above the sound of the groaning. He came face to face with infected dead more than once, but there was so much noise and so much movement, that he was fairly sure they were lost in the craziness that was happening around them. Before it registered in whatever thought processes drove the infected to react, Tom had slipped by again.

Molly clung to Tom's neck and held her breath for most of the run through the horde. She even kept her eyes shut for most of it, but Tom could sense from the racking sobs he felt shudder through her that she wasn't going to be able to keep it together much longer.

Tom said that he didn't remember when the pavement ended and the grassy median began. He also didn't remember when the pavement began or ended the second time. The fire truck was just suddenly in front of him.

There were infected on all sides of the truck, and although most of them were reaching in the direction of the huge pillar of fire and smoke, some of them could see him better now that he was not blending in with the crowd. With the truck as his background, he looked exactly like what he was......a living, breathing person who needed to be bitten.

Tom practically tossed Molly over the top edge of the truck to safety, and with his last drop of willpower he caught his foot in a rung of a ladder and gave himself a powerful shove to freedom. He felt more than one hand grab his trailing leg but not bites, and with disbelief he rolled over to find Molly sitting on top of coiled firehoses and ladders smiling at him. He looked around and saw that they weren't even visible to the infected dead surrounding the truck.

It was with no small measure of guilt that he remembered the four people who had been with him. He had become so caught up in keeping Molly alive that he had never even asked their names. A part of him wondered if he stopped asking people for their names because he had seen so many die in such a short time.

Tom looked around at us all and realized that he had become lost in his thoughts and had stopped talking.

Kathy said, "It's okay, Tom. You can tell us the rest later."

"No, no......I should finish," he said. "You need to know this if you don't already."

Tom thought for a minute before continuing, and he listened as his little girl was doing her duty in the next room at the short wave radio.

Tom said he didn't want to draw attention to where they had gone, and he was sure there were a few of the infected still trying to figure out where he had gone or how they could climb the side of the truck, but he had to see if the others had made it. He lifted himself up on his elbows and looked out between firefighting equipment to get a better look at the direction from where they had come.

Everywhere Tom looked there were the infected dead. There had to be hundreds of them, and they were mostly glued to the sight of the fire and smoke, but his heart sank when he spotted smaller groups that were more intent upon some other prey that could only have been the last members of his group. He couldn't see them, and there were no screams, but he could tell what was happening under so many hungry mouths. Tom rolled away from the view and just let the feeling of safety sink in.

He told us that he didn't know how long he laid there on his back just looking up at the gray sky and letting the weariness wash over him, but he gradually became aware of the building behind the big fire truck. He had come to rest with his feet facing the fire station and his head resting on a coil of rope by the cab of the truck. His daughter was sitting by his right hip and just watching him. Molly had a way of bringing calm to herself and to him at the same time, and when Tom was calm he thought more clearly. The back of the truck wasn't three feet from a second floor window.

Tom lifted himself onto his elbows and looked over the side of the truck again. There were still hundreds of infected dead moving toward the other side of Highway 17, and he figured they had to all be over there sooner or later. At least most of them would be.

Tom told us that he wondered if there were any inside of the fire station, and he was torn between crossing the small gap during the daylight hours when he would surely be spotted by the horde of infected, and waiting for the sun to go down. The inside of the station would be pitch dark, and would be a death trap if he stumbled into the bite of one or more of the infected.

It didn't take him long to decide because he didn't think they would do any better if they spent the night on top of the truck and waited for the horde to finally pass. Judging by the numbers still emerging from the trees as far up Highway 17 as he could see, Tom didn't have a great amount of faith in the theory that they were going to run out of new arrivals any time soon. It would have to be before it got dark.

Tom explained to Molly that he was going to go inside the building and then come back for her. Molly asked why she couldn't come too, but all he needed to do was to say he had to make sure it was safe, and that nothing could hurt her on top of the truck. Molly was worried, but she had learned over the last few weeks when her father really needed her to be brave.

He dug around in the cases of neatly stashed firefighting gear on top of the truck and found exactly what he hoped for. There were several working flashlights. When he clicked the button on the first one and it came on, he could feel his spirits soar. Next, he looked for something he knew firemen used to bring down walls and ceilings, and he wasn't surprised to find them, but he was glad to see they were still standard issue.

An axe might be too hard to swing in close quarters, so he was looking for something that resembled a pike. He found three fastened in a rack below the ladders. Each pike was about six feet long, had a sharp steel tip and a vicious looking hook. Tom told himself that he would prefer to thrust outward rather than swing an axe like a bat, especially in close quarters.

There was only one more thing Tom wanted. A fireman's coat would give him added protection from bites, and as a bonus he hoped to find a pair of heavy duty gloves. There was a locker full of spare protective clothing, and he helped himself. He felt a bit conspicuous in bright yellow clothing, but he couldn't have felt safer.

Tom and Molly gave each other a big hug, and then they found the best spot for her to wait for his return. The gray sky had turned to a slight drizzle, so Tom used extra coats to make a shelter where Molly could stay warm and dry. Once she was situated, he worked his way to the back of the truck and looked across at the window.

Tom said that he remembered thinking to himself that it was only one long step. It didn't matter that it was up in the air, and it didn't matter that below him were dead people who would shred him with their teeth if he slipped on the damp roof around the window. The roof was slanted on both sides of the window, and just a bit more level in the area directly in front of it.

He used the pike to steady himself as he made the step, and it was as easy as he had expected given that he was a professional baseball player, but he still felt like he was doing a high wire act at a circus. He decided that he wasn't afraid of heights, he was just afraid of falling from high places.

With one foot on the roof in front of the window and one on the truck, he tested the window to see if it was unlocked. Breaking it would be no problem, but if there was something inside, he didn't want to make more noise than he needed to. At first it stayed where it was, but with just a slight amount of effort, it slid upward.

Tom gripped the sill with one hand and then pulled himself the rest of the way from the truck to the window. He put his head close to the opening and tried to listen for sounds coming from inside. It was difficult because there was so much noise outside, and some of the noise was being drowned out by the blood pounding in his ears. He had his head turned sideways to the window and almost didn't see the hand that was reaching for his arm.

When Tom saw the movement in the corner of his eye, the infected was lowering its head toward his arm with its mouth stretched wide. He probably would have fallen backward from the window if he had tried to pull his hand away from being bitten. Instead, he held on with his left hand and threw a right jab to the side of the greasy looking head. The thick protection of the glove and coat sleeve would have stopped the teeth from tearing into his arm, but he was also grateful for the protection on his punching hand. To his surprise, his punch collapsed the entire left side of the infected man's head. Bone fragments would have shredded Tom's hand if he would have thrown a bare handed punch, and it would have meant the end for Tom. The creature went down in a heap and didn't move.

Tom was even more aware of the blood pounding in his ears as he tried to make himself calm down. He was more than a match for the weak monster that had just tried to bite his arm, but Tom was amazed by the fact that something so frail could be so deadly. It made him think about how silly it was to be afraid of spiders or even the cockroaches that grew extra large in South Carolina. They were gross and a nuisance, but they couldn't kill you.

He leaned back toward the window and listened, but this time he turned on a flashlight and aimed it into the darkness. He saw that he was looking into a large room, and his flashlight didn't seem to reach every corner. He could gradually make out the details of furniture and a pool table. There was theater style seating, and a huge movie screen on one wall. The room was obviously for the recreation and entertainment of firemen as they worked shifts of several days on duty in a row.

Tom couldn't remember how many days firemen worked in a row, but one of his fans had talked with him about being a fireman, and Tom always thought it would be a fulfilling career. The man had told him fire stations were supposed to be home to the men and women who worked there, so they were likely to be more comfortable than most people expected. The newer stations had even more amenities than the old ones, and this one appeared to be really new. At least it had been new. It had probably smelled a lot better before the infected had taken up residence.

After convincing himself that none of the shadows were infected dead waiting for him to step into their den, Tom put one leg in through the window. After all, the infected weren't exactly subtle when they saw living people within reach. The crowd of infected gathering around the back of the truck were making enough noise to attract anything inside, so Tom didn't have to worry about being too quiet. Still, he moved as quietly and carefully as he could.

He stepped over the infected man that he had dropped with one punch and began circling the room staying close to the wall. Playing the flashlight over everything he couldn't readily identify, Tom found that the room was as big as the first floor bay that held two fire trucks. The only difference was a lower ceiling. He could see two doors along the wall that ran from the front of the station to the back wall. He dreaded what he had to do, but he knew he would have to go through every room if they planned to stay for any length of time, and by this point he was beginning to hope they could.

After circling to the opposite wall, Tom turned off his flashlight and let his eyes adjust to the dim light that came from the open window. There was another window on the back wall, but there were curtains closed over it. As his eyes adjusted, he was able to make out familiar shapes and was certain that there were no more infected dead in the room. One shape wasn't familiar so he edged a little closer to take a look.

Older, more traditional fire stations had the pole for the firemen to get to the truck quicker. Some new fire stations still had the poles, and this one had a shiny pole enclosed by a railing that curved around the opening in the floor. Tom looked into the darkness below and strained to hear if there were any noises coming from the huge engine bay. It was quiet, but he wouldn't take that for granted. He thought about it for a moment, and it occurred to him that the best way to find out for sure was to be obvious. He walked over to a table and picked up a glass that had long ago been left behind. He walked back over and dropped the glass and waited.

The glass shattered at the bottom, and the groaning started a split second behind it. Tom told us that there was something really odd about the sound the glass had made, almost like it had hit something before it hit the floor. He clicked on the flashlight and pointed it at the base of the pole, and he was surprised to see an infected dead on the floor. He was looking up at the flashlight and reaching upward with one hand aimed at Tom. It took a few moments to figure out what he was seeing, but Tom was able to piece it together. The infected was on the floor instead of walking around because it had fallen through the hole and broken its legs.

Tom sat down on the floor and looked around the room. He was wondering how he was going to kill the infected that was sitting below him, and he was wondering how he was going to be able to clear the building of any infected he hadn't found yet. He figured one of the doors was going to be to the bunk room, and the other was maybe to a restroom, but knowing what each room was for was far less important than knowing what was in them.

He pushed himself up from his perch by the hole and walked over to check on Molly. He saw that the light drizzle of rain had gotten a bit steadier, but Molly looked like she was still doing okay. She gave him her usual little smile and wave, and he was impressed by how patient and brave she could be. He looked back toward the large room and it occurred to him that he had never tested the lights. The power station across the highway was going up in smoke, but there should have been emergency lighting somewhere. The only thing he could imagine was that the emergency lights had already been on, and that the batteries had gone dead.

Tom tested a light switch and wasn't surprised that the room stayed dark. He crossed over to the first closed door and said out loud, "Let's get this over with."

He leaned with his right ear up against the door and listened. He didn't hear anything, so he tapped lightly on the door. It was still quiet, so he knocked louder. He wasn't sure if he would have preferred to hear groaning or silence, but he got silence. If it had been groaning, he would have known for sure something was behind the door. He put his hand on the knob and turned it as quietly as he could. He pushed the door open and backed up in one motion.

Nothing came out through the door, but Tom mentally kicked himself. If something had been in the room, he wouldn't have been able to shut the door in time. He would have been forced to deal with whatever came out no matter how bad it was. He looked over at the other door and hoped he would be lucky at that door too.

He eased back up to the open door and used his pike to push it open further. The room was also large because it was laid out like a big efficiency apartment. There were bunks, a toilet area, and a community shower. Personal lockers had names on them, and Tom saw by the names that he was in the lady's bunk room. There were two windows with the curtains open, so Tom's eyes adjusted well enough to see the room was safe.

There was no sense in delaying the inevitable, so Tom walked back into the recreation room and crossed over to the second door. This time there was little doubt about where this door went because there had to be stairs somewhere. Instead of knocking, he just quietly opened the door and listened at the gap. It was dark, but there was total silence. Tom turned on his flashlight and aimed it at the darkness.

There was a landing on the other side of the door and then stairs that went down to a corner and made a left turn at the next landing. There may have been total silence, but the smell was so bad it was nauseating. Tom started down as quietly as he could, holding the pike out like a lance. He made it to the landing after the first set of stairs and put his back to the wall.

He saw the motion in the darkness before he heard the groans, and no matter how ready he thought he was to confront the infected, he wasn't prepared to see what had been a female trying to figure out how to walk up the stairs. It was an effort, but it was slow enough for Tom to regain his composure. He stepped forward and aimed the pike toward the forehead of the infected. One quick thrust, and the pike pierced completely through the head. Tom had to pull hard to keep from losing the pike as the infected fell back into the darkness.

There was a shuffling and dragging sound somewhere in the darkness ahead, and Tom had no idea of the layout of the station, so he didn't know where it was safe to put his back. He decided the only way to confront the problem would be to bring it to him. He let out a low whistle, thinking there was at least some hope that he wouldn't draw too many at one time.

There was an answering groan from somewhere straight ahead, so he aimed his flashlight there. Another infected was shambling toward him. This one was, or had been, a man. His head was tilted to one side, and it seemed to be looking down at the floor, but it had definitely responded to the whistle.

The landing that Tom had stopped on had two outside walls, and there was a shorter set of stairs that went down toward the left, but this infected was approaching from the other side of a metal railing instead of a wall. It was a bit more of an open appearance, and Tom's eyes were beginning to adjust to the light. He could see that he was looking out over a larger dining room, and on the other side of an island was a restaurant sized kitchen. Meals could be passed over the island to the dining room. The infected was coming from the direction of the table as if there were no stairs around to the left.

The infected dead man finally reached the railings that had widely spaced ranch style metal rails on it. Firemen probably sat with their legs hanging over those rails many times. Now it was the only thing separating Tom from the gaping jaws of a dead fireman. Tom felt sorry for the men and women in this station who had probably sacrificed their own lives trying to help others in the early days of the outbreak.

Tom stood back for a moment to give the infected the opportunity to lean through the railings, exposing his head to the pike. This time Tom would be stabbing downward from above. He raised the pike in front of him with both hands wrapped around the handle and started to jab downward, but just as the pike was about to find its mark, his arm was stopped as something came up under his armpit. He was so intent upon the infected man trying to climb up between the railings that he forgot there were just a few stairs going down to his left.

The infected that had caught him off guard was closing in on Tom just as Tom's arms came down from well above his head, and the result was that he had the infected in a headlock with his left arm. It wasn't the worst thing that could happen because he was protected by the heavy material of the fireman's coat and the gloves, but the infected in the headlock was snapping and biting at anything it could reach with its face, and right now it had its teeth firmly clamped onto the front of Tom's coat.

Tom's first reaction was to recoil and just push the putrid smelling creature away from him, but his common sense told him that this thing was no match for him. Tom tightened the headlock to stop the wild movements of the infected then put a gloved hand on its forehead and pushed and turned at the same time. He expected the loud snap as the bones in the neck were shattered. He didn't expect to rip the head free from the body. He also didn't expect to see the face on the head acting like it didn't matter. It continued to snap at the front of the coat and the gloved hand while the body dropped to the floor.

Tom couldn't throw the head away fast enough or far enough. He pushed it through the air and out across the dining room. When he looked down the other infected had pulled itself up between the railings and onto the landing and was taking aim at Tom's unprotected ankle.

By now Tom was reacting without thinking, which is what he was good at as a baseball player. He didn't try to pull his ankle back. Instead, he put his weight on that leg and lifted his left leg in the air. He brought his left foot down hard on the back of the infected dead's neck. For the second time he heard neck bones breaking, but the neck stayed attached. With his left foot holding the head in place, Tom stabbed downward with the pike and shoved the steel tip through the side of its head.

******

Tom had a dazed look on his face as he remembered where he was and looked around at each of us. He was searching our faces for understanding and found plenty. Kathy reached over and put her hand on top of his.

"Tom," she said, "we've had to kill a few of those things, but we really haven't gone out of our way to get into close quarters combat with them, especially in a dark building. You must have been terrified."

Tom looked grateful to hear a human voice interrupting his story. Reliving this part of the journey seemed to be taking more out of him than the rest. Then he got a thoughtful look on his face and asked, "Have you ever gotten fed up with it......so tired of the whole crazy thing that you just say to hell with it and just marched straight into it? That's what I did. I just said they could come and get me if they wanted, but there wasn't going to be anymore cat and mouse games."

Tom said he pulled his pike free and walked the remaining steps to the main floor. He walked through an open door to the big engine garage, passed the second fire engine, and found the unfortunate infected that had fallen down by the pole. He unceremoniously stabbed it through the face with the pike, just as yet another infected came toward him from the shadows. Tom lifted his right foot and sent the infected flying by kicking it solidly in the chest. Tom was stalking it even before it hit the floor, and once again he quickly ended its miserable existence.

There was a row of windows in the big doors to the engine bay, and there was still some light coming down through them. If he had been sitting in the front seat of the fire truck that was parked inside, he would have been high enough to see out through the windows. They were level with the windshield of the huge truck. He could see the back of the engine outside, but he couldn't see up on top of it where Molly was waiting.

Tom stood by the last infected he had killed and rotated in a circle. He had his head cocked slightly to one side and was breathing slowly and quietly. There were no more sounds coming from the garage. He went down on one knee and looked under the firetruck. There was a wall on the other side of the truck, so there were shadows, and he wasn't entirely sure, but it looked like there was a pair of legs near the front tire. When he had walked into the engine bay, he had walked so quickly and quietly that he hadn't drawn the attention of one more infected that was standing up by the front of the engine.

The infected moved toward the back of the truck but was making really slow progress. Tom moved fast to the side of the fire engine and used handholds to scale up to the top. Once he was on top he stepped over stowed gear and moved to the back. He looked down just as the infected stepped around the side of the truck and started to cross behind it. Tom drew the pike back like a spear, took aim and threw the pike so hard that the weight and force of the strike took the infected completely off its feet and flipped it to the back wall of the engine bay. His ability to throw a baseball through a doughnut hole made it an easy shot, but even he didn't expect to see it launch the infected so far after it hit.

Tom used his vantage point to look around the rest of the engine bay. He shone his flashlight at every suspicious shape or shadow, but only saw the three he had killed. He added them up and figured there could easily be more. He still had to check the kitchen, and his guess was that the men's bunk room would be somewhere on the other side of the kitchen. There was also likely to be an office on the first floor. There was still plenty of work to do.

Even though he had lost so many friends who were soldiers or police officers, he had learned from their training and from their mistakes. So, before climbing back down from the truck, he went forward to the area above the cab. He laid down across the cab and listened. Sure enough, there was movement below him.

He hooked his right foot through some ladder rungs and slowly lowered his face over the edge. He wasn't entirely sure, but he thought he remembered seeing the windows were up when he had climbed quickly to the top of the truck.

Upside down his blood was going to his head, so all he could hear for sure was the steady pounding of his own heart. His hair was hanging down ahead of his face, so whatever was moving around was going to see it before Tom's eyes were low enough. He hoped he was moving slowly enough to make a difference. Tom thought he was ready for it, but when the infected slammed its face up against the glass, he almost lost his foothold on the ladder. The infected couldn't get him, but Tom was still scared enough to get angry again.

Tom hadn't bothered to retrieve his pike, but there were more on top of this second truck. He didn't worry about being quiet, preferring to draw anything into the open that may have heard him. He took a new pike, and standing on top of the cab he reached down and slipped the point under the door handle. With just a touch of leverage and a little help from the infected that was ramming against the door, the door popped wide open, and the infected dead fell face first to the floor.

Because the infected aren't terribly coordinated, it took several moments for it to get itself untangled from its own legs, but just as it seemed it was going to get its feet under him, a second infected fell out of the truck and landed on top of the first. Tom mentally kicked himself for assuming there would only be one. This time he just dropped the pike onto the head of the one on top. Gravity and the weight of the steel tip did the trick. One wasn't moving, and the other one was pinned under it. Tom shone his flashlight into the cab while he looked in from above, and there weren't any more. There were rear facing seats behind the front seats, and there was gear stowed between the seats as if the truck was just about to respond to a call. Tom could only guess about the final moments inside the fire station, and he knew that somehow the infection had gotten inside the building.

Tom dropped down to the floor and pulled the pike out from between the ears of the infected that was keeping the other on the floor. Then he pushed it through the head of the second one. He was starting to feel fatigue and relief set in at the same time, but he knew that could be dangerous. He didn't waste time thinking about it and headed for the first floor area beyond the dining room.

He found an office up by the front door of the station, but he could easily see that it was empty. The kitchen was a large open affair, but there were two doors to deal with. Still feeling the pent up rage that he had felt earlier along with the feeling that he was almost done, Tom unceremoniously yanked open the first door. The door opened into the largest pantry he had ever seen, and there were crates of FEMA food supplies stacked wherever there was room. There were cases of bottled water, and medical supplies. If he could stay alive clearing the last rooms, Tom knew they would be safe for a little while.

Tom moved to the second door, steeled himself and yanked it open. He had to laugh at himself because it was just a small bathroom and sink. That left one more room to go, and it was a room where he fully expected to find company. He looked around the corner into the dining area and only saw the three Infected he had killed when he came down the stairs. He crossed to the door of the men's bunk room and started to just yank it open the same way he had the others, but he told himself this was not the time to blow it. He had survived so far, so stupidity wasn't going to cause him to mess up.

He laid his ear against the door and listened. It was totally quiet but even through a closed door, Tom could smell that musty smell that lingers on long after something has decayed. The infected dead that had been walking around in the building since the world had ended had their own smell. This was that after smell.

Tom eased the door open and could see more clearly than he had expected. This big room had two large windows with mini-blinds and curtains, but the blinds were up and the curtains were pulled back. He looked around and saw the remains of two large Dalmatians and one man. The dogs were both on dog beds, and the man was sitting in a chair with a 45 caliber pistol on the floor next to him. There were no infected in the room, so Tom figured it wasn't a stretch for him to assume the man had given the faithful dogs a merciful end, and then he had chosen to escape the madness in a split second. Tom wondered at least for a moment if he would have made the same choice if not for Molly. A moment was all it took. Tom decided he would want to fight for life as long as he could.

Tom approached the windows by moving along the wall as far out of sight as possible. He took the string from the blinds and lowered them so slowly that the infected outside wouldn't notice. He pulled the curtains shut over the blinds and then did the same with the second window. When he was done, he retrieved the pistol from the floor and checked the number of bullets remaining in the clip. There were four rounds in the magazine, and a quick check of the chamber showed there was still one round there. He thumbed the safety on and checked a couple of desk drawers for more ammunition. The personal locker of someone named Tradd produced two full boxes.

5 OUTSIDE CONTACTS

Molly called out from the living room and got our attention. She was motioning with her hand for us to get in there, and she was smiling like she had just gotten a present.

"Daddy, it's Dr. Bus. I'm talking with Dr. Bus," she said.

"It can't be," said Tom. "There's no way it could be him. What are the odds?"

Kathy asked, "Who's Dr. Bus, Tom? Do you know him?"

Without even asking we knew what Tom meant about the odds that Molly would make contact with someone he had known before the infected dead began killing everyone. We had all lost contact with our friends and family, some of us more than others.

There was an unspoken rule among myself, Kathy, Jean, and the Chief that we would talk about it when we felt like it, but there was a silent admission from each of us that we knew our families and friends were probably gone.

Tom still seemed to consider it a fact that Molly's mother, his ex-wife, was still alive because they had only been about forty miles from an Army base, despite the fact that he had seen the Army do no better against the infected than anyone else. He probably felt that way because the soldiers he had been with were on the run on a river. He was sure that a fortified position at an Army base would be able to survive.

Then again, he hadn't been with us when we saw the Navy base at Goose Creek get overrun.

We all arrived in the living room and gathered around Molly. She reached up and put the headphones over her father's ears and handed him the microphone. He keyed it and said, "Bus? Is that you? Over."

He listened for a moment and then excitedly pulled the headphone plug out of the jack on the short wave set and switched it to the speaker. A man's voice filled the room.

".....reading you loud and clear, Tom. I can't believe it's you and Molly. Allison will be so happy to hear that you're alive."

Tom didn't wait for the man to quit talking. He couldn't believe what he had already heard. "Bus, did you say Allison is alive? Do you know where she is? Can you contact her? Over."

The man answered, "Yes, Tom, it's really Bus, and Allison is here with me. She's okay, too. I can go get her now. Just wait right there. Over."

Tom looked like he was about to cry and Molly was grinning from ear to ear. She turned to the rest of us and said, "I found Dr. Bus. He said he's been taking care of Mommy." She looked totally pleased with herself.

The microphone keyed up on the other end, "Tom? Oh, my God, Tom it's you and Molly?" The woman kept the microphone keyed up as if she felt like letting go of it would make her lose them again. We heard Bus telling her to say, "Over" and to let go of the switch.

"Over......over, Tom. Oh, my God."

"Allison, it's Tom," he said as he wiped one hand across his eyes. "Where are you? Are you at the Army base in Huntsville? Over."

I looked at the others and saw that Jean and Kathy had both started crying along with Tom. The Chief had a big slap-happy grin on his face. I was somewhere in between because Jean was crying.

I noticed Jean glancing at Kathy, but Kathy avoided eye contact with her. I'm a man, but I'm not totally clueless. Jean and Kathy were crying because it was an emotional reunion, but there was just a hint of disappointment on Kathy's face. She could see that Tom was still in love with his wife even though she had left him. She wasn't the type to let jealousy run her life, but she allowed room for disappointment. I was sure she was happy for Tom, especially because of Molly, but I was also sure she had harbored some hope that she and Tom would be together. Knowing her, she would hide her feelings for his sake.

"No, Tom. We didn't make it to Huntsville." We could tell Allison had started to cry too, and they weren't happy tears.

"It was bad, Tom. People were attacking everyone and biting them. They were eating people, Tom. I saw most of my family get killed, and I thought you and Molly were dead too. Molly, where's Molly, can I hear her voice too? Over." Allison was talking at a hundred miles an hour, but she was remembering to let him know when she was done.

Tom held the microphone down to Molly and keyed the talk button. "Hi, Mommy, over." That caused us all to laugh. It was short and sweet, but music to her mother's ears.

"Oh, my God, it's really you, Molly. Where are you, Baby? Over."

Tom started to reply, but the Chief put his big hand over the microphone in time. "There could be someone else listening, Tom. Just tell her it's a safe place not far from where you were, and that this could be a party line. We don't want to give away our position."

Tom keyed up and said, "We started your way on the first day, but we didn't make it twenty miles. We met some good people and wouldn't have made it without them. Now we're in a safe place, but still a long way from home. Over."

"Can you come to us, Tom? I mean…is there a way for you to get home? Over."

Tom looked away from all of us. The reality was that there was no way he would be able to cross about five hundred miles with so many of the infected roaming around the country. Not to mention the fact that Atlanta had about six million people in and around it.

We all looked at each other when Tom looked away. I don't know what it was about our little foursome, but I could almost read their faces. They all three had this look that said, "Don't worry, Tom. We'll get you home to Molly's mommy." I think we all may be a bit crazy. Maybe we were all dropped on our heads when we were babies.

Tom keyed the switch and said, "I don't know yet, Allison. If there's a way, I'll find it, but for now we just have to stay alive. We have to stay safe. Are you safe where you are? Over."

"We're safe, Tom. The place isn't easy to get to, so we should be okay for a long time. Over."

Tom looked like he was puzzling over something. "Allison, are you saying Bus did that thing he was talking about all those years? Over"

Allison said, "Tom, he wasn't just talking about it. He was already doing it for years. Over."

Four of us were looking at each other like they were speaking Latin, but the light finally came on, and I asked Tom, "Is Bus like my Uncle Titus? Did he build a bunker somewhere?"

Tom was practically laughing as he tried to answer. "Ed, your uncle was a genius to put a shelter on an island, but I think Bus may have done something almost as good. He owns a large piece of property outside of town, and a lot of it is along the water. Guntersville has some incredible lakes, and some of the lakes are isolated by mountains with some equally incredible cave systems. Bus was always talking about building a bunker in one of those caves you can only reach by water. If he started building it and stocking it years ago, it must be pretty safe."

He keyed the microphone and said, "Tell Bus I always thought he was nuts, but we're in a place like his, so now I know he wasn't nuts. Over."

"Tom, it's hard to get here, so I don't know how you can find us." Before she could finish we heard Bus saying something to her. He took the microphone and said, "When you're ready to try, Tom, you know what to do. Over."

Tom answered, "Yes, I do, Bus. Thank you. Over."

We drifted away from Tom and Molly so they could spend some time talking with Allison in private. Jean put her arm around Kathy's waist as we strolled back to the kitchen. We all had a sense of satisfaction knowing that Tom's wife was still alive and holed up just like us, despite Kathy's secret disappointment. I could tell we all felt the weight lift off of Tom's shoulders. The unspoken question was how we were going to help them get back together again.

When we sat down at the table, Kathy and Jean handed out cold beers, and we all savored the feeling for a minute or two before the Chief broke the ice. He said, "Why do we always feel like we've got to do something? Why do we have to fix everything that gets broken?"

Kathy answered, "That's just who we are, Chief. We're wired that way."

"Funny thing," I said. "I didn't know I was wired that way until I met you three."

"So, just to be clear," said Jean. "Are we talking about trying to help Tom and Molly get back home to Allison?"

I answered, "What I can't figure out is how we knew that's what we wanted to do all at the same time."

"There's something seriously wrong with us," said the Chief. "We could keep this place up and running for years without having to leave."

Kathy said, "You know the answer, Chief. Sometimes it's not enough to just stay alive. Living isn't just staying alive. It's more than that."

"Who wants to tell them?" asked Jean.

"Let's break it to them gently," said the Chief. "This is going to take a bunch of planning. Our little trip down the coast was a picnic compared to this. I mean logistically it's not impossible. If nothing goes wrong, we could be back home in a few days."

If there was one thing the Chief could have said that would have stopped us in our tracks, that last sentence was probably it. He earned an expressionless stare from all three of us.

"What?" There was that innocent look again, like he couldn't possibly know what he had said.

"If nothing goes wrong?" asked Jean and Kathy at the same time.

Instead of answering them, the Chief looked at me as if I was going to bail him out. The cutest part was a man the size of a bear being stared down by two women.

"Don't look at me, Chief. They were saying it, but I was thinking it. We have millions of infected dead between here and Alabama. It's not like you just ask Google Maps to give you the best route. I know they would list road congestion, wrecks, and construction, but I don't think their app will tell you where the zombies are gathering in large numbers."

"They're not zombies," he said under his breath.

"Whatever," I said. "Call them Numb from the Ankles Up if you want to, but I think we can safely say that something will go wrong."

"I like that," said Jean. "We could call them NAU's for short."

Kathy said, "Yeah, that would strike fear into my heart when someone would yell to watch out for that NAU."

The Chief rolled his eyes. He finally caught on that we were pulling his leg. "Okay, Larry, Curly and Moe. I get it. We have to plan on something going wrong and then prevent it."

I wasn't done yet. I turned to Kathy and pointed at her top button. When she looked down I hooked my finger under her nose and flipped it upward. She swung at me, and I ducked, so she clobbered Jean in the left ear. Jean retaliated by pretending to spread two fingers and poke Kathy in both eyes. All three of us were going, "Whoop whoop whoop," like the Three Stooges. The Chief was loving it, but he wasn't going to admit it.

Tom walked in and watched the last part, and judging by the smile on his face, he really enjoyed it. Molly was peeking around him and started giggling.

"What did we miss?" asked Tom. "Looks like you guys found something to cheer you up."

Our foursome shared that knowing look we sometimes do when there's an insider secret, but there seemed to be this natural connection we had that made us pick a leader with our eyes. We voted for Kathy this time. Maybe we were subconsciously helping her to get by her earlier disappointment.

"Have a seat, Tom. You can join us, too, Molly. We have something we want to talk with you about," she said.

Tom sat in a chair and the Chief handed him a beer while Jean poured the chocolate milk. Tom reached for the chocolate milk and Molly lightly slapped his hand while letting out a single, "Whoop." We were such a good influence on kids, and of course we made it worse by laughing.

"Tom," Kathy began, "we were thinking about the possibility of trying to get you and Molly home to Allison."

Tom's expression stayed neutral, but Molly kept looking back and forth between Tom and Kathy. Some little kids have a way of knowing when to wait for something. Molly seemed to know it better than most. She knew it was up to her dad to answer, and his face was as unreadable as it could get.

"We just started talking about it," said the Chief. "We haven't filled in any of the blanks if that's what you're wondering."

"You can't do it," said Tom. "I won't let you risk your lives. I'd rather stay here with Molly and see all of you be safe."

Jean said, "So, what you're saying is that you don't think we could do it, right?"

"No, Jean, I'm saying I know you couldn't do it," Tom said. "There's a big difference between wishing we could go five hundred miles and actually doing it."

"Why couldn't we do it?" I asked. "We've gone out twice and made it back each time."

Tom said, "You admitted there were close calls, Ed. How far did you go the last time? Less than two hundred miles round trip?"

"The point is that we made it, Tom, and the difference is we have a plane," said Kathy.

"Which took a bullet and had to be abandoned," said Tom. "What would you do if you had to leave it behind again? Do you think you could go back for it a second time?"

Like it or not, Tom was wearing us down. Our desire to help him and Molly get back home was greater than our common sense, and we had to admit, we did feel like we were invincible. Maybe we needed Tom for the reality check.

Tom could see that we were disappointed by his reaction, so he said in a voice of total calm and reason, "When we left Conway, there were a dozen boats filled with seventy to eighty well-armed, well trained, brave souls. They were police officers and soldiers, and I couldn't have felt safer. We lost most of them when we stopped to try to help other civilians. It was in their nature to help, just like it's in your nature to help. I can safely tell you that every one of them felt good to know they were helping me and my little girl, but that didn't stop a single one of them from dying. When we made it to Simmonsville, there was only one of them left, and he gave his life for five civilians. When we reached the fire station, there were only two of us left. I'm not going to see anyone else die for us."

We couldn't argue with Tom about the facts, but for some reason I wasn't swayed, and I was sure my friends weren't either.

"Tom," I said, keeping my voice at the same level he had used. I wanted to come off as sincerely as he had.

"The soldiers and police officers made the same mistake repeatedly. They didn't think they could be taken down. They thought there was safety in numbers, and they expected civil obedience. The reason Kathy, Jean, and the Chief were the only survivors on a ship with five thousand people was because they knew something with certainty that everyone else ignored. They knew families would lie about who was bitten in order to protect loved ones. They got it then, and they get it now. This group knows that we survive together, but we don't take someone else down with us. That's why we've survived."

The Chief wanted to get his turn, too, and he quietly reminded Tom of what Jean had said when she had come within an inch of being bitten when they were dumping an infected dead off of the floating dock of the cruise ship. She didn't need to convince them that she was telling the truth when she said she would jump overboard with the infected that had bitten her before she would endanger someone else.

Kathy added, "Tom, there are still people out there, and plenty of them still think they won't die if they get bitten. No matter how many times they've seen it, they still think it won't happen to them. The difference between them and us is that we get it. We aren't ready to die, but we know we will die if we're bitten just as surely as we would know if we jumped from a plane without a parachute. That's what keeps us alive. We get it."

Tom asked, "And that's why I should believe that we have a chance of making it from here to Guntersville?"

The Chief said, "The only times we have to land are when we get there, and to find fuel for the trip back. I've played it really cautious with the fuel and had alternative fueling sites in mind when we flew to Goose Creek, but the de Havilland DHC-3 Otter can carry a payload just over a ton and still travel over seven hundred miles on one tank of gas. The combined weight of five adults and the Munchkin would leave us close to twelve hundred pounds of payload. Like I said before you came in, this is going to take some planning, but if Bus has fuel, we could go to the maximum cruising altitude of eighteen thousand feet for most of the trip, so we wouldn't be getting shot at. To economize fuel we could cruise at about one hundred and twenty miles per hour. That way we could detour for fuel if we had to. My best guess is we would have enough fuel for an extra one hundred and fifty miles."

Tom's eyebrows were raised at the thought of being with Allison in just over four hours. We could see that the Chief was beginning to sway him.

"Listen, Tom," said the Chief. "We want to do this or we wouldn't be talking about it. This group isn't a bunch of Boy Scouts and Girl Scouts even if Molly is getting lots of cookies."

Molly grinned at the reference and glanced at Jean. I don't know if it's some kind of mother radar or what, but Jean produced a box of cookies for Molly like magic. For some strange reason, that small gesture seemed to sway Tom over the tipping point. It was like Jean showed him that helping was our signature. His shoulders slumped a bit because he wanted to give in so badly. He just didn't want us to pay the price for it.

Kathy said, "You know what? We didn't talk about it this long the first time we went out."

We all laughed, but it was true. When we decided to go, we practically just went. The second time out we did some real planning, and we learned the rivers inside and out. This was going to be the same thing in some ways. We would need to get Bus's exact location without giving it away to anyone else, and we would need to have back-up plans for fuel. That would be the Chief's department.

"One last thing," said Tom. "I think you're forgetting about your problem back here? What about the water dropping in the moat and the nets collapsing your power cable?"

"We have two issues," said the Chief. "One of them is the power cables, and the other one is getting you home. The way I see it is that one of the issues we can do something about, and the other issue we can't do anything about. So, let's take care of the one we can do something about, and let's just hope for the best with the other issue."

It was settled, and by the looks on the faces of my friends, we were about to do what made us feel good about ourselves, and it was time to start planning. It had been a long day, and we could wait to hear the rest of Tom's story about the fire station. For now it was time to have a late meal and then get some rest......but that wasn't exactly how it worked out.

What started out as a simple late meal quickly turned into an all-out celebration. No real plans had been made, but the mood was the first thing that told us this was what we really wanted to do. To be honest, there was at least a small amount of selfishness. We could live a long time in the shelter even if we lost the mainland power lines, but the four of us who had brought Tom in didn't want to spend our remaining days hiding from the world. I was the least likely of the bunch to be a hero, but I was all in when it came to what my friends wanted.

Not that I always thought women should do all the cooking, but Kathy and Jean were wizards in the kitchen. They could make anything taste good, and we had more than enough in the way of quality food stashed in the deep freezer. Tonight they brought up a rack of prime rib that had been moved to the refrigerator to thaw. If any of us was thinking of it as a last supper, it didn't show. There was laughter, friendship, stories from the past, and more than a little love.

Kathy told us what it had been like at the South Carolina Law Enforcement Academy on the good days. She told how everyone got close and felt the bond that can only really be explained to another police officer or a comrade in arms. She didn't dwell on the days when she had to pay the price for being one of the prettiest officer cadets they had ever had. Those days were hard, but she rose above them and earned the respect of her peers, not only in the classroom, but in hand to hand combat training and small arms skill.

She told us that one of her best days was when a group of the male officers approached her during supper. She said it made her a little nervous because they came up to her at her table all together and didn't speak immediately. She thought it was a confrontation of some kind, but for the life of her she didn't know what she had done to earn it. Kathy said one of them spoke up for all of them and asked if she would consider running a study group. He explained that they were falling behind in some of the classes and they knew she was doing well. She remembered thinking there was a time when some of the big egos would have accused a woman of sleeping her way to good grades, but these guys weren't giving a hint that they felt that way. They really needed her help. So, she ran the study group, and every one of them gave her the credit for them passing.

She said that every graduating class nominated one person from their ranks for a special award. It was nicknamed the 'wingman' award, but it was officially for outstanding support of your fellow officers. She was nominated by her class, and she said she would have given up all of her marksmanship and academic awards for that one nomination. Kathy had one sad moment when she wondered what had happened to her friends in that class, but she shook it off and said this was a time to celebrate life because Tom and Molly were going home to Allison.

She passed the conversation baton to the Chief and asked him how he got started with his love for the oceans. Of course the Chief gave us an 'aw shucks' attitude at first, but he really did like telling sea stories. He said one of his favorite stories was our trip down to Charleston to bring back our plane, but we all knew that one.

Chief Joshua Barnes was six and a half feet tall and skinny as a rail when he went to Boot Camp at the Naval Training Center at Great Lakes, Illinois. None of us had ever been able to pry his age out of him, but the popular guess was around fifty. He kept his beard full but trimmed, and nothing ever seemed to faze him.

Kathy said, "Hey, Chief, how many times have you been in love?" She gave him a sly smile, and the rest of us kept quiet to hear the answer.

The Chief looked like he was thinking it over, and once in a while he would say something in a low voice like, "No, that's not right. Let me start over again."

I finally asked him what he was doing, and he said, "I'm trying to count the number of different cities where I've made port." He said it with a straight face, as usual, but we rolled laughing.

The Chief said, "Seriously, I fell in love with the sea, and I never met a woman to take her place."

The truth was, it was where he fit in the most. Navy food is healthy because they have limited storage space on ships. They don't waste space with things that aren't good for you. The end result was a bigger, healthier Joshua Barnes. He also loved the job, and he learned anything they wanted to teach him. He rose through the enlisted ranks as a machinist, and he was a natural leader when he was promoted to Chief Petty Officer.

The title stayed with him when he retired from the Navy and signed up to work on cruise ships. He could have been an officer on any cruise liner he wanted, but he liked being the senior enlisted man too much to accept the promotion. He was also popular with everyone who worked for him and trusted by every officer. Well, almost every officer.

"Hey Chief," I said. "Tell Tom about the time you had an officer locked up in the brig on the cruise ship."

"Not much to tell," said the Chief. "He got in Kathy's face, so I had him locked up."

Jean said, "He was great, Tom. The ship's doctor was a pompous ass who thought he was God's gift to the nursing staff, and he didn't like how Kathy had invaded his little kingdom by setting up an examination plan on the ship. When the Chief had him locked up, we were all ready to become Mrs. Joshua Barnes, but he wouldn't have any of us. It turned out to be a good thing because I was still single when I met Eddy."

"Oh," said Tom. "I knew you two were together, but I didn't know you were married."

I must have been my typical beet red because Chief Barnes looked like he couldn't get enough of where this conversation had gone. I looked at Kathy and it was obvious that she was waiting for something to come out of my mouth that would either make or break me.

Jean was also looking at me. Tom hadn't directed his comment at either one of us in particular, but it was obvious that everyone felt like it was my obligation to make it good. I thought to myself, "Sometimes when you lead a horse to water, he'd better drink."

I said, "We're not married yet, Tom, but I'm ready as soon as she says she is."

Maybe that wasn't the best thing I could have said, but it must have been close because all five feet of Jean was off the floor and wrapped around my neck. Kathy had both hands to her face in shock, and the Chief was one big smile.

"Was that a proposal, Ed?" the Chief asked around a mouthful of food.

I thought, "Man, is he enjoying this."

I looked down at Jean, and I knew it wasn't time for something witty. I said, "Jean Mitchell, will you marry me?"

Jean, however, wasn't going to miss a chance and said, "Can I have a day or two to think about it?" Before I could get too serious and think she really wanted a day or two to think about it, she added, "Of course I will."

Believe me when I say, that wasn't how I expected the evening to turn out.

The evening eventually wound down when Molly started to yawn. She asked in a sleepy voice if Jean and Kathy could be her aunts and if the Chief and I could be her uncles. We all agreed to her request just as Tom scooped her up to carry her off to bed.

Kathy said, "She's seen a lot for a kid, but she's taking it so well."

"Kids heal fast," said Jean. "She's got a lot of trust in her dad."

The Chief joined the conversation by saying, "An apocalypse has a way of bringing people together. Look what it did for you and Ed."

Beer went up my nose. I had come up with that one earlier but didn't say it because I thought it might get me clobbered, but when the Chief said it, it sounded funny.

"And I thought I was just a one apocalypse stand," said Jean.

I thought I was going to drown with beer in my nose.

......

Breakfast always seemed better when we had something we wanted to plan, and the next morning was no exception. Scrambled eggs, bacon, toast, pancakes smothered in syrup, and hot coffee were dished out around the table, and everyone dove in as if we hadn't eaten a prime rib feast the night before.

The discussion immediately went to logistics. The Chief made it clear that he wanted everyone to be thinking Plan B, Plan C, and Plan D. He said not to think about negative things as problems, but to think of them as barriers to be overcome. If the plane breaks down, think about where we would prefer to have it break down and where we could get another plane.

Tom said, "So we should anticipate that it will break down, and when it does, we should make sure it breaks down near an airplane dealership?"

"That's it exactly, Tom. If we run out of fuel, we should be able to see a fuel pump. If we run into weather that's too bad to fly in, we should have a boathouse big enough to hold a plane right there at our disposal. We don't need to be lucky. We need to be smart. Everyone getting the idea?"

We all nodded and told him we did, so we started working on lists of things we had to consider as barriers. At the top of that list we had to put the infected dead. A second list was started that would have the solutions to the barriers, so we listed guns, machetes, and protective clothing. Tom suggested that we should find something that fits easily in the plane like the pikes he had used at the fire station. The beauty of the pikes was that you didn't have to waste a bullet, and you didn't have to let them get too close.

Kathy said, "We have the oars for the raft. Can't we use them as weapons, too?"

"No, I think I know what Tom has in mind," said the Chief. "We could hold them at bay with the oars, but the pikes would kill them. I think we have room for a couple of them in the gear payload. Go ahead and add them to the list."

"Wait a minute," I said. "We have pikes? Where?"

"Believe it or not, on the houseboat," said the Chief. "Lots of gear is stowed up on the top of the houseboat."

I thought to myself that it was kind of funny that the Chief knew what we had better than I did, but I probably looked right at the pikes and never gave them a thought.

"Hey guys," said Jean. "I'm going to take Molly into the living room and get the radio tuned into whatever might be out there. It'll keep her a little busy while we plan the trip. The details might bore her just a bit."

"Sounds like a good idea," said Tom. "Molly likes to feel useful, too. Right, Baby?" Tom mussed up her hair a bit, and Molly gave him that look kids give their parents. She liked it, but she had to pretend she didn't.

I watched Jean take Molly's hand and walk her from the room. I couldn't help but think about how natural Jean was around children. I guess I was thinking ahead, and I could see her as a mom more than I could see myself as a dad.

The others had already gone back to planning, and I tried to figure out what project they had moved to after the pikes. The Chief had his maps rolled out onto the table and was pointing at different lakes. Some were in South Carolina, some were in Georgia, and some were in Alabama. There was no shortage of big water to land on. Now all they had to do was figure out where the fuel pumps were likely to be on each lake. The Chief had topped off the fuel when they had used the plane the last time, so they wouldn't need to refuel until the trip back, but like the Chief said, they needed a Plan A and a Plan B for fuel.

This morning reminded me of the day we decided to make the trip down to Charleston by boat. We laid out the maps and decided Plan A was the easy trip straight into the Charleston harbor and up the Cooper River. Plan B was to go further to the South and up the Stono River. As it had turned out, Plan A was cut short by snipers in Fort Sumter. If not for Plan B, we would have been forced to forget about the plane. For a longer trip like this one, the Chief wanted a Plan C and even a Plan D if we could think of one.

Without the internet to offer us satellite views of the lakes, we had to try to figure out from the maps which marinas were likely to have fuel pumps. According to the Chief it was really a no-brainer. If there was a convenience store at the boat landing, they were likely to also have a gas pump where people could fill up before putting their boats into the water.

The maps the Chief had were stashed in the shelter by Uncle Titus, and it looked like he had them printed professionally from satellite shots, but there was nothing like being able to zoom in and study the images. The Chief had a map spread out on the table that was about as high resolution as a map could get, and he was peering through a magnifying glass to get a closer look.

In the living room Jean and Molly had made contact with someone, and Molly was showing her uncanny ability to figure out foreign words. I heard her telling Jean that she knew a girl in school from Russia, and she had taught Molly a few words while Molly did the same for her. Molly told Jean that Russian was easier than English. She said English had too many rules and too many times that you had to break the rules, but she admitted our alphabet made more sense.

I drifted into the living room because something didn't sound right. I heard Molly say to Jean that the Russian man kept asking her where she was, and she kept telling him she was somewhere safe. Then he would ask again where she was. It sounded like even Molly was getting uncomfortable with his insistence. Jean was close to Molly listening to what the man said, trying to hear not so much what the man was saying but how he was saying it.

When I came up behind her, Jean turned around and gave me a worried look.

"This guy isn't being friendly," she said. "It sounds like he's demanding to know where Molly is calling from. He's scaring her."

I listened for a moment, and I could hear it in his voice even though I didn't understand a word of what he was saying. Molly was looking at me as if she wanted me to take over, so I just reached out and switched off the power to the radio.

It was when I turned around to go back to where the Chief, Tom, and Kathy were pouring over the maps when I saw what was on the outside monitor. I stopped in front of the screen and stared in disbelief. It was on the grid view that showed every camera on the island, and every view was filled with the infected dead. Even the camera directly in front of the main entrance to the shelter showed at least six. They weren't moving much, but there were more on the island than we had ever seen.

Jean called for the others to come see what was happening outside, but before they could even reach the living room, we saw the first one fall in the violent motion that could only have come from a head shot. It was in the view we had created when we moved the houseboat, and the infected were crossing the sand bar at low tide. As the rest of our group joined us, a second one flew backwards and disappeared, and a third head snapped back a split second later.

"The tide hasn't been low for too long. How could so many be on the island already?" asked the Chief. He didn't ask anyone in particular, but none of us had the answer anyway.

"A bigger question is who's shooting them," said Kathy. "Those aren't close up shots, and I don't see anyone in any of the long range views."

"Has to be a rifle," said Tom. "Could it be someone in the view we blocked with the houseboat?"

Kathy said, "No, the heads are flying back in the opposite direction, so the shooter would have to be somewhere in this camera view." She raised her finger just as a shot was fired from a sniper position on the beach facing the ocean. The shooter was so well hidden that they wouldn't have seen him if they had gone outside.

"Who the hell is that?" asked Tom.

We were all wondering the same thing, and as we watched he stood and advanced on his targets. He was wearing camouflage, but it was a uniform of some kind. There were patches on his left shoulder, but the camera view was too grainy to make out the details.

I said, "Chief, uniforms would be your territory. Any ideas about his?"

"Unfortunately, Ed, I've seen that style helmet he's wearing, and I think it's Russian."

Jean, Molly, and I all exchanged looks. That was just a little too much of a coincidence for me.

"Chief, I said, "we were about to call you into the room when this guy started shooting the infected like ducks on a pond. There was a Russian on the radio, and he kept demanding that Molly tell him where she was."

"This guy obviously isn't the dude she was talking to, so where are his buddies?" asked the Chief.

"I think that would be his buddies coming around the jetties right now," said Kathy.

A long ship was coasting into view around the northern jetty, and it was being trailed by two smaller boats that had fifty caliber machine guns mounted on their bows. They looked like Zodiacs that had probably been carried aboard the larger ship. It looked like a naval vessel about the size of a small destroyer, and it wasn't one of ours. We all looked at the Chief at the same time, and what we saw we didn't like. He looked the opposite of his normal self.

"That's a Buyan-class corvette," he said. "It can come in close because it only drafts about seven feet. It can carry those two Zodiacs on the aft deck along with a helicopter, and if you're thinking they're Russian, you would be correct."

"How many crew?" I asked.

"Anywhere from thirty to fifty, maybe a few more," he answered.

"We can't handle that kind of firepower," said Kathy. "What should we do?"

The Chief looked at each of us one at a time as if he was about to break some bad news, but all he said was, "Nothing. There's nothing we can do."

We settled back like a family that was getting ready to watch its favorite television show. Jean went to the kitchen and came back with some snacks and cold beer then curled up against me. The Russians didn't seem to know we were here, but they seemed very interested in our northern jetty.

The Zodiacs beached on the sand bar, and crew members got out into the shallow water to take a closer look. It seemed like they were trying to figure out how big the sand bar was and how fast it dropped off into the deeper water on both sides.

It didn't take them long to figure out that something had knocked a hole in the jetty, and that the sand bar was being formed by longshore drift. I had learned in a Geology class that longshore drift was when beach sand from the north was carried to the south where some lucky beachfront property owner could get luckier and watch his beach get bigger. The problem was it could be a double edged sword. You could lose your beach the same way.

The corvette stayed at the tip of the jetty waiting, and the advance party eventually turned its attention to our houseboat, the powerful twin outboard boat, and the plane. Tom wasn't letting it show, but he had to be thinking this turn of events marked the end of his chances to fly home. He just sat and watched with the rest of us. Like the Chief said, all we could do for now was nothing.

Both Zodiacs went into combat mode as they reached the dock, and they worked together using the same tactics any military group would use to clear an area. They went in weapons hot and cleared the houseboat first. One came out and signaled the others who had stayed back to provide cover. They relaxed and began checking the boat and the plane. Once they were satisfied that neither was operational, they boarded their Zodiacs and headed back to the corvette.

I glanced at the Chief and asked, "What do you make of that, Chief?"

"Pretty sloppy if you ask me," he answered. "First of all, the range of a corvette isn't so good. How they got on this side of the ocean is anybody's guess because they're more like armed Coast Guard Cutters than warships. They're relatively new and sophisticated, but without shore support, they're not something our Navy couldn't easily handle."

"What about the fact that they didn't even post a guard on the dock?" asked Kathy.

"That's what I mean by sloppy," said the Chief. "They think this place is deserted. Maybe the number of infected dead roaming around on the beach was an advantage. They must've dropped off the sniper and pulled back to let him clear the area first. Their crew compliment may also be less than they can afford for watch duty."

We watched for several hours as the corvette crossed to the opposite side of the jetty away from Mud Island and then came slowly closer to the beach. The hull was probably only clearing the bottom by a couple of feet.

One of the Zodiacs returned to the sand bar while the other Zodiac trailed the corvette until it was directly across from the hole in the jetty. Sailors played out heavy rope and grappling hooks until they had enough line to pull the hooks around the huge stones that had somehow been knocked out of place.

"Are they repairing the jetty?" asked Kathy.

"I was going to ask the same thing," I said, "but I didn't want to sound stupid."

Kathy gave me a mock stare and asked, "Did you just say I sounded stupid?"

"No, that's not what I meant," I said.

She looked at the Chief, and without looking at me he said, "Uh, huh. He said you sounded stupid."

Tom and Jean both nodded their heads at the same time without taking their eyes off of the scene that was playing out at the jetty. When I looked back at Kathy, she was just smiling.

"You're so easy," she said.

The corvette began to rotate until it was parallel with the beach, its stern facing almost straight at our camera. Then it slowly built up forward speed until the ropes began to get straighter and straighter. When they looked like they were about to break, the huge rock began to pull free from the sand that had partially buried it. It was like watching an iceberg being pulled to the surface. There was so much more of it than I had thought.

The men from the Zodiacs couldn't do anything but watch because the rock was too large for them to guide it. I couldn't help but wonder how Uncle Titus had found the resources to have boulders that big imported from some quarry all the way to this remote stretch of beach, and that was just one boulder. I didn't have a clue how many were in the pair of jetties that protected Mud Island from longshore drift.

With a tremendous splash, the boulder rolled over into its original hole and sealed the gap that had caused our moat to begin getting sealed off by the sandbar. I wondered how long it would take before the sand bar began to erode, but at least it wasn't going to get worse.

"So," said the Chief. "The Russians have repaired the sandbar, but why?"

Then he answered his own question. "There can only be one reason. They've already been around to the mainland side and know there's a deep body of water where they can hide a ship that size. They know this area must be crawling with US Navy ships, so they need to lay low. My guess is that they think they can go inland from here and find supplies."

"Boy, are they in for a big surprise," said Tom. "Those trees are crawling with infected."

"Chief," I said, "I'm going to guess you already know what's going to happen here. I mean you're the naval expert and all, but am I correct in saying that they'll check out the bottom of the moat with their sonar?"

"Ed, you're really coming along as a survivor," he said. "You're thinking ahead. They're going to sweep the bottom with their sonar. First, they'll see the big cables that hold the nets and wonder what's down there. Then they'll see the power cables and decide to investigate. If they send down some divers they might lose a few people to the nasty surprises hanging in the nets, but they'll eventually figure out that there are power conduits connecting the mainland to the island. When they do, they'll start looking for whatever those power lines are connected to."

"Can they get in here?" asked Tom. He looked at me since he knew my uncle had built the shelter.

I said, "As far as I know, Tom, there's nothing they can do to get in this place, unless of course they have the firepower to blow the front door open."

As I said it, I looked at the Chief, hoping he would laugh at the idea, but he looked deep in thought. He looked like he was working on a plan, so I waited for him to answer.

The Chief finally looked at us all and said, "We have to leave. Not immediately, but very soon."

I could see the disappointed looks on Jean and Kathy's faces. This shelter had been a refuge they could only have hoped for. Even though we had just been planning to fly Tom and Molly home to Alabama, we had planned on returning to our home. It had never occurred to us that we wouldn't have a place to come back to.

The Chief realized his mistake quickly and said, "Wait, wait. Are you guys thinking I meant that we had to leave permanently? I only meant if we're going to get a chance to leave, we have to do it now. They can sit there and try to blow a hole in the front door all they want, but I don't think that little pea shooter on the front of that corvette can do the job. Besides, if they try, they're going to make a lot of noise, and the Navy will hear them."

Kathy asked, "Why do we have to leave quickly, Chief?"

The Chief rubbed his hand across his beard and looked for once like he didn't know where to begin.

"Well, like I said, I think they plan to park the corvette in our moat. When they do, they're going to drop anchor."

The Chief just let his last sentence hang in the air for a minute while it sank in. It wasn't that we were being slow so much as it was that he had been down in the moat. His visibility wasn't the best, but he could see that there were two nets. One was just a shadow in the distance, but he could tell it was just as effective at catching the infected as the other had been. An anchor dropping in that mess was going to get interesting.

He smiled when he saw the lights start to come on over our heads like mine had when Jean told us she was pregnant.

"If the anchor catches a net, I'm not sure the corvette will be able to raise the anchor without getting totally fouled. It's either going to pull a net up and break it loose from its moorings, or it's going to get stuck for good. The other thing that can go wrong is that they will drop anchor right between the nets and catch on the power conduits. Personally, my money is on the nets because they come up closer to the surface. I also prefer the nets for obvious reasons."

Kathy connected the dots and said, "Either way, they're going to be stuck in the moat. This is going to get really interesting, Chief. We're going to have Russians as neighbors. That's the good news."

"That's good news?" I asked. "Please don't tell me the bad news, Kathy."

The Chief said, "In the long run, it means we have another buffer from the infected, survivors with bad intentions, and any other nasty thing that comes along. But that's why we have to leave now. Once they get stuck in the moat, we won't be able to get to the plane. We need to get it and fly out before they can stop us."

Tom let out a low whistle. "Any ideas about how to fly the plane out Chief? The water won't be deep enough at the northern entrance until that sandbar breaks down. We'll need to power up the plane and drive it the length of the island before we can even take off."

"Wouldn't they hear the plane before we can reach the southern exit?" asked Jean.

"They sure would," said the Chief, "and if they have good detection gear, they would be able to track the engine and shoot us down before we could gain enough altitude."

I asked. "So, waiting until they enter the moat is out of the question, and driving the plane out of the southern exit is out of the question. What option does that leave us with?"

"We can't get up enough speed to take off in the moat?" asked Jean.

The Chief shook his head, "No, the moat is too short, and we would lose too much speed in the turn. As soon as we would pop out at the end of the island, they would be tracking us with an anti-aircraft missile. We have to go out quietly."

"Wait a minute," I said. "The Chief has that look he gets when he knows what to do. What are you thinking, you old salt?"

The Chief had a smile he saved for special occasions, and he was putting it on display now.

"How fast can everybody put together emergency gear and supplies for about three or four days?" he asked. "Only what we can each carry."

"Only one trip to the plane?" asked Jean.

"Not to the plane," said the Chief. "Everybody get your gear together as fast as you can. When you're done let's all meet in the main bedroom where the tunnels lead to the surface. When we make our move, it has to go down like a well-rehearsed fire drill, and we don't have time for a rehearsal."

"When are you going to at least let us read the script?" I asked.

"It's a short plan," he said, and there was that smile again.

For the next hour we put together emergency packs with food, clothing, camping gear, weapons, and ammunition. The only verbal exchanges we made were when someone would ask if there was room for something else. In no time we were all gathered in the master bedroom with a big pile of backpacks and duffel bags.

When we were all together, the Chief asked if we were ready to go for a trip. Everybody nodded quietly including Molly, and the Chief had to lean over to see under the brim of her new Navy blue ball cap.

"We only have time to go over this once, and I'm going to make it quick," he said. "It's already starting to get dark outside. There's no moon, so it's going to get a lot darker out there. Everyone needs to stay together in case there are any infected dead out on the beach. Hopefully, the Russians did us a favor and cleared them all out, but we can take them on better if we stay in a group. When we get to the end of the tunnel, we need to get the Boston Whaler to the beach as fast as we can. No talking. Sound travels well at night over water. The gear can't go in the boat until we have it in the water. We don't want to get stuck in the sand. Everybody with me so far?"

We all nodded again, but this time there was no smile on the Chief's face. We had all moved into that zone where we were all business.

"Okay," he said, "once the boat is in the water and loaded with the gear, Ed and Jean will go back down the tunnel. Jean, you go all the way down and hang out with Molly. Not because of your condition, but because Molly needs company. Ed, you stay in the top of the tunnel and watch for us to come back. Kathy and Tom, you're going to use the long poles in the Whaler to circle the island in the moat. You can stay close to the oyster beds because the Whaler has a shallow draft and you won't be moving fast enough to damage the boat if you hit them. While you're doing that, I'm going down the tunnel and then back out through the front door. I'll get to the plane ahead of you so I can reconnect the wiring and let the moorings loose. The current will be moving your way, so I may try to drift in your direction. When we meet up, we're going to use the poles to get back out of the moat, and we'll tow the plane behind us. If we're lucky at all, we can make it out the exit and drift south far enough to bring the boat to low power and tow the plane faster. They won't know where the sound is coming from by then. Everybody ready?"

The plan was simple enough, but like the Chief said, we were going to have to do it like a well-rehearsed fire drill. The Chief opened the emergency hatch and disappeared into the tunnel towing a large bag of gear behind him. We each followed quietly. Everything that needed to be said had already been said. If we were going to go, it had to be before the Russian corvette dropped anchor in the moat.

The tunnel was long, but it wasn't a bad crawl. Uncle Titus had spared no expense when he built the shelter. The surface wasn't intended for sliding. That would make it easier to go down the steep tunnel, but it would be just as easy to go back up. There was a strip of rubber that ran down the middle about two feet wide and an inch thick. It made climbing out of the tunnel a breeze.

The Chief reached the hatch that came out directly under the Boston Whaler. There was an inner and an outer hatch. He stopped after quietly going through the inner hatch and listened for sounds coming from the other side. It wouldn't be a good idea to crawl right into the arms of an infected dead or a living Russian. Their cameras had been useful in telling them the Russians were all most likely on board the corvette, but the Chief wanted to be sure. After a few moments of listening, he eased open the outer hatch and took a look around.

When the Chief went through the outer hatch, we all followed with our gear and went straight for the surface. As the Chief had instructed, we stayed together in a tight group and carried our supplies down to the water's edge where the southern jetty met with the land. In a matter of a few minutes we were back at the place we called the garage and pulled back the camouflage covers.

One of my ideas that I was really proud of was the wooden planks under the wheels. I had suggested the idea back when the Chief and I had built the hiding place for the boat.

It had been a real pain towing the trailer up the beach through the soft sand, so I suggested to the Chief that we should put planks under the wheels in the hiding place and put spare planks under the trailer. We could line the spares up with the planks under the wheels as we rolled forward, retrieving the ones already used and moving them to the front.

Three of us moved the trailer forward while the other two ran back for the next two planks, and it was just like building a wooden road to the beach. We passed over the soft sand quickly without getting stuck even once. The trailer slid down to the beach and into the water. The Chief and I were unstrapping the boat as soon as it was able to float off of the trailer, and the others were tossing the supplies to Jean who had climbed inside.

As soon as the boat was loaded, we reversed our process and hauled the trailer back into its hiding place. We covered it and then went to work hiding our more obvious tracks in the sand. Footprints were no big deal because there were so many infected on the island the previous day.

The Chief dropped back into the tunnel to make his way through to the front door. He took a moment to mess up Molly's hair as he went by. Jean went back down the tunnel to keep Molly company, and I positioned myself between the inner and outer hatches. I kept the outer hatch open just a crack. With the boat gone from the hidden chamber we had made, I would be able to close the hatch quickly if I had to.

I didn't even have the chance to look back in time to see Kathy and Tom start muscling the Boston Whaler against the current into the moat. Since the water was coming outward, it was easy to coast with it, but they had to put everything they had into going in against it. It would probably become easier once they made it around the corner and started following the coast of the island over the oyster beds.

In the darkness of the moat, Kathy and Tom were struggling with the current but making progress. One of the advantages of the oyster beds was that they gave them something to push their poles against. They had a long way to go, but the Chief had to make his way to the dock and get the plane moving.

The island was about two miles long with the hidden shelter almost at the center, and it seemed like a hundred miles to Kathy and Tom's burning muscles, but on the other side of the island the Chief was moving quickly and quietly. He had a small bag of extra supplies and tools he would need to get the plane wired up, but he was also well armed. If the Russians had slipped someone onto the dock as a watchman without anyone noticing, the Chief was prepared to make short work of him. If he ran into any infected dead, he would probably run over them before he could stop.

He made it to the plane and didn't see any signs that someone was inside the houseboat, so he slipped quickly into the cockpit of the plane. Before he started working on the wires, he crawled into the back of the plane and watched the houseboat from the rear window. That was when he saw the faint glow of a cigarette and a shadow pass over a window heading in the direction of the front of the houseboat. It was positioned facing out to sea, and a dark figure walked out onto the sundeck on the bow with a flashlight. He blinked the light a few times in the direction of the corvette, and a few moments later there was a return signal. The Chief counted three flashes from each light.

The Chief checked his watch to see what time it was. If he was right, the Russian would be checking in with his crew on the ship every fifteen or thirty minutes. If he was really lucky, it would be an hour. He decided he would fix the plane first and then deal with the Russian, but he would have to keep an eye out for the next signal so he would know the intervals. He hoped it was at least thirty minutes so they would have time to get the plane most of the way around the island after he disposed of the guard, but thirty minutes would be cutting it really close. He also hoped Tom and Kathy didn't show up before the next signal was given. If it was an hour between signals, there was at least a chance of that happening.

At fifteen minutes the Chief was in position to see the fore deck of the houseboat again, and no one came outside to give the signal. He quickly crawled back under the controls of the de Havilland DHC-3 Otter and connected the remaining wires. He didn't need to test them because he knew he had it right. Now he just needed to be in position to take out the Russian as soon as he made the next signal.

With time to spare, the Chief stayed low and slipped from inside the plane down the full length of the dock to the door of the houseboat. He was counting on it being locked, but he had gotten the key from Ed before they started their escape. He eased the key into the lock and turned it just far enough to unlock it without opening the door. If the guard found it was unlocked he would probably think he had just left it like that since it was still shut. At least that's what he hoped.

At forty-five minutes there was no signal, and the Chief started getting a little nervous. He kept glancing into the darkness of the waterway behind the island hoping he would see Tom and Kathy before the guard saw them. He knew they would stay quiet, but he wanted to be sure. If they saw him down against the side of the houseboat by the door, they were smart enough not to keep coming, but he didn't know what the guy inside was doing. If he was watching out the back window he still might not be able to see them in the darkness, but if he did see them, it would be a race to get rid of the guard and out to the open water in the plane before the next signal was due.

Just before an hour had passed the Chief felt movement inside the house boat. He had his back firmly against the outside wall, and he felt it shift downward as the guard passed by behind him. There was a very slight sound from the metal joints, but it was barely audible above the sound of the water lapping against the side of the houseboat and the big twin outboard that was tied up behind the plane.

The Chief moved closer to the door just in case it opened, but the guard kept going toward the bow. He listened carefully for the sound of him reaching the sun deck, then he moved just far enough out from his hiding spot to be able to see the corvette. After several long seconds he saw the corvette flash its light, and he knew the guard would be going back aft again.

He timed it perfectly. As the guard walked by the door, he yanked it open and grabbed the surprised Russian before he could even guess what was happening. Chief Joshua Barnes was a kind and gentle man, but he was also powerful. His massive fist hit the man in his left eye, and he slumped to the floor. He dragged him further inside and used a roll of electrician's tape to tie him up. He didn't see the need to kill him because they would be long gone before he came to. As insurance he found the flashlight and took it and the man's rifle with him as he left the houseboat.

He was back at the plane ready to cast off the moorings when he heard movement out on the water. Tom and Kathy slowly materialized from the darkness, and he gave them just a short flash from the light. The Chief took a long coil of rope and went out onto the open dock in front of the plane. With a slight turn at the waist he heaved the rope through the air and across the Boston Whaler. Kathy grabbed the rope and tied it across two stern cleats. The Chief tied the other end to a towing hook just under the propeller housing and waved for them to reverse direction.

Kathy and Tom put their backs into the hard work of moving the boat back in the other direction, and as soon as the boat began to turn, the Chief gave the plane a hard shove and got it moving away from the dock. He flashed the light at them, and saw both of them look back.

In a low voice he said, "I'm drifting faster than you. Let me catch up."

The plane glided easily across the surface of the water and caught the current. When he was closer he said, "Trade places with me, Kathy."

Kathy was more than happy to let the Chief take over for her. She jumped across to a pontoon and grabbed a wing strut. The Chief said as he went by, "We have less than an hour to be out of here, and there's no time to explain why."

Kathy gave him a nod as he jumped over to the boat. Her job was just to use a pole to steer the plane and to give them just a little push now and then. The current had picked up a bit, and so had their speed. Going out was definitely easier than going in to the plane.

Over in the boat, the Chief told Tom that there had been a guard in the houseboat, and he had signaled the Russian corvette once per hour. Their timing had been good because the Chief had tied up the guard only minutes before they had arrived with the boat, but that meant they were going to have to travel two miles using nothing but the poles and the current.

They would probably get to the mouth of the southern exit to the moat around the same time that the Russian crew was expecting to see another signal from the houseboat. When that signal didn't come, there would be a few minutes of delay while the Russians decided how to deal with it, and then it would be a race to get the gear into the plane and get the plane into the air.

The Chief felt the current picking up even more than he thought it would, and he realized with a sense of irony that the current was swifter because the jetty had been fixed, and the sandbar wasn't slowing down the water that was coming into the northern entrance. The plane was gliding over the water so well that it wasn't putting any drag on the boat, and it even felt like the plane was going to pass the boat a couple of times.

Forty-five minutes later, they rounded the bend and could see the southern jetty. They had fifteen minutes to spare.

6 THE MISSION

It was a long couple of hours since the Chief had gone one way, and the Boston Whaler had gone the other. I had no way of knowing that the Chief was forced to wait for the guard to give his signal. I also didn't know how well Kathy and Tom had done getting the boat from one end of the island to the other using poles. My biggest worry was that they would cross over the nets and get tangled up in the infected that were stuck in them. After almost two hours, I couldn't stand to wait in the tunnel any longer, so I quietly pulled myself out of the upper hatch.

The pair of legs that I saw in the darkness couldn't belong to anyone I knew. The pants were torn and dirty, and the last I had seen of our group, they were all wearing new Navy blue coveralls. It had to be an infected dead, and he was standing just outside the camouflaged tarp that covered our secret garage. I figured I would use my machete to take out his legs at the ankles, and I was just about to swing when a second pair of legs came into view. These were in tattered shorts, and the legs were mostly decayed.

I watched as the legs turned left and right, and when both turned to face away from me at the same time, I stepped out from under the tarp and swung my machete twice. One went down with the first swing, and the other went down with the second. I couldn't help thinking how much I had changed.

When we had been forced to make a mad dash across the beach through a group of the infected, I just aimed and swung. Now I watched for my opening and took it.

I dragged their bodies over to the water and left them where the surf was just reaching them. If the tide came in higher it would carry them out to sea. If not, the crabs that were brave enough to come out in cold weather would be on them in no time.

Just as I finished disposing of the infected, I heard something on the water at the exit to the moat. The Boston Whaler came into view, and the de Havilland DHC-3 Otter was practically on top of it. I saw that the Chief had traded places with Kathy, and he was really digging hard with the pole.

As soon as the boat was beached, he and Tom jumped onto the sand and ran toward the plane. They each grabbed the plane by the wing struts and rotated it onto the sand. I ran back toward the tunnel to get Jean and Molly, and the others didn't waste any time. Before we could get back they had the gear loaded in the plane.

The Chief, Kathy, and Tom were standing in a tight circle, and Tom scooped Molly up in his arms. Kathy and the Chief blocked Jean and I from getting into the boat, and the Chief said he needed to do one last thing.

"What's going on?" I asked.

"Jean, you're staying here," said the Chief.

The protest was almost too loud. Jean said, "I'm pregnant, Chief. I'm not disabled."

The Chief cut her short. "You can stop arguing before you get started, Jean. Think about it a second. The last time we didn't know what we were coming back to. This time we're only going to be gone a day or two, and we'll know what we're coming back to if we leave someone behind on the radio. You're the logical choice."

The Chief didn't need to say it twice. He told us we needed to get clear of the island and have the plane in the air within ten minutes, so we didn't have time to discuss it. Jean needed to get back down through the tunnel, and we needed to see it sealed behind her. Jean wanted desperately to go with us, but she was too smart to deny the logic. If we needed to be warned to stay away, there had to be someone left behind in the shelter. She looked longingly at Molly and defied the Chief just a little by running over and hugging her while she was still in Tom's arms.

"You be a good girl for your dad, Molly. I already know you're very brave, and I'm so happy you will be able to go home to your mommy," she whispered. "I'll miss you, but I promise we'll see each other again."

Molly was crying just a little, but she was used to being strong for grownups. She hugged Jean back and whispered in Jean's ear that she hoped Jean would have a little girl so she could be a big sister.

Jean gave me a quick kiss. With tears streaming down her cheeks and her hand over her mouth, she ran for the tunnel just as the Chief said that we wouldn't be leaving if we didn't do it in the next few seconds.

As much as I wanted to comfort Jean, we didn't ask why. We just turned the plane around and got into the boat. With three of us digging and pushing with the poles, we were across the moat, around the beached trawler that had crashed ashore on the other side, and heading south along the coast in about four minutes. We didn't stop there because the further we were from the island when we started the engine on the plane the better.

The Chief kept glancing back in the direction of the corvette. It was at least a couple of miles away, and if they were listening, they would hear the engine start, but they wouldn't know where the sound was coming from immediately.

"Okay, everybody," said the Chief. "Get into the plane as fast as you can. Ed, stay with the Whaler long enough to cover it with the tarps and get an anchor down. Try to spot some landmarks so we can find it again."

Everyone scrambled over to the plane while the Chief helped me get the tarps spread out over the tallest part of the Whaler. It was dark, but I was sure I would be able to find the boat again. There were two trees up on the mainland that were larger than the others and were leaning toward each other. Even in the low light, they seemed to stand out.

I got the anchor into the water and hopped over onto one of the pontoons of the plane. As I did, I saw lights flashing on the bow of the corvette. Before I could even get inside, the Chief started the engine and began to move forward.

"Hang on everyone. I'm going to take off but stay low until I can turn inland. When I go for the trees, it's going to be a hard right turn, so be ready," yelled the Chief.

The water was splashing over the pontoons and soaking me as I tried to get into the plane before we were airborne. I didn't have the urge to be outside when the Chief banked to the right, especially since that was the side I was standing on.

Tom reached out and grabbed me by my belt. He yanked me in hard, but I wasn't complaining. The wind was beginning to pick up as the Chief increased the throttle, and I had to fight the door to get it closed and latched. Kathy was riding shotgun up front with the Chief, and Molly was in her lap. It seemed like gear was stashed everywhere because we had to load the plane so quickly. I shifted back packs and supplies around until I found a seat behind Kathy and strapped myself in just as the plane started to lay over on one side.

The Chief put us into a steep bank toward the mainland, and I was looking almost straight down at the water through my side window. Over the roar of the engine I heard Molly faintly asking for her daddy and Kathy telling her everything was going to be okay. We passed over water, marshes, and then trees in a matter of seconds as the Chief put distance between us and the Russian ship. I was missing Jean already, but I knew she would not have appreciated the take off any more than I did.

As we flew between big trees, the plane rotated to a more level position and then began to bank to the left. I could tell the Chief was getting us behind trees and down range as quickly as he could, and if he was flying low it was because we were still close enough to the ship for them to shoot us down if they acquired a clear target. I looked out the window and couldn't believe how low we were. For a moment I wondered if the Chief had forgotten that we didn't have wheels.

The last turn was a gut wrenching turn back to the right and then again to the left before the Chief finally leveled out. We were at least twenty miles inland before he began gradually increasing altitude, and looking over my shoulder at him I could tell he was beginning to relax a bit.

He smiled at me and asked, "Are you still here? I thought we dumped you off back at the start."

"I'm still here, Chief," I said. "By the way, is this your sleeping bag back here? I tossed my cookies in it."

Despite the tension involved with that take off, everyone was fighting back tears while laughing because Molly asked if she could have some cookies, too. Not to be outdone by me, the Chief said to give Molly some cookies.

We were all quiet for a bit after the fit of laughter, just letting it sink in that we were in the air again, and that we had defied my Uncle Titus one more time.

The man who had left his shelter to me in his will also left messages for me. His number one rule had been not to leave the shelter once the world came to an end. Despite the safety of the shelter which would at least add a few years to our lives, we had acted as if we were staging a prison break and had escaped into the night.

Of course there was the Russian corvette sitting off the coast. If their reason for fixing the jetty was to make the waterway behind the island stay deeper, they must be planning to try to hide their ship. There was no reason to expect them to wait another day, so we had to leave while we could. Once the corvette would be behind the island, there would be no way for us to fly the plane out of the area without being seen. They could shoot down a seaplane before it even lifted off of the water.

There was also likely to be some drama when the corvette dropped its anchor. One way or the other, it was going to get hung up on something, and they would send divers down to see what they had snagged. I wondered what we would find when we got back.

Kathy turned in her seat and got the Chief's attention. "What happened back there, Chief? Why the crazy take off?"

The Chief answered her loud enough for all of us to hear, explaining that the guard would be expected to signal the corvette in one hour, and that the hour was up. We were lucky the Russians had made it a one hour interval or we wouldn't have had enough time to load our gear before flying away.

The plane was gradually climbing higher, and all of us were glued to the windows. It was completely dark as far as we could see, and even though we knew why it was pitch black, it didn't change our hope that we would see living people below. When entire cities are dark the world looks like a lonely place.

Once we reached our cruising altitude, the Chief told Kathy to check in with Jean and then to start trying to get Bus on the radio. They needed to let them know they were coming and to find a way to get his coordinates without the wrong people getting them, too. He turned in his seat and told Tom that he should be thinking about places he and Allison had been to and maybe they could at least give a vague description of where they should land.

Tom asked, "You mean something like a place without naming it and then a distance and direction?"

"Yeah, something like five miles east of that place where we had our picnic the last time," said the Chief.

"Got it," said Tom. He pulled out a map of northern Alabama and started studying it with a flashlight. Guntersville had a large number of lakes and caves, and they had gone on plenty of picnics with Molly and her friends.

Kathy was tuning the radio through the frequencies and finally said, "You're coming through loud and clear, Jean. Is everything okay back there? Over."

She unplugged the headphones and put her on the speaker so everyone could hear. "I'm fine, Kathy. Tell Ed I love him, and tell the Chief I'm going to kick his butt the next time I see him, so he'd better come back in one piece. Over."

Kathy said, "They can hear you, Jean. I put you on the speaker. Over."

"She could do it, Chief," I said. "Don't underestimate her."

He could have laughed, but the Chief knew how to play the game. "I'll be sure to get us all back in one piece, Jean. I haven't had my butt kicked in a long time, and I could probably use it. Over."

"Hi, Aunt Jean," said Molly.

"Awwwww, hi Sweetie. I miss you already," said Jean.

Jean also knew when to get serious, and she said, "Your Russian friends are mad, Chief. I saw the deck guns turning back and forth. Were you zigzagging or something? Over."

"You could say that," said the Chief. "That bow gun isn't very powerful, but it's accurate almost to the horizon. I figured they wouldn't be able to track us too well on the other side of the trees, but I wasn't going to fly in a straight line for them and find out if they could hit us. What are they doing now? Over."

"They sent two Zodiacs full of people over to the houseboat. Did something happen over there that I should know about? The lights are all out, so I can't see anything through the camera inside. Over."

Jean was going to be completely safe inside the shelter, but she was sounding more worried than usual. I guess that's because this was the first time Mud Island was crawling with angry Russians who were probably looking for the Chief.

"I had to punch a ticket for someone they had hiding in the houseboat," said the Chief. "I didn't kill him, so they can't be too mad. They just wonder where I went and probably figure the radar contact they had was me. They also don't want me telling anyone else where they are. Over."

Jean said, "I've switched all of the cameras to night vision. I forgot they could do that. I can see armed men in the field of every camera except the one at the front door. Over."

I leaned toward the microphone and yelled over the engine, "Don't worry, Jean. Even if they find the front door, they won't be able to get in. Over."

The Chief added, "That deck gun of theirs would probably sound bad to you inside, Jean, but I've seen the specs on that door Uncle Titus had installed on the shelter. He wasn't kidding when he said it could probably take a direct hit in a nuclear war. Everything else might be gone, but that door will still be there. Over."

"That's reassuring," said Jean. "But I'd rather not find out. Over."

"Jean," said Kathy, "we don't know if they're listening or not, but it doesn't really matter. They can't get to you. Just stay inside, and stay quiet. We'll be back in no time. Just listen for our broadcast. We have to sign off for now and start trying to contact Bus. Over."

Jean said, "I hear you, Kathy, and bring back the father of my child for me, okay? Over."

"Will do, Jean. He's in good hands. Over and out," said Kathy.

Kathy switched off the radio and looked over her shoulder at me, and it was everything I could do not to get choked up. I could see in her look that Kathy knew what we all did. This was a dangerous thing we were doing for Tom and Molly. It was a unanimous decision to do it, but it wasn't the brightest or safest thing to do.

The hardest part wasn't getting away from the island, and the hardest part wasn't the trip anymore. The hardest part might just be getting back into the shelter now that the Russians were searching the island. If they searched long enough, they would find the door. They might not be able to get inside, but it wasn't going to be easy for us to get back in with them camped outside.

Tom said, "I've got it, Chief. There's a place where Allison and I were when we got the call from Dr. Bus about Allison being pregnant with Molly. It was during the off season, and I was back home. Our team didn't make it to the post season that year, so I was back home early. It was a cool day, so we were enjoying the fresh air down by one of the campsites. It wasn't far from Bus's property, as I recall."

"Okay, Kathy," said the Chief. "You know what to do. If my estimate is right, we should be in that area by two in the morning."

Tom said, "Not that it really matters, Chief, but they're Central Time Zone, so it will be one o'clock in the morning."

"Even better," said the Chief. "If anyone else is around, I want them to be sleeping for as long as possible while we're there. Maybe we can drop you and Molly off, top off our fuel somewhere, and be gone before people even know we were there."

"Hey, Chief," said Kathy, "you ever consider the possibility that Bus has fuel?"

Tom answered for him, "Bus was always talking about being ready for anything. I wouldn't be surprised."

"Did he have a plane or a helicopter that you know of?" asked the Chief. "If not, I wouldn't expect him to have the right fuel. The Otter 3 has a turbine engine that takes a specialized blend of aviation fuel. It's basically a really pure type of kerosene with additives."

"Why wouldn't he have just kept some on site?" asked Tom.

"The stuff is really bad for the environment, Tom. I doubt he could have gotten the permits needed to store it in a cave," said the Chief. "We're more likely to find aviation fuel in a truck parked by one of the convenience stores. There are probably a lot of seaplanes used on those big lakes, and the trucks would have to drive down to fill them up."

I said, "Do you really think Uncle Titus got a permit to have a fuel pump on his island, Chief? I didn't see any fuel trucks parked out by the dock."

The Chief thought it over for a moment and looked at me. "Ed, you never cease to amaze me."

"I lull everybody into thinking I'm not too bright, Chief. That way they never expect much out of me, and they're surprised when I think of something they didn't."

The Chief put on a really awestruck expression and said, "You mean that's all been an act?"

I was trying to come up with something witty to lay on the Chief when Kathy said, "Hold up on the manhood contest for just a moment, boys. Check out the view outside my window at about three o'clock."

We all looked in that direction and saw light, and not just a little of it. It looked like spotlights, most of which were facing outward around a series of barricades. I guessed the area in the center of the lights was a couple of miles across in all directions.

"That looks like Fort Jackson," said Kathy. "That's the Army Basic Training Center in Columbia. I wonder how they circled their wagons so well. Is that a wall around the entire perimeter?"

"Looks like it," I said. I had dug through the supplies and had a big set of binoculars pressed against the window. "Can you make out people, Kathy?"

"There's a lot of activity along the walls," she said. Then she just added in a low voice, "Oh, my god."

The Chief was trying to get a look past Kathy, and Molly was climbing into the back to be with Tom. Kathy and I had the best view, and what we saw was incredible. Outside the wall was a series of barricades. Concertina wire, concrete vehicle barriers, spiked personnel traps, and tank traps were spread all around the wall. It looked like each barrier had been overwhelmed one at a time by the sheer numbers of the infected dead.

Once the razors on the wire barricades had become completely full with trapped bodies, the infected started crawling over them. The vehicle barricades had slowed the infected better because they weren't climbers, but as more and more pushed from behind, the infected began to be literally pushed over the barriers by those behind them. Some were severally mangled by being crushed against concrete, and they didn't get up and walk toward the walls, but they still crawled. The area in between the vehicle barriers and the final line of defense was a mixture of crawling and walking infected, and the number was growing.

There was a bright flash of light along the western wall, and Tom asked, "What was that?"

"They're using flame throwers from the top of the wall," said the Chief. He had his own binoculars aimed at the drama taking place below, and he steered the plane to stay parallel to the base. We didn't need to pass too close and pick up a stray bullet. Besides, there wasn't anything we could do to help."

Kathy said, "Chief, I can't really tell from this high up, but I think those walls are nothing more than concrete lane dividers like the ones you see on highway construction sites. They're just stacked on top of each other, and the soldiers are using bayonets between the gaps."

"Where did they find that many lane dividers?" I asked. I knew it was a dumb question as soon as I asked. "Wait, don't tell me. Every interstate is under construction somewhere."

"They probably ran low on ammunition a long time ago and are having to do whatever they can. The flame throwers are probably the most effective things they have," I said.

As we got closer, we could see that there was a long line of helicopters warming up in the center of the base. Troops were climbing aboard in large numbers, and one by one they were lifting off from the tarmac and banking away to the East. There were clearly not enough helicopters for everyone.

"Kathy," said the Chief, "we have way more fuel than we need, and we have to give those guys a fighting chance. There's a knob up under your console. Turn it to the SPRAY setting. Then pump that red lever next to it until you feel it resist."

Kathy did as the Chief said and began banking the plane toward the base. He turned toward us and said, "I'm going to make one pass as fast as I can, and we're going to spray those suckers outside the walls with a little high octane hairspray. When the guys inside hit them with their flame throwers again, it should give them a chance."

We already knew that the infected were drawn to flame, but if everything outside those walls burned long enough, it was going to go a long way toward burning up all of the infected in the area.

"The helicopters could have done this themselves, couldn't they?" I asked.

The Chief said, "They were probably wanting to save their fuel to get as many people out as they could. For all we know, they may have a regrouping site somewhere, and they're coming back for more soldiers. We can buy them some time if that's what they're doing."

The Chief lined up the plane with the western wall of the Army base and dropped at high speed toward the dense crowd of the infected that was just beyond the reach of the soldiers. The idea was to wet down the ones coming up from behind those who had already breached the barriers. When they caught fire, it would spread toward the walls and away from them.

When we reached the thickest part of the horde below us, the Chief hit a switch and a fine spray of fuel went out behind us like a crop duster. We reached the first turn in seconds, and he threw the plane into a steep bank to the right. I practically rolled up the wall of the plane, and my face was against a window looking straight down at the huge horde of infected. There had to be well over a hundred thousand.

As we completed our turn and sprayed the infected approaching the northern wall, I caught a glimpse back toward the western wall. Someone had used a flame thrower and the effect was spectacular. The fire spread in all directions and engulfed the infected that hadn't even reached the concertina wire yet. I yelled at the Chief that it was working, and we all let out a wild cheer.

We could only imagine what the soldiers on the walls were thinking. Many of them were probably just praying that the troop carrier helicopters were going to make it back in time, while others were sure they were going to die. Suddenly, there was a seaplane with yellow stripes coming out of the darkness and passing the front wall, lit up by the flood light and fires, and it was spraying the monstrosities approaching the wall. When a soldier shot out a burst of flame toward the advancing horde, it was like someone threw lighter fluid on the barbecue grill, and the soldiers knew instantly what the seaplane had sprayed. They didn't know who we were or where we had come from, but more than a few were waving their thanks at us with flags and anything else they could find.

It was probably going to be warm inside the walls of the base, but warm was better than dead. We made our second turn at the eastern wall and then back along the southern wall again. We could see the soldiers along every wall turned toward us with their hands pointing to the right sides of their heads in a perfect salute. The Chief wagged the wings to return their salute as we finished our pass and began climbing again. He flipped the switch back to the off position and turned in his seat to look at us. We were all smiling.

He said, "Damn that was fun. I wish we had enough fuel for a second pass."

I'm not sure how long we cheered, but it was a good feeling to strike back for once. We were still overflowing with emotion when a brief burst came over the radio.

"This is the 17th Military Police Detachment at Fort Jackson, sending out a big thank you to the people in the seaplane. Over."

Kathy had it set on the speaker instead of the headphones, so we all got to hear it. She keyed the microphone and said, "For the history books, Fort Jackson, credit goes to retired Navy Chief Joshua Barnes for the idea, over."

"I read you, Miss. Please give our regards to the Chief. I hope we get to return the favor someday. I'm Captain Miller, and I have a long memory for heroics like I just saw tonight. We have incoming transport, so we'll be out of here soon, but we wouldn't have made it without you. I'm going to spread the word about you, Chief. Every living soul on the East coast is going to know who you are. Over."

The Chief was blushing because he never wanted or needed credit for anything. He did what he did because it was the way he was wired.

Kathy keyed up again and wished the Captain luck getting back to his people. She wanted to ask where they would be, but as grateful as he was, she would have been putting him on the spot by asking, and she didn't want to make him feel bad if he had to say it was a secret.

She had just signed off when the Captain's voice said quickly, "Twenty clicks southwest Norfolk Canyon. Over and out."

We all looked at each other without understanding. Everyone but the Chief, that is. He smiled at us and said, "The Captain may get an earful from a Major when he checks in next time, but I'm betting that's all he gets. He just gave a location within landing distance of a fully fueled helicopter out on the continental shelf. If anyone heard that message, they probably are thinking there aren't any canyons in Norfolk, but there are if you go out to sea. They probably have carriers off the coast receiving military, and you can bet they're screening them better by now."

"We only lost about thirty minutes of time and a little fuel to save maybe about two hundred soldiers," I said. "Not a bad day's work, Chief. What's next?"

No jokes this time. The Chief looked more at peace with life than I had ever seen him. When he had escaped from the Atlantic Spirit cruise ship, he had only been able to save himself and two other people, Kathy and Jean. Our gratitude wasn't enough to make up for the fact that he had never left five thousand people to die before, and this was his chance to earn some of those lives back.

We settled in as the hum of the big turbine engine caused Molly to drift off to sleep. Kathy put on her headphones and started listening for radio traffic. From time to time she would key the microphone and just ask, "Bus, do you have your ears on? Over." Then she would turn the dial to a different frequency and listen.

Once she listened intently for a moment and then took off her headphones. "Remember that preacher we heard near Goose Creek? There are still people out there like him."

Tom hadn't been with us, but we had filled him in about the radicals who managed to survive. He had told us that Darwinism always had a way of working things out. The nuts might survive for now, but they would find themselves on the trail to extinction sooner or later.

I asked the Chief where we were. I didn't know how he was navigating without being able to see landmarks and without air traffic control towers.

"We're almost to Atlanta," he said. "I wouldn't be too surprised to see a few lights coming from the tops of tall buildings. There would have to be some survivors in a big city like that."

We all started watching the ground below. It wasn't like we could do anything to help if we saw someone, but we felt more connected by knowing there was someone else out there. The tall buildings started to stand out in the darkness, and the Chief was right again. There were fires on top of buildings, probably oil drums that had been hauled up by survivors.

A few would improvise with the wrong thing, and then they would have a new problem on their hands. That would explain the smoke we could see even through the darkness. We had seen the same thing on our first trip away from the shelter. Homeowners didn't think before lighting their barbecue grills inside their garages. If the carbon monoxide didn't kill them, the fire would.

Tom said, "I've spent a lot of time in Atlanta. Some of those buildings would have tons of food in them if you could get to it. The OMNI Hotel has a convention center and a bunch of restaurants. If anyone survived in there, they might live through this, but if it was anything like the hotels in Myrtle Beach, it was a death trap."

I said, "Can you imagine how many buildings had survivors in them who are just trying to get to the supplies, but they're just out of reach?"

"Yeah, that's irony for you," said Kathy. "You live through a zombie apocalypse, and your apartment is across the street from a grocery store."

"Or a Walmart," I added. "You could have all the supplies you need right there in your apartment, but you would still have this crazy urge to go to Walmart."

We saw dozens of small fires on rooftops. Some were buildings close together, and when the lights were just right we could see ropes and even dangerous looking walkways made out of anything that would work. We couldn't see the streets below them, but we could guess what was happening down there.

On the edge of the city we saw headlights from a speeding car. By the way it was turning, we guessed that the driver knew what to expect on each road. The survivors wouldn't just get in a car and drive around the city. It had to be someone who knew where they were going. The car passed behind some buildings and disappeared.

There were no surprises as we skirted around the edge of the city. Even at our altitude we didn't want to tempt fate by giving someone an easy shot. If anything, we were probably the surprise for people on the ground, and we couldn't imagine how it made people feel when they saw the luxury and freedom of an airplane as it passed them by.

With the city receding behind us, the Chief adjusted our course slightly to the northwest. Guntersville was less than an hour away, and Kathy hadn't been able to get Bus on the radio. Our Plan B in the event that we hadn't made contact by the time we were over water was to use the satellite pictures Tom had been studying to find a possible fuel truck. The relative peace and quiet was disrupted when he almost shouted that he had found one.

"How can you sound so sure?" I asked.

He put the picture in my lap and shone a flashlight on it. I stared at it for a moment. First, I wasn't sure of what I was looking at, but then I was laughing because of the absurd good luck we seemed to have.

Tom showed Kathy the picture, and it was her turn to laugh. "I think that's the result of paying it forward," she said.

"What's that mean?" asked Tom.

Kathy said, "That means when you do something good for someone just because you want to, something good happens to you. We helped back at Fort Jackson, and this is our reward."

The Chief was listening but had no idea what Tom had spotted below. "What did you find, Tom? Is there a sign on top of a building that says aviation fuel?"

Tom held the picture over in front of the Chief. I expected the Chief to roar laughing, but instead he just got a quizzical look on his face. He turned and looked at me and asked, "Ed, did your Uncle Titus know any other bunker builders?"

"Not that I know of, Chief. Then again, I didn't know he was building one. Why are you asking?" I said.

Kathy made the connection before I did, but I was right behind her. I took the picture back from the Chief and borrowed Tom's flashlight. When I looked up, Kathy asked, "What are the odds that there would be a clear satellite picture that has a building that has Aviation Fuel written on top of it and a row of seaplanes parked along a dock?"

"I'm going to make a leap of faith here," said the Chief. "These survivalists all shared their information with each other and no one else. I'm going to bet that your Uncle Titus and Bus were both members of the same fraternity, and one last thing. Bus probably has a seaplane, too."

We knew why Bus hadn't told us over the radio that he had a seaplane. It was for the same reason that we didn't tell him about ours. If people were listening, we wouldn't want them looking around every drop of water for the planes, and we didn't want them hanging out by the fuel pumps. What we couldn't figure out was how the different shelters planned to stay in touch and realized it had to be some sort of code. Either Uncle Titus had taken the code with him to his grave, or it was in the shelter on Mud Island all along.

We were all so dumbfounded by this epiphany that we were surprised by Kathy holding up one hand to get our attention.

"Say again, over," she said as she keyed the microphone. "I hear you, Bus. Over."

Kathy pulled her headphones aside and said it sounded like they were having some kind of problem at Bus's shelter. She put them back on and keyed the microphone.

"Bus, we're looking for a good place to eat. Any suggestions? Over." Kathy was trying to let Bus know they were in the area without coming right out and saying it.

Tom leaned into the front and said, "Kathy, tell him we'll settle for a good place for a picnic near where Allison found out she was going to be a mother. We told him where we were when he called us."

Kathy repeated what Tom had suggested and listened. She whispered that the sound was a bit messy, so she wasn't going to put it on the speakers.

She said, "I hear you Bus. Stand by. Over."

She took off the headphones and told the Chief that Bus had said there used to be a good place to eat about two miles south of that campsite that was called the Catfish Grotto. It used to be a great place to eat, but now the customers don't eat catfish.

"What do you think he's trying to tell us?" I asked.

Tom said, "I think he's saying his shelter is usually a safe place, but there are more of the infected around than usual."

"Well, I think we need to take a look anyway," said the Chief. "Can you locate that campsite at night?"

"It's perfect," said Tom. "Look at the picture of the building labeled Aviation Fuel. That building is a resort area now. That's why there are so many sea planes. Straight south is the entrance to a huge cave that can only be accessed by water. That would be where Bus would have built his shelter because he owns all of that land."

"Can we get a big landmark, Tom? I need to find that building in the dark, and that land isn't flat down there. One rule of thumb for caves is to look for them in mountains.

These aren't really high mountains, but there's a lot of shadow down there."

Tom concentrated hard on the pictures, looking back and forth between them and his window. He finally spotted what he was looking for.

"Okay, Chief. We're really close. Bring us in lower and look for the most populated area straight ahead. Just after you pass over it you'll see a big bridge. That's Highway 431 North. About two miles up 431 we're going to make a sharp turn to the east. If we're lucky, it will take us straight at another bridge. You should come at it from the side. When you cross over the bridge, hug the shoreline on the right and get ready to land as it narrows. We're going to coast straight at a dead end, and that's the entrance to the cave. Believe me, you can't miss it."

"Where's that fueling station from the landing spot?" asked the Chief.

"That's easy," said Tom. "Go back toward the last bridge and cross it at an angle going straight north. Only about a mile across some land and water is the resort. It's just as easy to spot as the cave."

Despite the darkness below, the Chief could make out enough detail to tell when he reached the town of Guntersville. There weren't any really tall buildings with survivors camping on top, but here and there he spotted lights. He knew he had to be careful. This was definitely deer hunting country, and people were probably tired of shooting the infected dead. They were slow, easy targets, but above all, there were too many of them. Angry, desperate people with guns and no supplies would be very jealous of someone in a seaplane. The Chief didn't agree with their jealousy, but he understood their frustration.

As the plane got lower and closer to the buildings, the surrounding mountains seemed to close in. They weren't tall mountains, but they were bigger than hills. They were heavily forested even for this time of year because they were covered with ancient pine trees. The area was a fisherman's paradise, and for those who liked to live dangerously, there were massive caverns.

The shadows from the mountains made it difficult to spot the bridge that Tom had told him to look for, but the Chief spotted it and made a minor course correction to line up with it. Once he had the bridge in his sights, he increased power to get out of rifle range if someone had been taking aim at him.

The sudden burst of power would have been enough to make anyone miss, but the Chief didn't think anyone had taken a shot at them the way someone had in Goose Creek. When they were clipped by a bullet that time, they were forced to leave the plane behind and make their way back home in cars. If it happened this time, it wasn't likely that they would be able to drive home past Atlanta.

The bridge flashed by, and the Chief followed Highway 431 as it veered more to the northeast. Tom started hanging over the Chief's shoulder to watch for any familiar landmark, and the Chief was grateful for his help. This was seat of the pants flying at its best. At his present speed two miles would go by fast, so the Chief anticipated the tap on the shoulder when it happened. He banked hard to the right across the water and increased his speed even more. There was no reason to take his time now, and he knew he could either slow down quickly or come around for another pass if he had to.

Kathy had been listening to something on the headphones while Tom was leading the Chief through his maneuvers. Molly was watching out the windows because this was home to her, and she wanted to see her mother. I was lost in thought, wondering if Jean was okay, and wondering if she knew how much I missed her. I had just learned I was going to be a dad, and Jean and I were going to get married, but here I was five hundred miles away and getting ready to take risks that could kill me. If Bus was seeing more of the infected than usual, I could only guess what he meant by 'usual'.

Kathy keyed the microphone to the on position and exchanged a few words with Bus. She looked confused when she signed off and didn't say anything at first when she took of her headset.

She said, "Guys, all Bus said was to be careful because it was raining dead. What do you think he meant by that?"

None of us had a clue what he must have meant, but then Kathy answered her own question. "Chief, Ed, isn't that what the guy said to us on the Stono River when the dead started falling over the railing of the bridge? He said something about so many falling over the edge into the river that it was practically raining dead."

The Chief and I exchanged looks and agreed that Bus could mean something similar, but we weren't going under any bridges, so we couldn't figure out how it could be the same thing.

"Tom," I said, "did you say we're going to be able to use the seaplane to get to the entrance of the shelter?"

"Yes, it's a grotto, and the plane will be able to beach on the sand once we go inside. There will be an overhanging cliff that we will pass under to get inside. You can only get to the grotto by water," he said.

I said to the Chief, "After you land, don't go forward to fast, Chief. Just coast until we can see the entrance."

Kathy and the Chief both understood what Bus was trying to tell us just about the time that we crossed directly over the second bridge. It was so dark, and we were going so fast that we almost didn't see it flash by under us. The Chief made another hard right turn and descended at the same time. He expertly pulled the nose of the plane upward and eased the pontoons into the water. He kept the power up enough for us to keep moving forward, but he had plenty of room to stop or to make a turn if there was trouble. We all kept our eyes on the big, gloomy shadow of the mountain directly ahead.

"Chief," said Kathy, "do you think it's safe to use the spotlights?"

There was one located on each wing, and we could have been using them to navigate, but they also advertised our position better than we would have liked.

The Chief said, "This may be the perfect time to use them, Kathy."

He reached over and hit the switch that turned on the two high powered lights on the wings, and we were stunned by the view. What looked like the dark side of a mountain was actually a massive cave entrance, and the lights didn't even penetrate all of the way into its depths.

The Chief slowed our forward speed to a crawl as we took in the view. I wondered what it would look like during the day because it was such an enormous black hole at night.

We were still at least one hundred yards from the entrance, so my guess was that it was at least fifty yards wide and thirty yards high. Above the entrance was the sloping side of a mountain.

Our lights didn't penetrate the black entrance, but they did light up everything outside, including the trees above the entrance...and they were moving, or at least they looked like they were moving. As a matter of fact, the whole side of the mountain looked like it was moving.

We had to enter that grotto to get to the shelter where Molly would be reunited with her Mom, but there was something wrong, and I was beginning to understand what it was.

"Chief, turn around and get us airborne again," I said.

"Why?" he asked. He looked like he was going to say something else, but he started turning the plane away from the entrance to the cavern.

"Did you guys see that?" asked Kathy. She was pointing back toward the opening as we made our turn.

We all looked back in the direction she was pointing just as three dark shapes came from the trees above the grotto and fell into the water. Before they could sink totally out of sight, about six or seven more fell from above.

"That's what Bus meant when he said it was raining dead," said Kathy. "He was trying to tell us to be careful as we entered the grotto."

The Chief added, "Even one of those things falling into the prop could do enough damage to cripple the plane. How are we going to time it so that we don't have any dropping in on us as we go in?"

"I don't think that's our only problem," said Tom. He was watching the water through one of the side windows as we were making our turn. I joined him to see what he was talking about. I couldn't even make out the details around the dark cave, so I didn't know what he meant about other problems.

Tom pointed down toward the water, but it was too dark, so I told the Chief to rotate a spotlight in that direction. He reached up and pressed the switch that rotated the light just like a rearview mirror on a car. As the light crossed the water, I saw what Tom was talking about. The infected dead were so thick in the water that they weren't sinking......they were piling up.

"Chief," I said, we were just about to run aground on bodies. "How close can you get without having any land on top of us?"

"What have you got in mind, Ed?" asked Kathy.

"We need to be able to see further into the grotto," I said. "I'm not sure, but I think there's no current here to wash them away, so they're walking back up onto land. If they are, the closest place would be right on top of Bus's shelter."

The Chief eased the plane closer a little at a time until we were almost to the infected that were piling up so deep that they weren't even sinking. He brought the spotlights back around to shine on the same spot just inside the grotto.

We all stared into the darkness and watched our worst fears coming true. They were walking out of the water onto the soft shore inside the cave, and they kept going until they disappeared into the darkness. Even if we could get past where they were falling in and piling up, we weren't going to be able to deal with the huge number of the infected dead that were already inside. We had no way of knowing how long they had been increasing their numbers, but something was making them go inside instead of trying to walk ashore in other directions.

"Kathy," said Tom, "see if you can get Bus on the radio and find out what's happening in there."

Kathy keyed up and asked Bus if he was reading her. On the third try she switched to the speaker so we could all talk with him. She told him we were here but needed instructions. Bus came over the speaker and said he could see us, and he felt like we could assess the situation better because we could see the mountain.

"Bus, this is Ed. It's too dark out here for us to see anything. How can we assess the situation? Over."

Bus answered, "You're going to have to wait until daylight and then check the top of the mountain. I think you will have most of your answer then. Find a place to spend the night and assess the problem in the morning. We can't tell how bad it is from here. Over."

"Bus, are you and Allison okay? Can those things get into your shelter? Over," asked Tom.

"We're fine, Tom," he answered. "Allison is fine. Those things can't get in here no matter how many there are, but there's no way out past them, and I don't think you can get in here for the same reason. Over."

"We read you," said the Chief. "We're going to find a safe place to spend the night. We'll be back at dawn to see what's happening. Over and out."

The Chief turned the plane away from the entrance to the grotto and increased speed, but he didn't take off. He turned to us all and said he felt like the safest place to be was in the middle of the lake. It was deep enough and far enough from shore, and they didn't have long until dawn, so someone could stand watch.

7 JEAN

Jean kept telling herself that she was okay alone. She was independent even though she was in love with Eddie. At least that was what she told herself more than once in the first few hours after the others had left. She also understood why they couldn't check in with her by radio again. The Russians could be listening and might figure out that there was someone still hiding on the island.

Jean had the night vision cameras turned on, and so far so good. They hadn't come close to the entrance of the shelter. She looked at the camera view that showed the dock and noticed there were more armed men at that location than anywhere else. They also seemed to be more relaxed. They were sitting around smoking cigarettes and talking. There was even occasional laughing which told Jean they were less convinced they were in danger. She could see that they were boldly using lights out on the dock and in the houseboat.

She switched to the houseboat camera view and was surprised to see three men gathered around the small table that served as an eating area and a recreation spot. They had a map spread across the table and were pointing first at the map and then at the outside of the houseboat. She guessed by the gestures that they were pointing in the general direction of the moat that surrounded most of Mud

Island. The rest of the island was bordered by the Atlantic Ocean. There appeared to be some disagreement, and she didn't speak Russian, so she could only make more guesses about what had them so worked up.

They finally called for one of the men to come in from outside, and they pointed at the map and asked him several questions. He gave them the universal answer to what appeared to be the central question, a shrug of the shoulders, and they looked even more frustrated. He apparently said the same thing they were saying. "I don't know."

One of the men put his finger on the map at the northern entrance of the moat and traced it all of the way around the moat to the southern exit. Then he pointed at the jetties themselves and put his finger on the spot they had fixed. Jean was pretty sure they were debating the very existence of the moat, and they were coming to the conclusion that it was made by someone rather than carved out by nature. The men got up from the table and apparently had reached some form of consensus. One of then stuck his head out the door and barked an order at a man with a radio. He immediately snatched up the microphone and started speaking rapidly.

In the distance behind the man on the radio Jean saw white light. She knew it was not the moon, and she couldn't imagine what could generate that much light. Then she saw the corvette in the monitor that faced the open sea, and it was beginning to move. Spotlights located along the central part of the ship were aimed at the southern jetty, and the corvette was increasing speed quickly. In only a few minutes it reached the end of the jetty and made a sharp right turn headed straight for the opening of the southern end of the moat.

The Chief had been right. The Russians were going to hide from the US Navy by parking in the moat behind Mud Island. Even though the Chief hadn't told her what to do if he was right, Jean had been thinking about it. She was sure the Navy would investigate if an anonymous radio report said,

"Hey, Navy! There's a Russian corvette parked at these coordinates." She had the coordinates marked on a map, and all she had to do was make the call.

The problem was that she didn't necessarily want the Navy to bomb the moat. There wasn't much doubt that the sinking corvette would collapse the power conduits that crossed between Mud Island and the mainland. She supposed there was at least some possibility that the current state of affairs facing the entire world would make the Americans and Russians consider a nonaggression pact, but she couldn't take that chance.

The bright lights and activity on the dock had the expected outcome over on the mainland. Jean looked at the camera view that showed the spot where the houseboat used to be parked, and there were about six or even infected dead trying to cross the northern entrance to the moat by walking along the sand bar. The dead could see the men sitting on the dock and couldn't resist the temptation, but the recent repairs to the northern jetty had already started to have its effect on the current. One by one the infected were washed off of the sand bar and dragged under by the current.

The Russians on the dock were totally aware of the infected, but they couldn't have been less concerned. They just watched as the dead lost their battle with the current. When one made it just a little further than the others, one of the Russians reached for his rifle, but the others just laughed at him.

Jean switched back to the southern view and saw that the beach on the other side by the fishing trawler that had come aground there a few months ago was surrounded by the infected. The Russian corvette was around the end of the jetty and making good speed toward the opening. The infected were drawn to the lights on the ship like moths to a flame, and they just walked from the shore into the direct path of the warship.

There was so much light coming from the ship that Jean had switched to the normal cameras. Night vision was just a big, white flash. As the corvette reached the entrance to the moat, she saw the bodies of the infected popping up in its wake. There were so many in the water trying to get into the path of the ship that its propeller was probably stirring them up like fruit in a blender. A trail of body parts was washing up on the beach on both sides.

Jean switched to a different camera again in time to see the corvette make its final turn in the moat. She wanted to see if it would draft deep enough for the propeller to get stuck on the nets. Jean couldn't remember if the ship had one propeller or two, but that didn't really matter to her. The best possible outcome would be for them to park then successfully navigate back out of the moat when they were ready to leave.

With the bright lights shining from the corvette, the mainland beach was too dark to see, but Jean didn't doubt the trees were being cleared of the infected. Judging by the numbers on the southern beach, there were probably hundreds still staggering through the brush trying to reach the light and the noise.

Jean stifled a big yawn and saw the time. It was after three in the morning, and she was tired but too wired to shut her eyes. She knew she wouldn't be able to tell what was happening outside until daylight, but she was trying to watch anyway. Out of the corner of her eye she saw that the Russians on the dock were loading their gear into a pair of Zodiacs, probably to rendezvous with their ship after it dropped anchor.

She started to look back at the corvette when she saw that the last Russians on the dock were lagging behind the others and working with some small devices at key points along the dock. She saw one string some wire across the dock and draw it tight to the other side. It had to be a trip wire. She knew that Ed, the Chief, and Kathy weren't likely to approach from the North, but she didn't like the idea of them stumbling into booby traps when they got back. She wondered if they had put similar traps at the southern end of the island. She also didn't want to see their dock getting blown up because some infected dead managed to reach the dock and get hung up in those wires. She knew that Eddie would kill her if he found out she went outside, but she felt like she had to give serious thought to disarming those booby traps.

The corvette had reached the midpoint in its trip and began to slow its forward speed. All of the external lights went dark, and Jean quickly switched to night vision. She saw the big anchor begin to drop, and then it fell rapidly with a great splash. The corvette was at a complete stop as the Zodiacs pulled up along her side, and the armed sailors climbed aboard.

In the stillness that followed the disappearance of the crew into the ship, Jean was able to focus more clearly on the mainland beach. It was more than she had expected. The beach was so crowded with the dead that it could have been Memorial Day weekend at Myrtle Beach or Daytona. The bright lights on the Russian ship had drawn every infected dead for miles, and the moat was going to be full of them

Jean fell asleep on the couch watching the dead walk off of the shore and sink. The last thing she remembered thinking was that it was a good thing they couldn't swim. Then she had some really pleasant dreams about Eddie, being married, and having their baby. Despite the screwed up state of the world, she felt some measure of happiness.

When Jean awoke, she checked out the view through the camera facing the Russian ship and saw that it was daylight outside. She wondered if Eddie was safe, and of course she included the Chief, Kathy, Tom and Molly in that thought. She wished she could reach them on the radio, but besides not knowing if someone was listening on this end, there was always the possibility of causing problems on their end. Contacting them at the wrong moment could give away their position at a time when they needed to be quiet.

Jean made a quick trip to the bathroom, then to the kitchen to grab something to eat, and then resumed her watch to see what the Russians were doing. The corvette had been pulled by the strong current in the moat, and the anchor chain was stretched tight. There was a group of men standing on the bow above the anchor housing, and they appeared to be having exactly the problem the Chief had anticipated. The anchor had a firm hold on something. The men glanced from time to time in the direction of the beach. Even without being able to hear what was happening, Jean knew from first hand experience that the infected dead on the beach must have been making an incredible amount of noise. Stealth was not their strong point.

Someone on the ship made the decision that they should try to bring in the anchor. The motor on the anchor housing strained against the force that was holding the anchor in place hard enough to pull the ship forward until the bow was directly over the anchor, and the decision makers were all crowded into the bow trying to get a look at something below.

Jean looked at her camera controls and found the zoom function. She enlarged the image of the men, and her opinion was that they didn't have a clue about what could be hanging onto their anchor so well that they were pulled forward when they tried to raise it in. They were hanging over the side trying to see into the depths, but Jean also knew from experience that they weren't likely to see it well enough to figure it out. If they were hooked on one of the nets, the sheer weight of the net and that many bodies would most likely be more than the motor could lift. If they were hooked on a power cable, she hoped they couldn't lift hard enough, or the anchor would cut the power lines to Mud Island.

In the event the power did get cut off, Jean had placed flashlights around the shelter. She knew the battery operated emergency lights were supposed to come on if main power was lost, but she didn't want to stumble around in the dark if they didn't work. She knew the shelter well enough to find her way from room to room in total darkness, but it wasn't first on her list of things she wanted to do.

There was something happening out on the aft deck of the Russian ship, so she used the remote control to adjust the angle of the camera to see more in that direction. It was a clear morning and probably a little cold, but the Russians were used to a climate that was much colder, so they looked energetic and quite comfortable.

She thought of what the Chief said about Buyan-class corvettes being more like boats used for coastal defense and wondered again why she was looking at one sitting behind an island on the coast of South Carolina. It occurred to her that she had seen articles in magazines and on the Internet about foreign navies doing goodwill tours. Our navy had even sailed into Russian ports. She imagined that what had once been a visit in the spirit of building good relations could now be construed as an attempt to capitalize on the broken infrastructure of the United States, and the Russians didn't know if the US Navy would ask questions first or shoot first. That could be why they needed to hide.

When Jean had a good enough view, she zoomed in a bit more and saw that the Russians were about to have a really bad day. At least six of them were in wetsuits with full SCUBA gear on their backs. They were climbing down to one of the Zodiacs tied alongside, and they were obviously going to take a first hand look at what was hanging onto the anchor. If they were lucky, they would see the problem, slack up on the tension of the anchor chain, and watch the anchor drop free from the net. If they were unlucky, the anchor would need to be untangled. That would mean getting close up and personal with the infected dead that were also caught in the net.

The Zodiac pulled away from the stern and cruised the distance of the ship until it was directly over the anchor line. Jean saw the divers each give a thumbs up as they sat with their backs to the water. One by one they just leaned over backward and let gravity do its job.

Jean thought maybe if they had gone in head first the way the Chief had done, they would have been able to prevent the inevitable. Because the net was directly below them, they entered the water blind to the outstretched arms of the infected dead that were caught in the net close to the surface. Jean couldn't see them or hear them, but she remembered the video the Chief had made. She could only imagine what the divers saw once they oriented themselves and cleared the bubbles coming from their regulators.

The first diver resurfaced only seconds after the last diver entered the water, and there was nothing controlled about his arms and legs. They were thrashing wildly in an attempt to get something off of him. He tried to pull himself over the edge of the Zodiac, but slipped back under the surface again. Jean got a brief glimpse of a second diver. She had expected to see an infected dead hanging on to the first diver, but it was a second Russian who was so desperate to escape that he had wrapped his arms around his comrade.

On the deck above, the officers who had gathered to watch started shouting toward to crew members who had gathered along the starboard railings. They scattered and immediately began getting a second team into wetsuits. In a matter of minutes they were clambering over the edge of the corvette into the second Zodiac and going to the rescue of their shipmates.

At the bow, one diver had managed to pull himself out of the water and drop into the bottom of the Zodiac. Jean couldn't see him once he was completely in the boat, but she could see the trail of blood on the black rubber of the Zodiac. A second diver emerged, and he wasn't in any better shape. He had several tears in his wetsuit, and rivers of blood were running down his back. His diving mask was gone, and when he turned Jean saw deep scratches in his face that rivaled the rips in the wetsuit.

Jean didn't realize she was crying at first. She felt bad for the Russians and started thinking she should have warned them. She didn't know how they would have received the warnings. They may have completely ignored them, but she felt awful that all she could do was sit and watch them face such an incredible horror. She wiped at her wet cheeks and wished that she had at least given them an anonymous call and said not to go in the water. They would have been better off just cutting their anchor chain loose and driving back out to sea.

The second Zodiac arrived on the scene as three more of the divers surfaced. The crew of the second boat began pulling them on board. Two of the new group jumped over into the first Zodiac to give aid to their injured shipmates, and two others dove in to retrieve the last member of the original crew. They broke the surface only seconds later with his badly mangled body between them. He looked to Jean like he may still be alive but just barely.

With all six of the original group back in the Zodiacs, they rushed to get their boats back to the stern of the corvette. Crew members were already lowering stretchers inside wire rescue cages down to the water where they were quickly lifted aboard. Jean knew what they were trying to do. These were friends who had sailed halfway around the world with each other, and they couldn't just leave them behind. Despite the risks of spreading the infection, they were making the same mistake every hospital in the world had made on the first day of the apocalypse. They were trying to save lives that were already lost, and if they didn't realize it soon enough, they would all be lost.

Over the next three hours, there was very little activity on the Russian ship. The Zodiacs were hauled onto the stern and washed, but then everyone went inside with the exception of a lone man standing watch. He circled the deck with a pair of binoculars and a long rifle with a scope on it. From time to time he would stop and study something either on the mainland or the island through the binoculars or with the rifle scope, but then he would move on. He almost always stopped when he got to the bow of the ship above the anchor. He would just stare down at the water like he expected to get an answer about what had happened down there.

As that three hours passed, Jean was getting restless. It wasn't easy for her to sit still not knowing what was happening to her friends, wondering if they made it to

Alabama, or if they were even alive. Just the thought was enough to snap her into motion.

She said out loud, "If they make it back in one piece, I'll be damned if I will let them get their butts blown up by a stupid booby trap."

Jean wasn't really a stubborn person. She was more of a determined person. When she decided something was the right thing to do, she was hard to convince otherwise. She couldn't imagine a scenario where her friends would be forced to come back to the island from the North, but there was one possibility. If they lost the plane but made it back to the coast, they wouldn't be able to cross from the southern tip of the mainland without a boat. On the northern side, the jetty was repaired, but they could still cross using the sand bar at low tide. If they did, they could all be killed or badly hurt on the dock.

There was also the added advantage that the Russians were busy dealing with their own problems. She didn't know for sure what was happening out on the ship, but she imagined they were doing everything they could to treat the injuries in the hope that their shipmates would recover. The Chief had said the ship's compliment couldn't have been more than fifty-five, and six were likely to die. Everyone was below decks even if they were just hanging around for moral support. All Jean would have to worry about was the guard on the deck, and she was sure the ship was anchored far enough away that they wouldn't even be able to see the dock on the northern tip of the island.

Jean thought about the advice the Chief was always giving them about having a plan. She also thought about what Uncle Titus had said to Eddie about not leaving the shelter once you were safe inside, but she decided to ignore him because everyone else was outside, too. If they could do it, so could she, and it wasn't like she was going to go five hundred miles. She was only going a mile out and a mile back.

There were wet suits in all sizes in their supply lockers, but in the end she had to settle for one that would fit a child.

She felt more like a fearless warrior going off to battle before getting stuck with a child sized set of armor, but then she reasoned that she would be harder to spot. Besides, the wet suit was for protection against bites and the cold, because she didn't plan to go into the water. A wet suit alone wasn't a guarantee against the teeth of the infected dead, as was witnessed by the Russians first hand. She planned to add a few more layers of protection.

As Jean found combat boots, gloves, a jumpsuit, and a foul weather jacket, she thought about what tools she would need. She could go out there and simply disconnect all of the explosives and allow them to drop into the water. That might be a short term solution, as well as a giveaway that there was someone still on the island even though the Russians had searched for hours after the Chief had tied up one of their sentries.

Her best bet, she reasoned, was to deactivate the booby traps but leave them in place. That meant she would also need some wire and some cutters. She could cut the wires they had stretched across the dock and replace it with dummy wires. She had only seen the wires at night, so she would have to get a look at them when she checked the dock to see if it was all clear.

Jean also remembered that the Chief always said to have a Plan B, but she found out that it was harder to think of why she would need a Plan B without her friends around. She finally concluded that the only other thing to plan for other than the infected and the Russians would be the possibility of not being able to get back to the main entrance of the shelter. If she got stuck outside at night, she could freeze to death, so she needed to add a thermal layer to her clothing and an emergency kit with a foil blanket. Of course, she could always try to make it to the emergency tunnel on the southern tip of the island, but she didn't want to try to make it there in the dark. If something was preventing her from getting back inside, she didn't want to reveal the existence of the tunnel by using a flashlight.

Despite the fact that a flashlight would give away her position, it was still a necessity, but she put a red lens cover on it before using a clip to fasten it to her belt. Jean studied herself in the mirror and thought she looked more like someone's kid going outside to play in the snow than a commando, but she hoped she wouldn't run into anyone she needed to impress. For about the tenth time since she decided to do this, she questioned herself, but she kept coming back to that one fear, and that was seeing someone she loved blown to pieces by a bomb. The irony of such a loss was all she could focus on. You survive an apocalypse only to be killed by a bomb. You might as well get run over by a car or die from food poisoning.

The only thing she needed to add was weapons. The Chief had found a couple of silencers in the armory, but they had taken them along on their trip to Alabama. It wasn't like they expected her to need them. She rationalized that she should take a gun, but she wouldn't use it unless there was no other choice. She also figured if she used the gun on the ocean side of the island, she would be able to get back to the entrance to the shelter before the Russians could mobilize. She also slid a machete into a loop on her belt and strapped a knife in a sheath to her leg. Now she looked like a commando.

A quick look at the camera views showed one Russian still walking the decks of the ship but no other activity. Next she adjusted the camera on the dock to locate the trip wires. She zoomed in close and saw that the wires weren't exactly invisible. They looked like typical strands of copper wire. At night they would be deadly, but if you were looking down in the daylight, they were easy to see. The Russians probably just used what they had, and that was fortunate because copper wire was what Jean also had.

The other camera angles showed no activity on Mud Island. There were still plenty of the infected walking around on the mainland beach, but none had crossed the water to her side. A last look at the ship told her the Russian sentry had taken an interest in teasing the infected by yelling at them. They would walk out into the water and disappear with the current.

Jean said out loud, "Time to stop stalling and do this."

Before she could lose her nerve, she made her way to the big steel door and unlocked it. A big burst of cold wind hit her in the face, but the sky was clear. She grabbed her supply bag and stepped out, thinking the whole time that this was a stupid idea. She wondered which was closer to the odds of winning the lottery. Losing one of her friends to an explosive strapped to the dock, or her surviving a field trip in a world that had gone to hell. She grinned as she thought to herself, "Don't blow yourself up on the dock."

A mile doesn't really feel that long when you have something to think about the whole time, and she had plenty on her mind. Watching every moving bush, every overgrown path in front of you, behind you, listening for any sound that didn't belong on an island on a cold but clear day. Jean heard the sound that didn't belong before she spotted movement. Where this infected dead had come from she didn't know. It hadn't seen her yet, so she had the advantage. She chose the machete because she liked the longer reach. She gripped it in her right hand and began moving forward in a crouch.

Jean could smell the dead flesh on the thing standing with its back to her. She guessed she hadn't seen it because it was wearing a tan shirt that looked like it was made from the same material as the bushes. It didn't have any of the usual blue crabs hanging from it, probably because the weather and the water were so cold. She estimated there were only four more long strides before she would be in a position to plant the machete in the back of its head, so she took them quickly.

With her arm in its downswing, a hand grabbed her arm between the elbow and the shoulder, and her prey turned around to face her. She started to yell at the person who owned the hand, and locked eyes with another infected dead that had been standing virtually motionless in the middle of the bushes. It had a strong grip on her arm and had already begun to lower its head for a bite on her upper arm by the shoulder. She felt the pressure from its jaws as the teeth attempted to go through the layers of clothing, but even worse, she was afraid that her own struggles would cause the material to tear.

The infected that she had seen first wasn't moving as fast as Jean when she was closing the distance to kill it, but it wasn't having to fight its way free from the grip of something that was trying to eat it. Jean could see it was already opening its mouth in anticipation of the first bite. Everything seemed to slow down, and Jean remembered a discussion she had with the Chief. He had said everything would slow down when you were sure you were going to die, and if you wanted to live, you had to make yourself move faster because time didn't slow down for whatever was trying to kill you. Jean had asked him if he had ever experienced that feeling, and he had told her too many times.

Jean didn't have the benefit of past experiences to fall back on, but she made herself move. She let her feet go out from under herself so her weight would pull downward from the infected that was holding her. She heard the material of her foul weather jacket tear, but the feeling of the teeth gripping her was gone, and it wasn't replaced by cold air. That gave her hope that the material below the jacket wasn't pierced by the teeth.

As she dropped to the ground, she also reached across her body for the long knife in the leg sheath. The infected had a grip on her arm that was too strong to break loose, but apparently its elbows weren't what they used to be. The tendons made a loud popping sound as they tore free from their connections. The hand didn't let go, but Jean found herself below the two infected dead with a forearm dangling from her arm. It seemed to her that she had seen that happen before, but she was too busy to worry about when. She had already found the hilt of her long knife with her left hand and pulled it free as the infected in the tan shirt fell on her.

Jean didn't let time slow down, and she saw the blade of the knife go upward through the chin of the infected and out through the top of the skull. She didn't stop to admire her handiwork as she swung the machete hard to her right. It seemed to move slower because of the extra weight of the dead arm that flopped around when she moved, but she was only aiming at the knees. The machete made a satisfying crunching sound as it went through the right leg of the monster that had bitten her.

She wondered if the Chief was right about time not slowing down for the infected, because she was about to kill the one that had bitten her. The severed leg lost its last connection with its former owner and the infected fell over on its right side. Jean let the momentum of her swing and the extra weight of the arm hanging from hers continue in a long arc and brought the machete down just behind the left ear of the second infected dead.

Everything was quiet except for the breeze, and time slowed down again as Jean looked at the torn material on her arm. She needed to know for sure, but she was afraid to look. If she looked, and if she saw torn material with blood underneath, she knew what it meant. She remembered when the infected had tried to bite her on the Atlantic Spirit, and all it did was tear her shirt. It was on the same arm and almost on the same spot. She also remembered telling the Chief and Kathy if she was bitten she would throw herself overboard on her own. If she was bitten this time, she would have to take care of it before the others got back.

Jean pulled the knife from the head of the infected in the tan shirt and used it to pry the fingers loose that gripped her right arm. When it fell away, she hesitantly pulled her upper arm around in front of her face to inspect the damage. Tears streamed down her cheeks when she saw that the outer material was wide open. There were impressions of teeth in the rubber of her wetsuit, and she could guess there would be bruising later under the suit, but there were no holes. She knew she didn't have the luxury to sit and feel sorry for herself, but she couldn't help it. She sat and sobbed quietly with her knees drawn tightly to her chest and her head resting against them.

She knew she didn't stay where she was very long, but she still felt like it was far longer than it should have been. When she first made the decision to go outside, it had been enough to put butterflies in her stomach. When she put on her protective clothing, she had butterflies and a dry mouth. Now, the butterflies were gone, the dry mouth was gone, but her entire body felt wasted. She felt weak and mentally lost.

Somehow, she managed to lift her head and look around. Next to her were the two infected she had brought to a final end, and there was a stillness on the island she hadn't really felt before. She felt like she didn't know where she was because this strange island had become her home, and it had almost become her final home. She hadn't realized until this moment what an awful thought that was.

She managed to gather up enough strength and her old determination to push herself to her feet. She checked in all directions to be sure there wouldn't be anymore surprises. One thing in her favor was the knowledge that more infected dead would have shown up already if they were going to, because she had made enough noise thrashing around with the other two.

Jean looked up at the sky and guessed the time. Despite everything that had happened, she hadn't been outside more than thirty minutes, and she still had work to do. She looked around for her bag of supplies and found it under the infected dead in the tan shirt. She snatched up the bag and doubled her pace toward the dock.

When she reached the spot where the dock met with land she noticed that the ground was a bit more worn on the path than it used to be. With all of the foot traffic from the Russians, the path wasn't as well hidden as before. She sat down her bag and laid down on the ground facing out onto the dock. She wanted to be sure she could see all of the wires. As far as she knew, there were only two, but the reason they were called booby traps was because they trapped people who weren't bright enough to look for them.

Once she had the right angle to the wires, Jean could see both of them, and there weren't more of them that she had missed. She moved to the first one and checked to be sure that the wires were connected to one charge each instead of an explosive on both sides. She was happy to see they were only on one side. Next she studied the place where the first wire connected to its charge. She wanted to be sure that some trigger wouldn't be activated if she removed the wire. She saw that it was a simple pin with a ring on it, and everyone knew what a grenade looked like. If you tripped over the wire, it would pull out the pin, and the grenade would explode.

It made her angry that these people from another country were trying to leave traps for her friends, and whatever sympathy she had for the Russians earlier was gone now. Whatever was happening over on the ship was fine with her. If people were dying from the bites they had gotten in the moat, and if it killed the entire crew, it would be fine with her.

Jean got her wire cutters and a roll of string. The first thing she did was run the string through the ring on the end of the pin and then tied it around the grenade. This way the pin couldn't be pulled out. No matter what, someone would have to cut the string to make the grenade explode. Then she cut the wire at both ends and replaced it with wire that was only connected to the piling next to the grenade and across to the other side. It didn't take her more than a few minutes to set up the dummy wire once she decided how to do it. She moved to the next grenade and repeated the process in even less time. She inspected her work and was really pleased with herself. Unless the Russians got down and took a very close look, they would never notice that someone had rigged their booby traps not to work.

She picked up her supplies and was just starting to get up from her knees when something hit her in the back, knocking her flat to the dock with the air gone from her lungs. Something pressed hard between her shoulder blades, and she was only vaguely aware that it felt like a boot. All she really knew for sure was that it hurt.

Someone pulled a bag over her head, and her hands were roughly pulled behind her and tied. When she was lifted to her feet she could tell there was one man on each side of her. She felt herself being lifted into the air and unceremoniously tossed onto something that felt like rubber, and then her worst fears came true when she heard a motor start.

"No," she said. "Don't take me to the ship. That's not a safe place to be." Something hit her in the side of the head, and she blacked out.

When Jean woke up, the bag was gone from her head, and she was untied. She was in a cell. It was very small, probably because the ship wasn't very big, and a brig was only meant for temporary punishment. At least that's what she guessed, but she felt strangely safer than she should feel. She impulsively backed into the corner of the cell as far from the bars as she could get, and she knew why she felt safer. Nothing could reach her from the outside, and if things went the same way on this ship as they had on the Atlantic Spirit, this cell was going to be a safer place than anywhere else on the ship. She just wished she was back in the shelter.

8 GUNTERSVILLE

At dawn I woke up and looked over at the Chief. The plane was gently rocking because a small storm had kicked up the water a bit. Rain was streaking down the windshield. Some time after we had stopped to spend the night, I had traded places with Kathy so she could stretch out in back.

"Good morning, Sleeping Beauty," said the Chief.

Kathy added, "About time you woke up."

If the Chief didn't pick on me I would worry. It was just his nature to keep things light with a little kidding around.

"I was waiting for you to make breakfast for me," I said.

Tom joined in with, "I'll take my eggs scrambled, and make my bacon extra crispy."

I asked, "Any coffee left?"

A voice from in back said, "You guys are going swimming if you don't stop talking about hot food." Kathy emerged between us and held a finger up at me. "Don't tempt me again."

I smiled, and she laughed when we heard the sound of Molly getting the last drop of chocolate milk through a straw. Molly grinned around her straw.

"So, Chief, what do we know about the problem at the grotto? It looked pretty bad in the dark," I said.

The Chief motioned in the direction of the grotto and switched on the windshield wipers. Through the drizzle we could see there were still bodies falling from the tree line along the top of the cavern entrance, and they were still walking up onto the beach at the cave entrance. Some would linger where they came out of the water, but eventually they would start walking into the darkness and disappear.

I let out a low whistle. There was no way we were going in there. "Where are they all coming from?" I asked. "And don't tell me to ask Mr. Obvious."

"He's right," said Kathy. "We can see that they're coming from the top of that mountain. Does anyone else think that's a strange place to find that many infected dead?"

Tom said, "I may have an idea."

"Well, lay it on us, Tom. I think we've all had to develop open minds in the last year," said the Chief.

The Chief and I turned to face him, and we were all ears. Maybe if we knew where they were coming from, we would also know what to do about them.

Tom said, "I think you were right when you joked that Dr. Bus may have known your Uncle Titus, Ed. He was part of some super secret network that believed there would be an apocalypse of some kind. That's why he built the shelter, right?"

"Do you think he really knew Uncle Titus, or are you saying he just knew people like Uncle Titus?" I asked.

"Oh, I think he knew your uncle very well," said Tom. "As a matter of fact, I remember things he said that might give us a clue about how to deal with this."

"Like what?" asked Kathy.

Tom thought for a moment and then started listing things that we all thought sounded familiar. From his philosophies about being ready to the way his shelter was designed, it was almost like Bus and Titus had planned everything together.

The Chief said, "Then there would be another way in and out that only he would know about. When you think about it, we wouldn't have found our exits if Ed hadn't seen the emergency escape hatches in the bedroom."

Kathy said, "Look at that mountain. If there's a secret door somewhere, Bus will have to tell us where it is, and everybody and his brother will hear him tell us."

"We could just tell Bus to meet us at the back door," I suggested. "We just leave it at that and act like we know where it is. Bus will know that we don't have a clue where it is. If he can use his escape hatch, he will say so."

"Sounds good," said Kathy, "but how will we know where he's going to come out? Like you said, Chief, that's a mountain."

Everybody looked at me like I had the answer, and I relished the moment. There were so many times that I felt like a spectator in a room full of survivors. It felt good to be the leader for once.

"It's simple," I said. "We just tell Bus good morning, and to wave at us when he gets to the back door. We put the plane in the air and watch from above for him to signal us."

He laughed, but the Chief said, "That might actually work, Ed. As simple as it sounds, it might work because we would be the only ones to see his signal. The only problem we might have would be getting to his escape hatch from the water, but let's find out where it is before we worry about that."

The Chief started the engine and rotated the plane toward open water where we would have the room for a take off. The plane picked up speed fast, and we made a wide turn that gave us a good view of the mountain. We saw at once that the mountains in this area weren't as big as some people would expect. They were certainly higher than the flat land I was used to in South Carolina, but they weren't peaked or snow capped. As a matter of fact, they looked like a great place to ride out a zombie apocalypse.

Since we had arrived in total darkness, all we could see was the great mass of the mountain. It was all shadows from above, and we couldn't make out the difference between a man and a tree. Now, in the light of day we saw that it hadn't been just a tree covered mountain. The top of the mountain was broad and flat, and it had been cleared of most trees.

There was a circle of cabins and a larger building that looked like a barn. The entire compound was surrounded by a tall wooden fence that was strategically placed along the steepest edges of the mountain. A single, narrow road wound from the base of the mountain to a huge gate, and the gate was closed.

A low pass over the community gave us a better view of the buildings, and it wasn't hard to imagine what had happened inside the fence. There were bodies everywhere, and none were walking around trying to bite people. We passed over the trees on the side of the mountain that faced the lake where we had spent the night, and we saw there was a big gap in the fence. There were still a few infected dead near the gap, and we watched as they walked through it and dropped to a plateau about twenty feet below. The plateau had been cleared and fenced in just like the community above, and it was completely crowded from wall to wall with the infected.

"What in the world are we looking at?" asked Kathy.

"The houseboat and the moat," said the Chief.

I agreed. The houseboat was the little settlement on the top of the mountain, and the moat was the plateau, but it didn't look like it had worked out so well for someone. The plateau was supposed to keep the dead from coming up to the fenced in compound on one side of the mountain, but just like our moat, it had become a reservoir for the dead to either rot or fall into the lake below. I wondered if there were any predators like our sharks around that were getting their fill of the infected.

I pointed at the top of the mountain and said, "When we talk with Bus, he's going to tell us that the community on the top of the mountain was built as a distraction. People who would find the fenced community would be content not to look for anything under the mountain."

"What about that plateau?" asked Kathy.

"I have a guess about that," said Tom.

As the Chief brought the plane around for another pass, Tom pointed at the gap and said, "Look at the hole in the fence. You can see that the boards from the fence are still at the bottom where they landed. The lower fenced plateau was meant to be a buffer against people getting to the top, but it looks like it became a trap for the infected just like the moat around Mud Island."

"That's what I was just thinking, Tom," I said.

He looked like he was waiting for me to finish a sentence, so I explained.

"Let's say you decided to escape from the area when the attacks began. You're living down there in the valley along the river. You have a nice house, maybe you're retired and do a lot of fishing, or you live over at that resort and play golf. This stuff starts happening on TV, and you look out your window and see your neighbor snacking on the mail man."

The Chief looked at me like I had lost my mind, and when I looked at Kathy for help, I saw she was looking at me the same way. I didn't know how else to say it, so I guess I was saying it the way it had felt to me on that first day. I didn't see it on the news. I saw people biting people, and the police were shooting people who were biting people.

"Anyway," I continued, "where would you go? You already live in a gated community if you're the guy who plays golf, and that didn't do the mail man much good, so you know you're not safe. Or you're the guy who lives in a cabin down by the lake and you just fish, and these things are walking off your dock trying to get to your bass boat. Where would anyone around here go?"

Tom answered even though it was pretty obvious what the answer was. "People think it's safer on top of a mountain, but there are some drawbacks. For one thing, supplies don't last forever. There's only so much you can carry up a mountain, and water is going to be the first thing to go."

"And," Kathy added, "there are lots of mountains around here, but how many of them have a ready built community sitting on top of them? When the attacks began, people must have flocked up the hill to those cabins."

"What happened when they got full?" I asked.

Tom said, "It doesn't take long for someone to step up and take over as the leader, and it's not going to be your golfer or your fisherman. It's going to be some jerk with a big gun and some followers."

"We saw that happen with the houseboat before you moved in," said Kathy. "Some gang of halfwits with more guns than brains moved in."

"What happened to them?" asked Tom.

The Chief said, "The same thing that always happens to people like that. Darwin had them in mind when he talked about what species wouldn't survive. They got themselves killed thinking it couldn't happen to them because they had guns. Problem was, they didn't have the brains or the numbers."

The Chief was making another pass over the mountain, and we looked down at the cabins. The gate being closed meant the infection had gotten inside before they had closed their gates. Hidden by a family member, it wasn't discovered until it was too late. Judging by the large number of infected on the plateau, the mountain refuge had also far exceeded its capacity. By the time the infection started to spread, they were probably already out of supplies, and people were beginning to question the wisdom of hiding on a mountain.

There were still people who figured they could survive if the others decided to leave, reasoning that winter would freeze the infected, and all they had to do was wait them out. What they didn't remember to calculate in that little formula was the fact that people would keep dying, and even if they froze, and even if they killed the infected, there would be replacements. You wouldn't run out of the infected until you ran out of people.

The whole time we had been circling the mountain, Molly had been quietly listening and watching the scene below. She was such a calm child considering what she had seen since the day she and her father had escaped from the over populated area around Myrtle Beach.

Molly sighed and said with a touch of impatience, "Are we ever going to see Mommy and Dr. Bus?"

As difficult as it was to settle our predicament, Molly brought us back around to our mission. She couldn't have made it more clear if she had simply told us to focus. That made the Chief think about fuel, and about how we had used up most of our reserves helping at Fort Jackson.

"I think we should cross the lake to the resort and top off our fuel tanks before we ask Bus to pop his head out in the open," said the Chief.

I looked over at the fuel gauge and had no trouble agreeing with that suggestion. It was far to close to the red line for my tastes. I gave the Chief a thumbs up, not wanting to get everyone else overly concerned. Kathy and Tom saw what I did and nodded their consent.

Tom explained to Molly that we needed to go get some gas first, and she gave him just a little lower lip, but she said, "We can do that first."

That put just a touch of cheer into the cabin of the plane, and the Chief changed course in the direction of the resort.

In daylight it was easy to spot. We used the same way out of the lake that we used getting in, so we crossed the bridge going to the northwest. As soon as we were over the open water again we could see the unnatural green of the golf course. While everything else was in winter colors, the golf course looked like it belonged somewhere like Hawaii. The resort was on a peninsula that was shaped like Florida, and the western edge of it was occupied by an impressive marina. This one was probably packed with big boats until the day civilization came to a grinding halt. The boats would have made their escapes to the north and south, depending upon who was driving.

Wherever the boats were going, some must have made it to safety, but if Tom's experiences on the river were anything like the experiences of the average person, then maybe one out of every hundred had a chance. What was left behind at the marina was just what the Chief had hoped we would see. There were three full rows of slips that were occupied by seaplanes. Most of them were yellow and had an insignia on the side that we could read better as we got closer, and they all said TVA, but there was a real variety of colors and models parked around them.

I asked if anyone knew what TVA stood for and was surprised that everyone in our plane knew what it meant, including Molly.

Tom said, "The Tennessee Valley Authority is the controlling agency for the power generated by all of this water. Big lakes and rivers like this can either be damned up for power generating plants, or they can help to cool reactors."

"It looks like a lot of them didn't make it out before the infected showed up," said Kathy.

"Their loss," said the Chief, "but it means aviation fuel for us, and I may grab some spare parts from the avionics maintenance shop. It's that big building that sticks out over the water just beyond the marina."

"Chief, isn't that the building in the picture that had fuel written on top of it?" I asked.

"That's what I was thinking," said Kathy. "It's no small coincidence that Uncle Titus left Ed a seaplane, and there just happen to be seaplanes here."

Tom said, "What really is an odd coincidence is the way I wound up with you guys, and my wife happens to be holed up in a shelter with someone who knew Uncle Titus. I call that a small world."

The Chief gave us one of his really hearty laughs. He looked back at Tom and said, "First, we have Ed over here. He inherits a survivalist dream shelter complete with a seaplane just before the world ends. Second, the first people who find him and his shelter includes in its group a man who can fly a seaplane."

"I can top that, Chief," I said. "I'm going to guess that Uncle Titus also won the lottery and used the money to finance the shelter."

"This makes my head hurt," said Kathy.

That was funny by itself, but Molly made it funnier by holding a bottle of aspirin out to Kathy.

The Chief added, "Am I the only person here who has heard of six degrees of separation?"

It turned out the Chief wasn't alone with that bit of trivia, but sometimes he felt duty bound to explain anyway, and this was apparently one of those times.

"The theory behind six degrees of separation," he continued, "is not really associated with a number of degrees. It's the number of steps that supposedly can be taken by everyone in the world in order to connect people to each other. The theory says it would take no more than six steps for everyone to successfully relay a message to everyone else."

"I prefer to think of our connections as some really great coincidences," said Kathy, "and I like the idea that we're just an incredibly lucky group of people. I don't wish bad luck on anyone else, but I want to take their share of the good luck."

"Well, here's where we get to see just how much luckier we can be," said the Chief. "I don't see anything bad walking around down there, and we have to land for fuel sooner or later, so it might as well be now."

We circled the resort from the west past the seaplanes and made a big turn over land. Nothing was moving at the resort hotel or the clubhouse on the golf course. The greens were exceptionally bright in the morning sunshine even though the weather was cool. We came back around heading south, using binoculars to try to spot trouble, but it was totally quiet.

The Chief brought the Otter out of the last turn and made a steep dive for the water. He expertly pulled up on the front of the plane and neatly sat the pontoons in the water. I really had to admit, he was good at everything I had seen him do.

The Otter was just barely coasting as we pulled up next to the rows of planes parked in their own slips. We were only four slips away from the main dock, flanked on the left and right by yellow TVA planes. It was natural camouflage unless someone saw where we landed.

Kathy said, "I would almost prefer seeing some infected dead, Chief. This is too easy."

"I was just thinking the same thing," I said. "I would be satisfied to at least see some bodies. I think that this should tell us something."

Tom said, "It's like someone is still cleaning up around here. Someone picked up the bodies, and someone found a way to keep more infected from getting into the resort."

"Did anyone see a wall or really big fence around this place?" asked Kathy.

We all looked around and shook our heads, but Tom looked like he was thinking it over, maybe remembering something from when he lived in the area.

"That would be further north than where we went when we made our last pass," he said. "Besides, we were all looking back toward the resort area. This is a gated community, and the gate is literally a gate. There's no little guard shack with a crossbar across the entrance. If someone got it closed in time and then eliminated everything inside, they could have gotten control of this place."

Kathy was shaking her head. "Tom, you don't know how many places we have seen that were overrun even though they had gates. That has to be one strong gate to have kept out the infected. Not to mention staying supplied for this long."

"That's what's bothering me," said the Chief. "Whoever kept them out will be just as good at keeping us out." He killed the engine, and we all just sat for several minutes watching for the inevitable. It couldn't be this easy.

"All right folks, let's do this. The fuel pumps are up on the dock, and this place looks expensive enough to have catered to the whims of the filthy rich, and that would include not having to pull right up to the pump. Let's take care of business and get out of here."

We piled out of the plane onto the dock with our weapons drawn. We didn't know what we would find, but we would be ready for it. Tom told Molly to stay in the plane and to keep low. He latched the door shut and motioned for her to lock it from the inside.

With the Chief in the lead we went single file through the rows of seaplanes and up to the main dock. The Chief inspected the pumps while we formed a protective circle around him.

"We're in luck," he said. "There's a hand pump that you can use to prime the hose. The rest is just up to physics. There's also more than enough hose to reach the plane."

The Chief did all the work getting the hose into the wing of the plane, then he primed the lines and started filling up the tanks. It was a good feeling to know that there was going to be enough fuel to make it back home after we delivered Tom and Molly to Allison.

The hand came out of nowhere to grab the left ankle of the Chief as he stood on the right pontoon of the plane. As big as he was, when he started trying to shake the hand from his leg, the entire plane started rocking, and Molly started screaming. From where I was standing by the pump, all I could see was an arm. Whatever it was attached to, it was still under the water.

Kathy was the fastest to react, jumping from the dock and onto the pontoon of the yellow plane behind the Chief and pulling a machete from her belt. With one hard swing she removed the arm at the elbow. This was something we had seen before, but we didn't want to see it again. Severed arms of the infected tended to hang on afterward.

The Chief gripped the severed arm halfway between the elbow and the wrist and gave a hard pull. It resisted and held onto his leg for the first few pulls, but it finally came off. If we learned anything about the infected dead, it was that their grip was very strong. The Chief threw the arm in the water, and there was an immediate reaction. The water around where the arm landed began to churn with activity.

Both seaplanes where the Chief and Kathy were standing on the pontoons started rocking like they were on rough seas. They hung onto the wing struts as the water thrashed around them. As it started to die down, they leaped from the pontoons to the dock.

"What was that?" asked Kathy. She looked shocked, and I had never seen her look that scared.

The Chief didn't answer, and I saw that he was even a little unnerved. Tom ran down to make sure Molly was okay inside the plane, but Kathy stopped him from stepping out onto the pontoon and pointed down at the water. From where I was, I couldn't see what it was Kathy pointed at, but Tom visibly recoiled and backed away from the edge of the dock.

I looked around to be sure we were still alone. Satisfied that I wasn't going to let something sneak up on us if I left my post, I joined the others on the dock. I eased up to see what they were looking at, and I finally understood.

This wasn't salt water. This was lake water with no blue crabs. There had to be something in rivers and lakes that would eat dead flesh, but dead flesh would last a lot longer in the cold, fresh water of a mountain lake. The water was only about eight feet deep around the seaplane slips, and just inches below the surface of the water all around the docks and the pontoons were hundreds of hands reaching for the surface. The infected had fallen in and couldn't get back out, but they weren't decaying, either.

Kathy said, "Oh, my God, can you imagine what would happen to someone who came up to this dock in a small boat? Those things would tip them over just by pushing on the bottom of the boat."

"It probably has happened out here already," I said. "Are you two okay?"

"Surprised more than anything," said the Chief.

"Thanks for the hand," Kathy.

There it was again......dead people in the water bumping into each other trying to grab the next unsuspecting soul to come along and drag him or her down into what had to be a special type of hell, and what does the Chief manage to do? He delivers the world's worst pun or play on words, whatever you want to call it.

"Thanks for the hand?" she asked. "You are one seriously disturbed person, Chief."

Tom was standing there looking down at his feet. He looked so serious that he had me worried for a moment, but when he lifted his head I could see he was trying not to laugh. Of course that was exactly what the Chief had in mind.

Tom said, "Chief, what was the last thing Ed said to you before you pumped the fuel?" He gave it just a couple of heartbeats before he answered his own question. "He asked you if you needed any help, and you answered……."

The Chief got that big patented smile on his face and said, "I'll let you know if I need a hand."

Kids love to see grown ups laughing, and Molly was absolutely ecstatic watching us on the dock. She couldn't hear what we were saying or laughing about, but she knew it had to be funny.

Kathy caught her breath when she finished her laughing fit, and doubled over at the waist she said to the Chief, "Normally, this would be where I would push you in the water, but I'll give you a break this time."

She meant it as a joke, but all kidding aside, we were seriously unnerved by the sight below us. In clear water, looking down on the infected was a frightening sight. If they could find a way to walk up onto land, they would be unstoppable. I crossed over to the other side of the dock and looked down between two different seaplanes. It was the same thing there. Hundreds of dead eyes were looking upward, and when they saw me they started reaching. Some of the hands broke the surface, and I know just how lucky we were that we chose a slip at the marina that was in deeper water.

"Hey, guys," I said. "I think we have to check the water depth no matter where we go around here because these things can walk on the bottom. They just can't find a place to walk out of the water over here."

"Is there a boat ramp at this marina?" asked Kathy. "There has to be one around here somewhere."

We all started looking for it, but it wasn't down by the planes. It had to be there somewhere or the members of the resort who rented the slips would have to go to a public boat landing. That wasn't something people wanted to do when they paid for privileges.

"The avionics maintenance building is like a hangar," said the Chief.

He pointed toward the big building. "See how it extends out over the water so the planes can drive right up inside under power?"

"I don't know why I didn't think of it before," said Tom, "but people who pay to be members of places like this don't put their own boats in the water. The other side of the building probably has a big bay door on it, and the staff of the marina goes through the maintenance building with the boats."

Kathy said, "They probably clean the boats for the members, tune them up, and even stock them with refreshments all inside that building."

"Well, let's see what we can find in there that's useful," I said. "If they restocked boats for rich people, we might find a few luxury items we can use."

"Are you forgetting something?" asked Kathy. "If the boat landing is inside that building, that's why the infected haven't been able to walk out of the water. I'm not so sure I want to open that door."

The Chief was running his fingers through his full beard and looking at the maintenance building thoughtfully. "We could really use a few spare parts, Kathy. Uncle Titus didn't stock any at the shelter, probably because the plane was more of a decoy than anything. He didn't expect to fly it away from Mud Island as often as we have."

"He didn't expect it to be flown away from Mud Island at all," I said.

"If we need spare parts, this may be our only chance to get them, so I say we should at least check out the situation in the building," said Tom. "After all, if the infected are walking up a boat ramp into the building, wouldn't it be more likely that they were able to find their way out of the building by now?"

"I'm with Tom," I said. "Plus, those things don't think about things like that. There isn't one of those infected walking around down on the bottom of the lake thinking there's got to be a boat ramp around here somewhere."

Kathy looked at me like she was going to push me into the water, but she softened her expression and said, "I'm thinking there should have been plenty of them that have found the boat ramp by accident by now, Ed."

"How about we just go listen at the door for a minute or two?" said the Chief. "We don't have to go inside if it sounds populated."

No one could really argue with taking a quick look at the building. We could see from where we stood on the dock that there were windows. We could listen at the door and take a peek through the windows.

Tom tapped on the front of our plane to get Molly's attention and let her know we would be right back, and she needed to stay inside the plane no matter what. We formed up the way we had become accustomed to doing when we were covering each other and moved out. Our machetes were all through our belts because we could see a longer distance than in most places.

The dock was along the western shore of the peninsula, and for the most part it was all flat. The golf course dominated the view to the east with trees separating the greens where the fairways doubled back on each other. It was a beautiful day, and we were walking out onto the grass of an exclusive golf resort. Everything looked unnaturally normal, and it was bothering the hell out of all of us. It looked so normal that we half expected to see people teeing up to start playing a few holes before having brunch at the clubhouse. The only thing that looked as it should be was that the grass had grown, and the neat trimming done along the golf cart paths wasn't as nice as it had been in its better days.

In the distance, there was a hotel and the clubhouse where the members would kick back for drinks and talk about investments. It didn't look like anything had happened here, but plenty of those infected down there in the water had to have been lawyers, stock brokers, and realtors. Something was totally wrong with this scene because when the infection spread, they all wound up in the water. That couldn't have happened by accident. As a matter of fact, there must have been a large contingent of people who would have thought this was the place to go to be safe. A wall, a gate, surrounded by water, planes, and boats. Those were all good reasons why the average Joes and their families would have loaded up in their cars and tried to come here.

The maintenance building was about a hundred yards from the dock, so all we had to do was stay out in the open in order to see if anything was coming. The infected were too slow to be a problem if any showed up out in the open, so we were more worried that there would be living people with rifles taking aim at us. We stayed close to the water because we knew what the threat was on that side.

Kathy held up her hand for us to all stop, and we immediately began pivoting to our left and right looking for whatever the threat was that she had spotted. It turned out that she had seen something in the grass not far away and wanted to get a closer look. She was poking at it with her boot when we came up behind her and looked down.

"It's just clothing," she said, "but it's the first sign we've seen that something happened here."

"You mean besides all of those people in the water," I said.

"There is that," she said, "but it almost feels like everybody went into the water on purpose, maybe to get away from whatever was up here."

The Chief said, "Okay, let's keep that in mind. Something was up here that made everybody go to the water for safety, but why couldn't that have been the infected?"

"I don't know, Chief. It could have been the infected, and it could have been something else, too," said Kathy. "Something is making the back of my neck crawl, and I can't put my finger on it."

I took another look at the clothes on the ground, and I spotted what was bothering Kathy. Something had eaten whoever had been wearing those clothes. The infected dead would eat their victims, but this victim had been wearing a wide, leather belt, and there were long gouges in the leather. I hadn't really paid that much attention to the eating habits of the infected, partially because I had been so insulated from the carnage of the first days, but I didn't think they ate leather belts.

"Are there any other predators around here?" I asked the group.

"I was thinking that while we were flying in the plane," said Kathy. "I remember thinking that the predators most likely to go after the infected dead were also the predators most likely to go after living people."

That got everyone's attention. Tom said, "There are bear, bobcats, and a few mountain lions in this area, but they stay clear of the resort because it's too much civilization for them. They can stay up on the mountains and go after deer, so they don't come down here after people. Of course, that was before all the people started going up into their habitats. That many people trying to reach safety by going into the mountains had to drive the game down here."

"That's a good theory," said the Chief, "but I think Kathy is getting at something else. A mountain lion or two wouldn't have cleared this area so well. Maybe after we check the avionics maintenance building we could take a quick look around."

Kathy said, "I'd be content to just look around from the air, Chief. This place is giving me the creeps."

I had a sudden thought, and I wasn't sure why I hadn't thought of it sooner. "Chief, I think you're right about taking a look around. Maybe we should even go up to the hotel."

"Have you gone crazy, Ed? What could we possibly need from up there?" Kathy gestured toward the massive hotel that dominated the northern end of the peninsula.

"Information," I said. "We got to see the news when the infection first started to spread, but it never occurred to me that everyone and his brother was probably making videos with their cell phones. If we can find bodies, we might find cell phones."

"What about those clothes we saw back in the grass?" asked Tom. "Anyone see a cell phone?"

"That's what I was poking around for, Tom," answered Kathy, "but I figured the weather would have wrecked it by now. Ed might be right. Any useful information would be on a cell phone that's been inside since the first day. If the battery power hasn't bled off, it might be good to know what happened here."

"Okay," said the Chief. "If everything goes well at the maintenance building, we can take a quick look, but everyone keep your eyes open."

It only took a couple of minutes to cover the rest of the distance to the maintenance building, and the area between there and the resort hotel were just as clear and clean as the golf course. The only thing any of us had seen to show there had been anything to worry about was the pile of torn clothing in the grass.

As predicted, on the other side of the building there was a paved driveway that led to a large door. I had expected the door to open like a barn door, but this was like a huge garage. It was a roll-up door without any windows. At the bottom where the door met the ground, there was a padlock slipped through its steel frame, but no one had taken the time to squeeze it together and lock it.

I reached down and pulled the padlock out of its holes, but I didn't raise the door. "Too easy," I said. "Any windows we can see in through?"

I had just gotten the question out when something banged against the door from the inside, and the door started to go up a bit. Our mistake was that we backed up from the door and aimed our weapons instead of pushing the door back down and putting the lock back through the holes. By the time we realized the mistake, it was too late, and the Chief yelled for us to run.

The door was so large and heavy that it operated with counter weights. Once it was started in motion, the weights did all of the work and opened it the rest of the way. The padlock had been holding the door in a down position, because the counter weights put a constant pull on the door......pulling it upward.

We couldn't go back around the maintenance building because the door would be up too soon, so we all turned and ran as hard as we could toward the hotel. Something was trying desperately to get through the gap at the bottom of the door even before it was high enough. As a matter of fact, the something that was trying to get out was more than one thing.

We were almost to the hotel doors when the maintenance building door was high enough for the occupants to spring out into the light, and there was immediate chaos around the door as the guard dogs sprinted after us. If they had been faster breeds, we wouldn't have made it to the hotel, but these were the largest Rottwellers I had ever seen, and we had gotten enough of a head start. If we had tried to stand our ground, we would probably have been able to shoot most of them, but there were eight targets. Some would have been on us.

The door we chose was unlocked, and Kathy got there just ahead of Tom. She had her machete in her hand as she went through the door, and I was only vaguely aware that she had taken down the first of a few infected dead that were roaming around. It was a dining area, and it looked like it was occupied by eighteen to twenty of the infected.

All we could do was wade into the room and kill as we went. The Chief got the door shut in time, and the dogs began slamming into it. There was too much glass in this dining area, so it was only going to be a matter of time before they began charging at us through the windows, and they weren't likely to hold. We needed to get to higher ground where we could use our weapons to shoot the dogs and be reasonably safe from the infected dead at the same time.

The Chief, constantly strategizing, yelled at us not to shoot the dogs if they got in and to follow him. There was a staircase in the center of the dining area with infected piled up at the bottom of it. He jumped over the reaching infected that were pinned under other bodies and took the winding staircase to the second floor several steps at a time. He used his machete to slice the leg off of an infected dead that was at the top of the stairs and pushed it past us. It tumbled most of the way down the stairs where it joined up with others that had fallen.

There were less infected still in this area of the second floor, probably because they had been falling down the open staircase for so long. We saw that we were in the watering hole of the golf course. There was a huge sign over the bar that said we were in the Cavern Country Club and Resort.

The Chief yelled out his plan quickly, "Everyone keep your eyes out for infected, but Kathy is going to be at the railing as overwatch. When the dogs get in, let them attack the infected before you shoot the dogs. If any of them start coming up the stairs, go ahead and drop them, too. Ed, you've got our backs. Find a safe spot behind us where you can see if anything is coming toward us."

It looked like I had the easy job, but I had to keep my head on a swivel. Besides the bar, there were two long corridors that most likely led to meeting rooms. There were infected dead moving our way from both directions.

The once beautiful bar was a dirty mess. There was dried blood and long decayed bodies everywhere. If there had been a conference in progress in one of the meeting rooms, there could be hundreds of people on this floor alone, but it was more likely that people had begun to evacuate when things got bad. Those who were left here were like Tom and Molly when they got stuck in Myrtle Beach. They had no place to go. These people felt safe at their club, so they chose to go to the bar. The world was going to hell, so the best way to deal with it was over a glass of something strong.

I had a scope on my rifle, so it wasn't hard to clear the hallways, but it was a real mess at the bottom of the stairs. Kathy was holding her fire because the dogs were throwing themselves against the windows, and it was only a matter of time before they would break through. I made sure there wasn't anything on the second floor that could get to us and took a look over the railing at the dining area. There were well over a hundred of the infected below us and more coming.

I crossed through the bar and pulled the double doors shut to the corridor on the right. Luck was on our side because the doors could be pushed open from our side but had to be pulled from the other side. The infected dead didn't know the difference between pushing and pulling. As a matter of fact, they only seemed to know about pushing, and within a minute they were pushing from the other side. I took the curtain sashes from the big curtains on the windows that faced the golf course and tied the door handles together.

As I ran by Kathy on my way to the corridor on the left, I raised my voice over the chaos below and said, "We aren't supposed to be here. We should be dropping Tom off and Molly and flying back to Jean."

She casually answered, "We've got this Ed."

Kathy glanced over at the Chief and asked, "Think they're all in at the bottom of the stairs yet, Chief?"

"Yeah, but give it another minute, Kathy," he answered.

He nudged Tom and motioned for him to follow. They ran over to the bar and started hauling tables and chairs over to the top of the stairs and tossing them into a pile near the bottom. Most of them were landing on top of the infected that were already blocking the stairs, so an impressive barricade was being built.

I finished closing and roping the doors to the second corridor and went back to help when I noticed that nothing was coming down the stairs from above. I went part way up the stairs and saw that someone had come up with the bright idea of having stairs only to the second floor. The next level was nothing but rows of elevator doors on both sides. I imagined there would be emergency stairs, probably at the other ends of the corridors I had closed, but this place was strictly for the really rich and really lazy. They must have been seriously bummed out when this place lost power, and they had to use the emergency stairs.

When I got back to Kathy's side, I let her know we were closed in and safe. She whistled at the Chief who gave her a thumbs-up. I didn't know what they had cooked up, so I was surprised when Kathy fired a shot at the glass where they dogs were hitting it the most. The bullet had the desired effect as the glass shattered and dropped to the floor.

The dogs flew through the opening in the window and began ripping the infected dead apart. The infected had numbers by far, but they were slow and clumsy. By the time they could react to a dog, they were already being pulled to the floor. The noise level increased as the dogs barked with each attack, running from one body to the next. The infected were making a groaning noise that reminded me of the first days of the spread of the infection, but I had never heard it like this.

At times one of the dogs would let out a yelp when an infected dead would get lucky and its teeth would find flesh, but the yelp would immediately be followed by a renewed fury of snapping and barking as the dogs would get even for being bitten. There were still eight dogs attacking when the horde of infected had been reduced by half, and when one of the dogs finally went down, there were no more than twenty-five still on their feet.

I crossed over to the stairs where the Chief and Tom were keeping their eyes on the barricade. If any of the dogs decided they wanted living flesh, they needed to be dropped fast. We didn't need to find out what would happen if one of us was bitten by a dog that had just been biting the infected. There really wasn't much doubt, but we didn't think we could turn these dogs into pets anyway, and they weren't going to let us get back to the plane. They were doing us a huge favor, though.

I moved up next to Tom and asked him how he was holding up.

"Worried about Molly," he said. "She must be wondering why we've been gone so long."

"You've taught her the new rules well, Tom. I'm sure she's okay," I said.

Tom gave me a slight nod of appreciation, but I could see the worry on his face as he took aim at something below.

"Down to twelve infected," said Kathy.

One of the dogs looked up and saw her and immediately charged toward the barricade. We were all amazed to see the powerful animal easily clear the tables, chairs, and bodies at the bottom. It had moved so quickly that Kathy never got off a shot, but Tom was ready for it. The dog was almost on him when he pulled the trigger. He didn't have time to be sure that dog was dead because a second had jumped over the barricade right behind the first. The Chief got that one, and I heard Kathy open fire.

In the end there was one infected dead that was trying to crawl over bodies to reach us. It was almost pathetic to watch the effort it was making when there had been at least a hundred of them when the fight started. The four of us gathered at the railing and looked down at the remaining infected dead. It had been a young woman, and she was wearing the remains of a hotel uniform. She had probably been on the staff of waitresses and had been offered some overtime wages to stay and take care of the stranded rich people. Her own family probably never knew what had happened to her, and if they were alive, they were somewhere holding out hope that she was okay too.

The Chief walked over to the bar and looked through the remaining bottles of liquor.

"I can't believe this," he said.

He was studying labels with admiration. "I was only hoping to find something decent in their leftovers, but there isn't anything over here that isn't the best in its class."

He set up a row of glasses and poured two fingers of Royal Salute into each of them.

"My friends, that was too close," he said. "Let's drink one of these together and then get the hell out of here."

We each picked up a glass and studied the golden liquid.

"What is this stuff?" asked Kathy.

"In my opinion, this is the best Scotch whiskey in the world, and it probably went for about twenty-five dollars for a glass this size in this bar," he said.

We all downed our glasses, and even though I couldn't tell a good whiskey from a can of Dr. Pepper, I was willing to take the Chief's word for it.

Kathy said, "Chief, do me a favor and bring back as much of that stuff as you can carry. When we get back to Mud Island I want to get drunk with you on something that tastes this good."

The Chief wasn't going to argue with her about it and happily stashed several bottles in the supply bag he had brought along for the spare parts he hoped to find. It was when he remembered why he had the bag with him that he lost the cheerful look he had gotten when drinking the Scotch.

The Chief asked, "Has anyone else wondered how those eight Rottweilers stayed alive in that maintenance building so long?"

Up until this point, I don't think anyone had time to even consider it. We had been too busy running for our lives and then defending ourselves in the resort bar. When the Chief brought it up, you could tell it scared Tom the most because Molly was only about a hundred yards past that building. He grabbed his rifle and started down the stairs.

"Hold up, Tom," yelled Kathy. "We have to make sure nothing is still biting down there."

Kathy caught up with Tom and pulled out her machete. As soon as she moved the first table, hands started reaching for her from the tangled mess. She swung several times, removing hands but looking for the faces that went with the hands. There was such a mixture of bodies that she couldn't tell the infected dead from the really dead.

We joined her and began working our way toward the nearest door. Each one of us had to dodge at least one bite and then dispose of the biter so the others could get by. Eventually we made it to the broken window and stepped through one at a time.

We heard Molly screaming before we saw her. She was backing away from the open door of the maintenance building, and out of the darkness of the big open door we could see a large group of infected dead shambling toward her.

"Run, Molly!" we all seemed to be yelling at the same time.

Kathy put one knee on the ground to steady her aim and sighted on the infected closest to Molly. She was an expert shot with a hand gun, but she was beyond deadly with a rifle. She squeezed the trigger, and the first one went down.

Tom was running ahead of us, and was going to cross into Kathy's line of fire, so she had to keep moving at an angle to him to get off each shot. Molly had been too afraid to run, and even though Kathy wasn't missing with a single shot, more and more of the infected were pouring out of the building.

"Where are they all coming from?" she shouted. Even as she yelled the question she shot another infected in the head.

"The water," yelled the Chief. "They're walking up the boat ramp."

Molly finally overcame her fear and began running toward her father. As a professional baseball player in good condition, he closed the gap in a hurry and scooped her up.

The Chief and I weren't right on Tom's heels, but he was close enough to understand when the Chief yelled at him to keep going. Instead of running back toward us with Molly, he ran at an angle past the maintenance building in the general direction of the seaplane. Kathy would run to adjust her angle on them and then drop to one knee again. She was eventually in a position where she could make a run for the plane, too.

All three of us reached the dock in time to see Tom balancing on a pontoon and pushing Molly inside. I think we collectively held our breaths thinking a hand would grab him from below the pontoon, but he climbed in after Molly without giving us a scare. As we jumped down onto the dock and ran for the plane, I noticed that there were fewer faces looking up at us from the water. Apparently, once the boat ramp became an open door, they were drawn in that direction.

I helped the Chief cast off from the dock to get the plane out into deeper water. Up on the stretch of land between the dock and the maintenance building was a tremendous horde of water soaked infected dead, all moving in our direction. I jumped onto the passenger side pontoon and climbed into the seat. The Chief started the engine, and it was music to our ears when it roared to life, but he didn't back the plane away yet. We were just bobbing on the lake about twenty feet from the dock.

As the first of the infected began arriving on the dock and walking toward us, I saw what he was doing.

"Sort of ironic, isn't it?" asked the Chief.

He didn't even have to finish what he was saying. The infected were already falling off of the dock into the water, right where they had started from. The Chief waited until a large number of them had stepped over the edge before he began to back away just a bit, and they still followed.

"There's one thing I don't understand," I said.

"What's that?" asked the Chief.

"The infected aren't afraid of anything, so why didn't they walk into the maintenance building before we opened the door? I know they would have been walking right into all of those teeth, but there were only eight of them. Sooner or later the dogs would have died from exhaustion if not from being overwhelmed."

The Chief had spent most of his life around water, and he obviously had a history with seaplanes, so whatever explanation he gave, I could live with it. Kathy and Tom had nothing to offer, and Tom was still having a whispering exchange with Molly, probably about leaving the plane. I wasn't sure he was interested in an explanation no matter what it was.

"I can make a couple of guesses," said the Chief, "but that's all they would be."

Kathy said, "Lay it on us, Chief. It's not like we have a clue, and it was bothering me too."

"Well," he started, "the infected were the food source for those dogs. We know that much. I'm going to guess they haven't been in the maintenance building this entire time. I think they were put in there recently. Maybe there were three or four more of them when they were first locked inside. Whatever length of time they were in there, they were half crazy just to get out, and they were just a bit overweight from lack of exercise. That would explain why we were able to reach the hotel before they caught up with us."

"What about the infected?" I asked. "Why did they wait until we opened the door before they started walking out?"

He answered, "I have two guesses for that question, Ed. One, there's something that was only allowing them to get into the maintenance building one or two at a time, and the dogs could handle that traffic. It might be something as simple as them piling up on the ramp to where more couldn't get by except one at a time. Second, and I think this is the most likely explanation, the building was dark, so the infected in the water didn't see a reason to walk up the boat ramp. Remember, it's not like they were wandering around out in the lake looking for a way out. When the door opened, the noise of the door, the barking of the dogs, and the big rectangle of light that suddenly appeared over their water kingdom all attracted them to the boat ramp. Since they follow each other, the lake was giving up its dead."

As far as Kathy and I were concerned, that was a perfect explanation, and it made the whole thing seem even more ironic as we watched them drop off into the water once again. The Chief rotated the plane until we were facing a long stretch of deeper water and began to coast forward.

9 FRIENDS AND ENEMIES

Jean didn't know what deck her room was on. She just knew she was somewhere on the ship. There was no porthole, so the light came from a single fluorescent bulb in a recessed fixture. She was used to small accommodations on ships, but this wasn't a cruise liner, and she didn't think they would give her a stateroom. She also didn't know how long she had been a captive since there was no way to tell time. It could have been an hour or it could have been four. No one had come to see her yet. There was no food or water offered, and there was no toilet.

"This really must be a short-timer jail," she said out loud.

As if she had caused it, the door opened just as she finished her sentence. A man wearing an officer's uniform stepped into the cramped room with two armed guards in tow.

"Here it comes," thought Jean.

One of the guards bumped into the officer from behind, and he turned to look at the man. He barked something in Russian, and the two guards got out of the room as quickly as they could. The officer swung the door shut and turned to face Jean.

Jean asked, "Did you think I was going to jump you when you came into the room? Did they tell you I was tall and athletic or something?"

Jean was just under five feet tall, and she didn't weigh one hundred pounds soaking wet. He was likely to suffer more injury from a paper cut when she wasn't carrying her machete.

The officer glanced toward the door and said in perfect English but with a distinctive Russian accent, "No, they did not say you were tall and athletic. All they needed to say was there is a pretty American woman on board. Everyone volunteered to guard you just so they could get a look. I didn't even realize those two clowns were still behind me."

Despite her predicament, Jean wanted to laugh. Or maybe it was because of her predicament. She was so afraid of being tortured for information about her friends that she hadn't considered the possibility they might be civil. She studied him from her cell. He was young for an officer in the Russian navy, maybe only around forty years old. He had a slight build with thinning brown hair that he pushed back from his forehead with one hand. Not the mean looking Russian bear she had expected.

"My name is Abram Aristov," he said. "I am the captain of this vessel. May I know your name, please?"

Jean didn't think it would do any harm, so she told him her name.

"So, Jean Mitchell, what were you doing on the dock of this tiny piece of mud and trees?"

Jean thought it was ironic that he came so close to the name of the island. Since it had only been recently named, it wasn't listed on any of the charts they had in their shelter. She had been trying to think of a believable explanation for what she was doing on the island, and she did her best to pull it off.

She said, "I saw this island from over by the jetty, and I waded over at low tide. There was this houseboat, and I was so amazed that I had finally found a safe place to stay. Then I saw the wires across the dock, and I thought that was so dumb to put bombs out for those dead people and to blow up your whole dock in the process."

Aristov looked at her with a neutral expression but there was a hint of belief. "So, why did you put the dummy wires across in place of the trip wires?"

"Wouldn't you?" she asked.

She said it in such a matter of fact tone, that Aristov had to admit anyone with half a brain would have done it. "So, you didn't want anyone to know you had been there, but did you not plan to stay in the houseboat? That is what you call that floating home, yes?"

"Not right away," she said. "I didn't see anyone around, so I figured I could camp on the island for a couple of days and watch the houseboat to see if anyone was already living there. That was a nice boat parked next to it, too."

Jean almost said something about the Russian corvette not being visible from the dock, but she stopped herself in time. She wasn't supposed to know there was a Russian ship parked in the moat.

"Captain Aristov, where am I?" she asked. "You said that you were the captain of this vessel, but you didn't say where this vessel is or how I even got here."

"That is for another time," he said. He didn't sound rude or angry that she had asked a question. It was more like he had bigger things on his mind.

Jean thought this might be a good time to not ask any more questions. Captain Aristov looked like he was thinking about something else. After all, he couldn't really suspect that she had been living in a super shelter only a hundred or so yards away. It wasn't really so strange to find an American survivor in America.

"What do you know of this sickness?" he asked? "This thing that makes dead people try to bite living people."

"I know that it's the end of the world as we know it," she said. "I haven't seen anyone get bitten and then live, and after they die they get back up and try to bite you, too. I know that you can only kill them by shooting them in the head or hitting them in the head with something heavy. She left off the part about the machete so he wouldn't know she had any actual experience."

He looked bothered by her answer, so he studied her for a moment then said, "Do you know where this sickness began? Have you heard anything that may be useful for the treatment of this sickness? Is it always fatal?"

Jean knew what he was struggling with. He had several crewmen on board who had been bitten when they went diving to see what their anchor was stuck on. They were probably in some tiny little sick bay, and soon every one of them was going to die, wake up again, and start biting the nearest shipmates.

Jean stopped herself just short of telling him she was a nurse. The last thing she wanted was to be ordered to tend to the injured men. Instead, she told him she had started out on a cruise ship, and that they tried to control the spread of the infection unsuccessfully. In the end, she was the only survivor that she knew of.

Captain Aristov was studying her again, as if he was running some kind of personal lie detector test on her. She considered the possibility that he really didn't know what to do about her, his anchor, and his injured crew members. Jean did her best not to break eye contact with him as he continued to gaze at her through the bars. She also resisted the temptation to try to engage him in conversation. He obviously was preoccupied with his own problems, and what he was hoping for was answers, not more questions.

"Captain," she said, "what's happening? Why did your men capture me, and why do you have me in this cell?"

Jean figured those were the questions anyone would ask, and she couldn't just keep staring back at him, so she needed to keep asking him something. She also needed to keep from asking him about things she wasn't supposed to know, and the best way to do that was by asking about those other things.

After a minute, Captain Aristov let out a sigh, and his shoulders slumped. "I do not know what to tell you, Jean Mitchell. We have many problems, and I do not know what to do about any of them."

"Am I one of your problems, Captain? If so, you could just let me go." She figured it wouldn't hurt to try.

Captain Aristov gave her a faint smile and said, "I do not know what to do with you, Jean Mitchell, but I will not let you go just yet."

Jean tried not to look too disappointed, but she was. She knew from past experience what was going to happen if they didn't just do the humane thing and put those bite victims out of their misery. It could not be controlled once it got started, and she didn't want to be here when it did.

"Tell me, Jean Mitchell, if you were bitten by one of the sick people, what would you do?"

She could tell he really meant it, and she didn't want to answer too fast or too slow. So, she took a deep breath and let it out the same way Captain Aristov had when he sighed.

"I wouldn't want to turn into one of those things. I wouldn't want to be like them. I have thought of your question many times, Captain Abram Aristov, and I would hope there was someone I care about who would help me to end it."

"And if they didn't, Jean Mitchell?"

"Then I would do it myself," she said, "because if I didn't do it, then I would become one of them, and I would bite someone I love. It doesn't stop just because it's someone you care about."

Captain Aristov looked like he was going to say something else but stopped himself. He had been leaning up against a bulkhead, but now he pushed himself to a standing position and put his shoulders back. He looked more resolute, as if he had decided what he should do about his problems.

"Captain, you have someone on your crew who has been bitten, and you don't know what to do. Am I correct?"

Jean phrased it as a statement because she felt like he wouldn't answer, and it wouldn't take a genius to figure out why he was asking her what she would do.

"Yes, Jean Mitchell, someone on my crew has been bitten, but what would you say to the rest of your crew if you told them you were going to kill six of their comrades?"

"Six......you have six crewmen who have been bitten, and you have them on board? Tell them the truth, Captain. Tell them that a bite is a death sentence. Tell them anything you want to, but don't tell them you can save those men, because if you do then you are sentencing the entire crew to death."

It probably came out a bit more forcefully than Jean intended, but she was beginning to think Captain Aristov needed a reality check. He had to know by now what was happening, and he had to know by now the consequences of being bitten.

"Captain, I'm sorry for you and your men. I really am, but can you tell me something?"

"Maybe, Jean Mitchell, it is time for no more questions."

He started to leave, but Jean asked before he could open the door. "Have you been at sea this entire time? Don't you know that you can't do anything to save people who are bitten?"

The shoulders slumped again, and he turned to face her. Jean didn't know why, but he answered her question.

"We are not an ocean faring vessel, Jean Mitchell. We are more like your Coast Guard ships. We came to America for a goodwill tour. We were stopping at your port cities and meeting Americans. I must say, we have been pleasantly surprised by the reception we have received. Our countries......we have not been always such good friends, so we thought there may be some anger toward us. We were docked in Norfolk when the sickness began. We saw friendly Americans being killed by the sick people as we pulled away from the port. There were American Navy ships leaving as we did, and they did nothing to help, either."

"Captain, you knew what would happen and so did the US Navy. If one crewman gets bitten, everyone will die on board if you let him stay, and that means you also couldn't save those civilians."

This time Captain Aristov didn't pause when he began to walk out. Jean thought she had gotten through to him, but she couldn't be sure because he didn't even look at her. She turned back to the farthest corner of her cell and was just about to sit down when the door opened again. This time it was a young enlisted man who looked like he was still a boy. He came over to the cell and handed Jean a bottle of water and a bowl of something that smelled delicious. Jean didn't even know she was hungry until she smelled it.

He said, "Captain Aristov told me to tell you he will let you go after he has dealt with the other problem you discussed." His English wasn't quite as good as the Captain's, but it was pretty good. He was also being very polite and respectful.

Jean thanked him and gratefully accepted the soup. After he left, she went back to her corner and tasted it. She had to admit, it tasted as good as it smelled, and she greedily ate every drop. She was licking the bowl and wishing the young man would come back so she could ask for more when she heard the gunshots and the shouting. She froze and listened carefully for a clue about what had happened. She didn't think Captain Aristov would dispose of his problem by shooting the crewmen. Something a little more humane like a needle with a morphine overdose would be better.

She thought she heard someone go by outside the door, and she definitely heard someone scream. Her worst fears were just starting to overcome her when the door opened part way. At first she thought someone was just taking a peek at her out of curiosity, and then she realized what it was. It was an infected dead. It uttered a low moan and started to come into the room. Jean shrunk back into the corner of her cell as far as she could go. She had tears streaming down her cheeks because she knew this meant the Captain had waited too long.

Just as the infected started toward the cell, the Captain appeared behind it. He was injured and had blood running from a cut on the side of his head. He reached into the small room and grabbed the infected by the back of the shirt collar. Captain Aristov practically jerked the infected off of its feet and dragged it from the room.

He pushed the former shipmate to the deck outside the room and quickly said, "I am so sorry, Jean Mitchell. I should have let you go before it was too late. You would not make it to shore now. If we do not see each other again, I hope you find a way to escape from here."

Captain Aristov pulled the door shut hard, and Jean heard it lock. She knew he wasn't locking her in as much as he was locking them out. Either way, she knew she was going to die in that dark cage.

10 GREEN CAVERN

Allison contacted us on the radio almost as soon as we were in the air. Molly squealed with delight when she heard her mother's voice on the speaker.

"Otter, this is Allison. Come in Otter. Over." She sounded worried, and we couldn't blame her. We had already survived a rough morning and a really close call at the resort.

"We read you, Allison," I answered. "Good to hear your voice. Do we have a rendezvous location? Over." I sounded more like Allison than I had wanted, and my first thought had been not to worry her.

"Go to the same location as yesterday. Is everybody okay? Over."

Allison's transmission confused us at first, but we weren't going to dispute it with her. Maybe there was something we had missed because of the rain. The Chief had already gotten the plane in the air, and we were already crossing over the bridge at the entrance of the lake. He was going in for a landing before I could respond to Allison's question.

"We're all fine, Allison. No one is hurt. We're just a bit shaky. Will Bus be meeting us? Over."

Molly leaned into the front of the plane and pulled my arm toward her. She pressed the microphone button and said, "Hi, Mommy. We're all okay. Over."

"Hi Molly, I'm glad you're okay. Mommy will be seeing you soon. Over"

Tom said to us all, "Molly had just started calling Allison Mom, not long ago. I guess she went back to calling her Mommy because of what she has seen."

"Otter, park where you were yesterday and move in closer. Flash strobes on high beam directly ahead. Watch for activity and wait for a response. Over."

Allison was doing a good job of not giving away their position, but none of us could guess why we were returning to the same spot as before. The Chief did his usual smooth job of landing the plane, and we coasted to a stop at almost the exact same spot as yesterday.

There weren't any infected dead raining from the side of the mountain now, but there were still plenty milling around inside the grotto. Some were still walking up onto the beach and into the cavern beyond. No more than a hundred feet into the cave it was pitch dark, and it didn't look like a place where I would want to run into any of the infected.

The Chief let the plane coast a bit closer, but he didn't cross that imaginary line where the infected rained down from above the day before. Getting hit by a falling body would not be a good idea, although it was reassuring to know there was a ready supply of seaplanes back at the resort. Of course, the keys were probably all hanging in the maintenance building, and I doubted we could go back there any time soon.

Once we reached the closest position we could risk, the Chief turned on the emergency strobe lights above each wing. They were intended to make the plane easy to spot if it was stranded out on the water, but they were also good for distracting the infected that were wandering around in the cave and in the water.

Even though the lights flickered at high speed, we could still see deeper into the cavern. There was still blackness at the back, so we couldn't tell if there were tunnels, but we imagined any infected that were out of our view could still see our lights blinking.

Gradually, the sandy beach that served as an entrance to the cave was filled with the infected. They were being draw out by the light as moths to a flame, but in this case, they were going for a swim. As they walked into the water, they eventually disappeared into a deeper area and didn't resurface. It wasn't like our moat where they dropped off a shelf into deeper water and got carried away by the current, but it was deep enough to keep them from returning to the cave for a long time.

Since a zombie apocalypse wasn't the first thing on the minds of the designers of these shelters, their plans didn't take into account the need to prevent them from walking into the entrance of the shelter. Nor had there been a concern for them falling over the edge of the mountain and landing right at the entrance.

I said to the others, "When we finally get to meet Bus, someone remind me to ask him what that fenced in plateau up on the mountain was really for."

The Chief said, "I'm willing to bet it's several things, Ed. There's probably an emergency tunnel to that level, and maybe even one to the top level. That would have made one hell of a landing area for a helicopter."

"It could also have been a possible expansion area for survivors," said Kathy. "It may be like our moat in one way because nothing could climb that side of the mountain and get in through the walls, but if people had managed to survive they could have fortified it and squeezed in a couple hundred more people."

"Yeah, it looks like that worked out for them really well, didn't it," said Tom. "It got overcrowded up top, someone knocked a hole in the fence, and someone didn't tell the others they had been bitten."

"It's pretty easy to read that story from the looks of things," I said. "One way or another, when the group gets too large, the infection gets in."

We sat in silence for a bit, just watching the infected clear out of the cave. I imagined if Bus had it all to do over again, he would have made the entrance more like our moat. That way, the infected couldn't walk from the water into the cave.

Eventually, there was no more movement in the cave. There had been hands reaching above the water, but they slowly dwindled in number until it was just a quiet nature scene.

"Otter, come in. You should be clear to approach," said Allison. "Just check for clear skies first. Over."

"I'll do it," I said. I climbed out onto the pontoon from the passenger side of the front of the plane and moved backward along the body until I could see far enough up the mountain. It looked all clear, so I waved the Chief forward.

"We're moving into position now, Allison. Over," said the Chief.

The plane moved forward, and as we passed under the lip of the overhanging mountain face, I understood the sloping beach of sand at the entrance much better. The entire plane was able to slide into the relative safety of the cave, just as if it had been a garage. It occurred to me that Bus may have had a seaplane parked at this spot when the apocalypse began, and just like our plane, it couldn't be protected from everything.

Once the plane had come to a complete stop, the Chief cut the engine, and it went totally quiet except for the sound of air moving around rocks. It was like being inside a giant seashell.

I was still standing on the pontoon looking around at the back of the cave when the Chief switched the lights from strobe to steady bright. The walls were multicolored and beautiful. In the distance I could see stalagmites and stalactites that looked like a stone forest. I was particularly watching for a wall that would turn into a door, or a hatch to open in the floor. I wasn't thrilled with the idea of walking further back into the cave to find a big vault door like my entrance. There could be a few more of the infected dead lurking around in the shadows.

I was so focused on the floors, walls, and the back of the cave that I didn't see a large square in the ceiling of the cave was lowering down next to the plane. As a matter of fact, I didn't see it until I looked into the cabin of the seaplane and saw that the Chief, Kathy, Tom, and Molly were all looking at me. I was just about to ask them what they were looking at when I heard a voice behind me.

"Welcome to Green Cavern," said Bus.

I almost fell off of the pontoon when I jerked around. The cabin door did the rest and knocked me on my butt when Molly came flying out through the door and threw herself at Bus. The others came out after her, and Tom pulled me to my feet before going over to give Bus a big hug.

Bus was shorter than the Chief, had a full beard and a bald head, but like the Chief he had that perpetually broad, white smile that made you feel good when the world was going to hell all around you. He looked like he could wrestle a bear for fun even though he was probably in his fifties. He caught Molly in a big hug as she jumped into his arms.

He said, "Everybody grab whatever is important to you and hop aboard. This thing can lift a ton at one time. The Chief and I weigh about that much, but we should be able to squeeze the rest of you on, too. We don't want to advertise the location of the front door any longer than we have to."

We grabbed our gear as quickly as we could and jumped onto the elevator with him. It was a solid platform that had lowered down on four thick steel cables. Three sides were enclosed by nets rather than solid walls, and the fourth side was open.

"The ride is pretty smooth, folks, but if heights bother you, just get a hold on the nets. It won't take long." He pressed a button on a control cable, and the entire thing rose silently toward the ceiling.

I looked up and saw that we were ascending into a brightly lit room, and I could see the face of a slender woman with brown hair looking over the edge. It was undoubtedly Allison. She had to be beside herself, wanting to see her daughter again.

As soon as the elevator came to a stop, Molly and her mother were in each other's arms, and Tom was holding them both. The three of them were all laughing and crying at the same time, and we were in no hurry to see them stop. I looked at Kathy and the Chief, and I saw they felt the same way I did. We got Tom and Molly home. As crazy as the idea had been, as bad as they odds were against us doing it, we had gotten them home.

"Dr. Bus, I presume," said the Chief as he held out his hand.

"Please. Call me Bus. Even when the title was on my door, I didn't feel comfortable hearing it." He shook the Chief's hand and then mine and Kathy's.

He held Kathy's hand longer than mine and said, "My, oh my, she's a real looker. Which one of you gentlemen is the lucky guy?"

Kathy turned beet red. The Chief grinned and said something about her being his adopted daughter. I thought about Jean and said, "My looker is back at our shelter holding down the fort. As a matter of fact, I can't wait to get back home to see her."

"I'm sure you can't, young man. He clamped a hand as strong as a vise to my shoulder and gave it a squeeze."

We all looked over at Tom, Allison, and Molly, and it seemed that they had decided on crying for the moment. They were all shedding tears quietly while Molly attempted to soothe them by saying everything was all right now.

"Let's give them a few minutes," said Bus. "You must be tired from your trip, and more recently from your escapades over at the resort." He gave them a scornful look and asked, "What did you figure you were going to do over there after you got your fuel, play a few holes on the golf course?"

He didn't wait for an answer before he started down a gently sloping tunnel through what appeared to be solid granite. It was brightly lit by lights inside heavily reinforced fixtures, and the light made the granite sparkle. We followed behind him like a bunch of school kids who were being led to the principal's office.

The Chief felt like we should at least try to give him a rational explanation, so he said, "I told the others we should try to get some spare parts for the plane."

Bus turned around to face them and said, "The picture said Aviation Fuel on top of the building, but that didn't mean it was in the building. Didn't Titus teach you guys anything?"

He turned and started walking down the tunnel again while we stood and stared at him. The revelation shouldn't have come as a complete surprise to us because we had been noticing the clues. After sharing a look of disbelief we started to follow again, but Tom caught up with us.

"Friends, let me introduce you all to my wife, Allison."

Instead of waiting for him to say our names, she wrapped her arms around our necks one at a time and gave us each a really big hug.

"I already know each of you of course, and even if I didn't, you're the angels who brought my husband and child back to me. How many women can say that in this awful world?" She stepped back from them and gave them a look that was both happy and sad.

"I have to tell you the truth," said Allison. "I felt cheated by Tom's baseball career. It was supposed to be glamorous being the wife of a baseball star, and I let that get in the way of being a supportive wife. When civilization ended, all I could think of was making it up to him, and you've given me that chance. I can't thank you enough."

Bus came back from around a slight curve in the tunnel and gave them all a stern look, but the slight upward curve at the corner of his mouth gave away how he really felt. He had been living for this moment ever since he had learned Tom and Molly were still alive, and of all things they were in Titus' shelter.

We all started following Bus again, and we passed doors along the way, but he kept going. The tunnel started to slope upward a bit, and it changed directions left and right several times. It was wide enough for a golf cart, and I wondered if Bus had given any consideration to getting one from the resort. I thought better of it, though. He would think I was totally nuts.

The shelter on Mud Island had been like a really cool, well furnished apartment. When we reached the end of the tunnel we found ourselves in something that was more like a really cool, well furnished mountain vacation home. The tunnel became wider just before it ended, and there were doors to several rooms that were open. We saw all of the amenities we had, such as the workout facility, the armory, and a nice little hospital clinic, but the best was yet to come. The room that Bus called his living room had a vaulted ceiling and a feel of openness that our shelter didn't have. I don't remember ever feeling claustrophobic in the Mud Island shelter, but if this had been smaller, maybe the thought of a mountain sitting on top of us would have made me feel that way.

Bus flipped a switch on a console, and a row of windows appeared from behind a large panel along one wall. A breathtaking view of the valley appeared beyond the windows. I walked over to the windows and looked out at the scenery. The windows were hidden under an overhang that jutted out from the mountain at least twenty feet. Below was a sheer rock face that went straight down for hundreds of feet. It didn't look like anyone could climb up to the windows or drop down from above. The overhang also kept the windows in the shadows, and I doubted you could see them from below unless they were left open at night and the lights were on.

Judging from the view, I could tell we were not on the side of the mountain that had the winding road to the top, and we definitely weren't on the side that dropped onto the plateau that was filled with the infected the day before.

The room itself was furnished with plenty of comfortable looking sofas and chairs. One wall was full of TV screens just like ours, and there was an impressive library of DVD's. Up a set of stairs and overlooking the great room was a kitchen that looked like it had been designed by a chef. Just looking at it made me hungry. There was a large dining room through a door at the back of the kitchen. It also had a vaulted ceiling with ornate lighting hanging down over a long table that could seat about forty people. Dr. Bus apparently like to live in style.

On the other end of the great room was a set of stairs similar to the ones that went up to the kitchen. A study filled with books was visible up those stairs, and Bus explained that the bedrooms were all down a corridor past the study. We could see his shortwave radio set on a table in the study.

I said, "By the way, Bus, could we try to get Jean on the radio? We've been gone a couple of days, and I'd like to let her know we made it here."

Bus was more than glad to accommodate me. He led me up to the study and switched on the radio. "We get better range at night," he said. "It's called skip distance. The atmosphere is thinner and higher at night, so you can send a signal farther."

I sat down at the microphone and gave it a try, but all I got was static and something random I couldn't understand. I tried for about thirty minutes while Bus began working on a decent meal in the beautiful kitchen. Kathy and the Chief were given the go-ahead to explore the shelter while Tom, Allison, and Molly went off to get some family time. I couldn't say that I blamed them. I was really missing Jean, and we weren't even family yet. I was sure I'd be the same way once our baby was born.

The thought of a baby hadn't sunk in yet. In a private moment I had asked Tom when it had sunk in with him, and he told me it wasn't real until the day they brought Molly home from the hospital. Our baby was going to be born in the shelter, and he or she was going to be home already. I guess for me it would be the moment I became a father. I looked at the microphone and wondered for the thousandth time in the last thirty minutes why Jean wasn't answering. She had to be waiting to know if he was alive and if we had made it.

"Lunch is ready, folks," Bus announced from the kitchen. Something smelled really good, and I decided it would tear me apart if I let myself worry about Jean. We were over five hundred miles from each other, and worrying wasn't going to make it any easier. Besides, Jean would probably be on the radio soon.

Everyone climbed the steps to the kitchen and crossed into the dining room. Bus had put out a nice spread, and even though we had been eating well enough in our shelter, it had still been a couple of days since we had a good, hot meal.

Over lunch we talked about everything and anything. The topics went all over the place because there was just so much to tell each other. Tom told us about how he and Molly had holed up in the fire station for a long time, and they could have stayed there longer, but as the infected dead moved out of the area, the scavengers had moved in. People who only prepared for an apocalypse of any kind by stocking up on guns and ammunition began to look in the obvious places for supplies, and it didn't take a rocket scientist to figure out that fire stations would be a good place to find what they were looking for.

After Tom had retrieved Molly from the top of the fire truck, he made her comfortable and then went from room to room clearing out the bodies. It was bad at first because the only way to get the bodies out of the building was to carry them upstairs and then drop them out the windows. He had considered trying to open a lower window and quickly shoving out a corpse, but the outside of the building was surrounded. As soon as he parted the curtains at a window, a dozen or more infected dead had started for the fire station.

After clearing out the bodies, Tom spent some time covering all of the windows. He wanted to let Molly have some light inside when he could to keep her from becoming too afraid. By the time he was done, Molly was already sound asleep. At least he felt like she would have a good night of safe sleep for one night. He had found a large supply of flashlights that had strong batteries, so he spent a restless night searching through the FEMA supplies that were stored in the fire station. There was a huge supply of food and bottled water. He didn't know how much cooking he would be able to do, but he figured without power, the only way he was going to be able to do hot meals was to build a small fire on the floor of the empty engine bay.

Molly slept well, and by the time she woke up, Tom had found powdered milk and powdered eggs. There were lots of things like rice and instant mashed potatoes, and he only had to find a way to boil water. He was sure he would find something sooner or later, and it turned out to be sooner. The stove in the fire station kitchen used natural gas, and it meant Molly could have a hot breakfast. He found some pancake mix and syrup, and they had a real feast. He remembered telling Molly that she would be able to have chocolate milk again one day. Tom looked at the rest of us and told Allison and Bus that we helped him keep that promise.

Tom and Molly worked together to make the fire station a home, at least for a while. They cleaned it as best they could, and they carried a fair amount of the supplies upstairs. Tom figured there could come a day when they would be trapped upstairs, and if that happened, they would need food for a few days.

It turned out Tom was right. When the scavengers came along, they came in through the downstairs windows. Tom and Molly had no choice but to go out through the bedroom windows using rope ladders they had ready. Fire stations had some useful things, and Tom had made up some impressive bug-out packs for the day when they had to leave in a hurry.

Tom was just telling us that living in the fire station was a temporary thing right from the start when we heard something on the radio. I hadn't realized I had left it on receive and speaker settings, or maybe I had done it on purpose in case Jean called us. Whatever I had done, it was making noise now, but it didn't sound like Jean.

As a group we hurried from the dining room and crossed the kitchen, the living room and finally to the radio. It sounded like a distress call, and everyone recognized the European accent, but we couldn't tell what was being said. The only thing we knew for sure was that something terrible was happening, and a final scream came from the speaker just as we tried to speak to the person on the other end. There was only static coming from the radio.

"I wonder what that was all about," said Bus.

The Chief said, "I hate to say it, but it sounded like it could have been our Russian friends back at the island."

I said, "Have a seat, Bus. We need to be talking about getting back. Jean is there, and there's a boatload of Russians practically in our back yard."

Bus pulled at his beard and sat down across from the Chief. He had a thoughtful look on his face, and there seemed to be something bothering him.

"Chief, so far you haven't asked the obvious question," he said.

The Chief had his best poker face on, which meant no expression at all. He said, "I figured you would get around to telling us in your own time, but if you want me to ask, I will."

Bus said, "Allison is the only person I let in even though the whole town found out about the shelter and tried to get in. I knew a lot of those people out there, and I didn't open the door for them." He looked like he was ashamed of himself.

"How did you wind up letting Allison in?" asked Tom.

"Allison got separated from her relatives and friends who were going to try for Huntsville, and I guess I just always had a soft spot for you and Molly. It didn't seem right to let Allison die outside when I never doubted for a minute that you would survive."

"Were you outside when it all started to happen?" I asked. "I had left the shelter to go buy some......supplies, and I almost didn't make it back."

"Your Uncle would have been disappointed in you. Didn't he tell you to stay inside? Besides, what kind of supplies could you have possibly needed?" Bus gave me a stern look that made me feel like I was at the principal's office again.

"Yes, he did, but can you honestly tell me you were expecting a zombie apocalypse?" I asked. I probably sounded more defensive than I should have been, but it seemed like everybody knew there was going to be an apocalypse but me.

"To tell the truth," said Bus, "I was outside because I was still stocking my shelter. I was coming back when I ran into Allison, and I brought her along."

"Chief," I said, "what about us getting back to Mud Island?"

The Chief reached over and gave my shoulder a squeeze and said, "I think Bus has something he wants to tell us. Let's give him a few minutes to speak his mind, and I'll use a higher speed getting you home to Jean."

We all sat down around the radio to hear what Bus wanted to tell us, and to be able to listen for more contact at the same time. He had the look of a man who had a big burden on his broad shoulders.

"I built that stockade with cabins above us like it was my shelter, and everyone bought it. The whole town of Guntersville thought that was where I was going to go when the world ended. There were plenty of people who made fun of me or called me crazy, but when the infection showed up here, you can bet everyone was trying to get up that winding road."

"How did you and Allison get back in with everyone else trying to get in?" asked Kathy. As soon as she asked, she guessed the answer to her own question. "Everyone else was going up one side of the mountain, while the two of you made your way around to the real shelter door."

"Exactly," he said, "and my reward for outsmarting them was that I had to watch them die. The camera system here is like the one Titus put on Mud Island, and I was starved for local news. I needed to know what was happening out there, and once the Internet went down and the news channels went off the air, I only had the stockade to watch."

"Did they die from within?" asked the Chief.

"If you mean, did they have infected inside but didn't know it, then yes, they died from within," he said.

"And you feel responsible for that?" I asked.

"Yes, I do," he said. "You should have seen them fighting to get in, and then they were shutting the gates on people when the place was full."

"How long before an infected person started attacking other people inside the stockade?" asked Kathy.

He thought for a moment and said, "I think it was the third day, but I'm not sure. Time started to run together because I couldn't stop watching the news, searching the Internet for something encouraging, and watching the people inside the stockade go into a state of anarchy over the smallest things. A candy bar could get you killed if the wrong person saw you eating it."

Allison had been listening quietly, but she saw Bus was starting to relive the guilt she had already witnessed when it was happening. She stepped over to his side and said, "I've been telling Bus that he isn't responsible for what happened. How could he guess they would turn on each other so fast?"

She continued on for him, "Most of the people who got to the stockade first didn't bring anything but their guns. When people showed up with supplies, the people with the guns just took what they wanted. There were a few people who tried to assert themselves and establish order."

"What happened to them?" asked the Chief.

"The people with the guns put them out the front gate," she said. "They put whole families out when they had to. Then it got really bad when they figured out someone would have to go down to the lake for drinking water."

Bus said, "Titus was ahead of me building his shelter. He got his power, fresh water supply, and everything else done before me. I was going to put a well up on the mountain. Running a pipeline from the lake up to the stockade wasn't a problem. I just didn't get it done in time. I decided I should get the shelter done first."

The Chief said, "That worked out for you in the long run because you accomplished what you set out to do, right? You didn't have to save the world, just yourself."

Bus had his face in his hands when he answered, "But I'm a doctor. Now I know why Titus chose to put his shelter on a coastal island instead of the mountains. I'll bet you didn't have to watch people die on your island."

"I was lonely after only a few days," I said. "When Jean, Kathy, and the Chief came along, I felt like I had won the lottery for a second time. Then when Tom and Molly took up residence in the houseboat, it was a no-brainer to bring them inside."

"That's what I'm talking about," said Bus. "You were able to stay inside with your head down. If it had been one family up there, I would have brought them in."

"That would have been a mistake," said Kathy. "A family could have been protecting someone who had been bitten. When we brought in Tom and Molly, we got it out in the open immediately and dealt with it. If it had been a whole family on the houseboat, we would have watched them for days first, and we would have left them outside if one was infected."

Tom tried to brighten the mood by adding that the Chief told him he had to get naked if he wanted to come inside. That wasn't entirely accurate, but it did earn a small grin from Bus.

Molly had been sitting down below in the living room watching a movie on an iPad, but it turned out that the acoustics were good in this shelter, or she had exceptionally good hearing. She giggled and said, "I got a bubble bath and daddy got a shower."

I asked, "What happened up there in the stockade?"

Allison took over again because Bus was being overcome with grief. "When the first infected person died and attacked other people, the ones with guns started shooting. Children were shot like they were nothing but animals."

"How did the hole get punched through the back of the stockade?" asked the Chief.

"Someone had a chainsaw," said Bus. "There were infected dead making it to the top of the mountain at the front gate. The people still alive inside figured they could go down the back side of the mountain without running into anything that was likely to eat them, so they cut a hole. Of course they found out that wasn't such a good idea."

Allison said, "People who fell out the back were stranded on the plateau, and people who were bitten were tossed over the edge with them. It wasn't long before there were more of the infected on the plateau than uninfected. Because it was completely fenced in, there was nowhere for them to go."

Bus said, "That plateau was another big part of the plan that never got finished. If I would have had time, I was going to clear it and put a tarmac on it as a possible helicopter landing site."

"Well, we guessed that one," said Tom. "Is there an emergency tunnel that goes to the plateau?" he asked.

"As a matter of fact there is, but it doesn't look like there would be much use for it now," he said.

"And how did they get the fence to collapse on the side of the mountain we came in through?" asked Kathy.

"Sheer numbers," said Bus. "So, I guess you're wondering why I'm telling you all this."

"We were wondering," I said. I could tell the Chief and Kathy were thinking the same thing.

Bus asked, "Is your shelter big enough for us to come back with you?"

"You would leave all of this behind?" asked the Chief.

"You could use a doctor, and from what I understand, there's a baby due. I don't want to stay here after what I've seen. The view out the front windows might be beautiful, but the memories just make it look like a dead land to me. Besides, we could close this place up and use it as a fall back shelter if we ever have to leave Mud Island."

Tom looked at Allison to see if she was on board with leaving Guntersville, and she gave him a silent nod and a half smile.

Allison said, "I've also heard Molly talking about her aunts and uncles, and that makes you guys all family now. If you'll have us, I don't think we could do better."

There were nods of agreement all around, and with that settled, we started to pack essentials. I wished Jean was with us so she could tell Bus what medical supplies he should bring. Since we had extra people we decided to focus on medicines, MRE's, and ammunition.

As we packed, we talked about the pros and cons of making the move to Mud Island. The biggest advantage to Green Cavern was that you couldn't just walk up to the front door and knock, and being able to open the windows to get fresh air was an attractive thought. The disadvantages for those same things were that the elevator door wasn't impenetrable, and the windows were within range of anyone who got their hands on an RPG launcher.

The surgical suite was bigger at Green Cavern, but the important things were the supplies, so we considered it to be a trade-off. Green Cavern also had spare seaplanes not far away, but we figured that was something we could live without. Besides, the discussion brought out a little bonus fact that we hadn't known. Bus could fly a seaplane too, so there was no reason why we couldn't fly over and get another one for the trip back. After all, we had done the same thing with boats.

The Chief was also convinced there was one big reason for Mud Island to be the best choice. Besides being a warmer climate, which we all agreed was more easily tolerated, the Chief believed that the coast was where rescue would eventually begin. He believed the ships already at sea had to be where civilization was being rebuilt. I didn't think he had forgotten what happened on the cruise ship. I think he figured the military had handled it better. There were some ships that would have made the mistake of trying to treat bite victims, but even those that did might have done so under more controlled circumstances.

We had everything packed and ready at the elevator in under an hour. Bus had set all of the controls in the physical plant to just maintaining security. No heating or air conditioning would be needed, and all lights could be off. The only reason to leave power on was to operate the elevator.

The plan was simple. We would take everything down in one trip. All hands would load the plane except Molly and Allison. Molly would be safe inside the plane while Allison stood guard. If any infected showed up, everyone would stop to clear the threat using machetes. Guns would sound very loud in the entrance to the cavern. Once the plane was loaded, we would all shove it off and board.

Bus watched the elevator go back up and said, "I thought it would depress me to leave my shelter behind, but I'm feeling more alive than I have in months."

He looked really alive to me. I was sure I understood what he was talking about because there was the feeling you get from being with a group of friends that you can't get anywhere else. I didn't know how lonely I was until my friends came floating up to my island in a raft. Surviving and living are two different things.

Loading went smoothly, and it wasn't long before we were easing the plane away from the beach inside the cavern. We half expected to see infected in the water, but since they weren't raining off of the mountain anymore, there had been no reason for them to stay around. With nothing for them to bite, the infected in the water had simply walked away, while the ones that had gone into the cavern had probably just gotten lost somewhere in the dark caves until they either fell over a steep drop or got stuck in a hole.

We were still careful even though we weren't seeing any of the infected in the water, and we rotated the plane broadside to the beach to allow Tom and me to give the plane a shove as we jumped onto the pontoon. We climbed inside, and the Chief started the engine. I looked around the cabin, and everyone looked so happy with this decision that they were all smiles. If not for the way the world had turned out, we looked like a bunch of people going to Disney World on vacation.

The plane slowly rotated to the left until the Chief had it pointing straight out toward the middle of the lake. He powered up, and it began racing forward. The Chief was an excellent pilot, so his take-offs and landings were always smooth. This time was no exception. We were passing over the bridge toward the resort marina in only a couple of minutes, and we could see the huge expanse of the golf course stretching out toward the hotel.

"Uh, oh," I said as soon as I could make out the details at the marina.

"That's what I was thinking," said the Chief.

We had become accustomed to changing plans when we had to, and this was going to be one of those times. The docks of the marina were still overrun by the infected. We could probably land and coast up to the seaplanes that were parked in their private slips, but the risk to all of us just wasn't worth it. Not to mention the possibility of damage to the plane. Getting in close to the other planes meant we would have to watch where our wingtips were at all times. If we even bumped one against another parked plane, we wouldn't be able to take off until we did a complete visual inspection.

The Chief turned in his seat so he could see everyone and asked, "Is there anyone who would object to Plan B?"

"Do we have a Plan B?" asked Kathy.

"Not that I know of," answered the Chief. "This time Plan B can be to pass on Plan A. We don't need another plane that bad. Let's go home."

The Chief pulled back on his collective and gained altitude as he made a sweeping turn from the north to the east. I looked at my watch and estimated that we would reach the coast at sunset. I had to resist the urge to start using the radio to call Jean. It would be less nerve racking to start calling in when we were at least half way home.

I remembered there was something I wanted to ask Bus, and now was a good time. It would also be a nice way to make the trip go by faster because there were some things he knew that could mean a lot to us in the future.

"Hey, Bus," I said over the sound of the engine. "You and Uncle Titus knew each other because you were both members of the same group of bunker builders, right?"

He smiled at the term I used to describe his tightly knit little club. "Yes, I knew Titus because we belonged to a small group that believed it wasn't a question of 'if' the world ended, but 'when' it would end."

"And you tried to make the bunkers capable of withstanding whatever the 'how' was that made the world end, right?" I asked. "Did anyone in the group think it would be a zombie apocalypse?" I couldn't help but smile when I said the words because it still sounded ridiculous, even though it pretty much summed up what was happening.

Bus said, "You would be surprised how many of us would have preferred a zombie apocalypse over some of the more likely alternatives."

"Alternatives? What was the consensus in your group about the type of world-ending scenario?" asked Tom.

He answered, "Well, bacteriological or some kind of a virus has always been near the top, but the means of transmission has always been questionable. In so many ways, we might lose millions of people to a pathogen, but in the end there should be a way to contain it. The reason this type of transmission is so hard to contain is because people make the conscious choice to hide it."

"So, a virus was the number one choice?" I asked.

"No, not really," he said. "The number one choice has always been an event that wouldn't kill millions at the onset, but would kill hundreds of millions over time. We always figured one of our many national enemies would explode nuclear bombs in the atmosphere instead of the more common dirty bombs that blow up cities. The EMP, electromagnetic pulse, would fry just about every low voltage circuit in the country in seconds. Imagine, no cell phones, no smart TV's, no cars that have computer circuits or electronic ignitions, no microwaves, no computers, no tablets, no barcode scanners. Planes would drop out of the sky, reactors would go critical because their computers wouldn't withdraw the rods or flood them with cooling water. Traffic lights would stop working, and any vehicle that would keep running because it was made before all the electronics was added would probably plow into all the cars that just came to a complete stop in the road."

I said, "Bus, that would be bad, but how can you process the idea that someone who used to be alive now wants to sink its teeth into you?"

"I didn't say I find this all to be preferable," he said, "but in a way this is still somewhat limited. At least we do have a chance to fight back and still have our technology intact. Can you imagine what this would all be like if we didn't have the capability of flying or even using a modern boat? I would be willing to bet your boat even has circuit boards in the ignition."

"That's true," said the Chief. "We wouldn't have been able to travel to Guntersville to reunite anyone because it would have been a journey that could have taken months."

"I have another question for you, Bus," I said. "How many members were there in your club, or should I ask, how many members got around to building their shelters?"

Bus had a smile on his face like the one the Chief got when he was really amused. It was a cross between funny and the cat that ate the canary, and it usually had that innocent 'who me' appearance complete with the raised eyebrows.

He collected himself as if he was savoring the moment and said, "Thirty-two of us finished our shelters."

I hadn't expected that many, and judging by the mouths hanging open in the plane, I wasn't the only one who was surprised.

Kathy asked, "Do you know the locations of all of the shelters?"

He nodded his head and said, "Yes, and we liked to call them redoubts because it means the same thing as stronghold. A shelter is something that sounds weaker, and as you have undoubtedly noticed, they can withstand a siege. The supplies found in one redoubt would collectively be greater than some cities have been left with."

The Chief looked like he had some major questions he wanted to ask Bus, and I had already known him long enough to know he was making some plans. He turned almost completely around and looked at Bus before asking slowly, "Is there another redoubt in South Carolina?"

"Yes, there is, Chief, and from what you have told me about your adventures since this all began, you have been close to it a number of times."

The Chief started to ask Bus where it was, but instead he held up one hand and said, "Wait, save it for when we get back. I have an idea how we can use that information to do exactly as you said we can do. We can fight back. These redoubts can give our forces a foothold on the land, bases where we can take a stand." The Chief looked positively cheerful as he said, "First, let's get home to Jean. Then we have some people to contact."

11 DARK PASSAGES

It was quiet in the little room with the cell, but from time to time there was a noise on the other side of the door that sounded like something bumped into a wall. Sometimes it sounded like something being dragged along the floor. Jean had little doubt about what was making the sounds. She also had no idea of what she could do to save herself. At least the door was locked, but that also meant she would have to figure out how to escape the cell and then escape from the room.

Even if she could work some kind of magic with the cell door and the compartment door, she had no idea where she was in the ship. She could be on an upper or lower deck, but judging by the regularity of the noises outside her door, she was far from being alone.

Jean didn't know much about ships except what she had seen on cruise liners, but from what the Chief had told her military ships were much different from civilian ships. They were utilitarian, which meant nothing to her when the Chief had said it, but he explained there is no wasted space on military ships. There's very little privacy because so much space has to be sacrificed to machinery, storage, and weapons. He had also told her to expect to find cabinets in the strangest places, which gave her something to think about.

Jean got to her feet and decided she was going to inspect every square inch of the tiny room. She started with the door.

"I know what's behind door number one," she thought. There was some kind of storage locker in the bulkhead next to the door to the left, but that wasn't any help because it was much too far out of her reach. She put that door as first on her list of things to check after she got out of the cell.

"That's positive thinking, Jean," she said out loud.

As soon as she said it there was a groan on the other side of door number one.

"Think it, but don't say it," she scolded herself.

She continued her survey and saw there were two recessed latches along the wall on the right side of the door. Judging by the distance between the latches, she felt like she knew what those were for. If you opened them at the same time, a bunk would drop out of the wall. That would be number two on her list of things to do.

That brought her to the walls of her cell, and she had already been up close and personal with them. She inspected them, anyway, and she felt along the floor just in case. It didn't surprise her to come up empty handed. The cell would be positioned as far from anything as possible. As a matter of fact, the only thing she could reach from the cell was the light fixture.

Jean stepped over to the bars closest to the recessed fluorescent bulb and looked along the inside edge down the length of the bulb. There was a latch right in the middle. Something was beginning to make sense. The bunk was along one wall, and the light was along the other wall. "What if this had been an officer's cabin at some point in time?" she thought.

If she stretched far enough, she could just barely reach the latch, but she wanted to release it without having the whole fixture fall out of the wall. If she broke her only source of light it would be pitch black in the little room, and she felt like that would be the last straw for her. It would make her suicidal to sit in a totally black room with those things wandering around outside door number one.

Jean got a finger under the edge of the latch and eased upward on it gently. As she felt it release the locking mechanism, the entire recessed fixture pushed upward against her hand. She kept some pressure on it so it wouldn't raise up too quickly, and she said very quietly, "God bless you, Chief. It's a cabinet. Now it just needs to have a set of keys inside it, preferably within reach."

She felt around the inside of the cabinet and locked her hand around something that felt familiar. Cylindrical, flat on one end and a switch that could slide with a thumb. It had to be a flashlight. She pulled it out and carefully pulled her hand back through the bars. Even though she had enough light in the room, she knew she could be plunged into total darkness if power failed on the ship. The flashlight at least gave her the added security of knowing she could find her way around the ship if she got out of the cell.

After putting the flashlight safely in the corner of her little prison, she went back to the bars and stretched to reach the inside of the cabinet for a second time. There was plenty of paperwork in the cabinet, which was to be expected, but it was in the way, so she started bringing back whatever she could grip at one time. Most of it was Russian, but there were a few things that were souvenirs of their visit. The men's magazines were probably picked up in Norfolk.

"Men," thought Jean. "The world's coming to an end, but you can still find this stuff lying around. It's like styrofoam cups that never totally disintegrate."

Jean caught herself flipping through the pages, and even though no one was watching, she still got embarrassed and tossed the magazines into the corner. She kept pulling back paperwork until she had it all, then she went back to feeling along the deepest part of the cabinet she couldn't see. Her hand landed on something else that felt familiar. She pulled it out and was surprised to find another souvenir. This time it was something useful, though. It was a Statue of Liberty letter opener with about a six inch blade. It wasn't a machete, but it was something. She tucked the blade through her belt so she could get to it in a hurry if she had to.

On her next reach into the cabinet, she found what she was looking for. Almost out of her reach was the rim of a metal circle. She carefully dragged it toward her, and she was gratified when she discovered it was a key ring. She was already starting to wonder if she could use the letter opener to pick the lock, but she didn't have a clue how locks worked, and she would have been doing nothing more than just digging around inside the lock. Once she got a finger through the ring, she pulled it over with a death grip on the keys. There was no way she was going to drop her prize.

When she got her hand back between the bars, Jean finally quit squeezing on the ring so hard that it had started to make her hand hurt. If one of the half dozen or so keys on the ring didn't fit the lock, she was going to scream, and she didn't care if it woke up every infected dead on the ship.

She went to the lock and selected the first key. No luck, but with five or six to go, she hadn't expected to be that lucky. It turned out to be the fourth key, and when it slid into the lock, she felt her heart start to pound. There was always a chance it was just made for a similar lock, but her hopes were already up, so she gently turned the key. Nothing happened, and she held her breath. She tried again, and it turned, but it didn't unlock the door.

Jean was ready to do the scream that would wake the dead when it occurred to her to check to see if she was turning it in the right direction. Her head wouldn't fit between the bars, but she could get it against the bars well enough to see what her hand was doing, and she was both relieved and frustrated to find she had been turning it in the wrong direction. She mentally kicked herself until she remembered she was just as likely to turn a screwdriver in the wrong direction.

She forced herself to be mentally calm as she turned it back the other way. Aside from screaming, she planned to bend the bars with her bare hands if it didn't work. Then she was going to pull one of the bars out of the cage and go out that door and beat the hell out of every infected Russian sailor she ran into. She heard the click inside the lock, and the door swung open.

It was such a relief to be free from the cage that Jean wasn't even concerned with the fact that she was still in a little room, somewhere on a Russian ship and had no idea how to get back to the island.

She looked at the bars on the cage and said, "You're lucky. You were just about to get bent."

The sound of her voice caused a chorus of groans to start again on the other side of the cabin door, and for one moment she seriously considered locking herself inside the cage again. She wondered how many there were in this one corridor. She knew Captain Aristov had disposed of one, and if he was bitten, he probably took care of it himself. There were six in sick bay, but there was no telling how many there were all together. If she could let them into the room one at a time, maybe she could take them out, but she didn't know what she would be able to do against a group of them.

Jean thought, "There has to be something around here I can use as a weapon." She felt the letter opener she had stuck in her belt and pictured herself thing to stab one of those things with it.

"I'd probably bend it on the first one's skull, then I'd really be in trouble," she thought. "I wouldn't even be able to open a letter with it."

She looked around the room and remembered there was a cabinet by the door, and there were the latches to what was probably a bunk on the other wall. She very quietly pressed one hand against the cabinet door while she released the pressure on the latch. The last thing she wanted was to pull the door open and have stuff come falling out. Before she pulled the door to her, she wondered how long it had been since the last time she heard a human shouting or the sound of a gunshot. She thought it had been maybe an hour, but there was no way to be sure.

She pulled the cabinet open and blinked, trying to make sense of what she was looking at. There was a black handgun sitting on a shelf with a box of ammunition next to it. The box said it was nine millimeter ammunition, and she recognized the gun as a Glock 17. The Chief had found several of them in the armory and had shown her why it would probably be the best gun for her if she was in close quarters and couldn't swing a machete. There was also a bottle of Russian Vodka, and she really wasn't too surprised to find that.

Jean rotated her head and looked back at the cell. They keep the keys within reach from the cell, and they leave you a loaded gun. I can't wait to see what's inside the bunk.

"This must be the Russian version of Andy of Mayberry," said Jean, "but the Russian Barney had more bullets." She picked up the gun and ejected the clip to see if it was full, and a visual check showed there was a round in the chamber. The Chief had told her they were made to hold ten rounds or seventeen. She was lucky and got the seventeen round version.

Thinking it through, Jean figured the Russians didn't really have a discipline problem on this type of ship, and if someone was locked in the cell, it was probably to sleep off a good night in town. A guard was probably in here with the bad boys to keep an eye on them, and a gun wasn't likely to be needed. Captain Aristov was undoubtedly not worried about Jean escaping and taking control of the ship.

When she thought about Captain Aristov, she felt a little sorry for him. All he really wanted from her was to hear her say there was something they could do to save his men. She hadn't been able to give him that kind of false hope, no matter how much she wanted to say it. The last time she saw him, he was sacrificing himself for her. She hoped he had died in a way that would keep him from turning into one of those things. Her real fear was that she would find him outside the door waiting to bite her.

Jean tucked the Glock into her belt and emptied the box of ammunition into her pockets. If she was really lucky she wouldn't have to stop to reload, but if she did, it looked like she had enough rounds for the entire crew.

Her next stop in the tiny cabin was the pair of latches that looked like they would lower a bunk from the wall. She gripped both latches at the same time and squeezed them to the unlocked position. The weight of the door caused it to drop down on her, but it wasn't too heavy to lower by herself, and it was quiet. There wasn't anything remarkable about it, but the mattress gave her at least one idea, and there were two pillows that could be useful for the same thing she had in mind.

Jean pulled the bedding out into the open area by the cell, and that was when she figured out what she had to do. She dragged the mattress into the cell and added the two pillows. She took a quick look around to see if there was anything else she could do to make her plan better, but she didn't see anything she had missed.

The door to the cell opened outward, probably because the cell was barely big enough for one person anyway, but that was important to her plan. If it opened inward, then she would have to find a way to reinforce it. She didn't know how many times she had said a quiet prayer of thanks that the infected couldn't figure out the difference between pushing and pulling. All they knew was to come straight at you with their mouths open.

"Okay," she said. "Here we go."

Jean took the key out of the lock. If she had time when the fun started, she would lock the door, but she doubted there would be time. She left the cell door open and went over to the cabin door. She quietly turned the lock to the unlocked position and then backed all the way to the open cell door.

She drew in a deep breath and yelled at the top of her lungs, "Hey, dirt bags and scum buckets. Come and get it."

Jean backed in the cell and pulled the door shut behind her. She was just about to reach around and lock the door when the cabin door flew open. It wasn't like the infected dead rushed to get anywhere. It was just the sheer weight of them that made the door slam open harder than she had expected. Three of them were trying to come into the cabin at the same time. She had hope for one at a time, but there wasn't much she could do about it now.

The first of the infected to get through the narrow cabin door was one of the guards Jean had seen earlier with the Captain. He was missing a large piece of his neck, but his face was undamaged, so she knew it was him. He had been one of four that she had seen including the Captain. The next one was the young guard who had brought her the soup. Behind him was Captain Aristov and the other guard who had tried for a peek at her when the Captain had first come to see her. It saddened her because they were all so young.

When the first one arrived at the cell, it did exactly what they all do. It slammed hard against the steel bars of her cell and reached in as far as it could. Jean calmly held the pillow up to its face, pulled the Glock from her belt and pressed the muzzle against the squirming infected dead that was trying to push the cell door inward. She pulled the trigger, and it slumped backward onto the floor. Somehow the thing that had been Captain Aristov got to the cell door second. Jean now had the added insurance of the first one being in the way, so she had more time to compose herself before the infected dead version of Aristov reached through the bars.

Jean got the pillow in place and pressed the muzzle against it just as she had the first time, but just as she pulled the trigger, and as the former Captain Aristov flew backwards away from the bars, she felt a searing pain along her left arm. It felt like her arm was on fire, but she knew she hadn't been bitten. She looked at her arm and saw the trail of blood where the infected dead had left a deep scratch from her elbow to her wrist. It had somehow managed to reach in far enough to grasp at her shirt, and when it lost its grip, it had blindly tried to grab her arm.

In the split second that she had before the third infected reached the cell door, she realized her mistake. The cabin had been too warm, so she had taken off her thick, protective jacket, and it was still lying in a pile behind her in the corner of the cell. She only had time to think to herself that she didn't know if a scratch was fatal like a bite, or if she was going to be okay. All she knew for sure was that it wasn't like any scratch she had ever gotten before. This one felt like someone was cutting her arm off with a dull knife.

The third infected tripped over the bodies in front of the cell and literally stuck its head most of the way between the bars. Jean shoved the pillow against the head and pulled the trigger almost simultaneously. It had barely fallen free of the bars when the fourth one stumbled over the others for its turn. By now Jean was angry and afraid. She was taking care of her problems one by one, but she had gotten that stupid scratch, and not knowing if it was a death sentence was almost as bad as being bitten.

There weren't more infected trying to get into the cabin which meant one of two things. Either there were no more in the corridor outside, or no more of them had heard the muffled gun shots. Jean listened, trying to hear if there was anything moving out in the passageway on the other side of the door, but eventually understood that the ringing in her ears was real. The Glock had been quieter than it would have been if not for the pillow, but it had still been loud enough inside the small cabin to have messed up her hearing.

The dead were piled up outside the door in a very small area, and she had to work to get the door open far enough to squeeze through. She looked at the bodies and was grateful that she hadn't been forced to use Plan B. The Chief always said to have a second plan, and hers had been to hold the mattress up against the bars and shoot more than one at a time.

Jean very quickly closed the cabin door and locked it again. She opened the cabinet and grabbed the bottle of Vodka from the shelf. She knew it was going to hurt bad, but she needed to clean that scratch as soon as possible. Not to mention the fact that she felt like she could use a drink.

"I know," she said to herself, "you shouldn't drink when you're pregnant, but you shouldn't be on a Russian ship with over four dozen infected dead when you're pregnant, either."

She started to pour the Vodka on her arm, but she stopped herself and added, "You've got the order wrong, stupid."

Jean took a long drink from the bottle, rolled her eyes in appreciation of the burning sensation as it went down, and let out a satisfied sigh. She waited just a minute for the buzz to hit then doused her arm with the liquid. She thought she might pass out from the pain, and her head felt more than a buzz for a few moments, but she shook herself out of it. She tore off part of her sleeve from the other arm, soaked it in Vodka and did her best to tie it around the injured area. Where the scratch had broken the skin, the pain was unbelievable. Even if it wasn't fatal, it sure felt like it was killing her arm.

She remembered her jacket and knew it could give her more protection, so she wriggled back through the cell door to get it. Once she had it on, her arm felt a little better, but she found it so hard to push completely out of her thoughts. She was in love. She was going to have a baby. She wasn't supposed to die like this, and Eddie might never know what had happened to her.

Jean grabbed the flashlight and announced to herself and the empty room, "Okay, Jean Mitchell. Your pity party is over. Time to find your way out of here."

She listened at the door and then quietly turned the lock. When she pulled it open and stuck her head out into the passageway, she saw it was clear of more infected. There were a couple of cabin doors along the walls, and but she was looking at the space between them. Then she felt a little embarrassed when it occurred to her that she was looking along the walls for one of the maps she was accustomed to seeing on cruise ships. She had hoped to see something that said, "You are here." She had been incredibly lucky so far, but she didn't think she would get that lucky.

The first thing she had to do was find her way upward. Odds were that she was below decks somewhere, so she had to find a gangway that would at least get her moving in the right direction. Jean tried to find a rational reason to go either left or right, but nothing fit. If she would have had a porthole, maybe she would know whether it was better to go for the bow or the stern. From what she remembered about the Zodiacs, the stern was a better choice because one thing she wasn't going to be able to do was swim from the ship to Mud Island.

She decided to go to the left, but only because she didn't have a clue which way would be better. She walked as lightly as she could, not making a sound so she wouldn't attract attention and so she would be able to hear clearly if something came along. It looked like her corridor dead ended into a cross corridor that went left and right.

"Oh good," she whispered. "I get to make another fifty-fifty guess with no information. Maybe the 'you-are-here' sign is in that corridor."

About twenty feet from the next corridor she heard that shuffling sound that was easy to recognize as an infected dead dragging its feet. If she ever saw one walking normally by picking up its feet and putting them down one in front of the other, it might scare her more. She stopped going toward the corridor and lowered herself to the floor. If it was coming her way, she figured she had an even chance that it would go straight unless it saw her standing in the middle of her corridor. Once she was flat on the floor, she aimed her Glock down the hall and waited.

The dragging sound increased in volume, and for one wild moment Jean wondered if it was coming up behind her. She couldn't remember if she had checked her back since starting forward down the hall. She resisted the urge to turn around, and that turned out to be a good decision because a shadow appeared at the cross corridor in front of her, and the infected dead that followed the shadow would have seen her moving.

It came from her left, and Jean held her breath. It was another Russian sailor, and he looked liked he had been bitten several times before he died. It was dragging its left leg, and that made the infected turn its body slightly away from Jean, and since there was no reason for it to turn, it continued to walk straight ahead down that corridor.

"I guess I'm going left again," Jean whispered. She let out a ragged breath and slowly got to her feet. As she did, she looked back down the hall from where she had come and satisfied herself that nothing had been sneaking up on her from behind.

Her arm throbbed, and she wondered if it would be better to pour more Vodka on it or to drink more of it. She decided neither would be fine for now and started for the end of the corridor again. It didn't take her long to reach the turn, but the first thing she did was check the progress of the infected that had passed by. She got a chill when she saw the corridor to the right where the infected had gone was a dead end, and it was almost to a closed door. Once it got there, it was going to either push open the door or bounce off of it. If it bounced off the door, it was just as likely to get turned around and start back for the other end of the hall.

Jean glanced down the hall in the opposite direction and saw the gangway she was looking for. It sat slightly to the left of the hallway, and it went upward. Around the gangway, the corridor continued on to another closed door. Sooner or later, the infected would get around to walking back down the corridor on that side, and it would drop straight down to the deck below. Jean honestly didn't know if an infected could walk up a set of stairs, but she knew they could fall down stairs like pros. The good news was that the gangway was also steep. That would make it harder for her hallway friend to follow her if it turned around before she reached the stairs.

She sprinted for the beckoning gangway as quickly as possible without making noise and was just putting her foot on the first step when she heard the infected bounce off of the door at the end of the corridor. She glanced back and saw the infected was going to go for two. Instead of bouncing off and turning its momentum back the way it had come, it still had its back to her and was starting forward toward the door. Jean went up the stairs and thought to herself there were only about fifty more of them to get by.

The next level up was a nightmare, not because she could see more infected, but because she was looking to her right at a vast compartment that could only be the engine room. That meant she was somewhere in the back, lower decks of the ship. She had to find a way to go straight up, or she would have to cross through the engine room. Once again she had to remind herself that it wasn't all bad. Most of the ship was on the other side of the engine room, so most of the crew would also be in the forward part of the ship. There was still a generator running somewhere in the engine room, and she was just thinking how lucky she was that the power was still on, when she heard the generator start to sputter. The lights flickered almost in time with the sputtering of the generator, and as the generator stopped so did the lights. It went silent and dark at exactly the same moment.

Jean froze right where she was and just listened. Down below the stairs she could hear the dead crewman she had managed to sneak past. Its efforts to get through the closed door also seemed to be effected by the lack of light. It had changed course and was dragging itself back toward the stairs.

She wasn't afraid of the infected down below her deck. What bothered her was that they were drawn to noise, and it was making plenty......or maybe it was just noisier without the sound of the ship drowning it out. Either way, if she could hear it, so could the other infected, and that meant she couldn't just stand there and wait for them to come along. As much as she knew the flashlight would also give away her position, she also knew she wasn't going to go anywhere without turning it on.

Jean tucked the Glock back into her belt and fumbled the flashlight out of her coat pocket. She couldn't see an inch in front of her face so she was having to do everything by touch, the whole time listening to the infected dead at the bottom of the stairs. Jean didn't hear something come close to her as much as she sensed its presence. She felt the same feeling she had gotten every time she had to squeeze onto a bus or a commuter train and stand too close to men she didn't know. Her skin crawled, and the fine hairs on the back of her neck felt like they had a static charge.

Maybe it was from hanging around with Kathy, or maybe her knees just did what they wanted to do, but she dropped to the floor just as something bumped into her hard. She managed to hang onto the flashlight, but she knew she had been standing on the top step of the stairs so she reached out and grabbed at the air with her free hand. At first she found the metal railing of the gangway, and she gripped it hard. Then she felt the shin bones of the infected dead that had tried to wrap its arms around her. Her stiff grip on the railing acted like someone had strung a rope across the steps, and she felt it fall past her.

The tumbling noise of the infected falling down the stairs was enough to set off a chorus of groans from all directions, and Jean knew she couldn't lay there and cry about what was really hurting her, and that was her left arm. The scratch felt like it had been ripped open, and it hurt worse than ever. When she put her other hand to it, it felt hot and puffy like infection after scraping yourself on a rusty nail.

The engine room was too risky to cross, so Jean started crawling in the opposite direction in the dark. She kept feeling along the walls every few feet hoping to find something familiar. Hoping to find a door or a ladder going to the main deck of the ship. She wasn't hoping to find the pair of shoes her hand discovered.

Jean recoiled instantly, and whether the infected could see or not, it followed her. She didn't turn on the flashlight because she would have needed to search for the switch, but she had pushed herself away so hard that she went from being on her knees to being flat on her back. More out of instinct than anything else, she drew her knees up to her chest with her feet in the air, and she felt the weight of the infected fall on top of her. She had the wind knocked out of her, but none of the Russians were exceptionally large, and this one was possibly the smallest member of the crew. With every bit of strength she had, Jean pushed with her feet and felt the weight of the infected dead fly off of her.

She heard it land, and the last thing she would have believed was that it wouldn't come right back, because they didn't feel pain. Jean pulled the Glock from her belt and then thumbed the on switch of the flashlight just as it grabbed at her foot. She was at point blank range when she pulled the trigger, and the blast blew the infected over onto its back.

Jean took about three seconds to collect herself and then was on her feet running. She went straight over the infected that was now spread across the corridor, and as she did she hoped anything coming this way would trip over the body. Ahead she could hear more movement, and the ship seemed like it was too narrow for another corridor to be running parallel to hers. That meant she was likely to run into more of the infected as long as she was in a corridor. The best she could hope for was an empty cabin, and she hoped the Russian ship builders had the same way of thinking that most shipyards had. They tended to put accommodations areas aft of the engine room for the officers and crew to be nearer to the area where they worked. She didn't bother to turn off the flashlight because she had already advertised her location to the entire dead crew.

Only a few more long strides down the hallway brought her to a cabin door that was open. She panned the flashlight around the room and saw that it at least looked like it was empty of the infected. She decided she had enough of playing hide and seek in the dark with things that bite, so she ducked inside and locked the door. With her back against the door, Jean stood panting for a few moments, wondering if it was possible to get out of the ship. She shone the light around the room again and saw that it might have been the Captain's quarters. The best part was the porthole.

Jean checked the lock on the door again then went to the porthole. It was facing Mud Island. She tried to remember everything about her time on the ship so she could figure out how long the others had been gone, but time went by fast and it went by slow. She had no idea when they would be back. For all she knew they could already be back.

For the first time since the lights had gone out, she felt real hope. It was dark outside, and if her friends had returned, they would be watching the Russian ship through the security cameras. They would be wondering why they weren't seeing signs of life, but most of all, they would be wondering where she was. Jean lifted the light to the porthole and gave the universal signal for help......SOS. She may have only been a nurse on a cruise ship, but everyone working at sea had to know the basics.

Jean repeated the SOS several times, knowing that even if they had seen it, there was no way to signal her back. She could only hope they were getting their gear together for a rescue attempt. She didn't notice that she was dripping with sweat, partially due to her arm, and partially because the ventilation system was off. She also didn't notice she was already just randomly flashing the light, having lost the ability to remember the sequence. When the flashlight slipped from her fingers, she was already unconscious before she fell to the floor.

12 HOPE

The flight from Guntersville back to the coast was uneventful, but with each passing minute Ed was becoming more and more worried. The only break in the monotony was when they circled the area around what had been Fort Jackson to see if they had done any good when they sprayed fuel on the infected.

Bus looked down on the charred horde and let out a low whistle. "You did that?" he asked. "I think you wiped out a couple thousand of them. Maybe we could fuel up the plane and spray more of them along the coast."

The Chief looked like he was considering it at first, but when he weighed their need for the fuel against the effectiveness of the tactic, it didn't seem worth it.

He said, "Maybe if we could get them to all squeeze together in a nice little group, we could wipe out a bunch of them, but they're too spread out. I think there are too many of them hanging around in the trees, and a forest fire wouldn't be my first choice. So far the weather has been too dry to take the chance."

Small talk wasn't working very well. Everyone in the plane was thinking about getting home, and after Fort Jackson I had started trying to get Jean on the radio. No response didn't mean something was wrong, but any response would have made us all feel better. To make matters worse, Kathy reached up and rubbed my shoulders from time to time, as if she knew I was getting more and more worried. The usual smile was absent from the Chief's face. He was good at finding things to feel happy about but not today.

Molly was her usual astute self and asked, "Why is everybody so sad? Is Aunt Jean okay?"

I thought I was going to break down when she asked that, and Kathy came to the rescue. She asked Molly to tell her about when she had gone to school in Guntersville, and what was it like to watch her daddy play baseball. Allison and Bus even pitched in by keeping Molly busy with questions.

As we began to be close enough to the coast my anxiety grew because I knew we were in radio range. We were at a high enough altitude for me to see the ocean, and I started looking for landmarks.

The Chief could see me stretching my neck, so he reached over and tapped my arm to get my attention. He leaned closer and said we were going to approach Mud Island from the south to avoid detection as we retrieved the Boston Whaler. He was being patient with me because he knew I was worried, and he spoke in a soft but firm voice when he said Jean was fine. I was getting to see the Chief's fatherly side for the first time. He had always been like a protective big brother, but if he wasn't flying the plane he would probably have been rubbing my shoulders, too.

We reached the coast just south of Georgetown, and the Chief made a sharp turn to the north. He kept his altitude and began searching the coast with binoculars. Mud Island came up fast, and it was easy to see with the Russian corvette parked between the island and the mainland. None of us expected to see Jean outside waving at us, but the irrational side of me would have preferred that over nothing.

"There's no one topside on the corvette from what I can see," said the Chief. "I would expect some activity."

"Maybe they're just laying low," said Kathy. "Maybe they're playing possum in case they get spotted by the Navy."

"That would make sense," I said, but I think I was just trying to be normal by making conversation.

The Chief changed course again and headed straight out to sea. A couple of miles out, he turned south to bring us back around to where we hid the boat.

"Is there enough light for you to spot the Boston Whaler, Ed?" asked the Chief.

"Put us lower to the water, Chief, and I'll be able to spot the two trees I used as landmarks," I answered.

Allison leaned forward and watched as we rushed back toward the coast. "It looks so barren," she said.

"This time of year makes it look that way," said Kathy. "Cold salt air tends to take the green out of everything. Wait until you see how green it gets in the spring."

"There it is," I said. I pointed toward two trees that looked bigger than anything around them, and then drew an imaginary line down to where the boat should be.

The Chief started to throttle back as we got closer and then let the pontoons begin to skim the surface of the water. I had a momentary emotion that could only be described as the way you feel when you get over homesickness. It was strange to think that this had become home. It seemed like yesterday since I had gotten the call saying I owned an island. The lawyer had said it was good news and bad news. Little did he know it was good news for me and bad news for him.

The trees seemed to grow right before our eyes as we decreased speed but continued in a straight line for the coast. The Chief expertly turned the seaplane into a boat and began cruising toward the camouflaged Whaler. I heard Kathy explaining to Allison and Bus that we had left the boat hidden a little south of the island in case the Russians did as we expected and tried to hide their ship behind our island. She told them we called the waterway that separated Mud Island from the mainland our moat because it kept the infected dead and dangerous people from walking onto the island. It was deep and dangerous, and we had recently learned it was even more dangerous than we had realized.

The Chief brought the plane up alongside the Boston Whaler, and I was all too glad to climb out onto the pontoon and jump over to the boat. The Whaler was big enough to carry all seven of us and our gear, so everyone started tossing over backpacks and duffle bags. We hadn't discussed what we were going to do about the plane, but there was no way we could take it back to the dock. The Russians may be laying low, but we were sure they would come out at night to look around. The sun was going down, so we knew we had to move fast.

"We don't have enough tarp to completely cover the plane," said the Chief, "but let's anchor it and then cover the side that faces the island. If they've been looking this way, they saw something over here before, but they shouldn't really know the area well enough to tell that it's bigger."

With the help of Tom and Bus, we got the plane covered and were finally starting the engine on the Boston Whaler. I felt like I was holding my breath the whole time, and we worked quickly and quietly. The sun was going down, and we wanted to be back inside the shelter before the Russians sent out a patrol.

We steered the boat out of the tiny cove where it had been hidden and headed slightly out to sea. There was a fishing trawler on its side at the mouth of the southern entrance to the moat. I thought of it more as an exit because the current rushed from the moat out to sea and was very strong.

We had a bad moment when we turned the corner around the trawler and found a half dozen infected standing on the beach. We were in shallow water and not far from the beach, so they didn't need anyone to ring the dinner bell. They came straight for us with arms outstretched and gaping jaws moving.

Kathy had taken the helm from the Chief so he could prepare to pull us onto the beach of Mud Island, and she knew what to do. She turned to the right and put us back into deeper water where the current was the worst. The infected tried to follow us and began dropping out of sight as they were swept away by the current. I could have sworn one of them was wearing a Russian navy uniform.

Once we had led the infected from the beach into the water, Kathy turned us back to our original course. We stayed in deeper water only long enough to be sure there were no infected dead walking around on our side of the moat, then she pointed us toward the shore. As soon as we hit the beach on Mud Island, I was over the bow and running for the overhanging bank at the tree line where we had dug out a garage for the Boston Whaler.

I was hoping Jean was watching through one of the cameras and was inside the shelter doing a happy dance because we were back, but I had a responsibility to the other members of our group, and that meant getting the boat inside where no one would be able to detect that we had been on the beach. As bad as I wanted to, I couldn't take the time to pop down through the tunnel to see if Jean was okay. I also knew it would take more than a minute to say hello to her.

I pulled back the camouflage that hid the trailer from view and began pulling out the boards we had used to make it easier to cross the soft sand. A stiff breeze kicked up, and on the breeze I smelled the familiar scent of decay. Tom came up along side me and started helping with the boards. I could see by the look on his face that he smelled it too.

The infected dead came from the darkest corner of our boat garage but was still on the other side of the trailer. That didn't stop it from trying to reach us by climbing over the trailer. Kathy came up between the two of us and delivered a vicious blow to its head with her machete.

"How did that thing get inside?" asked Kathy.

"Better yet," I said, "isn't that a Russian navy uniform?"

Tom said, "It looks just like that one infected dead we just saw over on the other side of the moat near the trawler."

Kathy took a closer look at the body and said, "There are bite marks all over this guy. Something must have happened over at that Russian ship. I don't think this guy was bitten over here."

"What makes you think that?" I asked. "He could have been bitten and then crawled in here before he died. He got stuck behind the trailer and couldn't get out until we motivated him to climb over after us."

"Check out these bite marks," she said. "There are stitches in some of them. I think this guy was bitten and someone tried to treat the wounds."

Tom leaned in and took a closer look at the dead Russian sailor. He rolled the body over and said, "Pull his shirt back and look at this. There's blood coming through the material."

Kathy pulled back the shirt and exposed a large bandaged area that was soaked in blood. When she removed the bandage, the injury was obvious. Something had bitten the sailor deeply enough to rip out a huge chunk of his side, and stitches weren't going to help him. Both hands were also bandaged, and one hand was missing two fingers.

Tom said, "If I had to guess, before this guy died he was trying to defend himself using his bare hands, but when we do it, we grab at the infected dead by getting a handful of clothing somewhere around the chest. That way we can control the face and keep from getting bitten."

"What are you getting at?" asked Kathy.

"I think he was flailing at so many infected that he couldn't get a grip on one without being bitten by another," said Tom.

Kathy involuntarily looked around to be sure we weren't being surrounded by more infected dead. The Chief was coming toward us, probably to see why we didn't have the trailer on its way to the water yet.

"What's up?" he asked. "You guys find something in there?"

"You might say that," said Kathy. "Check this out, Chief. This guy looks like he had a really bad day before he died, and it's another Russian sailor."

The Chief took a quick look, and as he almost always did, he filled in the blanks for us. The Chief seemed to have a wealth of knowledge on more subjects than most people, so it didn't surprise us when he pointed out that the Russian sailor was wearing a ring worn only by SCUBA divers. It was silver, and engraved in the top on the flat surface was a trident spear.

"Russian navy divers all wear that ring after they've been in the water at least one hundred times for a minimum of thirty minutes. We're talking about fifty hours of underwater experience," he said, "and judging by his injuries, I would be willing to bet he went diving in the moat and got too close to the nets."

Tom let out a low whistle and said, "That would explain how he lost his fingers. He was flailing around in the water, and was getting bitten repeatedly. It looks like they grabbed him and pulled him into the nets."

"I can't even think about what that was like," I said. "Can you imagine dropping over into the moat and landing right on top of those things?"

The Chief shook his head slowly from side to side, "Remember when I went into the water, I went in face first so I could see what was in front of me. This guy probably went into the water the way divers usually do. He let the weight of his tanks pull him in backward and upside down. If he landed on the nets, he was bitten before he could even get right side up."

"Oh my God," said Kathy. "He's bandaged and stitched. That means they pulled him out of the water and back into the ship. I think we all know what happened next."

"Same thing that happened on the cruise ship when the infection started to spread fast," said the Chief.

"How many divers would they have put into the water to see what was keeping the anchor from coming up?" asked Kathy.

The Chief answered, "Never one diver by himself. They would have put at least two in the water, and then at least two more to pull them out."

"So they most likely had at least four divers who were bitten and then carried back on board, maybe more," I said. "Maybe that's why it looked so quiet over there."

"I imagine we'll find out in due time," said the Chief. "Let's get inside and check on Jean. We can worry about the Russians later."

The Chief spread one of the tarps out on the ground and then lifted the Russian sailor's body onto it. He didn't ask for help, and he was so strong he wouldn't have needed it, anyway. We watched him wrap the tarp around the body. He closed it at the ends as best as he could before lifting the body and carrying it out to the water. He walked out far enough for the current to start pulling at his legs before he lowered it into the water. One sailor to another, he paid his final respects.

We waited for the Chief to come back before we returned to our work. Tom, Kathy, and I put the boards in place ahead of the trailer wheels while the Chief pulled the trailer to the beach. Kathy jumped back into the boat, and as soon as we unloaded Allison, Molly, and Bus along with our gear, Kathy drove the boat back into deeper water and then came back taking aim at the trailer as the Chief slid it toward her. They worked well together, and the boat was centered on the trailer on the first try. We strapped it down and immediately reversed our process getting the trailer back into hiding. By the time we had it covered again, everyone including Molly had filled in the tracks and ruts left behind in the sand.

I took a deep breath as I dropped into the tunnel and dialed in the combination on the security lock. I was only a matter of moments away from Jean. I could picture her standing at the bottom by the emergency exit with a big smile on her face. She would tease me about something in her good natured way, and I wouldn't be able to think of anything to say back, but one thing was certain. I would be unbelievably glad to see her again.

I unlatched the door and swung it open. I figured the others would forgive me this time for not letting everyone else go in ahead of me, and I practically dove down the tunnel. I knew that the alarm system would have warned Jean that the outside hatch was opened even before I unlocked the inner door combination lock, but I was sure she had been watching us on camera the entire time, anyway.

When I reached the door at the bottom of the tunnel, I laughed to myself and thought she was just being herself.

Instead of opening the door before I got to it, she was giving me the chance to make a grand entrance.

I didn't want to disappoint her, so I dropped through the hatch, spread my arms wide as if I had just done a magic act by appearing out of nowhere and went, "Ta daaa."

The empty bedroom fueled my worst fears, and I didn't wait for her to rush in from another room to yell surprise. Somehow, the place just felt different. It felt like no one was there just as if it was something I could touch.

Kathy dropped in behind me just as I started to run from the bedroom into the main quarters. I didn't remember if I had already called her name, but I heard Kathy behind me yelling for her. By the time I came back from checking the living room and even the decontamination room, the others had checked the lower levels. Jean wasn't in the shelter, and Molly was sitting on the bed silently crying. For a child who had seen too much already, it was more than she could bear to even look at me.

"Where is Aunt Jean, Uncle Eddie?" she asked in a broken voice.

I couldn't even answer her. I knew if I tried my voice would break, too. All I could do was shake my head and shrug my shoulders.

Kathy was the first one to hug me and offer reassurances that wherever Jean was, she was sure she was fine. The Chief said we would find her as soon as possible, and we would start looking now. The thing that scared me the most was the feeling that she had somehow been captured by the Russians.

"We still have the houseboat to check," said Tom. "Maybe she got stuck out on the dock and had to hide."

I had to admit that Tom gave me some hope, and I looked at the Chief as if to say, "Can we go now, please?"

I didn't have to say it out loud. The Chief ran past me and slapped me on the back as he went by. He was carrying a rifle and pulling on a heavier coat as he ran for the living room. By the time I got there he was turning on the TV to check the security cameras. He brought up the view of the dock and panned around to see if there was a guard or anything unusual. The sun had set behind the trees, and there was enough moonlight to cast shadows, so he didn't turn on the night vision.

"Switch to the view inside the houseboat, Chief," I said.

"Hold on just a second, Ed. There's something on the dock. I've seen this view often enough to tell where the shadows should be, and that shadow isn't supposed to be hanging onto the side of the dock piling." He walked over to the monitor and put a finger on the spot he was talking about.

I looked closer at the screen and saw it too. Allison came up behind us and said Kathy had checked Jean's gear and felt like the boots and coat she would have worn if she went outside were missing. I don't know why it surprised me, but when I turned to thank her I saw Tom and Bus were both checking weapons and getting ready to go out with us.

Allison said, "Eddie, I haven't met Jean yet, but I feel like I've known her forever. Molly has been able to hold it together much longer because of all of you, but Jean has been special to her. We're going to find her and bring her back. I just know it." Allison was typically a quiet woman, and it was easy to see Molly in her, especially because she was a quiet girl. You could always tell she was thinking about something, though. Allison looked as worried as the rest of us, but she looked more confident than I felt.

"Chief," she said, "I think I see something on the dock." She walked over and stood next to him then traced her finger from right to left. "This line right here looks unnaturally straight, and look over here." She pointed at a line that was parallel to the first one and so straight it looked like it was drawn with a ruler.

"You have a good eye," said the Chief. "Those lines begin and end at shadows that shouldn't be there. I think those might be explosives strapped to the pilings, and the lines are trip wires."

"I'm glad you checked, Chief. I would've just charged out there and gotten myself blown up," I said.

"You can thank Allison, Ed. I was just making sure there weren't any Russians or infected dead walking around out there." He switched the view to the inside of the houseboat, but it was so dark inside that it was doubtful she was there. He switched to night vision, and there was no change. If she was hiding, I wouldn't expect her to be standing in front of a camera, anyway.

The Chief said, "Here's how we're going to do this. We approach carefully, and someone stands watch over the trip lines while the rest of us check the houseboat. It's too dark out there for us to disarm the explosives, and I don't want any infected dead stumbling out onto the dock and blowing us all to pieces."

Kathy had joined us, and she said, "Molly wants to make some cookies for Aunt Jean to eat when she gets back. Bus is helping her get started, but she wants her mom to show her how to do it. Bus wants to go with us."

The Chief turned to Kathy and said, "I hate not having my favorite cop with me, but I need for you to stay here and watch the monitors for me."

"What am I supposed to be watching for, Chief?" she asked.

"I need someone to keep a close eye on that Russian ship for me. I don't want to be out on the houseboat if they launch those Zodiacs full of armed men," he answered. "I'll have a radio on me. Give it a double click on the switch and wait for me to talk."

"Chief," she said, "find her and bring her back."

Chief Joshua Barnes had a look he would get when he was kidding around. He had a very special look he would get when he was up to something that involved a practical joke. He had a poker face you couldn't read if your life depended on it, but he had a different look when he was determined to do something. We were seeing that look now. No smile, steely eyes, and a set to his jaw.

He said, "I can promise you that Jean will be back in this shelter tonight, Kathy. Ed? Are you ready to go find your future wife?"

"You bet I am, Chief." I don't know if I could ever look as fierce as the Chief, but this was likely to be the closest I would ever come.

We checked the monitors for infected dead or living Russians at the entrance, and then we made it the fastest exit we had ever done. The Chief was in the lead with me close on his heels. Bus was third, and Tom was covering us from behind. It was about a mile from the shelter entrance to the dock, and I don't think we ever covered the distance so quickly. It wasn't really rough terrain, but we have left it as wild as possible so it would look like no one ever came to this island.

Half way to the dock there was a clear section that allowed us to stop and look at the ocean. It was typical for us to at least slow down as we passed that spot just so we could scan the beach for infected dead. To our surprise, the beach was dotted with the dark silhouettes of the slumped shouldered and shambling creatures that had once been human. It had been a long time since we had seen so many on our island. While it was still raining bodies in Guntersville, it had become much slower here. The moonlight made the beach even more eerie than it normally looked when the infected were out for a stroll.

The infected dead were too far from us to be a concern, but it did put us on guard for more to be near the dock. We passed the signal to each other to keep our eyes open by pointing at our eyes with one hand, and then at the beach. We were all heavily armed and ready for anything, but as usual the machetes were our weapon of choice, and we all had them at the ready except Tom. He had his rifle ready with the safety off. The Chief had pulled him aside and told him we needed to move fast and without delays. He told him to put a bullet through the head of anything if we missed it up front, or if there were more than two.

We arrived at the dock in record time, and the Chief dropped to a knee and put his right fist in the air with a bent elbow. We all stopped a couple of yards apart and waited for his signal to move forward.

He double clicked the button on his radio and said, "Kathy, we're at the dock. Any changes on the Russian ship?"

"That's a negative, Chief," she answered. "The dock looks the same, too."

"Okay, we're going in, Kathy. Keep and eye on Tom. He's going to be standing watch over the explosives."

The Chief moved only as far as the first trip wire where he laid down on his stomach and inspected the explosives. To his surprise, the wire was attached to the piling, and the pin in the grenade was tied in place with a piece of string. It wasn't going to explode no matter how many times someone tripped on it. The Chief scooted over to the other side and found the wire was attached to the piling on that side, too.

Even though it was a dummy trip wire, the Chief stepped over it and went to the second one. It was also tied to the pilings, and a string was tied through the pin. The Chief looked confused when he came back to where we waited, and it wasn't often that we saw him looking like that.

"The wires aren't even attached to the explosives," he said. "They're both dummy traps, but I can't think of a reason why anyone would want to even bother rigging something like that."

"Do you think we're being watched?" I asked.

"No," said the Chief. "I'm sure there's a reason, but I don't think we're going to get an explanation out here."

13 SOS

Kathy couldn't believe her eyes. She was watching the Chief and Ed on the dock. She knew Bus and Tom were somewhere just out of her field of vision, and the beach had more infected dead wandering around than normal. The moon was so bright that she didn't need to switch to night vision.

She almost missed it, but Allison had come up behind her and asked, "What was that?"

Allison pointed at the monitor that displayed the dark Russian ship, and Kathy looked at it just in time to see the message begin and end one last time. Then it became random. There was no mistaking what the first part said.

Kathy keyed the microphone and spoke with the Chief. As soon as she finished explaining what she had seen, she signed off and told Allison to take over watching the monitors. She ran for her room, strapped on her gear and went through the door of one of the several escape hatches that led to the surface of Mud Island.

......

We started forward as a group going over the trip wires carefully, but before we got to the houseboat, the Chief signaled for us to stop again. We watched as he pulled the microphone loose from the radio and keyed the talk button. He was wearing an earphone so we couldn't hear what Kathy said to him, but whatever it was made the Chief reflexively turn and look in the direction of the moat. Even though we couldn't see the Russian corvette, we all knew the Chief looked that way because it was somewhere around the curve. He keyed up and spoke several times before reacting, and we were surprised when he sprang from his crouched position by the door of the houseboat and jumped into the big boat we had tied to the dock.

I looked at the others, and I saw Bus and Tom were as much in the dark as I was, literally and figuratively. I saw Tom shrug his shoulders, but we stayed where we were supposed to be. I saw a flashlight come on under the dash of the big boat, and I moved a bit closer to see what the Chief was doing. It appeared to me the Chief was working on the wiring that he deliberately sabotaged to keep anyone from taking the boat.

The flashlight winked off, and the twin motors on the boat came to life. There wasn't any use for stealth anymore, and we didn't need an invitation from the Chief. It was obvious that we were going somewhere. Bus and Tom caught up with me as I was climbing over the rail into the boat. Tom grabbed the lines tied to the dock and tossed them into the boat. He gave the bow a shove and easily jumped over from the dock.

"What's up, Chief?" I asked.

Before the words were even out of my mouth, the Chief turned the wheel hard to starboard and hit the gas. I had to grab the back of a seat to keep from flying right out of the boat, and even Bus with his low center of gravity was pinned to the back rail practically on top of Tom. Wherever we were going, the Chief wanted to get there in a hurry.

The Chief aimed the boat toward the mainland dock, which happened to be a direct line for the Russian ship. He turned and yelled over the sound of the engines and the wind, but I couldn't understand a word until I pulled myself up to the front seats.

"Do you know Morse Code, Ed?" he yelled.

"Never learned it, Chief. Why?" I yelled back.

He answered, "Well, then it's a good thing Kathy stayed behind to watch the security cameras."

Tom and Bus had managed to pull their way up to the front of the boat, and they arrived just in time to hear the chief answering me.

He yelled loud enough for all of us to hear, "Kathy was watching the Russian corvette for signs of life, and she saw someone signal the shelter with a flashlight."

"Why would the Russians signal the shelter if they don't know it's there?" I yelled.

"Because it wasn't a Russian signaling the shelter, Ed," he answered. "Kathy knows Morse Code, and she said the message was spelled out SOS JEAN."

All four of us turned our heads in the direction of the dark ship that was rapidly growing in size as we sped toward it.

......

The Chief didn't look too comfortable knowing he was passing over the nets that ran across the moat because he had seen that particular form of hell first hand. There was no way to explain without guessing why that Morse Code signal had come from the ship, but the best guess was that Jean had sent it. To him and the rest of us, it was a no brainer that we had to board the ship to find out for sure.

The boat banked hard to port this time as the Chief pulled the steering wheel in that direction. I was almost ready to ask the Chief what he was doing when I saw a flashlight signaling us from Mud Island. It didn't take long for me to make out the shape of Kathy moving quickly to a stretch of beach that was beyond the dangerous oyster beds. If we were going to board that ship, we were going to need her training. She may have been a rookie when the infected dead had taken over the world, but she had become a pro in a hurry. Her blonde ponytail was bouncing as she jumped from the beach into the boat.

The Chief didn't wait for instructions on where to go. The best place to board the ship was going to be where the Zodiacs were tied up. They couldn't see any infected out on the deck of the dark ship, but they needed to make sure it was clear before they went into the belly of the corvette to find Jean.

Kathy squeezed up close to the Chief and said, "The signal came from a porthole directly below that big box-like structure between the middle of the ship and the stern. Does that help?"

The Chief got one of his looks, and to our relief he had a slight smile on his face. "Yes, that helps, Kathy. I've been thinking about what that corvette might be carrying in there, and if we're really lucky, it's a helicopter bay."

"Do we need a helicopter?" I asked.

I thought the Chief was going to laugh for a moment, but he said, "Sure we do, Ed, but one thing we need even more than a helicopter is a way to get into the ship that won't involve going through every level just to get to the space where that signal came from. The helicopter bay should have hatches we can use to get to the next level, and I'd rather shoot something looking down through a hatch than facing them head on."

We came to a stop between the Zodiacs. They were tied to the side of the corvette, so we could tie off to them. There was a body lying in the bottom of one of the boats, and Tom aimed his flashlight at it while Kathy, Bus, and I had our weapons pointed in the same direction. It didn't take long to see that the cause of death was a bullet through the forehead. We could see the tears in his uniform and the exposed bite marks on his hands. We knew there must have been a battle here, and from the looks of things so far, it was a total loss.

The deck of the corvette wasn't very high above us, and a section of railing had been removed for easy access to the Zodiacs. The Chief looked up and reflexively put reverse throttle on the boat. Everyone was caught off balance, but no one went overboard, and we were all just starting to yell at the Chief for the sudden movement when an infected dead bounced face first off our bow and then backward into the water. It disappeared below the surface just as quickly as it had appeared out of nowhere. It was a good thing that we hadn't tied our boat to the Zodiacs yet.

"C'mon, everyone," said the Chief. "We need to climb up there before another one finds his way to this section of the deck."

The Chief pulled us in close for a second time and switched off the powerful engines. We tied the lines to the Zodiacs, and before I could even reach the bow, Kathy and the Chief had gone up the chain ladders that still hung from above. The sound of a quick burst of gunfire was all I needed to get me up the ladder as fast as I could go.

The deck was broad and flat, and there had been some kind of confrontation judging by the amount of blood. There was a big white circle in the middle of it, and there were no masts or cables anywhere on the stern. The Chief had been right about the box-like structure just aft of amidships. We found ourselves facing a big hangar door just like the avionics maintenance building at the resort near Guntersville. The body of an infected dead was sprawled in front of the door.

The Chief said, "Hold your positions until Tom and Bus get up here. Keep Bus formed up behind our kill zone at all times. If Jean is hurt, she might need treatment before we can move her."

Tom and Bus came up behind us, and Kathy guided Bus to a position between us.

"Stay between us at all costs, Bus," she said. "You have your medical kit with you?"

He reached to the backpack he was wearing and gave it a silent pat. Kathy gave the Chief a thumbs up, and we moved together across the broad deck to the hangar door. There was a smaller door to the right of the big door. It had a big wheel lock in the center. Kathy positioned herself about ten feet from the door, ready to shoot anything that came out while the Chief began spinning the wheel counter clockwise to the open position. The wheel was silent, but the opening door would allow enough moonlight to splash into the helicopter bay to draw out any of the infected that had been trapped inside.

None of us were surprised by the loud groans that started as soon as the Chief swung the door outward. There had been over fifty crewmen on the corvette, and even though they could already account for a few, there would most likely be infected dead in every compartment. I just hoped Jean had managed to find a place to hide after she signaled the shelter for help.

The Chief quickly moved to Kathy's side, and both were taking aim into the dark interior of the hangar bay as the groaning got louder and closer. As we waited for the infected dead to appear, I couldn't stop myself from thinking that one of them could be Jean. Kathy had seen the signal, but after it had winked out, it never started again. If she was still able to send the signal, she would have kept sending it.

A shape appeared in the doorway, and my imagination was going wild. It looked like her. Before I could even yell her name, Kathy pulled the trigger on her rifle and the shape was gone.

The Chief said, "Let them come out in the open, Kathy. We don't want them blocking the others from coming through."

We all backed away from the door to give Kathy and the Chief a little more time to shoot, and even as we did, the dark shapes began emerging again. The light was playing tricks with my eyes, and even the tall ones looked like they could be Jean. I thought to myself that the Russian navy probably had women on ships just like our navy, and if she was captured, they may have put her in a Russian uniform. I didn't know that the Russians did not have women stationed on their ships yet, but that didn't stop me from worrying that we would mistake Jean for one of them.

"Kathy, wait," I said. "What if one of them is Jean?"

Everyone looked at me with sympathy, but I could see the hard set of Kathy's jaw, and knew the answer to my own question. If Jean came out of that door as an infected dead, she would want us to end it. She wouldn't want to exist as one of them.

Tom put his hand on my shoulder as Kathy and the Chief turned back to the door. One after the other, six of the infected came out of the helicopter hangar and were shot in the head.

We waited for about a minute after the last one had come through the door, then we started in. Kathy went to one side of the door, and the Chief went to the other. The infected didn't hide around corners, they came right at you. That gave us the advantage, because we always had time to take up a defensive position depending upon their numbers. The fact that no more were coming out of the door to the helicopter bay was a good sign.

Kathy shined a flashlight across the entrance to expose the inside of the bay immediately behind the massive door. She could see the back of the helicopter, but there wasn't anything moving behind it. The Chief did the same from his side of the door, and his flashlight illuminated the corner to the right of the door. He panned it along the bulkhead on the right and gave the all clear signal. Both of them aimed their lights to the center of the bay, and the Chief identified the craft as a Kamov Ka-27 helicopter. It wasn't heavily armed and was best suited for reconnaissance missions.

"That would have been my first guess," said Kathy.

The Chief looked at her to see if she was kidding, but he couldn't tell from her neutral expression. If he didn't know better, he would think she was teasing him because he knew so much, but she wasn't going to give him a clue.

They panned the flashlights back to the hidden spaces again, and the Chief went inside. Kathy was right on his heels, but she peeled off to the left as he went straight toward the helicopter. Tom went in on the right while Bus and I followed the Chief. He was carefully looking into the helicopter, and I could tell he wasn't going to assume there wasn't an infected dead inside.

"Chief, we can look at the helicopter later," said Kathy. "Right now we need to be finding the easiest way to get below decks and find Jean."

"That's exactly what I'm doing, Kathy."

269

He smiled at her in the dimly lit bay, and even though she couldn't see him well enough, she heard it in his voice.

"What is he up to?" She wondered.

The Chief worked his way forward from the cargo section of the Ka-27 to the pilot and co-pilot seats and didn't see anything inside. Tom and I kept guard over Bus in a safe corner while Kathy continued her sweep for exits. Without warning, the entire bay was lit up like broad daylight. The Chief had reached in through the pilot's side window and turned on the helicopter's landing lights.

"I was going to tell you to do that," said Kathy, but this time she had a grin on her face to match the Chief's.

With plenty of light we could see the hatches and doors that led from the helicopter bay to the other parts of the ship. There were three doors on the forward bulkhead, but we weren't interested in those. We were looking for the right hatch to use to go down one deck.

I asked, "What's below hatches one, two, and three Chief?"

"Believe it or not," he began, "I don't know everything about Russian ships, but if I had to guess, one hatch would go down to an accommodations section. That's where the off duty pilots would live. One hatch would go down to a service section. That's where the on duty pilots would be monitoring different stations while they wait for the orders to put the bird in the air. The other hatch would be a mechanical area, probably at the rear of the engineering compartment. That's where they would have the gear and the access to a refueling station. Helicopter fuel is different than the fuel that powers this ship, but the storage tanks would be located close to each other."

"If I had to guess what was below each of the hatches, I would have guessed down, down again, and more down," I said, "and no, I don't believe you when you say that you don't know everything about Russian ships."

Tom pointed to the hatch nearest to him and asked, "Which one is this, Chief?"

"That's the one where we are most likely to find people, whether living or dead," he answered. "That's most likely where we will find off duty crew, and just like on US Navy ships, off duty crewmen tend to gather with other crewmen. The on duty pilots have to be sharp and undistracted from their jobs. If they get the order to fly, they don't have the time to break up a party."

"So, that's where we should find Jean, but that's also where we're going to find the party," I said. "Why would she have to be in there?"

Kathy moved over to stand by the hatch. "We don't need to talk about it, we just need to do it. Every minute we stand here is one more minute that she could be fighting for her life."

The Chief was the strongest of our group by far, so he put one foot on each side of the hatch and got a grip. "I'm going to pull this thing fast, but we don't have to worry about them climbing up here if they're all infected. What I'm worried about is the possibility that there's a live one down there. If there is, then he's going to be jumpy. There's no sense in getting shot, so everyone stand clear until we know what's down there."

Everyone backed up a step, and the Chief pulled on the hatch. As it opened, he let it fall toward him, so he was able to back away at the same time. The stench that blew up into our faces was nauseating, and there was no doubt where it was coming from. The accommodations spaces had been full of crewmen when the infection had spread. The darkness below was a bedlam of infected dead who all wanted to reach whoever had opened the hatch and let the light come down on them. They were about fifteen feet below us, and they filled the corridor.

"Flashlights on single targets, please." Kathy had moved into position as soon as it was obvious that there wouldn't be anyone down there, jumpy or not, who was still alive. "You guys light 'em up, and I'll put them down one at a time."

We all shone our flashlights down in the hole and the noise level grew louder. We centered on the one infected dead face that seemed to draw our attention the most, probably because it was directly at the bottom of the ladder, and Kathy fired a shot through its forehead.

I couldn't help myself and had begun searching the faces below for the one I would recognize, but there were so many. They were pushing and shoving for position and stepping on the first one to go down. When one managed to get to the center that had been vacated by his former comrade, we all lit him up for Kathy. One by one the process was repeated, and the pile of infected at the center of the group became too deep for them to stand.

Kathy leaned in for a look, and I aimed my flashlight at the edge of the group. "Maybe we should have started at the outside edge and worked inward," I said.

"I'm not so sure that would have made a difference, Ed." Kathy sounded like she was thinking about something as she said it. There was a distant tone to her voice.

"Why?" asked Tom. "They're piling up so much that I don't see an end to them."

"Chief, would Jean have been able to isolate herself on this deck below us?" Kathy still had that tone as if she had something worked out.

"Only if she got here ahead of the infected," he said. "Why? What's on your mind?"

She shook her head as if something wasn't making sense. "Why would most of the crew be in this one section of the ship?"

Bus had been just listening to the trio because they had spent so much time together that they had started to think alike, but the thought had also crossed his mind that the crew should have been more spread out.

"Where's the sick bay located on this ship, Chief?" Bus sounded like Kathy.

"I don't think the Russians are much different from us, Bus. Sick bay is almost always located somewhere near crew accommodations because they don't have room for extra beds. They treat people, and then they put them in their own racks."

The Chief was explaining it to Bus, but as he did, he slowed down as if he was understanding the question and the answer at the same time.

"Kathy, Bus, you two are geniuses," he said. "Ed, you're pretty smart too, but I think they figured it out. The divers were bitten by the infected in the nets, and when they were brought back aboard, they were treated and then placed in their own bunks. When they turned, they had a target rich environment because there were so many crewmen around trying to save their shipmates."

"And that probably included the on-duty pilots who were in the ready room just down the corridor from crew's berthing," added Kathy. "They saw that the divers were coming back in bad condition, and since they hadn't been in the air on a mission for a long time, they left the on-duty ready room to help."

I looked toward the hatch behind the Chief and asked, "Didn't you say that hatch was likely to be over the on-duty ready room, Chief?"

"Yes, I did, Eddie, and that would mean the room was most likely abandoned when everyone started attacking each other. If Jean managed to get into that room and close the door, it's the only one with a porthole in the right place."

"Let's get back to work, gentlemen." Kathy took aim at another infected dead, shot it, and moved immediately to the next.

Even with every bullet counting for another infected dead being put to its final rest, it still took several minutes more to shoot every one that appeared below us. It was like shooting fish in a barrel, but we still had to go down that other hatch, and we knew the entire crew couldn't have been in the accommodations space. Counting the ones we had seen on our island, we still had many of the crew to account for.

One of us had to be first to go down that ladder, and as I started forward, the Chief got a gentle grip on my arm. He didn't need to say a word because they were all thinking the same thing I was. Jean couldn't be down there and still be alive, and it wasn't the best idea for me to be the one to find her.

While the Chief held me, more with his eyes than with his hand, Kathy sat feet first through the open hatch. She had slung her rifle across her back and had her Glock ready in one hand.

"Guys, I need a wide spread of lights down there. Chief, are there any portable emergency lights in your new helicopter? I don't want to step down into that mess and have my ankle get ripped open by an infected dead that can't move anything except its mouth."

The Chief looked at Kathy like she had just given him a new toy then went to look through the supplies in the Ka-27. He came back just a few minutes later with a large halogen light attached to a huge battery and had a handle on top.

"This is the best I could find, but it should do the trick. We can attach a line to it and lower it into the corridor. If any of those infected are still alive, it should cause them to move."

Tom produced a nylon climbing rope that looked like it was used as a safety line on the helicopter, and the Chief tied it to the handle. He turned on the light, and it would definitely do the trick. It lit up the helicopter bay even more than the exterior lights from the helicopter had done. When he lowered it past Kathy's feet into the corridor below, it was like broad daylight, and at least a half dozen heads began rotating and snapping.

"Look at that," said Kathy. "I would've looked like one of the infected walking down the beach covered by blue crabs."

I leaned into the hole head first and started counting. "Let me get you a moving count first, Kathy. You can count them off as you shoot them. Okay, I see eight."

Kathy unslung her rifle again and counted off eight shots. I did another quick look, and seeing no movement, she started down.

"It smells like a meat packing plant on a hot day down here, guys. I suggest you find something to put around your noses."

When she reached the bottom rung, Kathy searched for a spot to put her feet and couldn't see a clear piece of floor. She wasn't about to start stepping on them and have one wind up to be still capable of biting. She was just about to tell the men looking down at her that they had to find a way past the bodies when she felt the pressure on the back of her boot. She had never been bitten by anything in her life, and she was amazed by the power behind the jaws. It felt like her foot was being crushed, and the pain made it impossible to tell if the teeth were breaking through the material of her boot.

We all saw the head come through the rungs of the ladder at the same time, but from our angle there was no way to get off a shot that would get the infected in the back of the head. It was protected by Kathy's body, and shooting it in the back wouldn't make a difference.

Kathy didn't scream, but the pain did make her cry out. She pulled as hard as she could, but she couldn't get far enough away from the front of the ladder, hang on, and shoot all at the same time.

For a big man, the Chief was surprisingly agile. He dropped through the hatch and swung around to the back side of the ladder all in one motion. He took both feet off of the ladder, took aim at the shoulders of the infected dead that had its teeth buried in Kathy's boot and just let himself drop. He guided his fall down the hole by keeping his hands on the sides of the ladder, and his size fourteen boots landed squarely on each shoulder of the infected. The result was an awful tearing sound as the body was ripped free from the head and pushed the remaining distance to the floor.

The Chief reached through the bars with one hand and grabbed a big crop of hair in his huge hand and pulled the head back to the ladder where he could reach it. With his other hand he reached around and shoved his hunting knife through its head. Kathy pulled herself tight to the ladder and waited as the Chief used his knife to pry open the jaws that were as tight as a steel trap. The head dropped off to one side, and Kathy felt instant relief from the pain, but she was afraid to look down.

"Is there any blood, Chief?" she sounded more like a kid to herself than she could ever remember. It was like asking her dad to help her.

The Chief turned the powerful halogen light on the end of the rope toward Kathy's boot and looked at the marks the jaws had left in the leather.

"It was close, Kathy. As a matter of fact, you still have a tooth stuck in the boot. Get back up there and have Bus take a look at you. If nothing else, that's going to be one hell of a bruise."

Kathy pulled herself up the ladder with her arms and by hopping with her other leg. We caught her under her arms and pulled her the rest of the way. As soon as she was on the floor, we were working at the laces of her boot and getting it off of her. Bus drew a sigh of relief when he aimed the light at her ankle. The area was already turning black and blue, but there was no blood. As an extra test, I shoved a flashlight down inside her boot and then inspected the outside of the boot for light shining through.

"No light, Kathy. It would look like a Halloween pumpkin if the teeth had broken through."

"Thank God," she said, "but man does it hurt. I had no idea they could bite that hard."

Bus looked at the marks on the shoe and said, "The human bite can range from over fifty pounds of pressure up to two hundred and seventy-five pounds of pressure. I've got to get me a pair of these boots."

Despite her obvious pain, Kathy had to laugh at his remark, especially when he held the boot down to the bottom of his foot to see if they were his size.

Kathy snatched it away from him and said, "Hey, I'm going to need that."

"You're not going back down there," I said. "What are you going to do, hop around looking for Jean? Besides, with all that swelling, I don't think you'll be getting that boot on any time soon. You stay here with Bus while Tom and I go down there."

We hadn't even noticed that Tom had already joined the Chief below. They were still on the ladder using their flashlights to study the unmoving infected dead.

The Chief was also aiming his light down the corridor looking at the ceiling toward amidships.

"I can see the other hatch down by the on-duty ready room," he said. "I'm not sure we would have been able to get it open as easily."

He lifted the large halogen light higher and aimed it down the corridor. About thirty feet away was another ladder leading to the hatch that the pilots would have used in a flight mission, and there was a body hanging from the locking wheel in the center of the door.

To keep from taking on water, hatches on most warships use a wheel that expands a watertight seal as the door is locked. If we had tried to spin the wheel from above, we wouldn't have known what was holding the wheel in place, but the arms of the dead man were so entwined in the wheel that it wasn't likely we would have unlocked it without ripping out the arms.

The man hanging from the ladder wasn't moving, and from their angle they could see that someone had put him out of his misery as he hung from the ladder.

Tom said, "Looks to me like he was hanging onto the locking wheel trying not to be pulled down by the infected, and someone did him a favor."

The Chief nodded his agreement and rotated the light down the corridor. About twenty more feet away was the ready room, and the door was closed. With a little luck Jean may have made it to that door, and the room would have been vacant because the pilots would have been out trying to help control the mayhem that had broken out on their ship. It may have been her only hope for survival.

I looked down on Tom and the Chief as I climbed a few rungs down to join them. "What are we going to do, hang around and wait for her to find us?" It may have come out a little more sharp than I intended, but they knew what was at stake and gave me a lot of leeway.

The Chief pointed down the corridor and said, "There's a row of service areas, places where men worked at duty stations. Not everything is located in the operations center. If a ship takes a hit, command and control can be switched to another location. One of them would be the ready room for pilots, and that closed door down the corridor is likely to be the ready room. It's facing the island, I don't doubt that it has a porthole at the location Kathy saw."

"I think we're clear of any infected for the moment, but we don't know if the other compartments are closed off to them," said Tom.

As if inviting trouble by his observation, we heard a series of metallic rumbles. We looked at each other to see if anyone could identify the sounds. It was like identifying a song you only heard once every few years. The Chief was the first to get it.

"Ever hear a body falling down a set of metal stairs? I think we just did."

Groaning started from the corridor past the door we needed to get to, and as the groaning started, we heard the tumbling sound again. Apparently, there was a gangway at the end of the corridor that probably came down from either the main deck or from the operations compartment. The beauty of gangways, as far as we were concerned, was that they were always very steep. Sailors usually just put their hands on the railings and slid down them at high speed. Going up was another matter because it was more like climbing a set of stairs than walking up them.

"Let's move, and we have to control the area beyond the ready room before we open the door. I know you're hoping Jean is in there, Ed, but we can't just expect to open the door and have her rush into your arms." The Chief wasn't warning me that it could be too late, but I knew what he was saying.

We dropped onto the bodies piled up at the bottom of the ladder. There wasn't time to be sure they were all down for good, but it had been several minutes since Kathy had been bitten on her boot, and we couldn't wait all day. We turned and checked the corridor leading back toward the stern and saw a gangway leading upward. The Chief told us that set of stairs would exit away from the flight deck along the side of the box-like hangar structure.

The Chief explained, "It exits along the side of the hangar because it wouldn't be a great idea to have people popping out of a hatch near a helicopter that was landing on a ship that was going up and down in rolling seas. It must be dogged from above or we would have seen the moonlight coming down through it when we opened the hatch over the accommodations area."

Knowing we could focus on one direction was going to make it easier for us, and another light joined ours as Kathy hung down through the hatch above with her rifle aimed past the ready room ladder.

"I might not be able to get down there with you boys, but I can still shoot."

"How's your foot?" asked the Chief.

"Looks nasty, but Bus said it probably hurt the infected that bit me worse than it hurt me."

Somehow I doubted that, but we all appreciated the attitude. Kathy took aim and fired a shot down the corridor. We saw the first infected dead that had tumbled down the gangway somewhere up ahead. He disappeared back the way he had come from the force of the shot.

"Ed, when we get that far, check the guy hanging on the ladder. Tom and I will get more light down the corridor. He can stay there and pick off any that tumble down from above, and I'll check the ready room. Everyone clear about their jobs?"

We both acknowledged the Chief, including Kathy who knew she had overwatch. Tom carried the high powered halogen down the corridor, and we all saw the gangway appear about forty feet away. There was an opening in the bulkhead under the gangway that could only be the engine room. It was open and totally black beyond, but our immediate suspicion was that it was down another steep gangway. That was why nothing was coming out of it.

There were too many infected dead to untangle themselves from each other at the bottom of the gangway. Kathy shot them as soon as the area was illuminated. If any more dropped in, they would have to extricate themselves from the others before they could get up and come after the guys.

Kathy switched her light and her aim to the dead man hanging from the ladder, and she saved me the trouble of climbing up to check him by putting a bullet through his head. I gave her a wave and caught up with the Chief. Tom was half way between the door and the gangway giving Kathy a clear field of fire if anything else came down the gangway. He also wasn't going to take it for granted that there wasn't another entry to the corridor to the right of the engine room door. He couldn't tell for sure, but it looked like a corridor went toward the right along that bulkhead.

The Chief and I positioned ourselves outside the ready room. He had his hand on the doorknob while I put my back against the wall directly across from it. Being a narrow corridor, I was practically on top of the door when I raised my Glock to aim inside. The Chief turned the knob and pushed the door. I only had the moonlight coming from the porthole and the halogen in the corridor to see by, but I had enough light to tell there was a small body lying on the floor. I could also tell it wasn't moving.

The Chief clicked on his flashlight, took one look, and yelled for Bus. I was frozen for a moment as I held my breath in disbelief. I knew she was gone by the look on the Chief's face, and I somehow managed to break free from the wall and get past him into the room.

I turned Jean to face me, and when I pressed my cheek against her and pulled her to me, I was vaguely aware that something wasn't right. She was supposed to be cold, but she was burning up. Her hair and face were covered with sweat.

Bus pushed past the Chief and then gently took her from me. He began checking her over, and said, "She's got a really nasty scratch down her left arm, but there aren't any obvious bite marks. It looks infected, and her temperature has to be in the danger area. We need to get her back to the island as fast as possible."

Needing no other information, the Chief scooped Jean up from the floor like she was a feather and started for the ladder. Tom shot two more infected as they tumbled down the gangway, and all of us began moving up the ladder. Bus got to show off his compact strength by launching himself up the ladder first and then lifting Jean from the Chief as he followed.

Once we were in the hangar bay, I could see that Jean was alive but unconscious. Kathy had anticipated Bus's first instructions to her and was unpacking some medical supplies.

"Good girl, Kathy. We'll stabilize her here then get moving." He drew a syringe of clear liquid and found a vein. A second shot was given into her hip. He looked up at me and said, "Adrenaline for her heart and penicillin for infection."

"Is that okay for the baby?" I asked. I sounded out of breath, but I was afraid.

Bus gave me a sympathetic look and said, "It's a gamble, Ed. The baby won't survive if her heart isn't pumping enough oxygen to her own body, and we have to stop that infection from reaching the baby."

As Bus gave her the injections, Kathy wrapped the deep scratch in Jean's arm with a gauze bandage soaked in some kind of antiseptic. There was an instant cold compress in the medical kit, and she wrapped it onto the back of Jean's neck. Because Kathy and the Chief had worked with Jean on the cruise ship, he knew that Bus would want to check her vital signs before they moved her again, so he had the stethoscope and blood pressure cuff ready as soon as Bus reached for them. Tom and I could only stand by and watch, but I could see it had been a fortunate decision to bring Bus back to the island with us. If not for that decision, Jean would be at the mercy of a bunch of amateurs.

"Her pulse is thready, but we can move her. We need to be fast so we can get that wound irrigated and stitched as soon as possible."

Tom had to help Kathy as she hopped along on one foot, so I took the lead as the Chief carried Jean, and Bus kept a close eye on her. The moon was high as we left the hangar bay, and for some reason I felt like it was important to close the door behind us. Maybe it was because all that shooting had been like ringing a dinner bell in the middle of the moat. The beach along the mainland was dotted with the shadows of the infected dead that were wandering out of the surrounding trees. The cold weather had left the brush and undergrowth dry, so there was a rustling sound along with their constant groaning. At least they weren't coming out of the trees on Mud Island, so we wouldn't have to deal with them.

There was no way to move fast and gracefully get Jean down to the boat, so the Chief just put her over one shoulder and went down the ladder like Tarzan. I had to admit to myself that I had always had in the back of my mind that the Chief could have played the part of Tarzan after he grew up.

The rest of us were in the boat and casting off in seconds. The Chief turned Jean over to Bus while we got Kathy comfortable. It looked like she was going to walk with a limp for a few weeks. The Chief started the powerful motors and backed away from the Russian ship.

Kathy yelled, "Which is faster, Chief, the escape tunnel or the dock?"

"Good point," he answered. "The dock is still a half mile from the front door. Escape tunnel it is."

The Chief rotated the boat and brought us to full speed in seconds, and the full moon was bringing in a high tide, so we were able to get really close to the escape tunnel Kathy had used earlier. There was a gap in the oyster beds, and the Chief brought us right up to the soft mud with the bow. At the last second he put us broadside to the beach and cut the engines. We were able to scramble over the side as a group and locate the escape hatch. I dialed in the combination and then got out of the Chief's way as he and Bus guided Jean down the tunnel faster than an amusement park ride.

Kathy followed them while Tom and I tied the boat to some nearby deadwood and dropped the anchor in shallow water. I had no urge to get it caught on the nets. By silent agreement, we knew we could always come back for the boat, so we went down the hatch and sealed it as we went.

By the time I got to the bottom, they had already carried Jean to the infirmary. Kathy was explaining what had happened to Allison and hugging Molly, telling her that Aunt Jean was going to be okay. Tom took over with them while I helped Kathy to hobble from the master bedroom to the infirmary.

Bus had an IV bag hooked up to Jean and was working on her arm. It looked ugly because he had been forced to reopen the wound to clean it out.

"How is she, Doc?"

"We won't know until she regains consciousness, Ed. I don't know if the book was ever in on whether or not a scratch from one of those infected dead was fatal. Do you?"

"No, we never had a chance to test that theory," I said. "Do you know for sure what scratched her?"

"Not one hundred percent, but there are four parallel tracks, so it looks like a hand. The middle track broke through the skin and dug deep, so the scratch is ragged. It had to hurt like hell when it happened. The good news is that the ice bags and glucose have lowered the body temperature a degree already. We have her stabilized, but I need to get this stitched. It's probably better that she's not conscious for this part."

The woman I loved looked like she had been through hell, but in the short time I had known her, I knew she was tough enough to survive. At least with the help of a capable doctor, she had a chance. All I could do was stand there and watch, but wild horses couldn't have dragged me away.

Kathy was propped up on a tall chair in the corner of the tiny infirmary, and the Chief was using a roll of cellophane to wrap ice packs onto her ankle. He had given her a couple of pain killers, and Tom had joined us with a bottle of bourbon. Kathy was in the process of chasing the pills with the liquor, and she looked like she was already feeling the effects. There wasn't anything I could do to help at the moment, so I relieved her of the bottle and took a big swallow. My knees started feeling wobbly, and it was Bus who looked up in time to realize that I was about to take my turn at passing out. He jumped up and caught me in time to lift me onto a chair next to Kathy. Allison appeared out of nowhere and got a blood pressure cuff on my arm. The little infirmary was like a crowded Emergency Room.

I must have been out for longer than I realized because Bus had finished stitching Jean's arm and was wrapping it with sterile gauze when I opened my eyes. Kathy was leaning against me, and she looked like she wasn't feeling any pain. She handed the mostly empty bottle back to me.

"You didn't spill any," she said with a lopsided grin.

"What happened?" I managed to croak out through a dry throat.

Doctor Bus looked across Jean and said, "Adrenaline rush for too long. When you came down you crashed."

"Is he going to be okay?"

The weak voice that asked the question caught us all by surprise. At first we thought Molly had come into the room because it sounded like a little girl, but then we saw Jean had her head turned my way, and her eyes were open.

I fell down when I got off my chair, and the Chief had to help me to my feet. As soon as he did, I had my arms around Jean's neck and was crying.

"Have you been drinking, Eddie? You can barely stand up."

Her voice was music to my ears, and we all started laughing. She looked over at Doctor Bus and said, "Doctor Bus, I presume?"

"Yes, that would be me Jean. You've had a rough time, and I'm going to need for you to get some rest. Now that we know you're going to be okay, I want to give you a mild sedative that will help with the pain and let you get some sleep. You need to recover a bit before you move around. The baby's going to need you to be just a little stronger."

"The baby? My baby is still okay?" she asked.

Bus showed his best bedside manner and gave her a little wink.

"It has a strong heartbeat and is going to be fine…just like mom. The scratch of an infected dead is dirty and can cause a nasty infection, but it isn't fatal."

We all shared a satisfying moment of smiles, silent tears, and tremendous love for each other.

ABOUT THE AUTHOR

Bob Howard (1951-) was born in New Jersey to an Army Sergeant from Ohio and a mother from Romania. He was moved from one Army base to the next, and before he began high school in Huntsville, Alabama he had lived most of his life overseas in Germany and Okinawa with brief stays in Maryland and North Carolina. He credits his imagination to his exposure to different cultures and environments at an early age. He began reading science fiction and fell in love with post apocalyptic novels. He still has an original copy of the first one he read in 1966, The Furies by Keith Edwards. He joined the Navy after high school and continued to move from one base to another, including a submarine base at Holy Loch, Scotland. He eventually stayed in one place when he got stationed in Charleston, South Carolina. He graduated with a BS in Psychology from the College of Charleston and married his wife of 31 years. His son still lives in Charleston, but his daughter has married and made a home in Ohio where the Howard family has its earliest known roots. Through the years he has had one burning passion that he has wanted to fulfill, and through Alive for Now he is getting to live that passion. Creating a book is something so many people want to do but never have the opportunity, and after writing this book he believes the sky is the limit. He plans to write for the rest of his life because it is enjoyable beyond his wildest dreams. As for the zombie genre, he saw Night of the Living Dead when it originally hit the theaters, and until recently it didn't receive the attention it deserves.

www.ingramcontent.com/pod-product-compliance
Lightning Source LLC
Chambersburg PA
CBHW021957010726
47494CB00003B/781